THIS BOOK IS DEI
DOMESTIC VIOLE.

frederick Henderson

EARLY RETIREMENT
MURDER IN DAYTONA

F C HENDERSON

EARLY RETIREMENT
MURDER IN DAYTONA

A NOVEL BY

F C HENDERSON

Copyright September, 2012

fch32174@yahoo.com

"The price of hating others is loving one's self less"

ELDRIDGE CLEAVER

This novel is a work of fiction. The characters and events come from the author's imagination. Any resemblance to actual persons is purely coincidental.

OTHER WORKS BY F C HENDERSON

* Sisterhood of the Skull and Roses
* Unexplainable Things (a book of short stories)
* An American Idol (the illuminati conspiracy)

AVAILABLE FOR PURCHASE ON AMAZON.COM

PRELUDE

The lifeless body of a woman lies face down on the bed. Her wrists have been bound to the headboard, tied so tight her hands have taken on a blueish hue. Grayish matter oozing from an ugly crack in her skull leaves little doubt how she may have died. Her identity is concealed by blood splattered hair that covers the side of her face.

There's a tiny puncture wound below her left shoulder. It trickles blood, which pools in the small of her back. She appears to be made of candle wax, her skin an ashen white but for the welts and bruises covering the backs of her thighs and buttocks.

A wine bottle has been inserted into her vagina bottom first, made even more repulsive by the existence of a plastic straw, which grotesquely bobs in the decanters fermented remains. The bed sheets reek of urine. That and the stench of death permeates the air. Pillows placed under her midsection prop her up as if presenting her for view. At first it doesn't register...but then...then... OH GOD... NO... IT CAN'T BE... PLEASE GOD!

PEACE

EARLY RETIREMENT

MURDER IN DAYTONA

1

I'd just spent the day fishing on the Halifax River with a couple of friends. That is to say we'd become friends over the course of the day. When it was time to return dockside I was saddened a bit. It felt good to log in some male bonding time.

When my neighbor first invited me to join him on the fishing trip I'd been somewhat reluctant. The sport has never been my thing you see. I assumed I'd be bored out of my mind. Boy was I wrong!

Once we were tied up to the dock I didn't dilly dally. While my two fishing mates were popping the tops off a couple cans of cold beer I was making haste for my car. I promised my wife I'd be home in time to start dinner. Fifteen minutes after pulling out of the marina parking lot I arrive at the gated entrance of the 'fifty plus' retirement community I live in.

I approached the gate slowly, wanting to see which of the *Keystone Kops* the property manager hired to provide security is working today. They range from a former professional wrestler named Harley to a squeamish green party granola type dude whose chosen mode of transportation is a canopy covered recumbent bike. I find the safety of our enclave has been entrusted to Willis, an ex-army MP from South Carolina.

Willis waves to me from his comfortable position inside the air conditioned gatehouse then goes back to his newspaper. I give him a hearty thumbs up as I pass by.

Arriving home I choose to stay seated and enjoy a driveway moment. When I hear Paul Harvey say, "A*nd now you know the rest of the story"* I turn the radio off and pop the trunk. It's time to store my ages old but barely used fishing gear back in the shed for another period of long dormancy.

The fellow who invited me on the fishing excursion is recently widowed, having lost his wife to cancer. He always seems eager for conversation, and loves to boast about his boat. He's always telling me. *"You just have to see her, Richard. Salome is a beauty."*

She is something to behold. My neighbor christened the vessel *Salome* after buying her at a consignment auction in St Petersburg a few years back. I could tell by the way he treated her how special she was to him. Her mahogany skin is well oiled, and her engine finely tuned. *Salome* purrs like a kitten at his touch. I wonder if he treated his wife as attentively, and if she'd purred at his touch too?

Unbeknownst to me at the time my neighbor invited another friend of his to join us today. The guy was a retired priest from Michigan. They'd known each other for years. I was a little skeptical at first, but the padre turned out to be funny as hell. He kept the two of us in stitches most of the day telling risque jokes and salacious stories from what he referred to as his, *"Glory Days."*

One story had me laughing so hard I nearly fell out of the boat. The padre compared an old female parishioner of his to a large mouth bass, acting out the parts as he went. He referred to himself as the *Fish Priest,* which I later learned was a mallet used in the old days to kill a fish once it was caught. When I heard that it made the story even funnier.

8

It was obvious my neighbor enjoyed his friend's company. I was glad he had someone like him to talk to. Laughter has a way of equalizing life's heartaches. Putting things on an even keel so to speak. This friend of his, this retired priest, had a gift for making people laugh.

My fishing gear neatly tucked away, I meander down to the end of the driveway to get the mail. Fingering through the assortment of sale flyers and credit card offers I make my way back to the house. Just as I'm about to go inside I notice a sheet of paper sandwiched in the handle of the screen door. I toss the junk mail on the kitchen counter and go back for it.

I assume some small business owner went around stuffing flyers in people's doors to save postage. Instead I find a note from my wife. It reads... **Honey, I booked a room at the Pelican Inn on A1A. I need you to meet me there at five o'clock sharp. I have a surprise for you... Love, Veronica.**

It's not like my wife to leave me notes. If Veronica needs me she just calls my cell phone. Besides, we'd discussed our plans for the day over breakfast. She knew I was going fishing with the neighbor, and I knew she was going to be at the courthouse over in Deland. If she got out early she was going to go back to the shelter. There were some new intakes that needed to be filed. We agreed we would be home by five o'clock for dinner.

I didn't understand why she would drive all the way home to leave me a note? I give her a call. After several rings her voice mail picks up. *"Hello. This is Veronica. Sorry I can't take your call at the moment. Please leave a name and number and we'll talk later."*

Getting her voice mail doesn't surprise me. Veronica has a habit of carrying her cell phone in her purse. Quite often she doesn't hear it ring. Everyone we know complains about it.

My wife works as a volunteer court advocate for victims of domestic abuse. Her office is located inside the women's shelter in Daytona Beach. She doesn't like me calling her there. Says it's a safe haven for women on the lam and the number is supposed to be confidential. It was only given to me in case of emergencies. I call anyway, hoping to save myself a long drive. After spending the day in the hot sun all I really want to do is grab a cold beer and crash.

The person answering the phone tells me Veronica didn't come to the shelter today. I know she planned on going in. Friday is her busiest day. Veronica refers to it as Win-Win Day. She explains it like this. Judges need to clear their dockets and prosecutors know defendants can't post bond in time to avoid spending the weekend in jail. Her clients can relax knowing their abusers are behind bars. Win-Win Day... Everybody wins. I check my watch... It's half past four.

"What the hell is she doing," I wonder out loud as I grab the phone book from the kitchen drawer and find the number for the Pelican Inn. The telephone rings five or six times before someone with a husky voice answers. I ask to be connected to Veronica Stevens room. I get no response, but moments later I hear, *Brnnng Brrrng Brnng.* If she's there she ain't answering.

Accepting the fact I'm not going to get to relax I tear the page out of the phone book and head for my car. I estimate it will take me twenty minutes to drive there. *"I haven't even had time to take a fucking shower,"* I curse. *"I smell like a God damn fish."*

Driving across the Granada Bridge I see the Atlantic Ocean in the distance. When I get to A1A I turn right and head south. My thoughts turn to Veronica. I start thinking about how playful she can be and before I know it I begin to feel my anger melt away. I can't help but smile thinking about the potential results of my journey. This could turn out to be one hell of a night!

Several miles later I find myself in a rundown section of the beach. The blighted area is barren, but for a brightly painted motel located across from the ocean. The colorful lime green building sits in sharp contrast to its bleak surroundings. A sign tells me I've found THE PELICAN INN. I glance at my watch. It's a couple minutes before five.

Veronica's shiny red VW Beetle sits precariously between an old pick up truck with a flat tire and a station wagon with a cracked windshield. My wife's vanity plate, **RETRO-GIRL,** is easily recognizable.

An overflowing garbage dumpster sits in the far corner of the lot, the area around it littered with trash. It's obvious the trash has spilled from plastic bags torn open by scavengers of varying species. An out of business convenience store sits idly on one side of the motel. A vacant lot on the other. I can't help but grumble to myself as I head toward the office. This is definitely **not** the place I would have chosen to have a romantic rendezvous.

When I get there the office door is locked. I ring the buzzer and wait. After a second attempt I hear what sounds like a toilet flushing. Moments later this lethargic looking guy appears. He's slovenly dressed and desperately in need of a shave. The guy seems totally clueless. An unlit cigarette butt hangs from his lip, confirming my assessment.

Tossing what appears to be a *girlie* magazine on his desk he looks at me unenthusiastically and asks, *"Can I help you?"* I explain my wife checked in earlier today and I need her room number. The guy grabs a clipboard off the counter and in the same apathetic voice asks, *"Name?"* When I answer he looks up and says, *"I just took a call for her a few minutes ago... She's in twenty-eight."*

The Pelican Inn has two floors. Odd numbered rooms are down and even numbered up. Taking the stairs two at a time I quickly reach the second level. After locating the door with **28** painted on it I turn the door handle. The door's locked. I call out Veronica's name. No answer! *"Five sharp my ass,"* I complain.

I return to the office and buzz the clerk again. When he arrives I explain my wife must have stepped out and request a room key. The foul smelling paper shuffler responds, *"Sorry Pal. Two keys to a room."*

I point to my wife's car as I plead my case. *"She probably went for a walk on the beach,"* I suggest. She has to be around. After providing the clerk with a ten dollar enticement he finally agrees to let me in.

The late November sun is setting in the western sky as we climb the steel staircase. I can't help but notice how the impending darkness masquerades the grime of the place. Even the rusting vehicles parked alongside Veronica's beetle look good with the neon lights of the Pelican Inn reflecting off their dull sheen.

When we arrive at the room the motel clerk finger flips his unlit cigarette butt over the side of the railing then chooses a key from the ring on his belt. He unlocks the door then motions for me to go in. Just then all hell breaks loose in the parking lot below us.

Half a dozen police cars come speeding into the lot, their strobe lights flashing. I look at the clerk, who appears as confused as me. One of the cops jumps out of his cruiser and draws his weapon. When he points it towards me I duck into the room...

The image I see registers in my brain like freeze frame photography. My heart skips a beat and I feel my knees buckle. Anxiety replaces the oxygen in my lungs as I crumble to the floor in a state of disbelief. Half a moment later a female police officer rushes in. She points her revolver at me and screams *"**Don't you fucking move!**"*

A burning sensation rips through my stomach as I observe the officer from my crouched position. I watch as her gaze shifts from me to the woman on the bed. I see a horrified look come over her face. When she turns her attention back to me I try to explain who I am and why I'm there, but the words won't come out.

The motel clerk is out on the landing arguing with another police officer. The cop ignores his pleas. He wrestles him to the ground and cuffs him.

Two more officers rush into the room, their weapons cocked and pointed. They stop dead in their tracks when they see my wife's ravaged body on the bed. One of them asks the female cop if she's okay while the other one pulls me up by the scruff of the neck and pushes me into a chair. I knock over a glass table lamp in the process. It smashes on the hard tile floor.

Just then this giant of a guy enters the room. All three officers simultaneously take a step back, as if it were choreographed. His hair is cut short, marine boot camp style, and he sports a bushy salt n pepper mustache. The guy must be six and a half feet tall. He definitely has a presence about him. He's wearing a western style shirt and Levi's. Authentic alligator skin boots complete his ensemble.

I'm surprised when the big guy flashes a shield and identifies himself as Chief Detective Dan Brooks. First thing he does is walk over to check my wife's body for a pulse. Broken glass crumbles under his boots as he crosses the floor. Then he turns to the cop who shoved me and says, *"You'll be payin for that busted lamp, Son."*

It wasn't said in a threatening manner, but rather as a softly spoken statement made by a gentle voice of reason. I have to say I am immediately impressed by the placid nature of this oversized cowboy.

He walks over and places his large meaty palm on my trembling hand and starts asking me questions. I don't fully comprehend what it is he's asking. My senses are traumatized. Something about being right. *"Are you all right,"* or perhaps it was, *"You understand your rights?"*

Wiping snot and tears from my face I point to the plundered body on the bed and mutter, *"That's my wife."* The detective squats down and looks me dead in the eye. After studying my face for a few moments he asks me my name. Obviously in shock, I just stare back at him. Unfettered, the detective continues his questioning. He asks me when I last saw my wife alive. Then he asks if I'd had an argument with the victim... That's when I lose it!

"WHAT," I scream as I jump from the chair. ***"SHE'S NO VICTIM... THAT'S MY WIFE, YOU ASSHOLE!"*** I want to punch Goliath in the face. I want to hit somebody... Anybody! My anger restrained by handcuffs, I slump back down in the chair. *"YOU DON'T UNDERSTAND,"* I plead. *"MY WIFE'S BEEN MURDERED. PLEASE... HELP US!"*

The detective stops with the questions. He tells the two male officers to put me in a squad car and wait for further instructions. As I'm escorted away I hear him tell the lady cop to safeguard the room. *"No one goes in until the medical examiner arrives... Comprende?"*

Sitting in the back seat of a police car the reality of what's happened begins to settle in. *"How can this be,"* I ask myself? I need to question the cops and find out who did this to us. Problem is, they want to question me!

14

A van with a satellite dish attached to its roof comes flying into the lot. *Live Eye Action News* is emblazoned on the side panel. I recognize the woman who steps out of the van and approaches the cops assigned to watch me. She's a reporter. I overhear her talking to them.

"We received a phone call from someone claiming he'd just murdered his wife. He said they were staying at this motel." One of the cops told the reporter a call came into dispatch claiming the same thing. He said the caller even gave them his location. Then he turned and pointed up to room twenty-eight.

While the three of them are talking the television crew's camera operator opens the front door of the squad car and begins taping me through the glass partition. I holler for him to stop, but to no avail. The cops hear the commotion and order the guy away from the car. The reporter apologizes, then she heads off to visit the scene of the crime.

Several minutes later a canine cop walks by leading a german shepherd police dog. He's holding an aluminum baseball bat in his hand. The officer stops to talk to the two officers assigned to watch me. I hear him say, *"Rommel found it in the lot next door, didn't you boy?"* He pats the dog on the head then adds, *"There's dried blood on the barrel, right around the sweet spot."*

A yellow tape barricade is stretched in front of the motel to keep an assembling crowd back. Onlookers are pointing fingers at me. I can hear them mumbling. In the distance I can see the television reporter interviewing the big detective who'd questioned me up in the room. They're bathed in flood lights. After a while the lights dim and the news crew begins packing up. The detective walks over to the squad car and opens the door. He asks me how I'm doing, then instructs the two officers to take me to *The Resort.*

EARLY RETIREMENT

MURDER IN DAYTONA

2

I learn *The Resort* is a new jail facility that houses repeat felons and violent criminals awaiting trial. It had been christened *The Resort* by a couple of detainees when it first opened a few months back and the name stuck. The structure is located just off International Speedway Boulevard at the city line. Void of any windows above the first floor, *The Resort* is a cold foreboding place.

I'm brought in through the rear of the building and booked on suspicion of murder. Once shackled, photographed, and finger printed I'm enthusiastically welcomed by the staff. Because of the severity of my charges I'm not allowed to leave my private hell. A gunmetal gray five foot by eight foot jail cell. Most of the space is taken up by a metal frame bed bolted to the wall. Perpendicular to the bed is a combination stainless steel toilet and sink. The only other comforts afforded me are a pillow, a blanket, and a King James bible.

The next six days of my life are spent at *The Resort.* I am repeatedly questioned by an interrogator, a tall black man named Duval. Duval seemed like a decent guy at first. He provided me with cold drinks and casual conversation. He told me he played basketball at Boston University. Being a college basketball fan I was impressed. We talked sports, swapped stories, and it got so I looked forward to Duval's visits. Then things changed.

Five days in I'm brought to an interrogation room and chained to a table. An hour or so later Duval walks in and places a pen and a sheet of paper in front of me. He stands against the wall with his arms folded and waits. After a while he motions for me to pick up the pen. That's when things turn nasty.

Duval tells me I can't wiggle my way out of this one. He strongly suggests I sign the statement, *"For my own good."* The interrogator tells me things will go better for me if I do. When I refuse he gets very angry. After rattling off a litany of expletives Duval slams his fist on the table and informs me I will never see the light of day again.

Still I remain adamant about my innocence. Eventually Duval puts the *bad cop* routine to bed and pulls up a chair. We go over and over what happened a dozen times. I remind him I'd gone fishing the day my wife was murdered, emphasizing *"With some friends... One of them is a priest, for Christ's sake!"* I plead with Duval to let me assist in the investigation.

The following day I'm set free. I'd hired an attorney to represent me. I guess he did his job. God only knows how long I could have survived in that place.

My lawyer's name is Sheckstein. He's an old white haired Jewish lawyer from Brooklyn. Arty got his law degree from Stetson University. After he graduated he hung a shingle in downtown Daytona Beach, long before it became known as the *Historical District.*

Arty always runs ads in the Sunday edition of the local newspaper. He also leases one of those billboards on Interstate 95. His sign implores drivers to *Research the rest. Then call the best.* Arty's billboard features a twenty foot tall caricature of himself dressed as Uncle Sam. He stands there decked out in red, white, and blue, pointing a yard long index finger at passing motorists.

When I first saw his sign it reminded me of one of those army recruiting posters I'd seen as a kid. *WE WANT YOU.* Veronica and I used to make fun of Arty's billboard every time we drove down the interstate. Little did I know I'd one day be hiring him to represent me in a murder rap.

My release from custody came with a stipulation that I not leave the state pending resolution of the case. Arty was able to persuade the judge to grant me something lawyers call an *exceptio probat regulam.* The ruling would allow me to return to New York to bury Veronica once her body was released by the medical examiner. The four grand I laid out for Arty's representation was the best money I've ever spent, or so it seemed that day.

Shortly before being discharged Duval arrived at my cell to offer his condolences. He told me the city has a notoriously high rate of crimes against women. The interrogator sounded apologetic as he explained how Daytona Beach seems to attract that element of society. According to Duval his aggressive tactics were justified by the departments lack of success in apprehending perpetrators. I reassured him of my innocence and offered to assist in any way I could.

The sound of the heavy iron doors slamming shut behind me reverberate through the hall. My release from the resort results in a mixed bag of emotions. As I descend the stairwell leading to my freedom I feel elated. Conversely, I suffer intense misery over my wife's death. How can I possibly go on without Veronica? I would gladly spend the rest of my life behind bars if it meant I could bring her back. The reality of life without her will incarcerate my heart forever. How does a man recover from such loss? What does he do with his anger? I need answers. Who did this...and why?

Reaching the first floor I enter the lobby, appreciative of the sunlight passing through the floor to ceiling windows. There were no windows in the tiny cell I'd inhabited that week. The only light came from dull fluorescent fixtures that gave off a repressive hum twenty-four hours a day. It was impossible to escape the annoying sound. The consistent murmur mirrored the unrelenting angst I felt over the recent events that had put me there.

As I make my way toward the revolving doors leading to my freedom I hear my name. *"Stevens... Hey, Mr Stevens... Richard."* I turn to see a man in a grey suit walking briskly towards me. It's the detective who'd questioned me at the murder scene. He grabs my shoulder and says, *"It's a good thing I spotted you. Remember me? Detective Dan Brooks."*

He doesn't bother to offer his hand. He just continues with his diatribe. *"I was the officer in charge the night of your wife's murder, Stevens. I've been assigned the case. Actually I requested it."*

I ask him why he'd do that? The detective looks me dead in the eye and says, *"I've been a cop for nearly thirty years, Stevens. I've investigated dozens of murders. The memory of your wife propped up on that bed will stay with me the rest of my life. I won't rest until her perpetrator is brought to justice."*

A knot forms in my throat as I struggle to suppress my emotions. The detective continues. *"I was filling out my retirement papers when the call came in. As the senior officer on duty I responded. No way can I walk away from this job now. Not until this case is closed. It would haunt me forever. You understand?"*

Tears well up in my eyes. I start to sob, standing there surrounded by strangers busily going about their day. I half expect the detective to console me in my grief. I'm completely taken aback when instead he says to me, *"Murder is seldom a random act, Mr Stevens... It's a crime of passion."* Then the big lawman leans over and whispers in my ear, *"You're a passionate man, aren't you Richard?"*

I'm befuddled by the imputation. The inference I had anything to do with my wife's death is absurd. The detective pats me on the back and tells me he'll be in touch. Then he turns and walks away.

Once home I become a recluse. I refuse to answer my door or telephone. I'm at a loss... What should I do? My anger is morphing into depression, which results in my overindulging. If possible I intend to drink my pain away.

Some days later I receive a visit from Arty Scheckstein. My attorney pounds on my front door so hard he nearly splinters the wood. Seems the medical examiner has been trying to reach me. Unable to do so they contacted him. Arty tells me I need to certify my wife's body before it can be released. We share my last bottle of Johnny Walker Red, then Arty goes back to work.

Next morning I drive to the medical examiner's office over in Deland. I'm escorted to the basement where I'm asked to identify the body of my wife. Veronica is lying on a gurney behind a glass partitioned cubicle in an otherwise pleasant room. She looks so small and delicate lying there. I recall a trip we took to Niagara Falls before moving to Florida. We'd visited Madame Tussaud's wax museum. The museum's mannequins seemed so lifelike. Veronica could have been one of them today had someone applied make up to hide her bluish tint.

Once the certification papers are signed I'm provided with the official death certificate and a copy of the medical examiner's autopsy report. His report reveals the cause of Veronica's death as blunt trauma to the head. An aluminum baseball bat found near the scene was positively identified as the murder weapon. Samples of Veronica's blood and hair were found on it. No fingerprints were discovered... On the weapon, or on the body.

Her panties had been stuffed in her mouth. An apparent attempt to quell her screams. Knife wounds to my wife's back were superficial, presumably inflicted to instill terror. She'd suffered a horrendous beating about her lower torso, and she'd been sexually violated. No semen was found... On or inside her.

The autopsy report went on to say the victim had been dead less than an hour when discovered. Veronica undoubtedly suffered immense physical and emotional torture inflicted over an extended period of time. Surprising to me the autopsy also revealed there was a psychoactive drug present in Veronica's bloodstream.

After reading the report I made my way over to claims. The person behind the counter took my information and disappeared behind a partition. She returned several minutes later holding a plastic tub. Inside the container I find the pearl earrings I'd given Veronica on her fiftieth birthday.

Also in the container is my wife's purse. It holds her driver's license, credit cards, a twenty dollar bill, and a tube of lipstick. At the bottom of the tub are the clothes Veronica wore to work that day. A black pencil skirt, which she paired with a red blouse, a red bra and black heels. Her outfit had been found neatly folded in a dresser drawer in the motel room.

I stood there perplexed by the surrealism of the situation. I fought the urge to run back to the morgue, carry Veronica out to the car, and drive away from all this. Staring at the contents of the container I sense something is missing. At first I can't put my finger on it... Then it occurs to me. Veronica's wedding ring is missing.

I ask the woman behind the counter if there are any other items. She looks at me as if I'm confused and shakes her head, No. I tell her something's not right. My wife's wedding ring is missing. She hesitates, then lifts her finger to signal me to hold on. A few minutes later an unassuming figure appears from behind the partition. *"How can I help you,"* he asks?

The claims officer is a low key unpretentious looking guy of modest stature. His appearance seems to mirror his occupational status. He tells me he's responsible for cataloging the personal belongings of the deceased. When I tell him Veronica's wedding ring is missing he gets defensive, insisting all items belonging to the deceased were accounted for.

He explains when a body comes in all jewelry is removed, numbered, and recorded in the official register, then placed in a locked safe. *"If there was no ring recorded, then I'm afraid there was no ring,"* he insists.

I consider the possibility Veronica may have taken her wedding ring off. She would occasionally place it in a jar of jewelry cleaner she kept in the medicine cabinet. I thank him for his trouble and make a mental note to check the jewelry cleaner when I get home. The only unfinished business left is to make arrangements to have Veronica transported back to New York for burial.

After loading her things in the trunk of my car I decide to go for a stroll. It would be salubrious to my soul to walk away some of the pain. I'd learned from my days as a meter reader that one can have the most useful conversations with one's self when setting a fast pace and losing cognizance of those around him.

Victorian houses line the brick laden streets, most decked out with elaborate holiday displays. Eventually I find myself in historic downtown Deland. The once dilapidated buildings have been brought back to life with quaint little shops and welcoming haunts where one can imbibe. I happen upon a little Irish establishment, enchanted by a leprechaun Santa who stands on the street and beckons customers to come in and celebrate the holidays Gaelic style. Accepting his invitation, I set out to inebriate myself into the comforting arms of intoxication.

I can't recall how I got back to my car, but I wake to the sun shining in my face and a sore aching back. As I lay prone across the back seat I panic, thinking my wallet is missing. I find it safely tucked away in my jacket pocket. My trip home is hastened by the fact it's relatively early on Saturday morning. People are not yet out and about. My head is pounding and I need to take a leak. Both the result of a night dedicated to drinking my blues away.

Arriving home I make a mad dash for the bathroom. After relieving myself I go in search of ibuprofen. As I slide the medicine cabinet door open I remember Veronica's missing ring.

It wasn't an expensive piece of jewelry. Just a simple band of gold with diamond chips along the crown. I'd bought it at a jewelry store a few days before proposing. The night I gave it to her I laid the ring in the freshly opened bud of a red rose.

Offering Veronica the flower, I suggested she close her eyes and smell the sweetness. When she lifted the rose to her face she opened her eyes and saw the ring. You would have thought it was the most precious thing she'd ever been given. Veronica openly wept as she mouthed the words, *"Yes... I'll marry you."*

I reach for the bottle of jewelry cleaner. As I twist the top open it fumbles in my hands and drops to the floor. I get down on my hands and knees and wallow around in the cleaning solution desperately seeking any sign of the ring.

It is a wasted effort. The importance of that fact hits home immediately. The victim hadn't been wearing a ring. I determine that to find the victim's ring is to find the killer.

I'm momentarily taken aback by my referral of Veronica as the victim. The unforgivable depersonalization stuns me. Am I losing my compassion? The victim I was referring to was the love of my life!

23

Had no one noticed that the murdered woman, a married woman, was not wearing a wedding ring? It would be my link to the investigation. The police would be searching for her killer. I would be searching for her ring! My search would begin the minute I returned from New York.

EARLY RETIREMENT

MURDER IN DAYTONA

3

Typical of a late November day in Syracuse a cold rain is falling. A rainbow has formed high above the headstones and memorials honoring the dearly departed. Veronica loved rainbows. I recall the time she told me I was her pot of gold at the end of the rainbow. Under the circumstances it was a bittersweet memory.

Tears well up in my eyes as I make my way from her grave. Sitting alone in my rental car I begin to shake uncontrollably. *"Why God,"* I scream. *"Jesus... Why her?"* I was blaming the only person I could think of who could have prevented it from happening.

Everyone die's eventually. I understand that. No one lives forever. Who'd want to? I wasn't sure I wanted to go on without her. The horror she'd suffered at the hands of a deranged maniac haunted me. I remembered my vow. I wouldn't live forever, but I'd live long enough to see her tormentor pay for his crime.

After a while I regain my composure and head toward the exit. As I pull onto Grant Boulevard I notice the view hasn't changed much from the days when we lived across the street. The house we'd bought together some twenty years before was still there. It had been the first home we ever owned. At the time Veronica and I wondered if people would consider us morbid for living across the street from a cemetery. We joked about it, telling our friends and family at least our neighbors are quiet.

We used to go for long walks in that cemetery and talk about life. It was during one of those walks we decided we would be laid to rest there when our time came. Who knew it would come so soon?

As I approach the house I notice the beautiful flower gardens Veronica had planted were no longer there. They'd been replaced by a simple grass lawn. *"A shame,"* I mutter to myself.

The house had been repainted too. A dreadful shade of gray that blended in with the surrounding sky. I remind myself it wont be long before everything up here is covered in snow. This is upstate New York. Winters here are long and harsh. It's not at all unusual to get two or three feet during a winter storm. That's the main reason Veronica and I decided to relocate to a warm climate. A decision we... I, now deeply regret.

Driving back to the airport Veronica's memory fills my mind. How beautiful she'd been. How gracefully she'd aged. How she'd enjoyed helping people, often putting their needs before her own. I reminisce about our intimacy. How I miss the scent of her skin and the softness of her lips. The feeling of her body pressed against mine as we cuddle in at night.

I recall how she came into my life, and how she insisted it was divine intervention. How open and honest she'd been with me about her past. We spent many evenings drinking wine and sharing experiences. The more wine Veronica drank the more information she divulged. I'm sure I learned more about her past than I had a right to, but it brought us closer. Our lives were an open book to one another. I knew her better than I know myself.

Hancock International Airport is located ten miles north of the city line. Each mile I drive brings back memories. I pass by a house we once considered buying before finding the house on Grant Blvd. I remember we wanted to make an offer on it, but were told it had just sold. Minutes later I find myself driving past a little diner we used to visit on Sunday mornings. It was owned by a sweet oriental lady. Her diner served the best blueberry pancakes I've ever tasted.

When I got to this one intersection I recalled getting pulled over by a sheriff deputy years before. I had run the red light, hoping to beat it as it changed from green to red. I remember the deputy asking me, *"Where the heck you going in such a hurry, Sir?"* I told him the truth. My wife and I were late for a bible study.

He looked at me suspiciously before noticing there was a concordance and bible lying on the back seat. I remember him asking, *"New King James version?"*

I told him it was New American Standard. The deputy smiled at me in recognition of a brother believer and let me go with a warning and a spirited *"Praise the Lord!"*

Upon arriving at the airport I return my rental car then take the skybridge to the terminal. After checking my bag I grab a newspaper and search for my gate. Every time I have to take my shoes off and walk the TSA gauntlet I get pissed off at Osama Bin Laden all over again. This time is no different!

Once settled I pull out my newspaper and turn to the sports section. The Orangemen are preparing to host the Carrier Classic Invitational Basketball Tournament. This year's opponents are UNLV, Vermont, and Boston University. I instinctively think of Duval back at *The Resort.* I know he'll be watching the tournament, having played for the Terriers. I wonder if he'll think of me when he sees his alma mater playing Syracuse in the first round.

Upon boarding the plane I make my way to my seat. It's then I realize I'm sitting in row twenty-eight. The irony strikes me in an unsettling kind of way. I take my seat and finger my way through the rest of the newspaper. I'm thankful no one is sitting next to me. Before long I fall asleep. The remainder of my flight is spent in a state of perpetual tranquility.

EARLY RETIREMENT
MURDER IN DAYTONA

4

Veronica was the oldest of four daughters born to Jerome and Lynn Flowers. Her parents split up when she was fifteen. She vividly remembered the day her father left. He'd taken Veronica aside and explained how he and her mother were never meant to be together. When he tried to leave she blocked the doorway in a vain attempt to stop him. She begged her father not to go but he pushed past her, saying he needed to be with his *lady friend.*

According to Veronica her father always referred to his mistress as his *lady friend.* She told me the last words she ever spoke to him were, *"What about us, Daddy?"* She screamed them out as he drove away.

Mr Flowers had been unfaithful to his wife for some time. He'd made little effort to hide the fact. His desire to have a son had gone unfulfilled and he seemed unable to accept it. Jerome withheld affection from his family as if punishing them for being female.

Veronica's mom did her best to compensate for her failed marriage by devoting her life to her daughters. She rarely dated, and never entertained a man in her home. Mrs Flowers got no financial assistance from her ex-husband, and no child support. She never even took him to court. Lynn Flowers got a job to support her family.

My Wife told me her mother worked long hours, but she always made time for the important functions in her daughter's lives. Veronica, being the oldest, was relied upon to take care of things in her mother's absence. She'd prepare school lunches, get her sisters on the bus, and start dinner in the evening. There were always clothes to wash, beds to make, and dishes to do. Veronica made sure her sisters did their homework and said their prayers before being tucked in at night. She learned the true meaning of responsibility.

Veronica's personality mirrored her mother's. Outwardly both projected an air of confidence, but truth be known each carried the pain of abandonment deep inside. Veronica loved her father. She couldn't understand why he'd leave his family. Why he'd leave her. She told me there were times she wished she'd been born a boy. Maybe he would have stayed?

She often wondered if she'd done something wrong, or if she could have done something differently. Did her father love her? Would any man ever love her? Those questions haunted Veronica for many years. Her confident self assured outer crust shielded a fragile little girl yearning to be loved.

When Veronica graduated from high school a few years later she went to work for a local manufacturing plant. Her job consisted of inserting a screw into a piece of molded plastic then placing it on a belt and sending it down the line. She never got to see the finished product, or really understood what it was used for. She found the job tedious and unsatisfying. It was the kind of job one could do while lost in one's own daydreams.

One day she decided to go out for lunch. Normally Veronica brown bagged it. The Little Gem Diner was just a few blocks from the plant. When she walked there she had no idea she was about to meet the man who would become her future husband.

Lucky Focha was a construction worker on break from a building project around the corner from the diner. Veronica told me she'd seen him sitting at the counter when she walked in. He watched her in the mirrored wall opposite the counter as she was seated at a booth. Eventually he worked up the nerve to walk over and introduce himself.

I remember laughing when I heard his name for the first time. Veronica said she'd had the same reaction. *"Lucky asked me if I'd go out with him on Saturday night,"* she explained. *"How could I say no to a guy with a name like that?"*

Veronica told me she hadn't been asked out in quite awhile. It had been six months since she broke up with her last boyfriend, a guy she dated in high school. His name was Tom. He was a deputy sheriff, and considerably older than her.

According to Veronica this Tom guy could be very persuasive. She told me she lost her virginity to Tom in the back seat of his patrol car. Of course my wife had been drinking wine rather heavily the night she told me that. Like I said before, I learned more about her past then I had a right to.

My wife admitted she didn't know much about sex until she met Tom. He'd proven to be a very attentive lover. His patrol car became the scene of many of their escapades.

Veronica knew enough to insist he take the necessary precautions. Their relationship ended when Veronica found out Tom was two-timing her with another girl in school. He'd been making it with one of the cheerleaders. The girl ended up pregnant. *Ra-Ra-Sis-Boom-Ba!*

Lucky asked Veronica to meet him at Ed's Place, a local tavern that featured live bands on the weekends. New York hadn't raised the legal drinking age to twenty-one yet, though it had come up for debate. I've always found it ironic that an eighteen year old could be shipped off to fight and die in some foreign war but he couldn't legally buy a beer. Lucky was waiting outside with beer in hand when Veronica pulled into the parking lot.

Come to find out the tavern was owned by Lucky's older brother. Lucky spent most of his time there when not swinging a hammer. Veronica told me she had a good time with Lucky that night. The drinks flowed freely, deeply discounted by Ed, and she stayed till closing time. Afterward in the back seat of her car the passion of the moment overcame the promise she'd made to herself. There wasn't going to be any more back seat romances... Yeah, Right!

It was over rather quickly according to Veronica. Too quickly for her satisfaction. She liked Lucky but she was disappointed in his failure to consider her needs. He definitely wasn't a lover boy. He was no Tom! Having no other prospects on the horizon, Veronica continued seeing him.

Several months later Veronica learned she was pregnant. She'd started spending weekends at Lucky's apartment. She told me he'd developed a habit of waking up in the middle of the night to have sex. Lucky was usually good about using protection, but this one night she woke to find him on top of her. He hadn't bothered to take care of business and...well it was bound to happen.

Veronica's big concern back then was how to explain the pregnancy to her mom. The oldest daughter, the responsible one, was with child! Lucky may not have been a lover boy but he wasn't sterile. The living being growing in her womb proved that!

Her mother groaned when she heard the news. Mrs Flowers knew the father was Lucky and her disappointment showed. She'd hoped for more for her oldest daughter. Still, there was no way this pregnancy was going to be aborted. Mom was catholic and by God *"You make your bed, you sleep in it."* It was decided the best thing was for Lucky and her daughter to get married. Veronica Flowers would become Mrs Lucky Focha.

Mom's house had been converted to a two family years before, when Veronica's grandfather moved in. The small apartment next door had been vacant since his death several years back. It was about to be inhabited again. This time by Veronica, Lucky, and their newborn daughter. My wife told me they spent the next couple of years there, playing house and making believe they were happy.

Truth is Veronica and Lucky never really loved each other. They put on the pretense of marriage, but they both knew it was doomed to fail. According to Veronica Lucky showed less and less interest in being with her as time went on. He contributed little to the household, and even less to the relationship. She said his skills as a lover were never great and they deteriorated with time. Veronica remained unfulfilled, both emotionally and sexually.

I was told Lucky's older brother made inappropriate advances towards Veronica on several occasions. She told me she once considered having an affair with him, her desperation showing. Ed was something of a playboy. He always seemed to attract women.

Most of the girls working at his club were young and naive. He often bragged how his position allowed him to take advantage. Veronica told me she presumed he'd be a good lover, but that she found him kind of creepy. Ed knew Veronica wasn't getting it at home, and told her so. One time he backed her into a corner and felt her up. When she complained to Lucky he just blew her off, saying, *"Bullshit... That's just Ed being Ed."*

Eventually Veronica's mom helped her daughter get a job at the utility. It meant more money, but she found the work no more stimulating than her old job. Meanwhile the construction business had taken a downturn and Lucky was laid off. He worked at his

Ed's Place on the weekends to earn a few bucks, but he never contributed to the family finances.

Fortunately Veronica earned enough to support the family. Lucky showed no motivation in finding suitable employment, yet he refused to *babysit* the kid all day. He was content to sit home and watch television while Veronica dropped their daughter off at day care and went to work. Her frustration grew stronger with each passing day.

Veronica had an affair with a man who gave her the attention she craved. I assume it was her way of compensating for the lack of affection she got at home. Who am I to judge? Lord knows I'm not perfect... Who the hell is?

She told me she was in love with the guy, and thought he was in love with her too. The affair didn't last. His wife found out he was seeing another woman and he broke it off.

There were other men. Like I told you, we had no secrets from each other. Veronica told me when her needs went unfulfilled at home she went looking for someone to share a bit of intimacy with. Some were married, some were not. Some lasted a few days, others a few months. Veronica told me she felt guilty about it. I understood. She was a young attractive woman stuck in a loveless marriage.

Eventually Lucky reacted to what was going on. Veronica was spending more and more time away from home. After a while he couldn't continue to make believe it wasn't happening. My wife told me when he finally confronted her she didn't deny it. Rather than react violently as Veronica would have preferred, Lucky simply disappeared emotionally. Their marriage had become a burden. They were strangers sharing a bed. Her catholic upbringing aside, Veronica made the decision to end it.

EARLY RETIREMENT

MURDER IN DAYTONA

5

Men had been a constant source of pain for Veronica. Her father abandoned her, her first love got another girl pregnant, and her husband left her emotionally starved. Many of the lovers she'd taken turned out to be self indulgent narcissists. When Veronica met a woman who seemed to understand her she felt like she'd been saved.

Her name was Doris Van Fleet. Doris had turned from the opposite sex at a very young age. When she was nine years old her stepfather began sexually molesting her. The abuse started with inappropriate touching, but soon progressed to nightly visits to her bed. His visits continued for years. Not wanting to hurt her mother Doris kept her shame a secret. She never blamed herself for the rapes as some victims do, but she never dealt with them either.

Doris told Veronica she always felt her mother knew what her husband was doing, but she never stopped him. When Doris was old enough to leave home and fend for herself she did. Once gone she never attempted to contact her mother, and her mother never contacted her. That fact confirmed the unspoken truth. The silence was deafening!

She says she knew she was a lesbian since childhood. Doris insisted what happened with her step father didn't alter that reality, but you had to wonder?

A blonde with a gregarious personality, Doris was socially confident and uninhibited. As a young adult she developed quite a reputation in the local lesbian community. Word was Doris was good in bed. All the dykes knew she had no qualms about making a move on their partners
.

Veronica met Doris while shopping at a health food store. She was trying to improve her eating habits, and Doris was a health food nut. Veronica's story is Doris approached her with advice on healthy eating. The two struck up a friendship and she was invited over to enjoy a drink and continue their conversation.

Of course Veronica wasn't so naive that she didn't know where Doris was coming from. She'd never considered having a lesbian relationship, but the thought didn't repel her. She told me Doris liked the way she looked. Doris loved women with large breasts and ample bottoms. I joked about that as I recall, telling my wife Doris and I had more in common than she thought.

Veronica told me she was liberated that afternoon. She hadn't felt such passion in years. It was the first time she'd ever had multiple orgasms. It was only a matter of weeks before Doris invited Veronica to move in, convincing her it was the best thing she could do for both for herself and her child.

She made the move, but decided to leave her daughter with her grandmother until they got to know each other better. Doris had no experience with children. Veronica said she was led to believe her daughter would be welcome there when the time came.

Everything seemed to be falling into place. Veronica's divorce was moving forward, her daughter seemed to be doing well, and she was happy in her new relationship. Then a surprise came. Veronica was served a subpoena... Lucky was asking for custody of his daughter.

Ed Focha found out about Veronica and Doris and contacted his lawyer on his brother's behalf. He had a real issue with queers. Ed was more than happy to come to Lucky's aid. His tavern wasn't suffering the same economic downturn many businesses were. In fact Ed's bank account was overflowing. He instructed his attorney to do whatever was necessary to get his niece back with her father.

The attorney happened to be good friends with the family court judge hearing the case, and knew how he felt about homosexuals. Ed was assured the judge would never allow a little girl to be raised by a couple of lesbians.

The New York State Supreme Court granted Veronica her divorce, but child custody in New York is determined by the family court system. As expected, the judge gave custody to the father. Veronica would still be allowed to be a part of her daughter's life, in the form of child support payments and structured visitation. She was devastated when the ruling came down. How could such injustice prevail?

Veronica became deeply depressed, and her depression had a negative affect on her relationship. Doris tried to convince her she was better off. She argued that Veronica was now free to do what she wanted. Despite her vain attempts to encourage, Doris failed. Veronica became emotionally impotent.

They went on a vacation. Doris convinced Veronica she needed to get away for a while, insisting the change would do her good. She booked them a condo in Provincetown, Massachusetts. The resort town at the tip of Cape Cod is a haven for the gay and lesbian community. Doris wanted Veronica to experience a place where their lifestyle was celebrated as the norm rather than the exception.

Veronica noticed a change in Doris' behavior once they were there. It made her uncomfortable. Doris was beginning to display a much more aggressive personality. She insisted on calling her Vee, saying it sounded less *Fem.* She encouraged Veronica to cut her hair short and wear jeans and baggy tee's rather than the dresses she preferred. When she objected Doris angrily told her it was time she face up to who she really was.

Veronica told me Doris wanted to introduce her to bondage paraphernalia. That bothered her. She said she was always sexually satisfied by Doris and she didn't understand why Doris didn't feel the same way. The idea of using fake phalluses and an assortment of bindings was odd to her. She insisted she wouldn't enjoy the experience no matter how much Doris wanted her to.

When she refused to take part Veronica was accused of being a, *"Lipstick girl, A glam sister. Not a real lesbian at all."* It goes without saying the last few days of their vacation were spent in a tense, strained, state of silence.

The silence ended when they got back home. Doris tore Veronica down at every opportunity. She made groundless accusations of infidelity and questioned her parenting skills. She planned evenings out without her. Of course Veronica wasn't allowed to do the same.

Doris took to hiding Veronica's car keys, effectively isolating her from seeking any outside intervention. In Veronica's already weakened state, Doris' behavior drove her into an even deeper depression. What she needed most was emotional support and care and understanding. Instead she was with someone who wore two faces. Doris put on the facade of a loving partner, but in reality was a classic abuser. The protector and provider, the flattering and faithful lover, had morphed into a controlling malicious tyrant.

Veronica knew she had to get out of the relationship. To stay there would be to die there. It broke her heart that Doris, who'd originally been so attentive, changed so drastically. Veronica told me she could barely recognize the woman she'd shared a bed with. The level of cruelty had taken her completely by surprise. So much for sisterhood!

Veronica had loved this woman. She told me so. Now she found herself cowering to an onslaught of verbal abuse heaped upon her at every opportunity. Veronica told me she feared Doris would hurt her one day, possibly even kill her. I'm proud that she found the strength to pick up the pieces of her shattered life and make things right again.

It's ironic that Veronica's work life prospered as her personal life fell apart. She told me she immersed herself in her work as a way of compensating for the lack of control she felt over her private affairs. The desire to escape the reality of her situation lent itself to making the most of her career. She excelled in her job and was rewarded by being asked to take a higher level assignment.

The district manager needed help improving customer service scores. They'd slipped due to recent changes the utility had put in place to control costs. Veronica successfully performed duties far above her pay grade. She wasn't concerned with compensation. The fact she was doing work that stimulated her was more than enough incentive.

Her efforts didn't go unnoticed. The district manager was impressed, both personally and professionally. Veronica knew she'd made quite an impact. Even so, she was surprised when she learned she'd been selected for a promotion.

Veronica's lack of a formal education was overcome by her perseverance, intelligence, and strength of purpose. She was scheduled to attend management training school at the public utility's headquarters in Albany. The opportunity provided her with a chance to get away from Doris. She needed the time to sort things out in her mind.

EARLY RETIREMENT

MURDER IN DAYTONA

6

My first marriage ended in divorce too. It had been rocky from the start, but we endured. My ex-wife and I suffered from insecurity issues that often resulted in heated exchanges and physical altercations. In the early days our nights were filled with outbursts of jealousy and rage as we fell victim to our inner demons. We both knew our union was doomed to fail but we kept up the pretense of normalcy, as if to do so would cause it to miraculously work itself out.

Neither of us expected our relationship to survive, but the years rolled by. We eventually found a level of comfort we could coexist in together. There'd never been much physical attraction between us. Our sex life could best be described as intermittent. That is to say we seldom made love. Birth control in our house consisted of a combination of voluntary abstinence, timing, and luck. It worked like a charm for ten years. Then my ex got pregnant.

They say having children can't save a marriage that's doomed to fail, but having a baby brought a whole new perspective to our lives. Our son became the focal point of our relationship. One thing my ex and I could agree on was our love for him. The energy and commitment that might have been used to salvage our marriage was instead expended on raising our child.

Of course the truth remained, and one can only contain one's self for so long. Another ten years went by before the lie my ex-wife and I were living reared its ugly head. I'd come to terms with the fact our union had been doomed from the start. In my mind it was only a matter of time. I just didn't have the moxie to pursue it. My ex, always the strong one, did. When it came to time to make a decision it was she who made it.

My first wife had quit her job and returned to school five years earlier. She was an intelligent woman who, like me, entered the workforce after high school rather than continue her education. Her parents believed sons went to college, but daughters were expected to find a husband.

It was I who first suggested my ex take evening courses at the local community college, thinking she would enjoy the experience. I didn't mention that it would also provide me some alone time. She jumped at the chance, and ended up getting straight A's. Shortly after that she approached me with a plan to return to school full time.

She'd reworked our budget in a way that would allow us to stay current on our debts. After investigating the options available to non-traditional students we agreed she would continue her education. State grants would assist in the cost of tuition. My ex developed a bar graph that compared the potential earnings of future college graduates to her current salary. It was clear the best decision would be to tighten our purse strings in the short term to take advantage of the financial gains in the long term. There was no logical reason not to agree to it. Not to mention the hell I'd have gone through if I didn't agree.

She completed her course work in three years, excelling beyond even her own expectations. I knew my ex was smart, but she blew away the competition, finishing with a perfect 4.0 grade point average. When commencement day came my son and I sat in the auditorium and watched the procession of baccalaureate candidates make their way on stage to accept their diplomas. As they did they passed the honor students sitting on stage in recognition of their academic success. My wife sat among them as valedictorian of the graduating class.

Tears filled my eyes when she got up to give her speech. I'd spent the previous week helping her write the words she'd present that day. She spoke of education being a ticket to a better life. A path to higher consciousness. A college degree was a segway to a brighter future. What she didn't mention was how it provided her a way out of a marriage she'd become increasingly unhappy in.

I should have seen it coming. There were social functions at the college I wasn't invited to attend. Opportunities were provided for gifted students to network with representatives of upper echelon firms. I was just a blue collar worker, a meter reader for the state utility. I'd be out of my element, or so I was told. According to my ex-wife it would be embarrassing for her to introduce me to her colleagues.

Her accomplishments were a source of pride to me. I was appreciative of the benefits that would accompany a job offer, but it was painfully disappointing that I wasn't allowed to be part of the process. I wasn't allowed to share in the joy, or made to feel like I'd contributed to my wife's success. My behavior reflected that rejection. In hindsight, perhaps I got what I deserved.

Once my ex secured a fast track position with a large firm the dissolution of our marriage came swiftly. The frustration that had built up for twenty years was released in a fury of verbal abuse. One particular day was especially painful. She told me she'd never been satisfied by me. Not emotionally, intellectually, or sexually.

My ex-wife proved a formidable opponent during the divorce proceedings. My intent was to protect my son from being subjected to further outbursts of anger and hatred. At ten years of age he was both impressionable and easily damaged.

Her attorney, a cold calculating bitch of a woman, had no problem dragging my son into court and forcing him to choose sides. My natural response was to protect him from having to make such a decision. It was with heartache that I let him go. I would maintain my status as a custodial parent, but he would live with his mother.

It was during this tumultuous period that my work life took off. It's a curious anomaly that one's personal life can be going to hell in a hand basket while reciprocally their professional life can take off in the opposite direction. With all that was going on in my life I had unconsciously delved into my work as a way of escaping the pain. I happened to immerse myself at a time when my employer was looking to develop future leaders. As such, I was selected to participate in a management training program.

The training would be held at the utility's headquarters in Albany, New York. Unbeknownst to me, the future love of my life would be attending the same sessions.

EARLY RETIREMENT

MURDER IN DAYTONA

7

Veronica was at a table talking to the woman seated next to her when I entered the room. The chair across from them was open so I claimed it by placing my half filled styrofoam coffee cup on the table. After hanging my jacket over the back of the seat I sat down. As I did I glanced across the table. The two women had ended their conversation and Veronica was watching me. Our eyes met and time stood still.

I remember reading a magazine article that claimed no two people share the same eye color. An individual's eyes are uniquely their own. Veronica's eyes were like a glistening pool of melted chocolate. Big brown spheres that emanated warmth and enticed you to dive in. Needless to say I took the plunge. Veronica later told me she'd felt as though I looked straight into her soul that day.

I hadn't been searching for a lover. My marriage ended bitterly and I wasn't ready emotionally or financially to begin anew. In fact I'd sworn off women at that point. To much trouble and to much pain I'd decided. I needed to get my life back on track and avoid the pitfalls associated with a relationship. Of course that's before we shared what we would affectionately come to refer to as... *The Look!*

I'd seen a fragile person behind those eyes. Though outwardly Veronica appeared confident and self assured I knew better. She was attractive and seductive...but not vampish. I'd seen something else quite familiar... Pain! The kind of pain associated with loss.

Like the loss of a child or a parent. Or one's self respect. I knew the emotion well. I shared that with her.

Being somewhat shy it was the end of the week before I approached her. I'd returned from lunch a few minutes early and found Veronica sitting alone in the classroom. I introduced myself and we talked for a while. Eventually I worked up the nerve to ask her if she thought we'd shared a moment that first day of training. She blushed and said, *"Yes I do, and it frightened me a little."*

I apologized, explaining I didn't make a habit of staring down women I didn't know. She replied, *"That's not what frightened me. I honestly felt like you could see right through me. Do you know what I mean?"* Strangely, I did!

Our training group was being housed at a hotel near the district office. I asked Veronica if she'd join me for a drink in the lounge that evening. To my delight she agreed. We arranged to meet at 7:00PM.

I arrived a few minutes early, ordered a beer at the bar, and waited. At quarter past seven I began to worry. Had she had second thoughts? I decided I would give her another fifteen minutes before tossing in the towel and calling it a night. I ordered another beer and watched the game show playing on the television over the bar.

The final Jeopardy question had just been announced when I heard someone next to me say... *"Etruscans."* I turned to find Veronica standing there. I hesitated for a moment, then asked her what she'd said. She repeated ... *"Etruscans. The civilization that preceded the Roman Empire in what is present day Italy... The Jeopardy question, Silly."*

I was relieved to see her, and really glad she came. I had begun to think she may have changed her mind. Veronica pulled up a bar stool and ordered a glass of wine. We spent hours talking.

I felt completely at ease with her. Veronica told me she felt the same. We discussed our careers, and how we happened to be in this place at this time. We were both older than most of the other management trainees, and neither of us had formal educations. We'd succeeded through hard work and determination. Most of the other candidates had college degrees to justify their presence.

We talked about our families and our previous marriages. Both of us had children, and we'd both suffered the pain of losing them in custody battles. I began to understand what I'd seen behind those eyes. A thought crossed my mind. Might this woman be my soul mate?

I was falling in love, and it was wonderful. If possible I was going to sweep Veronica off her feet. Then without warning she knocked me off mine. It was a one, two punch. First Veronica told me she was living with someone. Then she said her partner was a woman!

She hadn't lead me on. Veronica only agreed to join me for a drink. We'd spent several hours sharing experiences and it was obvious we enjoyed each other's company. I presumed she was attracted to me. We'd both been somewhat flirtatious, but there'd been no overt advances. How was I supposed to react to this news? Like a prize fighter I took the hit, then reeled back on my heels and rebounded with both fists swinging. No way was I going down without a fight.

I turned up the charm and flirted unabashedly. I romanced her like she'd never been romanced before. It was almost midnight when Veronica asked me if I danced. She took my hand and lead me onto the dance floor. I was surprised to see so many people in the place. When I arrived it had been relatively quiet. Just a few people at the bar. Now the joint was jam packed full of weekend warriors. Having been enthralled with my conquest I was oblivious to what was going on around me. We reached the dance floor just as the band was slowing it down, *"For all you lovers out there."*

I took Veronica in my arms and held her close as we moved to the beat of the music. She buried her face between my cheek and shoulder, providing me easy access to her neck and earlobe. After a while she looked into my eyes. I could tell she was feeling what I was feeling. We kissed. A deep passionate kiss only two people falling in love can manufacture while in view of a hundred set of eyes.

We danced till closing time, holding each other and softly kissing the pain away. Afterward we went to my room where we continued our passion play. It felt right being with her, as though we shared one soul. Yet we were strangers. Two ships that collided in the night. We made love...without actually...*making love.* That is to say I never entered her. As sexually charged as the night had been I still respected the fact she was in a relationship.

Veronica told me about her partner. She said she was planning to get out of the relationship even before we'd met, but she needed time. Her partner was very jealous and Veronica was afraid of what she might do. I sensed her hesitation to consummate our relationship and silently agreed that the one with her current partner needed to end before ours continued.

At the end of the training session we returned to our respective work locations. An entire week passed and I hadn't heard from Veronica. Was she busy with her new job, or had she reconsidered? Taking the initiative I called her office. The person answering the phone told me Veronica was unavailable at the moment. I ordered a dozen roses and had them delivered to her workplace. The flowers ended up getting delivered on her day off. Word of their arrival spread fast and caused quite a buzz amongst the staff.

Evidently it was common knowledge that the new supervisor shared a home with a woman. Rumor was she was a lesbian. That made her prime gossip material. However the greeting card attached to the flowers had been signed with a man's name. Confusion reigned as the gossip mongers attempted to verify the validity of their information. The question of the day was... Is she or isn't she?

When Veronica arrived for work the next day she was informed the manager wanted to see her in his office. She had developed a unique relationship with her manager since arriving there some months before. He'd become something of a father figure to her, treating her like a member of his family. She'd been invited to his home numerous times, met his wife and children, and even offered a place to stay if needed. His motives were above reproach, the result of his own moral fortitude and belief system. He'd become very fond and protective of this young gay woman who'd been temporarily assigned to his office. When the time came he recommended her for advancement, seeing in her the potential for success.

Veronica knocked on her bosses door, took a deep breath, then entered. He immediately pointed to the vase of flowers on his desk and asked, *"Who's Richard?"* She blushed, then told him she'd met a guy. Her boss was well aware of Veronica's living arrangement with Doris, and he knew it had become an unhealthy situation for her. Under the circumstances his interference, one might suggest his intercession, was understandable. *"Mind telling me what this is all about,"* he asked?

Veronica explained how we met, and assured her boss I was a total gentleman. She told him how much she enjoyed my company, and promised that any relationship she had would never interfere with her job performance. Her manager told her the place had been buzzing with rumor ever since the flowers arrived.

"What about your girlfriend," he asked? Veronica shrugged her shoulders and told him she thought it had run its course. *"Well,"* he replied, *"you know if you need someone to talk to I'm here. Now get these roses off my desk and get back to work!"*

Veronica called me later that day to thank me for the roses. I asked her why she hadn't contacted me until now. She told me she would never call a man first, even if she did like him. Then she asked me why I hadn't contacted her? I explained that I had attempted to reach her at work, but she was never there.

"That's why I had to resort to the old send her flowers trick," I joked. *"Looks like it worked to! So how about having dinner with me sometime."* Veronica paused, presumably to consider my offer. I added, *"You do get hungry, Right?"*

I knew the comment brought a smile to her face. I felt it through the telephone line. Humor is a relaxant. I often use it to diffuse tension when dealing with situations on the job. I knew it worked when Veronica mentioned a little Italian restaurant down the street from her office. She told me she'd meet me there at 6:00.

Like most women, Veronica arrived fashionably late. She was as attractive as I remembered. Veronica had a flair for dressing casually sexy. Her style a mix of retro 50's with a touch of disco 80's.

She was a redhead that matched red lipstick and red fingernails with hi heels and black denim jeans. A black leather jacket completed her ensemble. She reminded me of the *'Sandy'* character from the movie Grease...only after the transformation. Veronica was an imposing figure, demanding of attention yet unpretentious. My senses salivated as I watched her walk towards me.

I stood and kissed her on the cheek, then pulled out her chair. While reviewing the menu Veronica noticed the restaurant served '*greens*'. Greens were a local delicacy. I knew one had to acquire a taste for them, and told her so. Anyway, I'd already decided on the lobster ravioli.

The waiter handed us a wine list and suggested the *Rose' of Isabella.* Veronica said it was her favorite so I ordered a bottle. Being a beer drinker I wasn't all that savvy on wine etiquette, and said so. Veronica smiled. I thought she appreciated my honesty. I deferred the wine tasting to Veronica. After she gave her approval the waiter filled our glasses.

Our relationship picked up right where it left off the week before. We were really comfortable together. I felt like I'd known Veronica all my life. It was like sliding my feet into a pair of warm slippers on a cold winter night.

Had we been younger we might not have considered the fact we were both struggling to find our way through the maze of a failed relationship. Should we not consider the rebound effect in assessing our feelings for one another? Should we be considering the fears of our children, and how our relationship might effect them? Might it be better to delay putting ourselves in a position of reliance on someone else?

Then there was the issue of Doris. Veronica had been planning to leave her partner long before I came along. The fact that we met only hastened her to get on with it. Still, Doris was a master of manipulation. She could be venomous to those she disliked. Her tenacious personality, self assuredness, and need to dominate made a break up not only difficult, but outright dangerous.

Veronica made her decision. She'd ask a mutual friend to come over to the house while she gathered her things to leave. Pam Sykes had known Doris for years. The two met at college and roomed together. They became lovers. After college they went their separate ways, but remain friends to this day.

Pam wasn't surprised when she got the call from Veronica. She told her she wasn't the first woman to run from Doris, and she wouldn't be the last. *"I knew you weren't cut out for this lifestyle long ago,"* she said. "*It was only a matter of time before this day would come.*"

Wanting Veronica to leave before Doris got home from work Pam hurried her along. She knew Doris would react badly. Pam hoped to avoid an ugly scene. She warned Veronica, *"Lovers don't dump Doris... Doris dumps lovers!"*

Pam helped Veronica pack the last few boxes in the trunk of her car, then told her she was going to stick around until Doris got home. Veronica apologized for getting her involved. *"That's what friends are for,"* Pam responded. *"Now get the hell out of here!"* With that she patted Veronica on the butt and kissed her goodbye.

Veronica drove aimlessly into the night. She hadn't decided where she'd go, only that she had to leave. Veronica knew she could go to her mom's, but the thought left a pit in her stomach. Her old apartment was available, but how could she stay there now? Ghosts would surely haunt her.

Her boss had mentioned if she ever needed a place to stay she was welcome there. He'd foreseen this day coming. He and his wife had discussed it in the event she ever showed up on their doorstep. Veronica considered getting a motel for the night. Instead, she drove the country roads listening to the radio and reliving the past few hours of her life. It was approaching midnight when she pulled into my driveway.

We'd discussed Veronica's options when she finally made the decision to leave. I'd told her there was plenty of room at my place if she wanted to stay with me. The small home I'd shared with my wife and son now seemed much to big for one person. It's funny how it never seemed big enough when I was married.

I'd fallen asleep in my brown leather recliner earlier in the evening. It was a habit I had developed since the divorce. My dog was my only companion these days. Jeter liked to join me in the recliner when I watched television. It had become something of a routine.

I woke to the sound of barking. Someone was tapping on the living room window, and Jeter loved company. I tried to focus on the figure standing on my front porch but my eyes were crusted over with sleep. Though the viscidity obscured my view I knew it was her!

I sprung from my recliner, tripping over the dog as I rushed to greet my guest. Jeter yelped, then raced me to the door. Upon entering Veronica knelt down and scratched Jeter behind the ears, thereby making a lifelong friend.

She told me she'd been driving around since suppertime trying to decide what to do. After I took her coat Veronica looked around my living room approvingly and said, *"I can't believe how clean this place is. I thought bachelors were supposed to be slobs."*

I put a pot of coffee on then we talked... Veronica told me she'd most likely end up at her mom's house, but she wanted to see me first. She said I had a way of making sense of things. Before we knew it the Seth Thomas on the wall was chiming it's 2:00AM.

I suggested it was far to late to drive all the way to her mother's house and offered to let her stay in the guest room. Veronica agreed. She went to her car to retrieve some personal items. When she returned I took her in my arms and kissed her.

Veronica responded like she had the time we kissed out on the dance floor. Our mouths melted together and we became one. Our passion carried us down the hall and into my bed. Neither of us could deny the other in that moment.

The awkwardness and uncertainty that often accompanies an initial carnal encounter simply didn't exist. We explored each other completely. My senses were heightened to new highs as I caressed the curves of her body and listened to the heaviness of her breathing. I inhaled her sweet scent and savored the taste of her lips. It wasn't long after entering her that I felt her body spasm deep inside. When the rolling contractions that held me tight subsided I continued my lustful assault. Our heated lovemaking continued until sunrise. It had been passionate, and it had been real.

EARLY RETIREMENT

MURDER IN DAYTONA

8

That was over twenty years ago. The memory replays itself in my mind often. The love we shared that night, the passion and intensity only grew with the years. A relationship that began with a single look became a lifelong obsession. We'd love each other forever, convinced we were meant to be together.

Certainly there were times when we fell victim to the daily grind. The monotony of life can takes its toll on any marriage. What never became routine was the love we shared. Veronica and I never took each other for granted. We nurtured our feelings like a gardener tends his roses. Our love was rooted in fertile soil.

Our lives changed with the announcement a reduction in force was going to be enacted by our employer. The RIF would effect management employees only. Veronica and I had completed the mandatory thirty years needed to qualify for a pension, but we were both a few years shy on the age requirement. The reduction in force would allow us to retire despite our ages.

The four additional years of freedom we'd gain far outweighed the additional money we'd receive if we stayed. Veronica and I both knew people who'd died before having a chance to retire, and we understood there was no guarantee of good health or longevity. We believe people should live their lives for today, for tomorrow never knows. That said, we submitted our paperwork and started making plans.

Our dream was to retire to the sunshine state. We would replace the gray skies and cold winds of upstate New York with warm ocean breezes and wild blue yonder. I had to shovel a ton of snow so the realtor could install his sign, but our home went up for sale.

It wasn't considered very savvy to put a home up for sale in February in our neck of the woods. No one goes house hunting when snow banks line the roads and freezing winds cut like a knife. Still, we went forward with our plan. We bought airline tickets, made hotel reservations, and searched for our dream home. We found it in Ormond Beach, Florida.

Thanks to the faltering economy home prices had nose dived. Houses were selling for half what they were just the year before. Ever optimistic, and knowing we still had a house to sell in upstate New York, we decided to buy.

Our little slice of heaven was located in an age restricted retirement community. We barely met the age requirement but we felt good about our decision. Tropical breezes brushed our faces as we walked in what would be our new backyard. Fish jumped in the little lake behind what would be our new home. Egrets and herons landed on the calm waters and songbirds chirped sweet melodies that soothed my savage beast.

The place was a virtual sanctuary of warmth and peacefulness. Veronica and I reviewed our financial situation, calculated what our housing expenses would be, and made an offer the seller couldn't refuse.

With our futures set we returned home prepared to sit out the winter and wait for offers. Our realtor took us by surprise when she informed us three offers came in while we were gone. Who knew there were people who house hunted in upstate New York in the dead of winter. We accepted an offer from a couple who not only gave us the full asking price, but wanted to purchase the contents of our home as well.

I wouldn't need to transport all of our belongings to Florida. We could simply pack our clothes in the trunk and set the cruise control. I was ready to begin the next phase of our life.

With furniture shopping to do, paint colors to choose, and tropical drink recipes to master, we settled into our new home. The dream I'd been living since meeting Veronica kept getting better and better. With no work related stress to contend with and the good vibes that come with blue skies and warm temperatures our love life took off. We were truly happy. Veronica and I made new friends, pursued new hobbies, and started living a life long imagined.

Then came the day my world came crashing in on me. The day my heart was ripped from my chest. I'd questioned why a note was left at my front door. The playful flirtatious undertone of the script was vintage Veronica. The reality however, had turned into unadulterated horror. I can't possibly describe the roller coaster of emotions I felt. My fear turned into anger before morphing into unrelenting determination. Veronica was gone. It took a while but I accepted that. What I would never accept was the way she died...and why?

EARLY RETIREMENT

MURDER IN DAYTONA

9

Panties had been stuffed down her throat. She'd been sexually violated with a wine bottle. The .75 liter bottle had been inverted into her vagina. I took a sip of now cold coffee and continued analyzing the medical examiner's report. *A drug known on the street as ecstasy was present in her bloodstream. The amphetamine had been ingested.* Sitting at my desk I was metaphorically transported back in time. The realism of the moment was frightening.

Veronica's body was on the bed. I could smell her scent mixed with the pungent odor of uncollected rotting trash. I could taste the salt in the air, remnants of the ocean's waves crashing ashore in the distance. Mostly though I could hear the deafening silence of a woman whose head had just been bashed in.

It had been over a month since I'd lost her. I knew I needed to begin the process of healing, of accepting what had happened. I knew I had to stop feeling sorry for myself. Stop living like a hermit closed off from the world. To continue my free fall would be equivalent to Veronica's killer having murdered both of us. I took a shower then sat on the edge of the bed to dry off. Today would be the day. Enough was enough.

The bedroom dresser I shared with Veronica was directly in front of me. A sudden urge came over me to open her lingerie drawer and finger through the pile of tantalizing delights. I found the pink satin baby doll Veronica knew was my favorite and lifted it to my face. As I inhaled I tried to recall the last time she'd worn it. I felt my way through the rest of her lingerie, drawn by the sensual feel of silk and lace. In the rear corner of the drawer was a small cardboard box. I pulled it out to find it contained the digital camera I'd given Veronica the previous Christmas.

The spell broken, I got dressed. On the way out to my car I grabbed Veronica's camera and stuffed it in my pocket. I didn't have a particular destination in mind, but the sun willed me to follow her. It was the Florida sunshine that initially drew me to her shores, and despite my current situation I still appreciated it. After stopping at a donut shop for an unhealthy dose of sugar coated pleasure I drove east towards the ocean.

The Intercoastal came into view and my thoughts turned to Veronica. What the hell were traces of ecstasy doing in her body? I'd done some research online and learned ecstasy was a hallucinogenic drug similar to LSD. It was supposedly an aphrodisiac. A love potion that stimulates sexual desire. Evidently it's popular with the club scene crowd, and often used as a date rape drug.

I'd even looked the word ecstasy up in the dictionary. It was defined as *Great happiness and joyful excitement.* Well, the woman lying on that cheap motel bed with her head smashed in didn't appear to be too happy...or excited!

Before I knew it I was driving down Atlantic Boulevard past the Pelican Inn. Something in my gut told me to turn around and revisit the scene of the crime and against my better judgement I listened. I sat in the parking lot for a few minutes. A Christmas song was playing on the radio. You know, the one where grandma gets run over by the reindeer. It was blaring from the speakers. Before the song was finished I turned it off wondering, whatever happened to jingle bells?

Sitting in my car in the middle of the parking lot I reviewed in my mind what had transpired that fateful night. It seemed like it had happened years ago. Conversely, it felt like it had just happened. How quickly a person's life can change. In the blink of an eye, a flash in the sky, everything you know as reality can be obliterated.

I got out of my car and walked over to the vacant lot next to the motel. I remembered the cop who'd found the baseball bat and how he'd rewarded his canine partner with a pat on the head as he pointed to the bloody barrel. Standing there amongst empty broken beer bottles, cigarette butts, and used condoms I looked up towards room twenty-eight. Lord knows how long I was standing there, but when I turned my gaze back toward the parking lot I saw the motel clerk staring at me. He had a cancer stick hanging out of his mouth and the same dumb expression on his face that I recalled from our first meeting. He was shaking his head in a slow, almost mocking manner. After a moment he went back inside, slamming the office door behind him.

I shrugged him off and headed back towards my car. As I did I remembered Veronica's camera was in my pocket. The Kodak had rarely been used. Veronica and I believed in living in the moment. It seemed to us that stopping to photograph an event often meant not being a part of it. Occasionally we'd bring it along in case we had a *Kodak Moment,* but more often than not the camera remained in my wife's purse. I decided to snap some pictures.

After fumbling with the mechanics of the damn thing I was ready to take a few snapshots. I took one of the neon pelican sign, then one of the dumpster, which still overflowed with trash. As I reached the parking lot I heard a noise coming from the dumpster. I assumed it was just some homeless pirate scouring around in search of hidden treasure. *One man's trash is another man's...* I chuckled at the thought and moved on.

I took a few shots of cars parked in the lot then turned and focused the camera lens on the office door. Just as the shutter clicked I heard the motel clerk yell, *"Get the fuck off this property. You're trespassing."*

Ignoring his orders I went upstairs. My hands were shaking as I focused the camera and took a picture of the coral colored door with the black number 28 painted on it. I reached for the door knob but then hesitated. Just as I did the door opened and I found myself looking straight into the eyes of a familiar face.

"Richard, what a surprise, won't you come in." Detective Brooks said as he stepped aside to allow me entrance. *"This is Jordan,"* he proclaimed, introducing me to an odd looking man sitting on the edge of the bed. The guy gave me a roguish smile and held out his hand. He was short and chubby with an impish face.

"Jordan is a good buddy of mine," the detective explained. *"We work together occasionally when I need someone with his special talent."* I got the impression the detective didn't like me very much. His comments back at the detention center, *"Murder is a crime of passion"* and, *"You're a passionate man, aren't you Richard"* had really rattled me.

I shook Jordan's too large for his body stub fingered hand then turned to the detective and asked... *"Special talent?"*

"Yes," the detective answered. *"Jordan here is a psychic. We've worked together on a number of cases. Police work is a science, Mr Stevens, and not an exact one at that. Now I don't claim to understand how Jordan does it, but I trust him. I think it's similar to a detective who uses his intuition. No one can really describe how it works but there's no denying it does. So Richard... What brings you here today?"*

I didn't have an answer. What was I doing there? I was standing in the middle of the room my wife had been brutally and viciously murdered in. What subconscious trigger had I tripped to lead me to this place on this day? My silence lingered until the detective broke it with an observation. *"You know Stevens, it's quite common for the perpetrator of a violent crime to return to the scene of his offense. It is also common he photograph the event. Sort of a memento of the occasion. By the way, that's some camera Richard. Is it new?"*

As I stuffed the camera back in my pocket I explained it had been Veronica's. I told the detective I'd been driving around trying to gather my thoughts and found myself driving past the motel. The urge to stop and look around had been strong. I wanted my wife's killer found more than he did.

I asked Brooks why he would imply my involvement. After all, I had a strong alibi. The detective's response? *"Experience! I've been at this a long time, Richard. I've learned things are not always what they seem."*

I reminded the detective we were on the same side, then turned to leave. Brooks repeated his response, *"Things are not always what they seem, Mr Stevens."*

My mind struggled to understand his gist. Tried to read between the lines. Jordan, the detective's clairvoyant friend, sat on the edge of the bed looking at me with a mischievous smile on his face. I couldn't help but wonder what he knew. I didn't mention my wife's missing ring. It was the one piece of the puzzle I had to go by.

As I stepped out onto the landing the motel room door slammed behind me. It hadn't been intentional. The wind just caught it. The ensuing bang gave the impression I was leaving in anger. As I descended the stairs I noticed the motel clerk was in the parking lot headed towards me. It was obvious he'd been waiting for me to come out of the room...and he was clearly upset.

By the time I reached the last step the clerk was there. He took his unlit cigarette butt from his lips and threw it to the ground, then got right in my face. He started yelling about all the trouble I'd caused him. I stepped back, partially as a defense mechanism, but mostly because of the disgusting odor of his breath.

"Do you have any idea what you've done to my business," he angrily screamed. *"You think my customers don't notice all the fucking cop cars sitting in the parking lot day and night? I may as well shut down thanks to all the fucking publicity you brought me. They even took me in for questioning, like I'm one of their fucking suspects."*

By now the poor SOB was red faced. Still, he went on screaming. *"Now you show up taking fucking photographs? Bad enough I got to let them into that fucking room at all hours of the day. Now I got you back here too! I NEVER should have given them keys!"*

EARLY RETIREMENT

MURDER IN DAYTONA

10

Dr. Jordan Downs is a nationally renowned psychic, admired by advocates and criminal investigators throughout the country. He earned his doctorate in paranormal research from Duke University. He is currently professor emeritus at his alma mater's Paranormal Research Center. In addition Dr Downs works as a consultant to police agencies throughout the United States and Canada. He utilizes his *gift* to denote events beyond the scope of normal scientific understanding.

Many in law enforcement are skeptical of psychics, but experienced investigators know the validity of their intervention. On several occasions the FBI has requested the doctor's help, and Jordan has been able to provide information that's resulted in a number of arrests. His involvement doesn't come cheap, but when a case goes cold Jordan Downs can be just the person to get an investigation back on track.

He has notoriety among his peers. Some question Jordan's motives but none can deny his ability. Occasionally Dr Downs appears on nationally syndicated television programs, most notably the Emmy winning, *Wanted; Dead or Alive.*

Jordan owns a home in Boca Raton. His oceanfront mansion is an example of the lucrative career one can have in the field of paranormal metaphysics. Jordan hosts a party at the mansion every year, inviting colleagues and friends from the field of criminal investigation. Some of the top investigators in the country attend.

The psychic considers his parties an opportunity to exchange ideas with people who share his passion. Detective Sergeant Dan Brooks was one of those people. He first met the detective at one of his parties a few years ago and they became good friends.

Both men share a passion for the game of criminal pursuit. Jordan admires Detective Brooks' low key approach, and the tenacious attitude he has when pursuing a suspect. The detective's imposing size can be intimidating but it is juxtaposed by his quiet unassuming demeanor. The contradiction often catches people completely off guard.

Jordan on the other hand possesses a vexatious personality. The short stocky clairvoyant is always loud and often obnoxious. He is the proverbial extrovert. The two men couldn't be more opposite.

When Detective Brooks is assigned a case he thinks will peak Jordan's interest he never hesitates to include him in the hunt. The Veronica Stevens murder was just such a case. He'd been waiting for an opportune time to approach him about it. This year's party was the perfect chance.

Unbeknownst to the detective Jordan was already familiar with the case. He'd received a phone call from a television producer who'd filled him in on the gory details. They were going to tape a segment on the gruesome murder for an upcoming broadcast, and the producer wanted Jordan as a guest consultant.

Jordan had appeared on dozens of programs over the years. Producers were aware of his unique ability to converse on the subject of paranormal activity in layman's terms. It's what made him an ideal guest. Jordan knew he possessed a flair for the dramatic, and he understood the public's fascination with it.

Detective Brooks cornered Jordan during a lull in the party and asked him for ten minutes of his time. He wanted to tell him about the homicide case he'd been assigned. Before Brooks could finish his sentence Jordan interrupted him. He asked the detective if he was referring to the Veronica Stevens murder?

Brooks was disappointed, and it showed. He'd wanted to wow Jordan with the juicy enticement. He shook his head and said to him, *"Damn it, Jordan... You are scary! How did you know I was... Ahhh, forget it!"*

Jordan laughed. It was an obnoxious nasally laugh that resonated in the famous psychic's nose before dying deep in his throat.

"I want you on the payroll for this one," Brooks continued. Jordan feigned amazement, then asked his friend if he'd be staying at one of those fancy Daytona Beach resorts if he took the case. The detective responded, *"No... You'll be staying in my ex-wife's bedroom, just like last time."*

Both men broke out in laughter. Jordan held up his stubby four fingered paw and gave Brooks a *high five.* Then Brooks got serious. *"This is a bad one, Jordan. I even put my retirement plans on hold. I just can't go out this way."*

Jordan could hear the passion in the detective's voice. He reminded him cops aren't supposed to get emotionally involved. He looked Brooks in the eye and told him not to worry. *"We are going to get this Son of a Bitch!"*

The next day Detective Brooks went to his division captain with a request to enlist Jordan Downs, explaining the case had turned cold. The detective knew the psychic would get involved regardless of whether he got paid or not. Payment for Jordan's services would definitely be appreciated, but the thrill of the hunt would be his true reward.

This was a highly publicized case and it warranted immediate attention. Wide spread stories of heinous crimes against women could wreak havoc on the local economy, especially in a popular tourist destination like Daytona Beach. The captain responded, *"If you think it will help, get him on board."* Brooks arranged to meet Jordan at the Pelican Inn the following Monday morning.

Realizing he would be early Brooks stopped for coffee on the way in. When the detective arrived at the Pelican Inn he parked his city owned sedan in the far corner of the lot then sat back and sipped his brew. His thoughts drifted back to the last case he'd worked on with Jordan.

A young runaway had fallen in with a group of gangland bikers calling themselves, *The Confederates*. She was from the Midwest. A teenage kid who thought Daytona was going to be a big party. Like many runaways she hung around the biker bars on Main Street, turning tricks to avoid starvation.

One night a member of The Confederates approached her with an offer to sponsor her membership in the gang. He enticed her by describing the gang as being a close knit family offering love and companionship. The only requirements would be her pledge of allegiance to the gang and her promise to serve and obey its leaders...which she did.

Several weeks after joining The Confederates she broke a gang directive. Female members were to provide for the needs of male gang members **only**! When the young runaway showed up at the gang's haunt with a college boy in tow their leader got pissed!

The college kid had been drinking heavily. He had no idea who he was dealing with. When several gang members confronted him he got belligerent. He warned them he played football for the Georgia Bulldogs, and threatened to come back with some of his buddies and kick some biker ass.

When he left the bar that night it was on a stretcher. Five of The Confederates, at the direction of their leader, kicked the living shit out of the kid. Among his injuries were a shattered knee, a broken collar bone, a broken nose, and several fractured ribs.

The college kid would recover eventually, but he would never play another down of football for the University of Georgia. The runaway was taken to a remote location and gang raped, then viciously beaten to death.

Brooks was assigned the case. He attempted to interview members of The Confederates but they were uncooperative. They realized their lives were dependent on their silence. It was Jordan who got the investigation on track. He *saw* the figure of the young runaway lying in an open field surrounded by thick brush. The trees had been scorched by brushfire. Jordan told Brooks he could smell the charred scrub.

Somehow Jordan was able to place the scene as being a few miles south of Daytona Beach, just west of Interstate 95. A massive search was conducted, lead by state police canine units. They located the teenager's badly beaten body the next day. It had been severely disfigured by animals, and had begun to decay in the hot Florida sun. Thanks to Jordan five members of The Confederates were now serving long prison sentences. The gang's Pres' is sitting on death row.

Jordan pulled his Mercedes into the motel parking lot and slid alongside the detective's unmarked sedan. Brooks was so entranced in his thoughts he never noticed him. Jordan got out and tapped on the detective's window, effectively breaking the spell. When he got out of his car Jordan joked he'd caught the detective napping on the job.

They made their way across the lot to the office. Jordan took in the surroundings. He noticed the vacant lot next door and asked

Brooks if it was where the murder weapon was found. The garbage dumpster caught Jordan's attention too. Seeing it was heaping with trash he questioned whether it had been emptied since the murder. When Jordan asked Brooks where the crime had been committed the detective pointed up to room number twenty-eight.

Detective Brooks went to get the room key while Jordan started up the stairs. He arrived moments later to find his friend rubbing his hands all over the door, caressing it as if it were flesh and blood. Brooks waited for Jordan to finish. When the psychic was done he turned to the detective and devilishly said, *"You ready? Let's go in."*

Jordan sat on the edge of the bed and looked around the room. He asked Brooks to describe the scene on the day of the murder, saying he wanted as detailed a description as possible. When Brooks finished Jordan paused, then asked the detective if he could recall any particular smells. Without hesitation Brooks answered, "Yes... *Piss... The poor woman had pissed all over herself."*

As Jordan pondered Brooks noticed movement on the balcony. He peeked through the window curtain and saw someone standing there. The person he saw was holding a camera in his hand. "Well, *I'll be God damned,"* he said as he opened the door.

EARLY RETIREMENT

MURDER IN DAYTONA

11

I could feel an anxiety attack coming on. The presence of the detective and his impish friend in the motel room had taken me completely by surprise. I hadn't planned to revisit the scene of my wife's murder that day. The emotional consequences of doing so had been nerve-jarringly surreal. As I drove up Atlantic Boulevard my breathing became labored. I felt my throat tighten and my hands started to tremble. Knowing I couldn't continue driving in that condition I turned when I saw a beach access sign at the next intersection.

Toll booths set up to fleece motorist wishing to drive on *The World's Most Famous Beach* are not staffed in the winter months. I drove right up to the water's edge and killed the engine, then gazed out at the liquid horizon.

My anxiety grew. I could feel the pressure building. Eventually I screamed out in pain. Mercifully the sound was muted by the roar of the ocean's waves. The physical exertion I expended effectively soothed my angst and I felt my breathing return to normal. I began wondering if finding my wife's killer was simply a self induced fantasy?

Salt water licked my front tires as the tide came in. I fired up the engine and put the car in reverse. After parking up by the dunes I got out of the car to stretch my legs. I noticed someone standing by the toll booth. They were holding a set of binoculars to his face. Whoever it was appeared to be observing me.

I yelled... *"Hello."* Whoever it was put his binoculars down then turned and walked away. I assume it was a cop assigned to keep me under surveillance. It boggled my mind to think the police thought I had something to do with my wife's murder.

That evening I downloaded the pictures from Veronica's camera onto my computer. Photos my wife had taken appeared alongside the ones I took this morning. She obviously used the camera more often than I thought because when the download was complete there was over a hundred images. I spent the next several hours grouping them into albums.

Veronica had taken snapshots of clients she assisted at the women's shelter. None of them appeared to be from very affluent backgrounds, which didn't surprise me. Not that domestic violence doesn't exist in upper class America, I wasn't so naive as to believe that. It's just that anyone with the means would most likely make alternate arrangements rather than subject themselves to the bureaucracy of a government run shelter. Besides their indigent circumstances, the women seemed to share one other unfortunate trait. The facade of their posed smiles failed to hide the haunting sadness in their eyes.

One particular group of photos was quite disturbing. Veronica had taken pictures of several clients who'd suffered vicious attacks. One middle aged woman had deep savage teeth marks on her neck, shoulders, and breasts. Another woman, younger than the first, had been brutally beaten. Her buttocks and upper thighs were covered with dark purple welts and bruises. They lined her backside from hip to hip. I winced at the sight of such a lovely female specimen so violently treated.

A second grouping featured pictures of myself in various states of undress. I felt my face flush at the remembrance of posing for my wife as we childishly played with her new camera. Even a few unauthorized *nudies* had been taken. Veronica must have thought it would be funny if she pulled the blanket down while I was sleeping and captured the moment. I couldn't help but wonder who amongst our friends may have seen them.

I set the computer's photo lab on slideshow and turned off the lights. Sitting back I watched the images appear and disappear before my eyes. Eventually the pictures I'd taken appeared. One shot revealed several letters in the motel's neon sign weren't illuminated. Another picture I took of the vacant lot was out of focus and indistinguishable. On the other hand a photo I took of the trash dumpster was so clear it picked up the brand names of the empty beer bottles laying about.

A fourth image showed two vehicles sitting in the far corner of the motel's parking lot. I zoomed in for a closer look and was surprised to see the late model sedan had an official city license plate. Parked next to it was a shiny silver Mercedes roadster. Its Florida license tag read **SIX-CENTS**. I realized the vehicles must belong to Sergeant Brooks and this psychic friend, Jordan Downs.

Returning to the slideshow I just caught a glimpse of the motel office door before the computer advanced to the next photograph. A pink door with a number 28 painted on it. I hit the pause key and sat silently staring at the screen.

After a while it went black as the computer timed out. In the dark, lost in my thoughts, I found solace. It felt odd being soothed by the very darkness I used to fear as a child.

When my self induced coma ended I tapped the keyboard and the photo reappeared. A chill ran down my spine as the **2** and the **8** stared back at me as if they were eyes. Total recall rushed through my brain. It all came back. Every detail of that day. Who and what I'd found on the other side of that door.

As I studied the image on the screen I simultaneously heard a voice. *"Get the fuck off this property... You're trespassing."* I arrowed back to the previous image, the photo of the entrance to the motel's lobby. To the left of the entrance I could see a partially opened window. The curtain was pulled aside and a face was visible. When I zoomed in the face became lucid. It was the motel clerk, but he wasn't looking at me. His attention was directed towards the garbage dumpster in the corner of the parking lot.

At that moment I realized the clerk's outburst hadn't been directed at me, but at someone near the trash dumpster. Zooming in on the image even closer I was amazed to see a reflection on the office window pane. The reflection was superimposed over the face of the motel clerk. It appeared to be that of a man. A big, muscular man with thick black hair he pulled back in a pony tail.

"Sometimes things are not always what they seem, Mr Stevens." Those words came rushing back to me as I recalled what Detective Brooks had said just before I left the motel room that morning. I turned back to the image on the screen.

EARLY RETIREMENT

MURDER IN DAYTONA

12

Chief investigator Dan Brooks assembled a crack team to assist with the enormous task of compiling information, interviewing witnesses, and making sense of a senseless act. His superiors were under a lot of pressure to bring closure to this case. They wanted answers. As the detective poured over the evidence he knew the case wouldn't be solved any time soon. There were no viable suspects, nor was there any substantial evidence to work with. The forensics lab hadn't given him much in the way of analysis. Hair follicles, organic samples, and partial fingerprints taken at the scene could belong to almost anyone. They found nothing that could be directly linked to the crime.

Jordan Downs had felt some conjectural impulses during his investigation. The psychic said one impulse, an emanation he described as *"a figure without form,"* was present when he stood in the parking lot looking up at room number 28. According to Jordan the emanation returned when he touched the door handle of the room, but it dissipated when the two men entered. The only other comment the psychic offered was his strong impression that the victim's husband was not responsible for his wife's death.

Detective Brooks decided a trip to upstate New York was inevitable. If the investigation was to go anywhere the trail would start there. He chose William (Spider) Durance, a young assistant he'd worked with previously, to accompany him. The youthful detective reminded Brooks of himself as a hungry young cop. He had a bloodhound's nose for police work and a burning desire to get the bad guy. Brooks wasn't looking forward to spending the holidays freezing his ass off in the snow capital of America but duty called. His assistant on the other hand, being Georgia born and raised, was all *gung ho* about experiencing his first White Christmas.

Jordan assisted the detectives by using his F.B.I. connections to find a contact person in the bureau's branch office up in Syracuse. Will Durance was both surprised and delighted to find their contact was a young female agent. Her name was Mary Clarice Sheldon.

Agent Sheldon had been named after her Aunt Clarice, a retired FBI psychologist and profiler. Interestingly, Agent Sheldon's aunt was the inspiration for the character played by actress Jodie Foster in the movie *'Silence of the Lambs'*. Will was hoping Ms Sheldon might be available during a few of those harsh upstate New York winter nights, or so he fantasized.

Sheldon arranged to have the two investigators use a vacant office in the basement of the federal building, and got them limited access to the bureau's computer files. Local law enforcement provided them with a car. The automobile had been involuntarily forfeited by a drug dealer during a recent drug bust. Consequently, it was christened, *The Coke Mobile.*

With his support network in place Brooks began the arduous process of trying to piece together a puzzle of possible suspects. He started with the victim's ex-husband. Brooks knew Lucky Focha had reason to be angry with his ex-wife. She'd dumped him for another woman. The humiliation and embarrassment of losing your wife to another woman could be devastating to a man's psyche. The fact it happened so many years ago didn't negate the fact that it happened. The detective understood such feelings could fester in a man's soul. He'd seen it happen.

Brooks found out driving a vehicle in upstate New York in the winter took special skills. Before they reached the on ramp to I-81 south he assigned his protege the position of designated driver. Snow had been falling since the day they arrived. Brooks was amazed people actually chose to live here.

While Will cautiously headed down the Interstate Detective Brooks did a little research on his laptop. A google search of the name Lucky Focha resulted in some interesting findings.

He learned his given name was actually Lucken, a Dutch derivative of the German name Glucken. It literally meant, *"To lock up."* His family name, Focha, was originally a Dutch derivative of the German slang word for copulate. So in German the name Glucken Focha literally means *"One who is locked up and fucked."* Brooks found humor in the irony, as he was hoping to do just that.

Lucky lived just north of the city of Binghamton, New York. Driving in the snow it took the detectives nearly two hours to make the seventy mile journey. During questioning Lucky didn't try to conceal his feelings. As far as he was concerned his ex-wife's death was well deserved. He told Detective Brooks he considered Veronica an obscene degenerate. He asked the detective what kind of woman would abandon her family to be with another woman?

Despite his obvious contempt Lucky insisted he had nothing to do with his ex-wife's death. He told the detectives he'd gotten over the pain she'd caused long ago. *"Getting custody of my daughter gave me all the justification I needed,"* he added. When Brooks asked Lucky where his daughter lived now he responded *"I don't know... I don't care."*

Detective Brooks knew Lucky's daughter had left home when she was of age. The lack of affection provided by her father seemed to have more of a negative affect on her than did her mother's choice of partners. The child suffered the same emotional void that Veronica had during her marriage to Lucky. The detective changed the subject. He asked Lucky if he could recall where he was last November, fourteen?

Lucky responded to the detective's question by asking one of his own. *"Am I a suspect?"* Brooks told Lucky at this time he was only considered a person of interest! Lucky asked him if he should hire a lawyer before answering any more questions.

Detective Brooks informed Lucky his questions were routine to the investigation, and suggested if he was innocent he shouldn't have a problem answering them. Will Durance spoke up, telling Lucky he had a right to have an attorney present. He reminded him he was not under oath. Lucky considered his situation for a brief moment, then answered the question. *"Yes... I was deer hunting."*

Lucky and Ed always set aside the third week of November to go deer hunting in northern Pennsylvania. Ed Focha owned a camp a few miles outside the village of Montrose. They would haul down coolers full of beer and spend the week roaming the country-side shooting at anything that moved. In the evening they'd go down to the village and raise hell at the local taverns. The Focha brothers were well known in town as free spending, free spirited, good old boys from New York.

Susquehanna Valley is known for its excellent deer hunting. Several of the bigger camps surrounding the valley are owned by professional football players. Mainly members of the New York Giants. It isn't uncommon to see players and coaches in town during bye weeks in the schedule. Ed was always bragging to them about his place up in New York. He'd invite the players to come party at his club. So far none had taken him up on his offer.

Lucky told Brooks he and his brother left for camp early that Sunday morning, November 13th. They wanted to arrive in time to unload their gear and drive down to the village so they could watch some football at the Montrose Tavern. He tauntingly told the detectives he had plenty of witnesses to verify his story.

Will Durance took down the information and asked Lucky to sign a deposition. Brooks thanked Lucky for his time, and the two detectives headed out. As Will was pulling out of the driveway Lucky stuck his head out the door and gave them a pseudo wave, hollering out, *"Have a safe drive home, Boys."* The detectives ignored the gesture.

Detective Brooks knew Lucky's story was easily verified, and he mentally deleted him from his list of possible suspects. He instructed his protege to continue with the process of interviewing other sources. Brooks wanted to question Ed Focha alone. The detective knew where to find him.

When the detective walked into Ed's tavern he saw two men sitting at the end of the bar. They were huddled together, giggling like a couple of school girls. Something was laid out on the bar in front of them. They ignored the detective when he walked up and took a stool next to them. A deck of cards, the type that features young women in various sexual poses on the back, was spread across the bar. Brooks noted all the Hearts were redheads. All the Diamonds, blondes. Clubs were brunettes and Spades...black girls.

Feigning ignorance, Brooks asked the young fellow tending bar if the owner was in. The kid snickered, then pointed to the guy sitting at the bar in front of him. The two men stopped giggling. The thinner one turned around and rudely asked the detective, *"What's up, Dude?"*

Brooks expected Ed Focha would be a cocky little prick, and he wasn't disappointed. He introduced himself, then asked the tavern owner if he'd mind answering a few questions. Ed replied,

"Geez, I don't know man... Why don't you ask my lawyer?" He pointed to the guy seated next to him.

Ed Focha's attorney was dressed in a rumpled pinstripe suit that, despite his size, appeared to be too big for him. He asked Brooks what the questions pertained to? When the detective said he was investigating the murder of Veronica Stevens, Ed jumped off his barstool and exclaimed, *"That fucking dyke! She got what she deserved, Man!"*

The tavern owner's attorney attempted to calm him down, but Ed hollered over him. *"That bitch made all kinds of moves on me when she was married to my little brother, Bro... Guess she must be, AC-DC."*

By now Focha's rumpled attorney was standing between his client and Detective Brooks. He pleaded for him to quiet down. Ed completely ignored him, shouting, *"No way, Man. Let me answer his fucking questions. I got a rock solid alibi."*

Brooks secretly wished Ed was his man, but he knew the only way the little prick could be involved would be if he'd hired the job out. Ed's attorney told Brooks the only way his client would answer any further questions would be with a subpoena.

The detective wondered if this guy was the same lawyer that represented Lucky at his custody hearing. He knew Ed had paid for his brother's attorney, and he knew the guy had a vehement hatred for homosexuals. Brooks thought it was possible Ed Focha had contracted a hit on Veronica Stevens. Sure, it was a long shot, but it was possible.

He made a mental note to have his FBI contact run an inquiry into Ed's financial records. It would have to be off the record of course. For now the Stevens case was still a local matter. The FBI had access to information that made the detective's mouth water.

Brooks thought about all the things he could accomplish with that kind of authority.

While he was busy with Ed Focha, his protege was inter- viewing people who'd known Veronica Stevens. Past employers and coworkers, neighbors, friends, and relatives. Many had learned of Veronica's demise through news reports on television. The story made national headlines.

Will compiled quite a large portfolio on the life of Veronica Stevens. It turns out she didn't have many enemies. Everyone he interviewed described her as being a gentle, kind, caring person with compassion for those less fortunate. The young detective knew it only takes one.

The two men discussed their findings over dinner that night. Brooks began to understand what a loss Veronica Stevens was to the people she touched. His experience told him any list of possible suspects in a murder investigation had to start with those closest to the victim. He wasn't prepared to let Mr Stevens off the hook just yet, but he did have empathy for him. Meanwhile back in Daytona the investigative team had come across some valuable information.

One of the suspects on the shortlist lived less than an hour from the scene of the crime. Doris Van Fleet had relocated. She now lived in a community just outside Mount Dora, Florida.

Previously from Binghamton, Ms Van Fleet had moved to Florida the year before. The information was discovered by a police analyst assigned to match persons of interest with computer files of travelers flying in or out of Florida airports.

He learned the suspect had flown into Sanford the previous afternoon. The records showed Ms Van Fleet landed at the airport just outside Orlando on Empire Airlines, a small regional carrier based out of Ithaca, New York. That information was forwarded to the second in command, who verified the data then contacted Detective Brooks with the news.

The entire team was ecstatic. Van Fleet was near the top of the list of possible suspects. Their investigation had revealed Veronica Stevens was not the only woman Ms Van Fleet had terrorized. She had a history of violent behavior, and it was well documented.

While posing as a lover of women Doris had proven to be just the opposite. She was involved in a number of altercations where the police had to be called. In one case she was arrested and put in jail, charged with domestic battery. Her lover at the time refused to testify against her in court, which resulted in the charges being dismissed. Less than a year later Doris was arrested again, this time for violating a court order of protection.

Her live in girlfriend had been having an affair with another woman. When Doris confronted her about it the girlfriend admitted it. That sent Doris over the edge. She told her lover she would kill the other woman if the affair wasn't ended. When the other woman heard about Doris' threat she took it seriously. She filed papers in court seeking an injunction.

A few months later the girlfriend walked out. Doris assumed she'd left to be with the other woman so she showed up on her door step looking for trouble. The police were called. When the woman produced a court order of protection Doris was led away in handcuffs. As a condition of her release Doris was required to seek counseling and take anger management classes. Ironically her girlfriend had ended the relationship with the other woman long before. The affair had absolutely nothing to do with her leaving.

There were other skirmishes over the years. Doris had a penchant for flirting with the lovers of other dykes. Her behavior resulted in numerous cat fights where the authorities were called to restore order. Those in the lesbian community knew Doris had anger issues. Some accepted her for who she was, while others avoided her altogether. In either case Doris commanded their respect. She was a sister. One who was tough as nails and feared no one.

Brooks instructed his second in command to discreetly put a tail on her. He didn't want him to bring Doris in unless she tried to leave the state. The detective knew there was no real evidence he could use to tie Doris Van Fleet to the crime. Besides, he wanted the opportunity to interview her himself.

EARLY RETIREMENT

MURDER IN DAYTONA

13

Investigators learned Doris never submitted a change of address with the post office. She never officially become a Florida resident. Matter of fact her car was still registered in New York, and she still filed New York State income taxes.

Doris was collecting disability benefits for an injury she suffered while working as a mechanic. She'd been employed for over twenty years by Sam Foxx transport headquartered in Binghamton, New York. The company was owned and operated by a woman, Ms Samantha Foxx.

Brooks investigation revealed that Ms Foxx was a lesbian. That explained the Doris Van Fleet connection. He made plans to make another trip down Interstate 81 first thing Monday morning.

Despite being in her mid-fifties Samantha Foxx was a striking figure. Nothing like the stereotypical female trucker Brooks had envisioned. When the detective entered her office she was sitting behind a desk smoking a cigarette.

She stood to greet him. Samantha was a tall woman, with shoulder length chocolate brown hair and deep blue eyes. Dressed in a knee length skirt, cardigan sweater, and heeled boots, she looked anything but gay to Brooks. He noticed a pendant hanging from a thick gold chain around her neck. The pendant featured a skull smiling up at a bouquet of roses. It contrasted sharply with her outfit, and the detective consciously gaped at it longer than he should have. Finally he said, *"Interesting piece of jewelry."*

The trucking magnate snuffed her cigarette out and approached the detective with her left hand extended. Brooks noticed she was wearing a gold band on her wedding finger. Had the information he received been incorrect? Was she married? Was she not a lesbian?

"Love and Death," Samantha said as the two shook hands. The detective looked at her questioningly, so she explained her previous comment, *"My pendant. The rose and skull represent love and death. I'm sorry, but were gaping!"*

Brooks thanked her for the explanation, calling her Ma'am in the process. *"Please, Detective... It's Sam,"* She insisted! *"Now tell me, what brings you here."*

The detective told Sam the gruesome details of Veronica Stevens murder. He studied her facial expressions as he spoke. He was an expert at analyzing body language, and had a knack for knowing one's thoughts by reading their faces. He asked her if she had any information that might assist his investigation.

Dumbfounded by the question, Sam told him this was the first she'd heard of it. She asked him why he thought she'd have any information. Brooks explained a past employee of hers was a person of interest in the case. A Doris Van Fleet. He hoped she might have some insight.

Cutting to the chase, Detective Brooks asked Samantha if she ever had a personal relationship with Doris. He suggested he'd find out anyway. Sam told him Doris had been with her firm since the early days, and that she was both a good employee and a good friend. Not willing to leave the question unanswered the detective repeated his question. At that point Ms Foxx responded with an emphatic, "ABSOLUTELY NOT!"

Sam told Brooks it would have been inappropriate under the circumstances. Reading her body language, the detective believed her. She went on to tell him about the time Doris brought Veronica to a company Christmas party. It had been many years ago. She said Veronica seemed sweet, but that she was just one of many partners Doris had over the years.

He asked about the injury Doris suffered while working for her. Sam answered, *"That was devastating to Doris. The woman had no patience for weakness, and that included her own."* She told him she hadn't heard from Doris in over a year, adding, *"After her surgery she disappeared from the face of the earth."*

She mentioned another person Brooks might want to talk to. *"You should get a hold of Pam Sykes, Detective. She and Doris were really close."* The detective asked Sam if she knew where he could find this Pam Sykes person. *"Yes. Of course,"* she answered. Then she went to her computer and printed a file containing Pam's address and phone number. She handed it to the detective.

When Brooks went outside there was four inches of snow covering his windshield. He cleared it off with his coat sleeve, all the while grumbling how he should have brought Will along. The detective hated driving in this crap. Once the Coke Mobile was cleared of snow he got behind the wheel and entered Pam Sykes' address into his GPS. He had to wait another five minutes for the car to warm up enough he could see out the windshield, then he headed for the highway.

The GPS led him to a mobile home park called 'Highland Meadows'. It was sixteen miles north of Binghamton. Brooks located the single wide and knocked on the door. When a woman answered he flashed his badge.

Pamela Sykes was a petite woman. She had a sagging face and a bulbous nose. Age had taken its toll. She'd once been a good looking lady. She appeared nervous, but invited him in.

Detective Brooks declined Pam's offer of hot coffee and got straight to the point. He asked her if she knew Veronica Stevens. When she replied she did, he asked if she knew Veronica had been murdered. Without so much as a blink of an eye Pam told him, *"Yes... I have a friend living in Florida. She called me with the news the day it happened."*

The detective continued. He asked if this friend of hers knew Ms Stevens personally? Again Pam answered affirmatively. *"Yes... but it was a long time ago!"* Brooks finally asked what he knew was obvious. Who was this friend? *"Doris"* Pam answered. *"Doris Van Fleet."*

Brooks explained he was in New York because he was investigating the Veronica Stevens homicide. He told Pam that Doris was a person of interest in the case. Tears welled up in her eyes.

The detective gave Pam a moment to compose herself by apologizing for being the bearer of bad news. Once he felt he could proceed he asked her how she knew Ms Van Fleet. Pam told him she and Doris had attended Tech school together years ago. As an afterthought she mentioned they were roommates.

Brooks asked Pam if they were ever lovers. After a long pause she answered, *"Yes, we were. A long, long time ago"* She told him she and Doris remained friends over the years. She said Doris struggled with severe back pain, and that she'd moved in with her after she had surgery, just to help out. Pam told the detective Doris would have been placed in an assisted living facility if no one had been available to help her. *"That would have killed her for sure,"* she interjected.

"Doris wasn't able to deal with weakness in people," Pam explained. *"That included her own... Detective, her back issue was a disgrace to her pride. Doris found her disability humiliating. Believe me, it wasn't pleasant living with her again after all those years. Eventually I had to leave."*

Brooks asked Pam if she could tell him anything about the relationship Veronica and Doris had. She responded, *"I was there the day they split up. Veronica called to ask if I'd come over while she loaded her things... You know, just in case."*

Pam said she tried to tell Doris that Veronica wasn't cut out for the lesbian lifestyle. *"Doris was infatuated with Veronica. She insisted she could turn her on to it."* Pam hesitated, as if second guessing what she was about to say, then she blurted out, *"She always did like girls with big boobs."* Brooks couldn't help but snicker at the unsolicited comment.

Pam Sykes went on to tell the detective that it had been extremely tense the night Veronica left. *"When Doris came home and found Veronica gone all hell broke loose. I'd been watching for her from the kitchen window. When I saw her pull in the driveway I came out on the porch. Doris got out of her truck and asked me what I was doing there. Then she asked me where Veronica was... What could I say? She was gone!"*

The frail looking woman shuddered, as if she'd caught a chill. She asked Brooks if he'd like coffee, forgetting he'd already declined once. Then she continued. *"Doris gave me a blank stare. Like she didn't comprehend what had happened. After a minute she screamed,* **Is she gone?** *Then she froze!"*

A moment of silence passed between them. The detective thought Pam was finished. He almost went to stand up, but before he could Pam started talking again. *"I saw a look come over her face that scared the shit out of me, Detective. I held out my arms hoping Doris might accept my embrace, but I knew better. I prepared myself for her wrath."*

Brooks asked Pam if she could recall if Doris made any threats that day. She said she remembered exactly what Doris said. *"She screamed as loud as her lungs would let her, THAT FUCKING UNGRATEFUL BITCH! ... I'LL KILL THAT FUCKING SOW!"*

"Eventually it subsided," Pam stated. *"We uncorked a couple bottles of wine and spent the rest of the night indulging. Doris had no idea Veronica had left to be with a man. If she had God only knows what she might've done."*

Pam told the detective at one point Doris claimed she wanted Veronica out anyway, but on her terms. *"Doris admitted she'd already found a fresh little kitty as a replacement. She often bragged about going on the prowl"*

She told the detective Doris used to brag about leaving Veronica home alone. Pam said Doris was a good looking dyke, and full of confidence. She knew there were lot's of young women looking to experiment with their sexuality. She never had trouble finding a girl to lure into her bed... *"How do you think she got Veronica?"*

Brooks felt he'd gotten all the information he could. He thanked Pam for her help and handed her a business card. Then he got to his feet. Before leaving he asked Pam to notify him right away if she heard from Doris. He suggested she not mention anything about their conversation, reminding Pam that Doris was only a person of interest. *"When I return to Florida I'll bring Doris in for questioning,"* he explained. *"We have a number of leads we're following up on. Doris is just one of them."*

The detective hoped to reassure Pam that her friend was in no eminent danger. He headed for the door, but then hesitated.

Turning back, he asked Pam if she knew if Samantha Foxx was married? She answered, *"Not in this State she's not."*

Brooks sat in the driveway thinking about the conversation he'd just had. Before leaving he needed to ask Pam one more question. He went back and knocked on the door. He could see Pam through the blinds. She was talking to someone on the phone. He opened the door a crack and hollered out, *"Ms Sykes...When was the last time you saw Doris Van Fleet?"*

Pam quickly hung up the telephone and rushed to the door, her face flushed. Brooks had a stupefied look on his face as he absorbed her answer. *"Two days ago... I dropped her off at the airport."*

That night Brooks and his protege reviewed all the data they'd gathered. Their work was nearing completion. The detective was eager to get back home. The freezing temperatures and endless snowfall were wearing on him. It seemed no matter how much he fidgeted with the thermostat in his hotel room he was cold. Wearing thermal socks and long johns to bed just wasn't his style.

He decided Will would stay and finish up. There were still a few interviews that needed to be done with assorted associates of the victim. Brooks booked himself on a morning flight and packed his bags. At the top of his agenda once back in Florida was his intention to question Doris Van Fleet. He pondered whether he should have her picked up. In the end the detective decided there just wasn't enough evidence to justify it.

EARLY RETIREMENT

MURDER IN DAYTONA

14

Mount Dora is a quaint little village located some fifty miles southwest of Daytona Beach. It's home to many artist and craftsmen. The town's population swells during the winter months when an influx of snowbirds from New England and Canada take up residence.

The community of Mytilene sits on the outskirts of town. It was conceived as a retirement haven for affluent lesbian women wishing to spend their golden years in the sun. Mytilene was developed by a contractor who'd foreseen the demand for such a community. Investigators learned Doris Van Fleet lives there.

Dan Brooks took a drive out to Mount Dora the day after he arrived home. He considered asking Jordan to accompany him but decided Doris would probably be more responsive one on one. Though it wasn't really necessary the detective entered the address into his GPS. He'd been to Mount Dora many times before. It's just that his fascination with global positioning technology made every trip another excuse to use it.

The device's coquettish female voice kept the detective company on long drives. He'd named the voice *Lorelei,* after the mythological 'femme fatale.' She communicated articulately, never mislead him, and was a very good listener. During one very long solitary trip he'd jokingly told *Lorelei* it was a shame she didn't cook. Otherwise he might propose.

Upon arriving Brooks gave the Mount Dora Police Department a courtesy phone call letting them know he was in town conducting business. Being it was nearly lunch time the local police chief invited him to stop by the station. He ordered his desk officer to run across the street and pick them up some lunch. *"Get us sum dat fried groupa an southern slaw,"* he said. The chief didn't bother to take out his wallet. There was never a charge on orders placed from the police station. It was sort of an unwritten town ordinance.

While the two men waited for their food to arrive Brooks told the chief about his investigation. He asked him if he knew anything about the place on the outskirts of town that was supposed to be populated by gay women? The chief responded, *"Ya'll must be talkin bout Mytilene? Sure I knows bout it."*

He told Brooks Mytilene was started by some oil baroness about eight years ago. *"Dis ole Texas broad rides inta town an approaches da plannin commission wid dis grand plan to build dis retirement community,"* he says. *"It gonna generate lot'sa tax money an provide lot'sa jobs. She neglected ta mention it twas gonna be built for a bunch of friggin lezzies,"*

The chief went on. *"Dere be some gorgeous homes oud dere, Detective. Dem lezzies gots money. It no wonda dey don' need no man around."*

Brooks asked the chief if he knew how the place got its name. The chief answered, *"I undastand it some town in Greece where dat Sapphro woman come from. You know, da one started all dat lezzie crap."*

The detective thanked the chief for the history lesson. Then he asked him if he ever heard of someone named Doris Van Fleet. She supposedly rented a home in Mytilene. The chief told Brooks the women in Mytilene tend to stay to themselves. He'd never had to answer a call there himself, and his patrol officers rarely ventured

90

onto the property. *"Dat entire deevelopment be self sufficient,"* he stated. *"Da village don' even maintain da roads in dere."* Then the chief asked, *"Dis here Doris lady your suspect?"*

The two men finished lunch and Brooks headed out. He asked the chief to keep the investigation hush for a while. The detective understood how fast news can spread in a small town. As his GPS device led him toward Mytilene he heard *Lorelei* say, *"Turn left at the next intersection."*

As he approached the community the detective came upon an eight foot high coquina stone wall bordering a coral colored iron gate. An azure blue sign to the right of the gate read, **'WELCOME TO MYTILENE.'**

Brooks noticed a motion activated camera attached to the top of the gate. A detector activated the camera as traffic approached. There was a bright pink kiosk to the left of the gate that held maps of the community and a speakerphone. The detective pulled up and grabbed a map, then pushed a button on the kiosk. A moment later a female voice said, *"Good afternoon. Welcome to Mytilene."*

The voice sounded eerily like *Lorelei.* Brooks found that kind of creepy. It instructed him to help himself to a community map and continue on to the sales center at the end of Zephyrus Drive.

Studying the map as he passed through the gate the detective saw that the community was diamond shaped. Roads divided the property into four quadrants. As he drove up Zephyrus Drive he passed by a large park. He saw there were walking paths and a beautiful swimming pool. Women were sunning themselves on the pool deck, oblivious to a man driving by.

Brooks slowed as he drove past a Spanish style villa with a SALES CENTER sign prominently displayed on the front lawn. As he approached the next intersection he heard *Lorelei* say,

"Right turn ahead." A hand painted street sign informed him he was on Boreas Lane. Halfway down the block the GPS announced *"Arriving at destination."*

The detective pulled to the curb and climbed out of the car, taking in the expansive building before him. The architectural style could be described as modern minimalist. The huge home was constructed of prefabricated concrete slabs, and framed with cedar siding. Straight line windows ran the entire length of the forty-eight hundred square foot structure, which featured a flat, slightly angled metal roof. The simplicity of the design contrasted sharply with the elaborate landscaping that enveloped the property.

In the center of the courtyard was an enormous sculptured fountain. The sculpture depicted a Grecian goddess driving a golden chariot led by huge male lions. Brooks thought it looked beautifully out of place. He had to stop and admire it. After a while he made his way to the front entrance.

Brooks rang the buzzer, which was mounted on a hand painted Mexican tile. The motif on the tile... Skull and Roses. A pretty young latino woman in a housekeeper's uniform answered the door. Brooks identified himself and asked if Doris Van Fleet was in. The housekeeper nodded and motioned for him to follow her.

She led the detective through a portion of the gardens not visible from the street. In the far corner of the garden sat a white stucco cottage. The housekeeper told him to wait there, then entered the cottage through a side door. A few minutes later she reappeared in the company of another woman. The woman walked with the assistance of a cane.

Detective Brooks ran a quick assessment in his head. The woman appeared to be around sixty years of age. She had short blonde hair, greying at the temples. He estimated her height at about five foot, eight. She wore a baggy white tee shirt with blue jeans and white sneakers. The woman's tee shirt had a blue star emblazoned over the heart. It perfectly matched a blue star tattoo on her left arm.

She wasn't wearing make up, and the only jewelry Brooks noticed was a thick gold necklace that disappeared under the woman's tee shirt. Her body was well toned and she appeared to be in great shape. The detective extended his hand as she approached and asked, *"Doris?"*

Doris led Brooks to a bench in the middle of the garden. She sat down and pulled out a pack of cigarettes, offering him one before lighting up one of her own. Brooks declined the smoke, joking, *"It might stunt my growth!"* He always tried to interject humor when making these kinds of visits, believing it would help de-stress a situation.

The detective looked around and said, *"Real nice place you have here, Ms Van Fleet."* Doris didn't respond. That told Brooks this wasn't going to go as smoothly as he'd hoped. Pointing to some foliage across from where they were seated he asked, *"What kind of flowers are they?"*

Purposefully directing her response towards the flowers Doris reluctantly answered him, saying the plants were mostly salvia and bromeliads. Then she turned to face the detective. She looked him straight in the eye and asked, *"You here because you like flowers Detective, Or because of what happened to Veronica?"*

Brooks smiled. He responded with a question of his own. *"Why do you think I'm here, Doris?"* Doris told him she expected that somebody would be out asking questions eventually. She said she reads the newspapers every day and knew there'd been no arrests made.

The News Journal ran editorials on the unsolved homicide quite often. Most were critical of how the local police were handling the case. A recent article questioned how the murder might affect the upcoming tourist season.

Before Brooks could respond Doris told him she'd just returned from New York and the story was in the news up there too. *"Tell me about Veronica,"* the detective replied.

Doris asked him what he wanted to know. Detective Brooks responded, *"Whatever you'd like to tell me, Doris"* After contemplating a moment, she spoke.

"When I first met Veronica I could tell she was unhappy. She was a very attractive woman, Detective. I hated to see her waste it on an ungrateful man."

She went on for some time, bragging how she was there for Veronica through thick and thin. She told Brooks she tried to educate Veronica about men, and tried to be a parent to her daughter. Detective Brooks sat back and listened, hoping Doris might compromise herself with a statement she wouldn't be able to retract.

He asked her to tell him about Veronica's divorce and subsequent custody battle. She responded, *"I tried to get her to see the positives. To let it go and start fresh. She just kept getting deeper and deeper into her depression. I even took her on a vacation. We ended up fighting the entire time."*

Doris continued. *"That was the beginning of the end as far as I was concerned, Detective."* The two sat on the garden bench quietly staring at the ground. Minutes passed without a word being said. The detective could tell Doris was getting agitated. He decided to push the envelope. He asked her to tell him about the day Veronica left.

"You mean the day I threw her out," she corrected him. *"I told her to get her stuff and be out of my house before I got home from work! I wouldn't have tossed her out on the street, Detective. I knew she could go to her mom's. Her mother owns a two family house. No one lives in the other apartment."*

After another brief period of silence Doris looked over at Brooks and said, *"I loved Veronica, Detective...but I couldn't put up with the crying and moping any longer. She needed to snap out of it. If I wasn't good enough to make her happy... Then the hell with her!"*

Brooks wasn't sure what to say next. How could he lead Doris where he needed her to go? A full minute passed with no conversation between them. Finally the detective broke the silence.

"Let's be honest," he said. *"You know very well Veronica met a man...and you know the night she left she went to see him!"* Brooks could see Doris' hands were starting to tremble. He watched the veins in her neck begin to constrict. The detective knew his tactic was working. He continued turning the screws. *"You do know she was in love with him... Don't you Doris?"* The detective hesitated for effect, then plunged the proverbial dagger straight into her heart. *"Doris... Veronica left you because she fell in love with a man!"*

Doris exploded! ***"FUCK YOU"*** she screamed as she jumped up off the bench. She threw her cane clear across the garden, then got right up in the detective's face and screamed, ***"VERONICA WAS NOTHING BUT A GODDAMN WHORE."***

Her spirit broken, Doris collapsed back down onto the bench. She reminded Brooks of a wilting flower. A rose that had outlived its ability to impress. He pulled a handkerchief out of his pocket and wiped her spit from his face, then handed the hanky to her. After wiping the tears from her cheeks and blowing her nose Doris turned to Brooks and said, *"I loved her, Detective. Why didn't she love me back?"*

Brooks took Doris by the hand and compassionately told her it doesn't work that way. *"Love is a two way street,"* he explained. The detective let the thought sink in for a moment before adding, *"Unfortunately, some of us are one way people."*

At that point Brooks thought he might have his conquest on the ropes. He changed gears and went back on the offensive. He asked Doris point blank, *"Did you have anything to do with Veronica's death?"*

She froze up like an icy cardboard cut out. Her hand slid from his grasp... The movement hardly detectable. *"That's why you're here?"* she asked. *"You think I killed Veronica?"*

Again there was silence. This time it was Doris who broke the spell. *"Am I under arrest,"* she asked in a whisper? Detective Brooks informed Doris she was a person of interest, but he wasn't there to take her into custody. At least not yet. He asked her where she was on the 13th of November. At that point it was Doris who switched gears. She curtly answered, *"I don't remember... Do you, Detective?"*

Driving back to Daytona the detective reflected on the strange conversation he'd just had. Doris Van Fleet was obviously intelligent. She possessed a mental toughness that he truly admired. Still, the woman concealed an explosive personality the detective knew could be exploited. If he were to push the right buttons she would react in a way counterproductive to her best interests. That could definitely work in his favor when the time came.

Before leaving he'd informed Doris his investigation would require her to come down to the station for further questioning.

When she hesitated Brooks told her she'd be subpoenaed, adding he would prefer it if she came voluntarily.

Her inability to recall her whereabouts the day of the murder bothered him. It was relatively easy to disprove a lie, but when a suspect plays dumb it's much more difficult. Doris reluctantly agreed to meet with the detective the following Monday morning.

Meanwhile back in Syracuse, New York Will Durance had turned up something of significance. The young detective's main purpose had been to tie up loose ends before returning to Daytona. Not one to take anything for granted, Will had taken it upon himself to interview a number of people not on Detective Brooks list.

Two of those people were women who claimed they knew Veronica Stevens intimately. Interestingly, both claimed the affairs happened while she was living with Doris Van Fleet.

Betty Otis was a fifty-six year old nurse Will Durance thought looked no older than forty. She was tall, with a shapely figure and long dark hair. She'd come in to give s statement after her shift ended at the hospital. She arrived still wearing her nurse uniform.

She told the young detective she'd met Veronica years ago at a lesbian friendly bar in Syracuse. He must've had a dumbfounded look on his face because Betty stopped mid-sentence and said, *"Yes, Detective. I'm a lesbian."*

She continued her testimony, *"I met Veronica's partner first. A few weeks before I was at this dance club, and Doris was there. She'd been hitting on me all night and we ended up leaving together. I took her back to my apartment and we got it on. Doris waited till we finished before telling me she was in a relationship. Not that I cared. Sorry, but I was horny, Okay? Anyway, she told me I was very talented. Then out of the blue she asks me if I would do her girlfriend!"*

Will cleared his throat. This was an uncomfortable interview, but it was obvious it would cast new light on the investigation. He asked Betty if it was common for lesbians to share their partners with other woman. She answered, *"Most dykes are very jealous, just like you guys. Not me! Hell, I figure to each her own! I wasn't about to turn down an offer like that."*

The young detective found himself getting excited. He fidgeted with his pencil and shuffled around in his chair. As the aging, sexually stimulating nurse continued her testimony Will couldn't help thinking, *"Why the hell can't I find a straight woman like her?"*

Ms Otis continued, *"Doris was going to tell her girlfriend she was taking her out Friday night. She wanted to check out a new dance club in Syracuse. When Friday came, Doris would call to say she had to work late. She'd encourage the girlfriend to go on her own and she'd meet her there. Of course, Doris wouldn't show up... I would!"*

Betty could see the detective was getting excited. *"Down boy,"* she said to him, *"there's more."* Will laughed nervously, as though he didn't know what she was talking about. Betty continued giving her testimony. *"I found out later that Doris' real intention was to see if her girlfriend would take the bait."*

Will's interest piqued. He looked at the nurse impatiently and asked, *"Did she?"*

Betty answered, *"Oh Yes, Detective. She sure did. Hook... Line...and Sinker."*

After taking a sip of water from the bottle Will had given her Betty continued. *"Doris called to let me know her girlfriend had arrived. I spotted her as she came in the door. I ordered a couple of beers and went to work. I can still remember what Veronica was wearing. A red lace cami that enticingly left her belly button exposed. She paired that with a pair of skin tight blue jeans and red high heels. I could see why Doris chose her. She was hot! Very voluptuous for a gay girl, Detective. WOW, she had a great ass."*

Will felt himself blush. He cleared his throat but didn't say anything. Betty could tell the detective was uncomfortable. She said to him, *"We were young and crazy in those days, Detective. Remember, it was the 80's. The whole world was crazy!"* Will smiled, then asked her to continue.

"We had a few laughs," Betty reminisced, *"and ordered more drinks. I flirted with her. I don't deny it. Veronica tried to phone Doris several times, but she got no answer. Eventually I got her out on the dance floor where I could really turn up the heat. Later that night we stumbled out of the bar and into the back seat of my car."*

Betty took another sip of water, then continued her story. *"Unbeknownst to us at the time, Doris had driven up to Syracuse. She parked her pick up across the lot from where I was parked and watched."*

Will took a deep breath. He shook his head in disbelief. *"That's it,"* he asked? Betty nodded. The young detective stood up and extended his hand, thanking the attractive nurse for her statement. He assured her the information she provided was valuable to the investigation, and promised he'd keep in touch.

Up until then Veronica Stevens had come across as something of a saint, despite her promiscuity as a young woman. The Betty Otis interview shed more light on the real persona of Veronica Stevens. Will watched from his desk as the curvaceous nurse walked out of his office. Once alone he said to himself, *"Holy Mother of God... What a waste!"*

The interview not only shed more light on the character of Veronica Stevens. It also exposed Doris Van Fleet as a devious manipulative person. The woman had secretly arranged for her lover to have a sexual escapade with a stranger. Such an endeavor could provide invaluable ammunition to someone wanting to humiliate, disgrace, or discredit a significant other.

The detective thought Doris Van Fleet would be just the type to do it. Veronica's *pseudo* affair definitely gave a psychological advantage to the controlling neophyte, in case war were ever waged.

The second person to testify was someone who'd contacted the detective stating Jesus told her to. Will had originally blown her off as a nut case. It wasn't that unusual in high profile cases to get a few kooks seeking their fifteen minutes of fame. Only after the woman had written a letter explaining how she knew the victim did he agree to interview her.

Her name was Lois. She and Veronica had worked for the utility company together. At the time they were the only two women on staff locally. According to Lois they'd become good friends.

Lois told the detective when she first met Veronica she was living in sin. *"We used to take our lunch breaks together,"* she testified. *"Like most women, we usually spent it gossiping. Sometimes we would talk about our love lives."*

She told Will she remembered when Veronica first mentioned she was a lesbian. Lois said she warned Veronica that being a lesbian was a sin, and said she'd ask God to forgive her.

"I didn't know if she would listen. Veronica told me her lover was better in bed than her husband had ever been," Lois testified. She said Veronica asked her about her own husband, wanting to know if he was good in bed.

"I lied," Lois admitted. *"I told her my husband was great in bed."* Will could tell Lois was beginning to relax the more she talked. He asked her if Veronica ever said anything derogatory about Doris? Lois responded, *"I was just getting to that, Detective."*

"When Veronica found out her husband had been awarded custody of their daughter she called me. She was very upset. She asked me if she could come over, saying she didn't want to be alone. My husband was working and my son was in school so I said yes."

Lois stopped to clear her throat before continuing. *"When she got to my house Veronica looked heartbroken,"* she testified. *"We sat on the couch and cried together. Veronica blamed Doris, saying her partner never wanted her kid around."*

Lois looked to the detective for understanding. She told him she was going to admit something she'd never told anyone. Taking Will's hand in hers Lois whispered, *"Veronica and I were lovers."*

After the words came out Lois felt the need to explain. She'd tried to comfort Veronica that day. *"I held her hand and stroked her hair,"* she said. *"I tried telling her how lucky she was to be with someone that loved her. I cradled her in my arms."*

Then Lois blurted, *"God forgive me... I bent down and kissed Veronica on the cheek. Veronica looked up at me and smiled, so I kissed her again. This time on the mouth."*

Ashamed and frightened, Lois took a deep breath before continuing. *"That's when things got carried away, Detective. I told Veronica I'd lied about my husband being a good lover. I told her we rarely touched anymore. Then, God forgive me, I asked her to make love to me."*

Lois looked at Will and started to weep. *"I was young and foolish, Detective. Veronica gave me what I'd desired for so long. Her hands were so gentle, and she knew just where to touch me. She took her time with me, you understand? Veronica stayed until she knew I'd been satisfied."*

Will smiled at her in a nonjudgmental way, giving her the courage to continue. *"I never really understood how two women made love. When Veronica pulled me on top of her that day, I learned. I've never told anyone about this, Detective. I'm a married woman! I'm only telling you now because Jesus told me to. We never did it again after that. I swear! We never even talked about it."*

After some hesitation Lois said, *"Honestly Detective...I felt compelled to come forward. The last thing Veronica said to me that day has stayed with me all these years. She told me If Doris ever found out about them... She was dead!"*

All the interviews Will conducted were taped, with the consent of the participants. The young detective downloaded the testimony given by the two women onto his computer and forwarded them on. When Brooks listened to the tapes he was ecstatic. The investigation was beginning to take shape, and all the evidence was pointing directly to Doris Van Fleet.

Brooks telephoned his young protege to commend him for a job well done. He instructed Will to gather his belongings and come home. The young detective was a little disappointed about leaving. He'd come to appreciate the beauty of freshly fallen snow.

Will loved how the frigid air rejuvenated him when he inhaled. Someday he'd return, he convinced himself. Snowmobiling and ice hockey would replace surfing and biking as wintertime hobbies.

The following Saturday morning the team got together to share information and cross check facts. Will was asked to share the information he'd gathered during what was described as his *'Winter vacation in New York.'*

The novice detective decided to turn the tables on them. He thanked his boss for scheduling him a holiday in the snow capital of America. To prove his point he held up a photo for everyone's amusement.

Detective Brooks was shoveling snow and ice from around the wheel wells of their *'Coke Mobile.'* Another photo showed Brooks standing next to a street sign buried so deep in snow you couldn't read the name of the street. The photographs were passed around. Will pointed out how his boss had put his tail between his legs and run back to Florida leaving him to finish the job alone.

Everyone laughed. It was stress release time. The entire team had worked vigorously for the past two months. Now with some light at the end of the tunnel, it was good to relax a little bit. After a few off color remarks concerning the testimony of a certain nurse named Betty it was Detective Dan Brooks turn to speak.

He told the team about the talk he'd had with Doris. He informed them they were dealing with an intelligent, manipulative, and very dangerous woman. Brooks explained that he based his presumptions not only on his interview, but on the facts. The details the team had collected about her life.

He said there was damning testimony from persons close to the suspect. Finally, he suggested there were his instincts. *"I can feel it, Folks. In my bones... I'm telling you, Doris Van Fleet is our killer!"* Brooks displayed a flip chart for the team to review. He strongly suggested they focus on her.

EXAMPLE:

DORIS VAN FLEET
AGE 59
MOUNT DORA, FLORIDA

* RAPED BY STEPFATHER - AGE 11

* RAISED BY SINGLE NON SUPPORTIVE MOTHER

* VERIFIABLE HISTORY OF VIOLENCE

* PREVIOUS ARREST RECORD

* VIOLATION OF A COURT ORDER OF PROTECTION

* KNOWN TO HAVE MADE DEATH THREATS AGAINST THE VICTIM

* KNOWN TO BE INVOLVED IN SEXUAL DEVIATION

* VERIFIABLE PUBLIC OUTBURST OF ANGER

* UNABLE TO VERIFY HER WHEREABOUTS ON THE DAY OF THE MURDER

* UNABLE TO PROVIDE A CREDIBLE WITNESS WILLING TO VERIFY WHEREABOUTS

Once everyone in the room had a chance to review the chart the detective continued. *"All the evidence points to Doris Van Fleet. She is our number one suspect, People. We all know that the majority of murders are committed by folks who know their victims. Gentlemen, I surmise to you. Doris Van Fleet is our gal."*

The detective paused for emphasis. He picked up a pointer and walked over to the flip chart. *"The proof is in the pudding, Fella's. Doris is our killer, but we need proof... It's our job to find it! Take a good look at this chart. As a small child this lady was raped by her stepfather. She was disowned by her mother. She has a history of criminal violence. She can't even come up with a damned alibi. Where was she the night of the murder, Boys? Yes, it was her all right! Now lets get back to work and prove it!"*

Detective Brooks was well aware a person in custody is much more inclined to cooperate than one roaming free. It was time to start turning over rocks and rattling cages. Everyone has skeletons in their closet. There had to be something Doris could be held on. He didn't care if it was an unpaid parking ticket. Whatever it takes to get her in a compromising position, that's what they'd do.

EARLY RETIREMENT

MURDER IN DAYTONA

15

Jordan Downs was at a psychic fair being held at the recently opened Amway Arena in downtown Orlando. The SCI-FI channel was televising several of its programs from the event and one of the producers had asked Jordan to appear on a segment. During a break to reposition cameras one of the crew members handed him a post-it note. The message said, *"Call me ASAP - Dan."*

He waited until the show's director called it a wrap before responding to the message. Detective Brooks, excited about locating his prime suspect, had been pacing the hallways in anticipation of Jordan's call. When he finally got it he hollered into the receiver, ***"We got her, Jordan! I need you in my office Monday morning."***

For the next five minutes Jordan couldn't get a word in edgewise as Brooks pleaded his case against Doris. Eventually he stopped for air. That's when Jordan dropped his bombshell. ***"It wasn't her, Dan!"***

The silence on the other end of the line was deafening. The detective was momentarily stunned. Brooks struggled to give his friend a response. He valued Jordan's gift. Lord knows he'd been around the psychic enough to know he was the real deal. Upon regaining his composure Brooks asked Jordan how he knew it wasn't her? *"I just do, Dan,"* the impish clairvoyant responded. *"Your killer is a man, Detective!"*

How could he be so sure? The two men closest to the victim, her husband and ex-husband, both had an alibi. Doris Van Fleet was a viable suspect! Brooks wasn't prepared to discount her just yet. Besides, the honchos at city hall were pressuring him. They wanted an arrest, and they didn't care whether it was a man or a woman in custody. The upcoming tourist season depended on it.

Detective Brooks told Jordan he intended to interrogate Ms Van Fleet just the same, and that he'd like him to be there. He reminded Jordan he was on the payroll. Jordan snickered at the comment. *"Okay Dan, I'll be there,"* he replied, *"but I'm going to turn in an expense account."*

"The killer is a man!" The thought remained on the detective's mind as he pulled down the sheets and hopped into bed. The brutality of the crime certainly pointed to a male perpetrator. Women rarely went to the extent their male counterparts do when carrying out violent atrocities, even though the results are the same. The staging of the victim's body was in itself a clue, as doing so was preeminently male behavior.

Brooks fluffed his pillow and killed the light. Laying there in the darkness he wondered, could Jordan have been picking up on the *'maleness'* of Doris Van Fleet? After all, she is a dyke!

He woke up sweating profusely. The clock on the night stand read 4:00AM. His dream had seemed so real. So much so that upon waking the detective was surprised to find it wasn't. Then again, it couldn't be.

Brooks got up and poured himself a cup of yesterday morning's coffee. The bitter taste helped transform him from half asleep to fully awake. The detective took paper and pencil from a kitchen drawer and began writing.

In his dream Veronica Stevens was lying next to him, exactly as he'd found her in the motel room that day. The back of her head was caved in, and it oozed brain and blood. Thankfully her face was turned towards him. When he reached down to feel for a pulse she opened her eyes and spoke. *"Please help me, Detective. It hurts... Please... Won't you help me?"*

The detective heard himself say, *"That's why I'm here. I'm going to find out who did this to you, Mrs Stevens."*

She lifted her head and twisted around. *"What in God's name is that"* she exclaimed, looking at what appeared to be a wine bottle protruding from between her legs. The detective reached over and removed the bottle. He held it up for Veronica to see. The corners of her mouth curled up slightly and she coyly simpered... *"It's a Rose' of Isabella. My favorite."*

His dream continued. *"Do you know who did this to you, Mrs Stevens"* Brooks heard himself ask? He placed the wine bottle on the night stand. *"Was it Doris?"*

Suddenly a look of surprise came over Veronica's face. She repeated his words back to him, *"Was it Doris?"* The detective saw her eyes widen as she spoke. They seemed to focus on something behind him. He turned to see what it was. As he did someone smashed the wine bottle across his forehead. The blow knocked him unconscious.

The dream had been so surreal, and yet his recollection so vivid. Brooks knew he wasn't going to be able to fall back to sleep. If the dream didn't keep him awake, the stale coffee would. He went to take a shower, stopping along the way to turn the television on. The detective hoped the noise would alleviate the ominous presence he'd felt since waking.

Once dried and dressed Brooks decided to take an early morning walk on the beach. It was a few minutes before six when he backed out of the driveway and drove east. After making his regular routine stop at The Donut King to flirt with the girls behind the counter he crossed over to the beach side.

Arriving at high tide the detective decided to forego the walk. This morning he'd just relax and watch the sunrise. He stayed until the sun peaked above a line of pink clouds clinging to the shore, then drove to work.

When he got there the detective pulled the Steven's folder from his file cabinet and tossed it on the desk. After making a fresh pot of coffee he opened the folder. An eight by ten color photograph of the victim lay on top of the pile staring back at him. Brooks slammed the folder shut and took a step back. His thoughts returned to the dream he'd had. He wondered what Jordan Downs would have to say about that?

He went to the men's room and splashed cold water on his face. After gathering his wits Brooks returned to his desk. He reopened the Stevens file and sorted through the pile of glossy eight by tens, arranging them in the order he wanted Doris to see them when she came in. The detective wanted to be sure she'd view the most horrific shots last, hoping to shock her into a state of remorse. He knew it was a long shot, but Brooks had seen it work before.

Having Jordan present during the interrogation heightened the detective's anticipation. He would introduce Jordan to Doris. She might recognize him. The psychic's television appearances had made him a bit of a celebrity. If she knew of his powers the intim-adation factor could increase substantially in Brooks favor. He decided he'd mention Jordan's upcoming appearance on the Sci-Fi Channel. *"I might as well mess with her head right from the get go,"* he chuckled to himself.

Just then Will Durance walked into the office. *"Good afternoon Greenhorn,"* Brooks joked. *"Forget to set the alarm clock?"* Will laughed, then questioned why his boss was there so early? The detective shrugged his shoulders and responded, *"Couldn't sleep."*

Will walked over and poured himself a cup of coffee, then turned and facetiously asked his boss, *"Your conscience keeping you up at night?"* Detective Brooks didn't respond. He just stared out the window as if he were a million miles away.

Twenty minutes later the analyst who'd identified the whereabouts of Doris Van Fleet walked in with a manilla folder in his hand. Brooks had been impressed with the young man ever since hearing about how he'd located Doris. The detective knew good work ethics were scarce these days. As far as he was concerned the kid had a promising future in the department. Brooks had favors to call in before he retired, and he planned to take care of this one.

The young analyst handed Brooks the folder and said, *"I think you are going to want to see this, Sir."* When Detective Brooks opened the folder and viewed its contents he nearly dropped his coffee. Inside was a copy of an outstanding arrest warrant... It was issued to none other than Doris Van Fleet.

"I found it online, Sir," the analyst stated. *"She was stopped for driving without a license. I spoke to the trooper who issued it. He told me the driver was pulled over on the shoulder of the turnpike for some reason. Assuming she needed assistance he stopped to investigate."*

"Evidently she got belligerent," he continued. *"She started accusing the trooper of harassment. When he asked to see her license and proof of insurance she refused to provide it. Detective Brooks, the trooper could have taken her into custody immediately. Instead, he gave her a break. He issued her an appearance ticket. Well, guess what? She didn't show up for court!"*

110

Brooks stood there studying the document in his hand. He checked the dates, made note of the justice's signature, and verified the charges. The detective knew the town justice who'd signed the warrant. He'd been a Lake County deputy before retiring back in 1998. Brooks decided to give him a call. He picked up the phone and started to dial just as Jordan Downs walked in.

The detective hung up the phone. He walked over and greeted his friend with a bear hug. Jordan disappeared in the big detective's grasp momentarily, then suddenly reappeared. Brooks told Jordan the news he'd just been handed. The existence of the arrest warrant played right into their hands. Jordan responded by reiterating, *"It wasn't her, Dan."*

Detective Brooks grabbed Jordan firmly by the arm and told him Doris Van Fleet was totally capable of committing the crime. The psychic responded, *"That don't make her guilty...Dan. I'm leveling with you, my friend. Your killer is a guy."*

Brooks sat there, not uttering a word. After a while he spoke. *"What if the signal you're picking up, or whatever it is you pick up, Jordan. What if it's confused? What if you're picking up the male side of Doris? Remember Jordan, the woman is a dyke. She has masculine features. Her aura probably does give off a male manifestation. At least consider the possibility!"*

Before Jordan could respond Brooks said, *"I need you to give me the benefit of the doubt, Jordan... I need this!"* The detective explained how he planned to use Jordan's presence to get inside Doris' head. He needed to rattle her cage. See if he could get her to lose her temper. He asked Jordan to go along with his scheme, just in case he was right.

The detective had reserved the conference room to conduct his interrogation. He didn't plan to arrest Doris immediately, even though the outstanding warrant allowed him to. Brooks wanted to interview her first, hoping she might cooperate. If she refused or he sensed the interview was not going well he would present her with the warrant and and take her into custody. The detective expected she'd be accompanied by her lawyer. He would have Jordan and a female officer attend the interrogation also. It was scheduled for 10:00AM.

At 10:15 Brooks started to worry. It was unusual for a suspect to be late for this type of meeting. Attorneys always try to present their clients in the best possible light. He didn't panic, but decided if Doris didn't show by 10:30AM he needed to act.

At precisely 10:31 the detective contacted the Mount Dora Police Department. The Chief told Brooks he'd drive over to Mytilene and find out what was going on. At 11:00 the chief reported back. He was at the little stucco cottage on Boreas Lane talking to a young latino woman who identified herself as the housekeeper.

She told him in broken english the homes owner was in Paris and wasn't expected back for some time. Detective Brooks asked about Doris. Was she inside the cottage? He could hear the chief talking to the housekeeper in spanish. After a few minutes he got back on the line and told the detective the bad news.

"According to the little girl here, your suspect packed her bags and left last Friday morning. The housekeeper says Doris didn't leave a forwarding address, or any other contact information. She says Doris didn't even say good bye."

Brooks asked the chief to personally verify the cottage was vacant. He told him he'd be out later in the day, and thanked him for his assistance. As he hung up the phone Brooks hollered to anyone within hearing distance... ***"Get an APB out... NOW!"***

EARLY RETIREMENT

MURDER IN DAYTONA

16

Though retired Veronica still had a burning desire to make a difference in people's lives. She'd always been interested in helping women of low self esteem. She decided to put her efforts towards helping victims of domestic abuse. A phone call revealed a desperate need for volunteer advocates to accompany victims to court. The position required volunteers be available a minimum of two days per week, four hours per day. The opportunity excited Veronica. She eagerly pursued it.

Her training taught advocates not to get emotionally involved with their clients. Their role was to be a resource. I knew Veronica would end up getting involved though. She would make their problems, her problems. I also knew there was a danger in getting too entwined in people's personal lives. I told her so. I tried to explain when emotions become part of the equation it can always be dangerous...

One client Veronica took a particular interest in was a young Mexican girl named Teracita. She'd been brought to the shelter several days before, badly beaten by some psychopath she refused to name.

Veronica told me she first saw the girl when she was all alone in the community room. She'd found her blankly staring out the window. Veronica introduced herself and asked the girl if she'd like to talk. She could see she was in trouble. Fear was written all over the young woman's face. Her body trembled. Veronica said despair smothered the light in the girl's eyes.

According to my wife Teracita was wearing a Liz Claiborne dress, paired with fashionable heels and not to cheap costume jewelry. Veronica said she complimented Teracita on her outfit and attempted to put her at ease. Most women at the shelter wore cut off shorts and tee shirts, that sort of thing. Occasionally a girl from a more affluent background would show up, but not often.

My wife knew domestic abuse wasn't limited by class boundaries. It's just that those with the means usually avoided the shelter. The few that did come normally stayed just long enough to arrange for more dignified surroundings.

Veronica's heart hurt for Teracita. She wanted to be involved in her case but unfortunately it had been assigned to one of the other advocates. She decided to read her file anyway. Veronica told me she waited for the case manager to leave for lunch one day, then went through the file cabinet and pulled Teracita's folder.

Reading through the file Veronica learned Teracita had been brought to the shelter by a priest. She'd gone to *The Little Lamb of the Sea Catholic Church* seeking help. The poor girl had been brutally beaten. She claimed she didn't know her attacker, and had no place to go. That's when the priest contacted the shelter. After assessing her case a social worker instructed the priest to bring her in.

Upon arriving a nurse treated Teracita's injuries. Afterwards she was interviewed by a domestic abuse counselor. Teracita told the counselor she didn't know her abuser, claiming it was a random act. She feared deportation if the police were called.

Veronica returned the folder to its proper place, then signed herself out to lunch and headed for the community room. Teracita was in her usual spot, watching the world go by. This time when she saw Veronica approaching Teracita smiled, albeit timidly. The smile quickly left her face when Veronica told her she'd reviewed her file. She looked into Veronica's eyes and studied them intently, then whispered, *"Why?"*

Veronica told her she too had been in abusive relationships. She talked about her father, explaining he'd deserted her as a child. She told Teracita about her first boyfriend, and how he'd broken her heart when he got another girl pregnant. She told her about Lucky, her first husband, and how he'd manipulated and used her. She explained how emotionally distant he'd been, and suggested that type of abuse could be just as painful as any physical beating.

Veronica teared up when she spoke about her relationship with Doris. She told Teracita women can be just as abusive as men. She said she understood what it was like to fear someone. *"There was a time when I feared for my life,"* she told her... *"That's why!"*

She needed Teracita to know there was hope. She told her about the love she had for me, saying *"There were times when I wondered if I'd ever be happy... Now I can't fathom not being so!"*

Veronica tried to convey her message by using an old adage... **You can't see the forest for the trees**. *"The forest is a place of wonder and beauty,"* she told her. *"It is filled with foliage and fauna and flora. From above or beyond it is a glorious spectacle of magnificence. However for someone lost the forest can seem a hostile place, full of menacing sounds and unsympathetic terrain. If the lost could only step back and change their point of view they could see the forest for what it really is."*

The look on Teracita's face suggested she didn't have a clue what Veronica was talking about. Still, she knew she meant well. She agreed to answer Veronica's questions...off the record!

Veronica asked the frightened young woman if she knew the man who'd hurt her. Without answering, Teracita motioned for Veronica to follow her back to her room. Once there she closed the door and removed her dress. Veronica tried to conceal her horror. The documents in the file hadn't prepared her for what she saw.

The backs of Teracita's upper thighs were swollen and badly bruised. Her buttocks were lined with deep purple welts that ran from hip to hip. Veronica began to cry. When she did, Teracita did too. The two women stood there embraced in each other's arms weeping.

Veronica couldn't shake the memory she had of the beating Teracita suffered. She questioned whether there should be some record, some proof of her injuries. Photos depicting the intensity of the abuse. Had the police been involved they'd surely have taken pictures.

If Teracita came forward with the name of her attacker after her wounds healed would anyone care? Veronica fumbled around in her purse and pulled out a camera. She'd brought it today to take pictures of one of the residents celebrating a birthday. Veronica looked at the abuse victim as if silently asking for her permission. When Teracita nodded, Veronica swallowed the lump in her throat and started taking photographs.

It was a painful chore, but one Veronica felt compelled to finish. She put the camera back in her purse and sat on the edge of the bed. Both she and Teracita recognized they'd made a lasting connection. The look on the frightened girl's face answered Veronica's question. She definitely knew the identity of the man responsible for her injuries, and she definitely feared him. Veronica gave Teracita a hug and told her they'd talk later.

EARLY RETIREMENT

MURDER IN DAYTONA

17

Teracita Goncalves grew up in Delicias, Mexico. The city sits just across the border from Texas. It is home to over one-hundred thousand residents. Delicias has experienced rapid growth ever since the North American Free Trade Agreement was signed into law in 1994.

NAFTA allowed American corporations to take advantage of cheap Mexican labor and non existent safety regulations. By constructing hastily built manufacturing plants and hiring low paid workers to work in them companies could increase their profits. The goods they produced would then be exported back to the United States for consumption. Dozens of these maquiladoras line the northern edge of Delicias. They employ thousands.

Teracita's parents work at one of the maquiladoras, each earning the equivalent of six American dollars a day. Those not fortunate enough to find work in one of the maquilas often turn to the drug cartels for their livelihood. There is always a need for field laborers and armed guards to protect cartel interests. A high turnover rate guarantees employment to anyone desperate enough to take the risk.

One of nine children, Teracita was the first in her family to graduate from high school. She finished a full semester ahead of her classmates, thanks to an accelerated program for gifted students. Even for someone with an honors diploma there were limited opportunities for employment. Teracita feared she'd end up working alongside her parents in one of the maquiladoran sweat shops. She was determined to make a better life for herself. Teracita decided to look for work across the border in the United States.

International employment agencies often sought out qualified applicants for careers abroad. Many of them had begun recruiting high school graduates in northern Mexico. Most of the students were bilingual, making them particularly appealing to english speaking employers. By graduating early Teracita got a jump on her classmates, who wouldn't be eligible for recruitment until their June commencement.

Teracita spoke with representatives of an American Au Pair agency whose program was sponsored by the State Department. They encouraged Teracita to apply. She had plenty of experience taking care of children. She'd been responsible for her younger siblings while her parents worked.

Teracita's high school diploma qualified her for a J-1 visa. The document would allow her to work as a domestic in the United States for two years. She would be required to live with a host family and continue her education at a government accredited school. With her prospects limited in Delicias, Teracita completed the application.

According to her recruiters she'd receive a five hundred dollar bonus if she was accepted into the program, as well as a minimum salary of six hundred dollars per month, with room and board furnished by the host family. Teracita would earn more money than she ever dreamed possible.

At the end of her two year commitment she would be certified in household management. Many in the Au Pair program applied for permanent residence status at the end of their two years. Once she established residency Teracita could apply for citizenship. At that point she could sponsor other family members desiring to come to America. Teracita Goncalves was a young Mexican woman fulfilling her dreams. Her parents couldn't have been more proud of her.

Several months after applying for the Au Pair program she was accepted. Teracita was placed with a host family from South Florida. Salvatore and Camilla Conti lived in Coral Gables, an affluent city a few miles south of Miami.

Mr Conti was a Cuban exile. He'd made a considerable fortune in the import/export business. His wife of three years was an Italian-American whose family owned an art gallery and auction house in Miami Beach. Nicolina, Camilla's five year old daughter from a previous marriage lived there with them.

Camilla was something of a social butterfly. She sat on the boards of several charitable organizations and served as official hostess for the Miami Art Guild. Her agenda kept her quite busy, leaving little time for child rearing. Nicolina was mostly raised by nannies. Her previous nanny, a Dominican woman named Leta, had returned home after learning of her mother's sudden illness.

The Conti's took little time choosing the outgoing nanny's replacement. Teracita's file had been presented to them by an agency rep along with several others. Camilla Conti fingered through the files for a few minutes, then chose one and handed it to her husband. Salvatore opened the folder, shrugged his shoulders in agreement, and arranged to have Teracita flown in the following day.

A chauffeured limousine picked her up at the airport and drove her to the Conti home. The driver slowed as he entered Coral Way so Teracita could take in *The Miracle Mile*. The wide, tree lined boulevard was home to some of Miami's most famous residents.

Emilio and Gloria Estafan of Miami Sound Machine lived there, as did several members of the Bee Gees. Before he married Jay-Lo pop singer Marc Anthony had a home there too. As the chauffeur drove the limo under a long canopy of moss covered live oak trees he opened the sunroof so Teracita could enjoy the breathtaking view.

A few minutes later they turned onto a gravel road. It ended at the gates of an impressive mansion. The Conti home was an Italian Renaissance Villa. It was constructed of Cuban limestone and accented with coral colored architectural trim. The home sat on the edge of a lagoon and featured a Tuscan inspired garden filled with subtropical plants native to the area.

Varieties of cycads and palms were surrounded by flowering anthurium and philodendron meticulously placed and cared for by a professional gardener. When Teracita exited the limo she was met by a well dressed dark haired woman with a small child by her side.

"I'm Camilla," the long legged beauty said as she extended her hand. *"This is my daughter, Nicolina."* Camilla instructed her chauffeur to take the new nanny's luggage to the *Mariposa* suite, then led Teracita through the gardens to the back entrance. When they got there Mrs Conti said, *"All employees use this entrance when coming or going, Capisce?"* Once that was understood the lady of the house invited Teracita inside.

Teracita entered into a brightly appointed vestibule. The large room was furnished with eclectic Caribbean pieces that her host bragged she'd hand picked for the space. The vestibule emptied into a large kitchen, where the family's Haitian cook stood waiting.

Rosita was a heavy set woman with a thick Haitian-Creole accent and a large unpretentious smile. She motioned for the two women to be seated. She'd prepared a midday snack consisting of

120

fresh fruits, buttered croissants with salmon spread, and iced tea. Camilla asked Rosita to take Nicolina to the nursery, then turned to Teracita.

"This room is where the employees eat their meals. I will post your schedule for the week here every Sunday evening." Camilla methodically chose a small croissant, spooned some salmon spread on it, then continued. *"I do have things come up unexpectedly from time to time, so I will need you to be flexible."* When the women finished eating Camilla said, *"Let's get you settled in, shall we?"*

The Au Pair was housed in a suite of rooms on the second floor. Painted jasmine white, the *Mariposa* suite was larger than the entire Goncalves home back in Delicias. It featured a Queen size rattan bed placed in the center of the room surrounded by high end furnishings and tropical accents. A walk-in closet would easily provide more than enough space for Teracita's meager wardrobe, and a small bathroom would provide privacy the other domestics lacked.

A separate sitting room adjacent to the nursery offered cable television and an internet connection. Teracita learned some of the furniture pieces had been manufactured in Chihuahua, Mexico. She presumed by cheap Mexican labor working in a maquiladoren sweatshop. Using it would feel strange, knowing the conditions under which it had been made.

It didn't take long for Teracita to become comfortable with everyone. She was the youngest, and according to Mrs Conti, the brightest of the bunch. Camilla told Teracita the way she handled her daughter was wonderful. Nicolina was well behaved, and Teracita enjoyed their time together.

She rarely saw Mr Conti. He spent many nights traveling in support of his business. Teracita thought it must have been a lonely existence for Camilla, which explained why she kept so busy with her social functions. Camilla Conti treated Teracita more like a friend than an employee. She hadn't been there two months when she was asked to join the family for dinner in the dining room.

To meet the educational requirements of her temporary visa Teracita enrolled in a course at Miami University. The campus was just a few miles from the Conti home. She became friends with a classmate who happened to be in a situation similar to her own.

Celeste Montoya was a domestic worker for a family in nearby Coconut Grove. She had use of a car, and liked to go to the beach on her days off. She invited Teracita to join her one afternoon. Celeste took her to Haulover, a clothing optional beach north of Miami.

Haulover is a two mile long strip of sand and surf located in Bal Harbour. It is a popular destination for young professionals eager to expose their bodies to the ultraviolet rays of the South Floridian sun. The clothing optional park beckons eight thousand visitors to its shores almost every weekend.

The girls made the hour long drive from Coral Gables to lay in the sun and check out the sights. At their age they were more than interested in the opposite sex and, being clothing optional, Haulover allowed them the opportunity to see exactly what they were getting. It became the girls destination of choice most Sunday afternoons from then on.

Teracita was an attractive young woman. She had long shiny black hair that cascaded over her cinnamon colored shoulders, and large dark eyes that glistened in the sun. Not to mention a gorgeous curvaceous figure could rouse the dead. Teracita got plenty of attention from the many men who frequented the beach. It was her strict catholic upbringing and strong parental influence that kept her from falling victim to the unsolicited advances inadvertently bestowed upon her. That is until she met a hunk of a man that happened by one afternoon.

Carlo Santiago was a thirty-five year old Miami Beach attorney. Originally from Havana, he'd attended law school at Florida International University. He was employed by Galen Rose Associates, a prominent Miami law firm.

The attorney struggled with three vices. Gambling, women, and self conceit. Saturday afternoons would find him at Gulfstream Park making exotic bets. Sunday afternoons were always spent at Haulover.

To him women were fleshy pieces of boneless fillet to be savored...then devoured. Haulover Beach was where Carlo went fishing for that evening's catch. He was handsome, confident, and blessed with the equipment to impress. When Carlo Santiago walked the beach people noticed. The women and the men. Hey... This was Miami!

Teracita had been baking in the sun for over an hour. Streams of perspiration were forming between her breasts and pooling in her belly button. She pulled her bikini bottoms from her beach bag and slid them on, then told Celeste she was going in the water to cool off. A fear of sharks wouldn't allow her to go in very deep.

Down the beach Carlo Santiago was walking in the surf and enjoying the sights. His reasons for not going in very deep were more elemental. It would prevent his admirers the opportunity to feast their eyes on him. He happened to see Teracita wading in the water, her firm brown breasts inches above the surface.

Carlo watched as she cupped pools of turquoise water in her hands and splashed it across her chest. The playboy attorney appreciated how Teracita's nipples responded to the shock of the cool water. He felt himself begin to perk up at the sight. He quickly turned to face the waves.

Once sufficiently cooled off Teracita returned to her beach blanket and removed her bikini bottoms. Lying there with her eyes closed she fumbled around for her bottle of sunscreen. A moment later she heard Celeste flirtatiously say, *"Well, hello there."*

Teracita opened her eyes to see her friend looking up into the sun with a big grin on her face. When she turned to see what had made Celeste so giddy she saw a gorgeous guy looking down at her. His position directly in front of her blocked the sun, allowing her a full unadulterated view. He was handsome, well built, and... All man! Teracita self consciously thought she'd taken a moment to long admiring him and embarrassingly looked away.

"Hi. I was walking up the beach and couldn't help but notice you," he said to Teracita. *"I've never seen you here before. Are you on vacation?"*

Teracita smiled shyly. She told him she'd been coming to Haulover Beach with her friend from college the past few weeks. She pointed to Celeste as she spoke.

"I see," Carlo responded. *"So you are college students? That's fantastic... Coeds!"*

He told her he was a graduate of Florida International. A Golden Panther. *"That makes me a predator,"* he joked. *"So watch yourselves."*

Carlo swiped his paw in the air and mockingly lunged toward Teracita, who giggled like a school girl. She told him she went to the University of Miami. She didn't bother to mention she was enrolled in just one class there. Nor did she mention she was employed as a domestic.

Ten minutes into their conversation Carlo asked if it would be okay to join Teracita and her friend. He sat down between them and offered to help with tanning lotion.

Carlo was smooth. He knew how to seduce women, and he thought Teracita might be special. There was something about her. She was gullible...innocent...naive? He contemplated, wondered... Could she still be a virgin?

The three of them spent the rest of the afternoon together, talking...tanning...and flirting. When the sun sank below the roof lines of the condo across from the park Carlo suggested they go for Chinese. Celeste, realizing she was a third wheel, opted out. She made up an excuse for why she needed to get back.

Carlo told Teracita if she agreed to join him for dinner he'd be glad to drive her back to her dorm. Not wanting to lie to him about her true vocation, she declined too. She did however promise to meet him again the following Sunday.

The playboy escorted the two women to their car and kissed Teracita goodbye. It was a passionate kiss. One that would normally be considered inappropriate for a first time meeting. Teracita returned it with vigor. The throb she felt deep inside would not be self stimulated away... Not this time.

The following Sunday Celeste called to say she wouldn't be able to go to the beach. Her employer was attending a function and needed her to watch the kids until she returned. Teracita panicked. She'd been looking forward to this day all week. The throbbing still dwelled deep inside her. She went to the kitchen to ask Rosita how much a taxi would cost to take her to Bal Harbour. The Haitian cook looked at her questioningly then said, *"Yuiz talkin bout Alluver Beach, Child?"*

Teracita blushed. She admitted she'd met someone, and had promised him she'd be there today. Rosita asked Teracita if she was on good terms with Ramone? When she got nothing but silence in response she waved her hands in the air and said in broken Creole, *"No mine no way, I iz. Go git yuself reddy."*

Ramone complained the entire way. *"If I lose my job over this,"* the chauffeur kept fretting. *"Damn it, Rosita knows better."* He dropped Teracita at the entrance to the beach and told her, *"Find your own way back."*

Teracita rushed to the spot she'd met Carlo the week before. She reclaimed it by spreading her beach blanket on the sand. She waited for over an hour, but Carlo didn't show. Teracita had enough cash on her to cover cab fare. She never really expected she might have to use it.

She fingered her way through a couple magazines, using them as props. Her heart hurt. The twinge deep in her belly subsided. Teracita had never been in love before. Hell, she'd never known a man before... Not intimately.

Carlo watched from his perch some fifty yards away. Sitting in a rented beach chair and holding a set of binoculars he could see the hurt on Teracita's face. He watched as she wiped away tears from behind a Spanish language copy of Allure. *"This is going to be easy,"* he thought to himself. Not like the last time. *"That Cunt deserved the beating she got."*

He'd thought that being so young, the little cunt would be naive, but she'd proven to be anything but. The bitch actually laughed when he tied her to the bedpost. Face down and spread eagle, she'd begged him to spank her. When he dropped her battered body in that dumpster in Liberty City she wasn't laughing any longer.

When Carlo saw Teracita get up to leave he made his move. He sprinted towards her gasping for breath. *"I'm so sorry, Teracita. Please forgive me. I got here as fast as I could... I was so afraid I'd miss you."* The lying lawyer kissed her on the cheek and noticing a tear said, *"You've been crying? Sweet girl, I'm so sorry."* Carlo licked the tear off Teracita's cheek, then kissed her passionately. Several bystanders mockingly applauded and yelled for them to get a room.

"Do you like horse racing," Carlo asked? *"I go to the casino up in Hallandale and place a few bets when I leave here. Are you hungry... We could stop for dinner?"*

Teracita was enamored. This man some eighteen years older than her was the sexiest guy she'd ever known. The thought of having sex with him both aroused and frightened her. She regretted not being honest with him the previous week. He thought she was a college student. How could she tell him she was just a domestic, here on a work visa?

Carlo helped Teracita stuff her beach bag, then they walked to the parking lot. Teracita stood dumbfounded when Carlo pulled out the keys to a midnight black Ferrari Spider F-50 and motioned for her to get in.

Recognizing Teracita's hesitation, Carlo explained he'd bought the car used. He told her he paid less for it then she thought, only a hundred grand. He said if it made her feel any better they could go dutch on dinner tonight. Teracita got in the car and Carlo headed up Collins Avenue.

Reaching his destination, Carlo pulled up to the valet. A tuxedoed attendant opened Teracita's door and took her hand. The valet was obviously acquainted with Carlo, greeting him by name. He took the keys that were handed to him, as well as the twenty dollar bill attached to them. Carlo escorted Teracita into the Versailles.

According to Carlo, the Versailles was the best Cuban restaurant in Miami. The maitre d recognized him immediately. They were seated at a table with a gorgeous view of the inter-coastal waterway. Carlo ordered for both of them, not bothering to open the menu.

The waiter brought fresh mojitos. Carlo told Teracita they were made with the finest Cuban pineapple liquor. The two sipped their drinks and watched million dollar yachts pass by on their way to...wherever.

Teracita thought she was in heaven. She wondered what her parents would say if they could see her now. She finished dinner, a traditional offering of mango gazpacho, ropa vieja, and arugula salad. Carlo had romantically ordered a Mexican chocolate tart for dessert. When the bill came Carlo reminded Teracita of his promise to go dutch. He slid the check over to her, then excused himself and went to the men's room.

Teracita picked up her purse while simultaneously looking at the check. Her jaw dropped when she realized her half would cost more than she earned in a week. She'd brought fifty dollars to cover a cab ride home had one been necessary.

When Carlo returned he saw the look on Teracita's face and broke out laughing. *"What's the matter, my little chingona"* he asked? Teracita, flabbergasted by the cost of dinner, told him she'd get the tip. *"Don't worry about it, Doll,"* he replied. *"I've got it covered. I forgot you're just a poor college student."*

Carlo continued laughing as they waited for the valet to bring his car. He told Teracita she was a good sport, and confessed he'd survived on plantains and black beans all through college. *"We're going over to the casino, so don't worry about it, Sweetie"* he insisted. *"We're gonna win it all back."*

Gulfstream was ten minutes from the restaurant. During the drive there Teracita told Carlo she'd not been completely honest with him, admitting she was just a part time student, here on a work visa. Carlo parked his Ferrari, then took Teracita's hand. He looked her in the eyes and said, *"Baby, we all got skeletons in our closet. I knew you weren't going to school full time, and I knew you were here on a J-1... So don't worry bout it. Okay?"*

Teracita let out a sigh. She asked Carlo how he knew? He gave her a stock answer. *"I'm a lawyer, Doll.. That's what I do."*

Over the next month Teracita saw Carlo with increasing regularity. He took her out several times a week, usually to the clubs on South Beach. Sundays were reserved for Haulover Beach and Gulfstream. Carlo still had his vices to contend with!

The fact he'd even consider falling for this young Mexican peasant surprised him. He'd intended to treat her the same way he treated all the other ones. Like a dirty whore. He'd truly meant to follow his normal routine. Identify, stalk, delude, and unveil. This time though, his routine had failed him.

Teracita's purity and innocence had somehow soothed the savage beast that lay just beneath Carlo's surface. If he wasn't careful he could fall in love. That would be dangerous. Carlo Santiago could love only one person... Himself.

The attractive Mexican Au Pair had managed to postpone having sex with Carlo. She'd wanted to abandon the pledge she'd made to her parents to save herself for marriage, but she hadn't. At least not yet! She and Carlo often engaged in long sessions of mutual stimulation, but always stopped short of consummation.

Teracita was surprised Carlo wasn't more aggressive sexually. It was almost as if he was saving himself for marriage too. She knew that wasn't the case. A man like Carlo must've known many women.

Camilla Conti was aware her new nanny had met someone. She and Teracita discussed the rules of the house in detail, especially the one banning overnight guests. She warned Teracita not to get involved with an older man, telling her *"Your guy is older than I am, for God sake."*

Camilla suggested Teracita invite Carlo over for dinner so she could get to know him, saying, *"As your sponsor I'm obligated to watch out for your best interest."* In actuality it was Camilla's curiosity that prompted the suggestion. She had to admit Teracita had impressed her. This nobody, this Mexican immigrant, had somehow managed to attract a handsome, single, well connected Miami lawyer. Most of Camilla's girlfriends would've done anything to be in Teracita's shoes.

A dinner party was set for the following Friday evening. Camilla would invite a few friends over, and Rosita would serve one of her Caribbean Island specialties. They'd dine on the veranda overlooking the tropical Tuscan gardens.

When Carlo arrived in his Ferrari he was wearing a custom made Ted Fisher suit. It was fitted perfectly and expertly matched with a coral colored silk shirt and azure blue tie. His jet black hair was pulled back in a ponytail, stylishly held in place by a fuchsia colored holder.

Camilla Conti watched inquisitively from her second floor office window as Carlo exited his vehicle and made his way to the front door. When she heard the doorbell chime she closed the shutters and went to greet him. She stopped briefly to check herself in the mirror. Camilla contemplated how she'd approach her guest. She smiled at her reflection then went downstairs.

Carlo was standing in the foyer talking to Ramone. The chauffeur had originally balked at Mrs Conti's request that he be available to help out tonight. It wasn't enough being her driver/ gofer/ boy-toy. Now he was expected to be an official greeter too? *"Appearances, Dear boy,"* she'd told him. *"Appearances."*

Camilla looked stunning as she walked down the stairs. An elegant lady to begin with, the knee length chiffon dress she'd chosen for the evening's festivities only confirmed it. She approached Carlo with her hand extended. He met her halfway.

After softly kissing the back of Mrs Conti's hand Carlo thanked her for the invitation. Teracita, who'd been nervously fussing with her make up, hadn't heard his arrival. Camilla took advantage of the moment and playfully flirted with her guest of honor. Putting a finger to his chest she said, *"If things don't work out with your little girlfriend... Come see me!"*

Teracita entered from a side room and saw Mrs Conti talking to her lover. She walked up to Carlo and kissed him on the cheek, then asked, *"When did you get here, Darling?"* Camilla suggested Teracita get the guest of honor a drink while she checked on dinner. Ten minutes later they were all out on the veranda toasting the amazingly gorgeous moon over Miami.

Just as dinner was being served Salvatore Conti showed up. He'd not been expected until Sunday morning, but an argument with a business acquaintance had shortened his trip. *"What's the occasion, Darling,"* he asked his wife? *"Did I miss a birthday?"*

Camilla feigned her delight at seeing him. She explained she'd invited some friends over for dinner. Mr Conti noticed his recently hired Au Pair, and walked over to say hello.

Teracita introduced Mr Conti to Carlo. Camilla intervened, telling her husband Mr Santiago was an attorney with the Galen Rose law firm over in Miami. Conti shook Carlo's hand, then bluntly asked him, *"Why are you dating my Au Pair?"*

Camilla abruptly changed the subject. She instructed Rosita to set another plate, and told Ramone to get her husband a drink. Mr Conti rejected the offer, saying he needed to take a shower and get changed. He promised to join them later for dessert, then headed inside. *"We were going to put some dance music on after dinner,"* Camilla hollered after him.

Rosita made a simple but delicious Dominican shrimp gumbo for dinner. It got rave reviews. True to his word, Salvatore Conti appeared as if on queue, just as dessert was being served. The caramel and rice souffle Rosita had created for the occasion went particularly well with the caramel coffee liqueur being served as an accompaniment.

After dinner the men enjoyed a cigar while the women talked about how the evening had gone. Once they'd given their meal time to digest Mrs Conti put some preselected CD's into the sound system. She'd chosen a selection of romantic Latin music for tonight.

The couples danced a few numbers, then stopped to enjoy a Baby Doc cocktail. The Haitian drink was something Rosita had concocted. When the couples returned to the dance floor a few minutes later they switched partners. Mr Conti maintained a respectful distance from his daughter's nanny as they swirled around the dance floor to *Spanish Eyes.*

Salvatore Conti seemed oblivious to the close embrace his wife shared with Carlo. Camilla whispered the romantic words of the song in Carlo's ear, *"You and your Spanish eyes will wait for me."*

Teracita wasn't nearly as incognizant as Mr Conti. She noticed how Camilla clung to Carlo. She watched as her lover explored Camilla's body with his eyes. When the song ended Teracita excused herself and briskly walked to the powder room.

She had a conversation with herself in the mirror. Was she being silly? Was she acting like a little jealous child? These were sophisticated people. Was she out of her league? Teracita washed her hands, then took a deep breath and returned to the veranda. She hadn't been gone ten minutes, but it seemed Carlo had disappeared.

Mr Conti struck up a conversation with Teracita, and had Rosita replenish her Baby Doc cocktail. Teracita spotted her nemisis walking in the garden talking to her chauffeur. Camilla looked up at her, smiled a killer's smile, then turned and walked away.

Teracita felt a hand on her waist. She turned to find Carlo standing next to her. He kissed her passionately, then led her to the dance floor. Nothing was said about his absence, or why she'd rushed off earlier.

The next day Teracita went shopping for new clothes. She'd finally earned enough money to purchase some outfits. It was a short cab ride to The Falls, the upscale shopping mall that bordered the Eastern edge of UM's campus. She phoned her friend from college and asked if she wanted to join her, but Celeste had other plans. Teracita went alone.

After buying a couple outfits and a new bikini Teracita decided to visit Madrid's. The recently opened Spanish restaurant offered lunch specials. She ordered the paella saffron with a glass of Cava. While waiting for her meal Teracita scanned the scene. Her table overlooked the outdoor patio, offering a birds eye view of the customers seated below. One of Teracita's favorite past times had become people watching. Americano's were an interesting breed.

Not expecting to see anyone she knew Teracita was surprised when she recognized a familiar face. Camilla Conti was seated at the Tapas bar talking on her cell phone. Her chauffeur Ramone stood next to her fiddling with a book of matches. It was obvious he was bored.

After a few minutes Ramone patted Camilla on her behind and whispered something in her ear. She reached over and kissed him on the cheek, then playfully scolded him for interrupting her conversation. He got up and headed towards the men's room.

Teracita decided she was in the wrong place at the wrong time. She left cash on the table and headed out. Walking away she turned to see if Camilla had noticed her. She did. Her employer smiled and did a little finger wave to acknowledge she'd seen her. Teracita waved back, then quickly looked away. She headed for the taxi stand at the other end of the mall.

Carlo had been dating Teracita a little over three months when they finally gave in to their desires. It took place in the balcony of an art house movie theatre in Lincoln Square. Carlo was a fan of film classics, and the original version of King Kong was being shown.

He told Teracita he loved the movie because it correctly portrayed man as the superior predator. *"The beast's downfall came when he looked into the face of beauty,"* he explained. *"A weakness once revealed can be taken advantage of."*

Teracita was about to agree with Carlo's statement when he added, *"From that point on Kong may as well have been dead."* She responded by putting her finger to her temple and mockingly pulling the *trigger.* Seeing that, Carlo half kiddingly grabbed her by the throat and squeezed. Then he kissed her...deep and hard. Teracita submitted to his forcefulness. The two lovers threw abandon to the wind.

Three months of unabated passion were released in a fifteen minute torrent of lust. The physicality of the event wasn't what Teracita had expected. Carlo's aggressive performance had felt like an assault on her femininity. Like trying to stuff a size ten foot into a size seven shoe.

When the closing credits rolled at the end of the film Teracita removed her torn and soiled panties. She used them to wipe herself clean, then she stood and unsteadily tottered out of the theatre. The encounter would be the first of many sexual tryst the two would have together. Teracita would come to despise the pain and discomfort of having sex with Carlo, while simultaneously enjoying the eroticism and intense orgasmic fervency.

Carlo never took Teracita home. He rarely mentioned he had one. She'd once asked him to, but he'd refused. He claimed he lived like a bachelor and it would be embarrassing. Unbeknownst to her, Carlo had a rule. Never take women home!

He'd have liked to, but he was way to smart for that. It wasn't his normal routine. Carlo knew when you break your routine you make mistakes. Besides, the abundance of motels in South Florida made the point moot... A bed was a bed.

The lawyer rented a condo in Coconut Grove, not far from Coral Gables. Property in South Florida was extremely expensive. Especially waterfront. Even an established attorney like Carlo couldn't afford a decent place on the water. His high end tastes outmatched his finances. The home he envisioned himself owning was out of reach at this point. Besides, his other vices ate up a considerable amount of salary, and he wasn't about to give them up.

Carlo wasn't exactly committed to his little Mexican *portulaca*. His sexual compulsion demanded a submissive who thrived on humiliation and pain. Teracita was a work in progress. She was nowhere near ready to satisfy his ego, or his urges. She was learning sexual satisfaction came with strings. Orgasms were expertly induced by Carlo, but they were contingent on her willingness to subject herself to the whims of her mentor. Her involvement was consensual, but it was encouraged and nurtured by Carlo, the master of deception.

To accommodate his inflated level of dominance, Carlo occasionally hired prostitutes to role play his fantasies. There were plenty of women willing to submit themselves to his masochistic proclivities if the price was right. For their fee they were expected to perform various deviant acts, and subject themselves to sexually humiliating behavior. When his compulsive urges couldn't be satisfied sufficiently Carlo would resort to plan B.

The nightclubs and sandy beaches of South Florida flourish with young attractive women seeking someone to share a night of steamy carnality with. Plan B was to find one stupid and horny enough to accompany a total stranger to a motel. Of course Carlo had love potion pills for the few who resisted. They were the ones who normally woke up the next day covered in scat and viciously beaten.

At six foot, three Carlo commanded attention. His masculine features and washboard abs attracted plenty of women, but it was what he was packing underneath his jock strap that kept them coming back. His preference for younger women didn't stop him from enjoying the fruits of an occasional cougar.

Such was the case with Camilla Conti. The woman knew how to dress to impress. Her flirtatious behavior had impressed Carlo, and the beast within him insisted he handle the merchandise. It was less than twenty-four hours after he'd enjoyed dinner on her veranda that he had her squealing like a pig in a room at the Holiday Inn.

Camilla blamed it on her husband. He'd been so attentive the year they dated, but once married he'd backed off. When she tried to talk about it he'd blow her off. It didn't matter. Camilla knew how to use what she'd been blessed with to get what she wanted. You don't live in a mansion in Coral Gables and drive a Bentley if you're naive. In some ways this was better. Her husband couldn't compete sexually with Ramone, or the younger husband of her next door neighbor, much less Carlo Santiago.

In the three months following that first dinner invitation Carlo made Camilla feel like a disobedient schoolgirl at least two dozen times. She'd never known a man with the ability to maintain like he did, not to mention his package. Camilla agreed to submit to a few of his unusual requests rather than risk losing him to someone who shared his interests.

Some of the devices had been uncomfortably restraining, but overall she'd enjoyed the experience. His fascination with her derriere had been painfully interesting, but she'd enjoyed that too. Camilla even enjoyed the cat and mouse game of avoiding Teracita when Carlo came over.

Carlo didn't share Camilla's exhilaration. His preference for young starlets was all consuming. The affair with the aging Camilla was beginning to bore him. She'd been a good fuck, but it was time to move on. He couldn't simply ignore Camilla because Teracita was involved. Besides, she was a wealthy socialite. They could always cause trouble. Carlo would need to let her down easy, and to do that he needed to talk to her in private.

Teracita and Carlo had planned on making their normal Sunday afternoon visit to the beach, but Carlo said he had to stop by the office for a few hours. He persuaded Teracita to meet him at Haulover, and paid Ramone to drive her there. Upon reaching her destination Teracita spread a beach blanket on the sand and poured herself a Captain Morgan, then she laid back and waited.

Back in Coral Gables, Camilla Conti was entertaining her Au Pair's boyfriend in her bed chamber. As far as Carlo was concerned this was going to be the last hurrah. He'd treat Little Miss Socialite to a good time, then break the news. Camilla was particularly horny this day. She'd purchased a new costume she hoped would bring added excitement to what, even for her, had started feeling routine. The patent leather cat suit featured access zippers that covered each breast, and another longer one that ran from her pelvis all the way around to the small of her back.

Camilla's ankles were shackled to a thick metal D ring, which hung from a hook in the ceiling. She was blindfolded and gagged with proper masochistic paraphernalia. Carlo found the sight of Mrs Conti's restrained body hanging upside down exhilarating. He was eye level with her patent leather covered ass.

Carlo slowly unzipped Camilla's cat suit, fully exposing her. Taking his time he tasted and teased for half an hour before bringing her to orgasm. Then he picked up a leather strap!

Teracita continually tried calling Carlo's cellphone, but she got no answer. After nearly two hours she decided waiting any longer would be futile. She gathered up her things, dumped her drink in the sand, and hailed a cab. Any enjoyment the beach might have provided was stolen by her concern for Carlo anyway. As far as she was concerned it had been a wasted day.

Carlo decided to break the bad news to Camilla while she hanging upside down in her bed chamber. She didn't take it well. The bastard had just subjected her to a thrilling, erotic, painful beating. She'd climaxed multiple times while hanging there like a freshly gutted slab of meat. Now she wouldn't be able to sit for a week, much less let anyone see her below the waist.

Still, Camilla knew he was right. She'd been getting a little bored with him too. That wasn't the problem! The bastard was using his Mexican whore as his excuse. "*It isn't fair to Teracita,*" he said as he released the pin holding her in the air. Turning Camilla right side up he continued, "*I care for her. I can't continue doing this.*" After loosening the bindings and bagging his device, Carlo simply turned and walked out.

Camilla chased after him, spouting threats of revenge. He responded arrogantly, laughing at her, all the while knowing she could make good on all of her threats. The argument carried out to the side yard by the garage.

"*BULLSHIT*" Camilla screamed. This handsome hunk of a man, this sick sex god, was choosing an ill-bred, uneducated, Mexican slut over an intelligent, attractive, sexy lady of substance like her. "*BULLSHIT.*"

The cab driver dropped Teracita at the end of the long driveway. As she walked the three-hundred feet to the house she heard the commotion. Someone was arguing. It sounded like Carlo, but she wasn't sure. The other voice definitely belonged to Mrs Conti. She couldn't make out what was being said, but as she got closer a figure turned towards her. She could see it was Carlo.

Why was he arguing with Camilla Conti? She stopped walking when he looked at her. His Ferrari was parked fifty feet away. He made a mad dash for it. Teracita started running towards him, but he jumped in the Ferrari and fired up the twelve cylinder turbo charged engine. Then he zoomed past her. All Teracita could do was watch as Carlo fishtailed down the driveway and disappeared.

Camilla stood in the doorway looking at her. She was dressed in some sort of black leather outfit with zippers all over it. It reminded Teracita of a Madonna video she'd seen as a little girl. It looked better on Madonna, she thought. Camilla glared at Teracita for a moment, then turned and disappeared inside the house.

Teracita stood on the pavement looking at the space where Camilla had been moments before. She turned and looked down the driveway, hoping Carlo might come speeding back towards her. *"What the fuck just happened,"* she said aloud. Whatever it was, it couldn't be good.

Things slowly deteriorated from that day on. Mrs Conti became increasingly short with Teracita, and increasingly critical of her. It seemed Teracita could do nothing right when it came to caring for Nicolina. Every decision was the wrong decision. Camilla informed her husband of her dissatisfaction with Teracita, and suggested they look for additional help. He acted surprised, telling her he'd thought she and Teracita had bonded, but that the choice was hers.

Mr Conti was no fool. He knew why Teracita was on the outs. He'd suspected his wife was somehow involved with Carlo, but figured the feelings would dissipate like they had with the others. Considering the amount of time he was gone he didn't really blame her. After all, it wasn't like he spent his nights away from home all alone.

Conti knew Camilla wasn't going anywhere. The extravagant lifestyle he provided would keep her around long after her lovers faded away. He felt bad for Teracita though. He'd taken a liking to her, and she was really good with Nicolina. It would have been more humane to just make the cut, but Camilla didn't. Instead she made the poor girl's life miserable.

It was a progressive fall from grace that hung in the air like a dark cloud. Teracita found herself walking on egg shells trying to avoid upsetting the proverbial apple cart. To be sent home in disgrace was not something she could bare, nor was the thought of spending the rest of her life back in Delicias.

Teracita didn't hear from Carlo for three weeks. She didn't dare contact him. She wasn't sure he'd take her call if she did. Her imagination ran wild with images of what might have transpired that afternoon. After seeing Mrs Conti at the mall with Ramone Teracita knew her employer was capable of adultery. She'd once asked Rosita if she thought Mr Conti spent too much time away from home. She'd been told to mind her own business. *"Ms Conti does what she do, Child. Das all to'it. Ain't nowun's bezness but deys own."*

Eventually Carlo phoned. He spoke in a quiet, monotone voice. *"We need to talk,"* he told Teracita. She was so glad to hear from him she cried. *"Stop... Please. It's gonna be okay,"* he told her. *"Have you spoken to Mrs Conti? What did she tell you? Don't believe a word that Bitch says, You hear me!"*

The two lovers agreed to meet at Madrid's Spanish Restaurant. Before hanging up the phone Teracita told Carlo she missed him, and that she loved him. He responded *"I know you do, Doll. I miss you to."*

Teracita snuck out of the house shortly before eight. She was free to go of course, but she didn't want to have to explain where she was going, or with whom. It was a fifteen minute walk to Coral Way, where she called a cab to take her the additional mile to the mall. Carlo was there waiting. He dishonestly explained what had happened that day. It'd been three weeks since she'd seen him go flying down the Conti's driveway like a bat out of hell.

Carlo told Teracita he'd planned to meet her after finishing up at the office that day. He said he was preparing to leave when Mr Rose walked into his office with a client. *"Nobody says no to the senior partner,"* Carlo interjected. *"Not if they value their job."* He told Teracita Mr Rose introduced the client, Mr Jose Gacha, and instructed Carlo to take good care of him.

"Come to find out Mr Gacha was being sought by homeland security," Carlo continued, *"Due to his ties with a drug cartel that had settled in Little Havana."*

Part of Carlo's story was true. He had gone to the office to meet with Jose' Gacha that morning. Gacha was a high level member of Los Norte del Valle, the last remaining remnant of the Medell'in drug cartel. He was being threatened with extradition back to Columbia. Carlo would be representing him.

Carlo continued his partial fabrication, telling Teracita by the time he was finished with the client it was too late to meet her at the beach. He said he went to the Conti home, hoping to find her there.

Carlo could tell Teracita was falling for his story. He continued lying, *"Mrs Conti answered the door in a housecoat. She told me you weren't there. I could tell she'd been drinking, she slurred her words. When she asked my opinion on new bedroom furniture she'd recently bought I should've known better. Instead, I followed her upstairs."*

"She pushed me on the bed and got on top of me," Carlo continued. *"I didn't know what to do. I pushed her away."* Carlo seemed sincere. Teracita found the story somewhat humorous, and encouraged him to go on.

"That's when Camilla got nasty," he lied. *"She told me if I didn't have sex with her she'd see that my little whore got shipped back to Mexico."* Carlo embellished the story a little, blurting out, *"She unzipped my pants and performed oral on me."*

He gave Teracita a minute to visualize it, then said, *"She was serious, Teracita. She was going to use me for her own personal pleasure, and if I refused she was going to hurt you. In that moment I wanted to kill her. I slapped her across the face, but she*

142

just smiled at me and took off her housecoat. That's when I saw she was wearing a black cat suit."

"Camilla handed me a leather strap then walked over to the bed and bent over. I lashed her with it... It's what she wanted! I hit her naked bottom half a dozen times, hard as I could. Then I got scared and ran, but Camilla ran after me. I stopped to catch my breath and we argued back and forth. I told her she'd never see me again. She informed me she'd see me the following week, or else! That's when I looked up and saw you running towards me. I panicked!"

Teracita was lost in thought. After a few minutes of intense contemplation she looked at Carlo and said, *"I believe you."* Teracita honestly thought his story made sense. Camilla would be capable of such behavior. She ruled that house with an iron fist, and she knew the domestic workers would play dumb. Teracita felt guilty for thinking Carlo had been having an affair. She loved him, even though she found his sexual predilection...a bit strange.

The problem now would be how to work around Camilla. Carlo certainly wouldn't be welcome at the Conti's any longer, and neither would the idea of them being a couple. Teracita realized her job, her entire future, was in jeopardy.

Rather than fire Teracita, Camilla downgraded her. She brought in another girl, someone referred by a friend. The new nanny was American, and some ten years older than Teracita. The woman was given the *Mariposa* suite, relegating Teracita to a small bedroom on the third floor with the other domestics.

She hadn't lost her title, and she still received a salary, but the ordeal was humiliating. Teracita became the person assigned the most monotonous, tedious tasks in the household. Her days consisted of washing and folding laundry, relieving the new nanny when Nicolina was napping, and running errands. Everyone in the house shunned her, as if instructed under threat of removal.

Her choices were limited. Teracita could continue doing what she was doing, collecting a paycheck and biding her time, or she could quit and ask the agency for another assignment. The likeliness of that happening was nearly non existent.

Without a reference from the Conti's Teracita wouldn't stand a chance. With no job and no host family she'd be deported back to Mexico. The thought of that frightened her more than anything.

She would shame her parents and be relegated to a life of poverty in the barrios of Delicias. In the scheme of things she decided her best option was to lay low. As long as Mrs Conti kept her on the payroll she was safe. The only question was...for how long?

EARLY RETIREMENT

MURDER IN DAYTONA

18

Back in the 1970's jobs poured out of the rust belt like a blood letting at a slaughterhouse. Many of the mills and manufacturing plants closed their doors or relocated to southern *'right to work'* states. North Carolina was one of the states that benefited the most. In the late 1950's, and throughout the 60's and 70's the Tar Heel State lured large northern companies by creating tax exempt zones and providing cheap nonunion labor. It experienced an economic expansion that lead to dense population growth throughout the period.

In 1994 the North American Free Trade Agreement was passed into law. One by one companies that originally left the rust belt in search of a more advantageous corporate climate migrated even further south. This time not stopping at the border. The hemorrhage of good paying jobs continued for years afterward. People who'd dedicated their entire lives to one employer suddenly found themselves unemployed.

Such was the case of Diedra Daniels. At age seventeen she'd gone to work for a furniture manufacturer in Thomasville. Now a week shy of her thirty-seventh birthday Diedra learned the company was consolidating operations and moving to a facility in Juarez, Mexico. The plant would be joining hundreds of other American manufacturers that folded operations and sprung up on the other side of the border. She learned about her employer's plans to close the plant the same time as everyone else.

Like she had every day for the past twenty years Diedra reported for work five minutes early. She put her jacket and bagged lunch in her locker, then went straight to her tufting console. In the old days she would have had to *run the gamut* between the ladies locker room and the manufacturing floor. Back then most female employees were the recipients of unwanted, unwarranted, and undeserved verbal forays thrust upon them by the mostly male staff. All under the watchful eye of management. Often it was management who were the culprits.

It was different nowadays. Women had proven their worth. Many had risen in the ranks and held management positions themselves. One such woman was Diedra's current supervisor.

Lynn Cox was a former machine operator who started at the plant a year before Diedra. The heavy set supervisor gestured for her employees to gather in the center of the workroom floor. The workers assumed Lynn was going to put them through yet another motivational speech on productivity. When a trio of club carrying security guards walked in and flanked the supervisor Diedra knew something wasn't right.

It was short, but bitter. Lynn announced the plant had ceased operations effective immediately. Employees were to quietly and orderly leave the premises. With that they were summarily escorted out of the building. There'd been no warning, no mention of severance, and no explanation. It didn't matter if you worked there three days or thirty years.

Diedra stood outside the gate looking in. She had to consider the possibility she could be out on the street. No one was hiring. A rumor was circulating around town that other manufacturers would be closing before long. She had three hundred bucks in a Christmas Club account at the plant's credit union. Not even enough to cover the next month's rent. Diedra didn't have a back up plan, but she knew she had to get out of Thomasville.

146

She always wanted to go to Florida. Her mom supposedly lived there. Diedra had never forgiven her mother for running off with the truck driver she met at the diner where she worked. Her father, an alcoholic who couldn't hold a steady job, had shot himself shortly after his wife left. That's when Diedra quit school and took the job at the plant. She'd been on her own ever since. A few guys had come into her life over the years, but she didn't trust anyone enough to commit.

Diedra would have loved to fly the friendly skies to Florida, but after paying for the flight there'd be no money left for food. Nope, she'd drive... All the way to Key West. Once there she'd find work in a motel or restaurant and get herself a small apartment.

She didn't waste any time. Diedra loaded up on non perishable groceries, gathered her belongings, and left. The new Ford Taurus she'd bought seven years ago was a bull of an automobile. Diedra figured it could handle the thousand mile journey no problem. She'd spend a hundred dollars on new used tires and an oil change before she left...just in case.

The newly unemployed furniture upholsterer hadn't actually sat down and figured out how much fuel might be required to make the journey. She spent the last of her cash refueling at a gas station just outside Bunnell. According to the road map she'd picked up at the Florida welcome center she was just a few miles from Daytona Beach.

It wasn't Key West, but there were bound to be opportunities in a place like Daytona. The tourism industry alone must employ thousands, and unlike Thomasville those jobs were recession proof. So she thought...

Diedra drove another fifteen miles before seeing a billboard beckoning her to visit The World's Most Famous Beach.

When she got to the beach the first thing she saw was a big metal sign. It warned visitors NO OVERNIGHT PARKING VIOLATORS SUBJECT TO $500 FINE.

She wouldn't be sleeping on the beach tonight. Diedra made a U-turn and headed back towards the highway. Just before reaching it Diedra saw a dirt road. For no good reason, she took it.

The dirt road wound a quarter mile through scrub brush before opening up to what had once been an orange grove. An old shanty sat in a corner of the grove, vacant and neglected. Rotting porch boards led to an entrance door that hung forebodingly on one hinge. Diedra got out of her car and shouted *"ANYONE HOME."*

When she got no answer she walked up on the porch, careful to avoid a board that had a long crack where someone had obviously put too much weight on it. Diedra surmised the next person to step on that board would be going through it. She stopped short of the door and again bellowed, *"IS ANYONE HOME?"*

It appeared the property was abandoned. Diedra went back to her car and foraged through her remaining groceries looking for some semblance of nourishment. She found it in a can of diet coke and a jar of applesauce. Lying in the back seat with her head resting on a pillow Diedra listened to the radio and enjoyed her meal.

She woke to the sun peeking through the branches of scrub pine that grew wildly around the shanty. At first discombobulated, she soon recalled where she was and how she'd gotten there.

Suddenly Diedra sprung up like someone had stuck her with a hat pin. *"OH SHIT"* she hollered, realizing she'd left the radio on all night. She'd wanted to listen to some music, promising herself she'd turn it off before falling asleep. Diedra tossed her blanket aside and crawled into the front seat. She tried the ignition. Nothing! The battery was dead as a year old corpse.

She spent the next several days walking the beach. Diedra stopped at every motel and restaurant on the strip seeking some type of employment. She got the same responses from every prospective employer. *Fill out an application and we'll call you. Do you have reliable transportation? Are you a permanent resident? Sorry, only experienced need apply.*

What was wrong with these idiots? It was a catch 22. You were damned if you did and damned if you didn't. Diedra wasn't having any luck. She was thankful for the warm weather though. At least her sorry ass wasn't freezing.

Diedra realized she did have one ticket she could cash in. She'd loiter around some of the beach side establishments and strike up conversations with people. Invariably she'd ask for spare change. When the pain in her stomach overcame her pride she resorted to offering her services for a meal. Even at her age she still looked good in a bikini.

She found there were plenty of guys who'd anxiously trade a good meal for some female company. Diedra never accepted cash. She wasn't a prostitute...but a girl had to eat, right? Eventually she fell in with a cadre of young transients who wallowed in the shadows, scavenging an existence wherever one could be found.

She spent her days scoping out potential habitats where the chances of being caught seemed slight. Snowbirds who wintered in the area surely wouldn't mind if a few hungry vagabonds borrowed their accommodations while they were up north. After all everyone needs shelter from a storm. It was in one such home that Diedra witnessed a storm she'd never have thought possible.

It wasn't a fancy place. The little house sat on the edge of Bulow Creek a couple miles north of Daytona. The closest neighbors lived a half mile up the road. A perfect setting for a group of young vagrants.

The six nomads figured they'd gotten lucky, having occupied the home for over two weeks with no interference from anyone. Just when they let their guard down the skies opened and the tempest struck. In the name of the law...

Diedra had just taken a bag of trash out to the shed when she heard someone holler *"POLICE."* A moment later half a dozen deputies stormed the house. The four occupants inside the house were taken by surprise.

The one who'd spotted the cops coming down the driveway got away. He ran into the woods behind the house and disappeared in the thick foliage. Two deputies gave chase but returned minutes later empty handed.

Meanwhile the two male vagrants inside were taken out the front door and made to strip and lie spread eagle on the ground. One of them opened his mouth to complain and a deputy viciously kicked him in the groin. Another deputy, this one a big beefy guy, approached them and calmly said, *"You've been bad boys!"* He removed his thick leather uniform belt and proceeded to give each of them a good walloping.

Back inside the house a deputy found two girls hiding under a bed in the back bedroom. The creepy cop had an enormous gut and a bald head. He unzipped his fly and ordered one of the girls to perform oral sex on him, saying *"It's either that or jail, Sweetie."* The young homeless runaway wasn't surprised by his callous request. She'd been down this road before.

150

The officer sworn to serve and protect wasn't satisfied. When he finished ejaculating on the young woman's face he urinated on her too. The slob stood laughing as he emptied his bladder. When he was finished he warned the girls to keep their filthy mouths shut, then marched them outside. The four transients were escorted off the property and told to keep going. If they were seen in the area again they'd be arrested.

Diedra remained in the shed until it was dark. Then she snuck back inside the house and cleared the kitchen pantry of anything she could carry. With no place else to go she headed for the abandoned orange grove where she'd left her car. She pledged that from now on she'd take care of herself... Just like always.

She spent the next several weeks clearing out the shanty. Diedra cleaned whatever could be salvaged. She repaired the front porch so it could be walked on without fear of collapse. A blue tarp found neatly folded underneath the front porch was used to cover a gaping hole in the roof, which effectively stopped the rain from leaking in.

There was no plumbing, but a shallow creek on the property provided water for bathing, cooking, and cleaning. An outhouse stood some fifty feet beyond the shanty. It was hidden from view by an overgrowth of firebush.

A Walmart store sat a mile or so down the main road. It provided Diedra with a few necessities. Groceries and supplies were usually acquired illegally. She was always amazed when she walked out unscathed.

Of course Diedra still did her share of panhandling, and when necessary she still provided her services in exchange for a meal. Several times a week she would visit the Salvation Army soup kitchen. One could trade a prayer for a cup of minestrone. It was a battle of survival living in this underworld. She, and those like her, were invisible to those with the means to make a difference.

Diedra accepted her lot. She was neither angry nor jealous. *"It is what it is,"* she'd tell herself. Most evenings she'd toss a few orange tree scraps in the fireplace and curl up to read a newspaper she'd confiscated from someone's driveway. A crib mattress someone had put out to the curb provided a comfortable bed. Before she knew it, spring arrived.

Packets of seeds borrowed from Walmart began sprouting. Tomatoes, okra, and broccoli, along with strawberries and cantaloupe all grew like weeds. Diedra never realized she had a green thumb. Her garden grew so abundantly she started taking baskets down to the soup kitchen as a way of paying them back for the meals they'd provided.

The Salvation Army officer in charge of the pantry insisted on paying her. It was he who suggested she set up a table at the local farmer's market as a way of earning additional income. Eventually Diedra earned enough money to purchase a new battery for her car.

She found one at Walmart. The shear size of the damn thing prevented her from slipping it under her shirt and walking out. Even though her Ford Tauras had sat lifeless for nine months it started right up the minute she turned the key.

It was George Bernard Shaw who wrote, *"The only thing wrong with the poor is poverty. On the other hand what's wrong with the rich is uselessness."* Diedra Daniels had certainly proven that. She did what she needed to do to survive. Her heart was pure, though her confidence shaken. The life she lived was simple. It was void of love and bounty. It had been a life spent giving rather than receiving.

She counted as a blessing her *new home,* as well as the opportunities she'd been presented. Problem is, it wasn't her home... It seemed opportunity had passed her by. Then again... Perception is reality!

It was one evening in the middle of August that two men appeared at her front door. Diedra was in the process of making a vegetable stew when she heard someone say, *"Hey there."* She looked up to see a tall thin deeply tanned man wearing a black sombrero. He was smiling at her. The guy humorously lifted his nose in the air and inhaled the scent of fresh stew. His partner, shorter, heavier, and more unkempt than he, looked at Diedra approvingly, but said nothing.

She invited them in. There was plenty for everyone. Both of her guests wore the look of life on the run. Their hair was long, their hands were strong, and they both had a twinkle in their eyes. As if they knew a secret they'd be willing to share if you only dared ask them. Both men carried guitar cases.

They claimed to be traveling musicians. Wandering American rovers. The tall man's name was Cass, the shorter one called himself Zeppelin. Cass told Diedra they'd passed this way some years ago and stumbled upon this place. *"We didn't expect anyone to be here,"* he laughed, *"especially a pretty young lady like you."*

He asked Diedra if she owned the property. The squatter explained how she'd come to be there, and how she'd tried to make it a home. Diedra told him about the incident out at Bulow Creek, and how it had changed the way she viewed the world.

After dinner Cass started a fire, then the two men took out their instruments and put on a show. The three of them spent the rest of the evening singing songs and sharing stories. The guys could really pick their guitars. When Cass added his harmonica to the mix it really took off.

They spent the next two months together. The abandoned orange grove was home. The two drifters helped Diedra fix the place up. The roof was patched, the windows repaired, and the garden expanded to include a few cold weather crops. Onions, turnips, and potatoes were added to the ever expanding catalog of homegrown vegetables.

Occasionally Diedra's roommates would go into Daytona and set up on a street corner to play favorites and take requests from vacationers. Their pay would depend on who'd tossed coins into the hat.

Zeppelin had been giving Diedra a little more attention than she desired. Every once in a while she would look up to find him staring at her. One time she thought he was peeking at her through a small crack in the outhouse door, but she couldn't be sure. Truth is the guy was starting to creep her out.

Besides his quirky behavior Zeppelin was a heavy smoker. It gave off a distasteful smell and yellowed his teeth. Then there was the issue of his clothes. The man rarely changed them. Diedra knew he took his clothes off before going to bed. The problem was he'd put them right back on again the next morning.

Zeppelin had a rotund body. Beefy and thick. Diedra had accidently seen him naked on several occasions, so she knew he had the equipment to provide a woman with pleasure, assuming his partner could ignore the rest. Diedra simply couldn't.

One day Zeppelin asked Diedra if she wanted to go to a movie. He would drive, if her car would start. She politely declined. Unfazed by her rejection the portly minstrel kept on asking. Truth is he wouldn't take no for an answer. Diedra just kept refusing until eventually the two had a heated exchange. Fortunately Cass happened to walk in before it got out of hand and broke it up. He told Zeppelin to go for a walk, suggesting he not come back until morning.

That night Diedra woke to a noise coming from across the room. It was a moonless night. One could barely make out the slightest of shadows. Diedra knew it was Zeppelin though. What she couldn't see, she could smell.

The old blanket she used to cover herself up with had fallen off during the night. Diedra lay on her tiny mattress, her only covering a stained Tee shirt. Unable to relax she sat up and spoke into the darkness, *"Is that you Zep? I know you're..."* Before she could utter another word he was on top of her.

Large, strong hands tore at her shirt. Diedra heard the flimsy material tear as it was ripped from her body. She tried to turn away but it was useless. She was no match for Zeppelin's strength. He pulled Diedra over on her back and tried to kiss her, but she bit his lip. Zeppelin responded by going into a rage, pummeling her with both fists. She only felt the sting of the first two blows before being rendered unconscious.

She came too several hours later. Diedra's face was badly bruised and her left eye socket was fractured. The blood splatter smeared across her face had coagulated, the result of a ruptured nasal cavity. She felt like she'd been hit with a sledgehammer.

In addition to her physical injuries, she'd been raped. Semen leaked from Diedra's vagina and congealed on her mattress like a messy gob of phlegm.

Diedra was certain if she did nothing she would die there. Unable to dress herself she managed to wrap her blanket over her shoulders, then made her way to the door. The sun hadn't yet risen. The coolness of the hour felt good against her red hot skin.

The hood of Diedra's Ford Tauras was raised. Someone had messed with her car. The bastard had not only stolen her dignity, he'd stolen her car battery too. She forced herself to walk the quarter mile to the main road. Hell, she'd walk all the way to Halifax Medical Center if she had to.

Thirty minutes after leaving the shanty Diedra was spotted by a police officer in a patrol car. He called in to request immediate medical transport, then went to her aid. She was taken to a trauma center where an intern treated her wounds. The maxillary bone in her right eye socket was fractured in two places. It would need to be grafted. The intern realigned her nose as best he could and treated her other contusions.

With her injuries tended to, Diedra was subjected to series of questioning by two detectives. She refused to give them an address, insisting she was homeless. She knew if she mentioned the shanty it would be over. They asked Diedra if she knew the person responsible for inflicting her injuries, and if she'd been raped. Not sure how she should respond, she told half truths.

Diedra said she knew the man who'd beaten her. His name was Zeppelin. He was a drifter she'd befriended a few months before. She gave a detailed description of him, but didn't say a word about her missing car battery, nor did she mention Cass.

She never did answer the question about whether she'd been raped. Wasn't it obvious? The detectives never mentioned it again. Diedra wasn't sure which was the bigger crime, being raped...or being homeless?

The detectives provided information she'd need to arrange for her surgery. She was surprised to learn the operation would be performed by a dentist, rather than a plastic surgeon. Even worse, it would be done at a public clinic on an out patient basis. Only the best medical care for a citizen of the richest country in human history... Right?

It was around three in the afternoon when she was taken to the domestic abuse shelter. The police department wasn't about to release someone in her condition back on the streets to fend for themselves. This woman would spend a minimum of ten days in the relative comfort and safety of the county shelter before being returned to her cardboard bedroom underneath some highway overpass.

While at the shelter Diedra was interviewed by a domestic abuse counselor, who forwarded her file to the court advocate's office. Volunteer Veronica Stevens was asked to familiarize herself with the file. In all likelihood, criminal charges would be lodged.

EARLY RETIREMENT

MURDER IN DAYTONA

19

Carlo Santiago enjoyed living in South Florida. Being an attorney afforded him a comfortable lifestyle and brought him immediate respect. With a diverse population of some three million people the area allowed him to delve deeply into the unsavory aspects of his personality with little fear of exposure. The single upwardly mobile lawyer could become a secretive, evasive, dark stranger.

He could be the Casanova of the beach, or the dedicated lover of a poor immigrant girl. Carlo was for all intents and purposes a faceless stud, picking up young women to satisfy his masochistic lust. With hundreds of disco's, strip joints, and nightclubs to choose from his options were almost limitless. Once satisfied he could morph back into his Cuban persona and disappear amongst the masses.

The one grievance Carlo had was the belief he would never make it to the top. In his mind others considered him a minor leaguer working in a major league city. He was a sail boat in a sea of ocean liners. In Miami you didn't break on through to the other side. You were either invited or born into it.

His position at the Rose law firm was secure. Carlo knew he was liked by Galen Rose and respected by most of the senior partners. Unfortunately he also knew he'd never be offered a full partnership. He simply lacked the blood line and the background. Unless his ticket was stamped by one of the high ranking members of the cartels the firm represented he'd remain a staff attorney. Carlo wasn't sure he wanted their endorsement. A cartel endorsement always came with strings.

Galen Rose was gay. He didn't hide the fact. It was public knowledge. He didn't hide the fact he was attracted to Carlo either. Mr Rose had done a lot for the young, self made attorney, and Carlo was appreciative. Still, he knew his ticket to the top lie elsewhere.

He hired a headhunter he knew from his college days at FIU. His one time pal ran a thriving job placement firm in D.C. Seems the market was bursting with discontented legal eagles. Attorneys seeking shortcuts to stardom.

The inquiry would need to be done with the utmost discretion. Even the rumor of someone seeking a position outside the Rose Law Firm could be disastrous. Galen Rose wouldn't be happy, not to mention *Los Norte Del Valle.* Carlo was privy to information some would want to keep quiet. Once out of Miami he'd be fine. At least that's what he told himself.

Nearly a month passed before Carlo heard from his Washington connection. When he did he wasn't exactly thrilled with the news. Headstrom & Downs, a law firm in Daytona Beach, was looking for a bilingual attorney with experience in immigration law. He'd have to go through the interview process, but Carlo's college pal was confident the job would be his for the taking.

Carlo's perception of Daytona was an unsophisticated beach town known for biker bars and stock car racing. He wasn't that far removed from reality. If it hadn't been for the headlines in the morning edition of the *Miami Herald,* he'd have told his friend to forget it. Under the circumstances Carlo was willing to pursue the opportunity.

Splashed across the front page of the widely read newspaper was a photo of a young woman who'd been beaten to a bloody pulp and sadistically raped. Her body was found stuffed in a trash dumpster behind a warehouse in Overton. She'd been there for several days. The article went on to describe the condition of the decomposing body, which had been feasted on by vermin.

Carlo recognized her. He'd picked her up the previous weekend while carousing the *Calle Ocho* festival in the Latin quarter. She'd appeared to be alone, so he approached her. She was a tall blond from the Midwest. The girl had come to Miami in search of adventure. Carlo recalled taking her to one of the seedy *pay by the hour* motels on Flagler Street. They did lines of coke together.

He'd parked his Ferrari amongst the BMW's, Jaguars, and other luxury automobiles that lined both sides of the street most weekend nights. The owners were preoccupied, but only for an hour or two.

Carlo knew he and the blond had sex, but he remembered little about it. Was it possible he'd killed her? Could he be responsible for what was now the talk of South Beach? Had he been involved in a cocaine induced slaughter?

A job interview was scheduled. The Headstrom & Downs Law Firm was highly respected, and by all accounts successful. Carlo was one of several candidates being considered for the open position. His experience in immigration law stood out. Several of the firm's senior partners were familiar with a few of Carlo's cases.

A spanish speaking attorney with experience in immigration law was highly sought after in Florida. Latino's were leaving the Miami area for opportunities further north. Though educated, many of them didn't speak English. The chance to open a business and assimilate into American society was what they sought. They wanted what we all seek... The American dream.

Carlo could read the writing on the wall. Headstrom & Downs needed him as much as he needed them. Attorneys start out in places like Daytona, using the experience as a springboard to lucrative deals with big city firms. The fact Carlo wanted in could be parlayed into benefits not offered most job seekers. Before leaving the interview he'd managed to secure himself a benefits package unlike anything he could have hoped for.

His salary was inline with what he earned at Galen Rose, but he'd also negotiated perks. Those perks included a two thousand square foot oceanfront condo in Ponce Inlet, exclusive use of a Mercedes CLS-550, and a time share overlooking the strip in Las Vegas. He'd also get a percentage of all new revenue he generated for the firm.

The King of Daytona! Carlo crowned himself sovereign over the biker bars and leather shops as he drove up Main Street. Sure the mountain wasn't as tall here, but it was his mountain. Today he sat on top of it. He'd give Galen Rose a two week notice, but Carlo knew he'd be asked to leave immediately.

Carlo convinced himself this was a new beginning. The cocaine loving piglet he'd tossed in that dumpster in Overton had shaken him. The Miami Herald newspaper story had spooked him. He knew he couldn't continue assaulting young women just because they deserved it. Sooner or later everyone makes mistakes, even him. Daytona would be a fresh start. A new life. Carlo knew who he wanted to share it with.

He hadn't mentioned his plans to anyone, with the exception of his Mexican girlfriend. Carlo never felt the compulsion to punish her. She was different. Teracita reached him on a deeper level. Perhaps it was because he'd been her first lover. It is possible her chastity drew him to her.

He'd introduced Teracita to the wonders of sadomasochism, though in a somewhat restrained way. She hadn't yet seen what he was really capable of. Carlo found she was an easy target. Too easy! There'd be no satisfaction in punishing an innocent. It would be like crucifying the mother of Christ.

Still he couldn't help but toy with her. It was his nature. Carlo summoned Teracita to meet him at Madrid's, the spanish eatery in The Falls Shopping Mall in Coral Gables. When she arrived Carlo ordered her a margarita, then told her he had an announcement to make.

He put on a performance. Like a lawyer toying with a jury. If you want to get someone's attention tell them you have an announcement to make, then don't make it! After the delay of game infraction had run its course Carlo finally said, *"I know it's bad timing. Things aren't going very well for you at the Conti's. I want you to know I blame myself for that, but... I'm leaving Miami."*

Teracita didn't take the news well. She teared up, and began shaking. Carlo found enjoyment in her pain. So much so he lashed out again. *"I've accepted an offer from a firm up in Daytona. It's a great opportunity for me, Teracita. I'm tired of being a small fish in a big aquarium. You do understand... Right?"*

The Au Pair swallowed hard and gathered her wits. She wiped away the tears and forced a smile. It was just the response he'd hoped for. This little lamb could be led to the slaughter without so much as a whimper. She'd do anything he told her to do. Carlo had a mystical power over Teracita that couldn't be bought, not even with blood. He was acting like a spoiled little boy at his birthday party. All the gifts were his, as well as all the attention.

Carlo pretended not to notice Teracita's dismay. He told her he'd be notifying his employer in the morning, and would most likely be escorted out of the building. *"If that happens,"* he warned, *"I'm going to drive up to Daytona and get acclimated. No sense waiting... Nothing for me here!"*

Teracita did her best to contain her emotions. Carlo called the bartender over and ordered another margarita. When it came he slid it over to Teracita, then got up to leave.

That was it... She'd invested so much of her time. She'd given up her virginity. She'd subjected herself to his strange sexual proclivities. Yes, she'd enjoyed it some, but she never would have ventured into it without his encouragement. Now he was just going to pick up and leave? Even worse, he was being flippant about it! She'd thought Carlo loved her, though in retrospect Teracita realized he'd never actually said so.

"Enjoy the drink, my little chingona," Carlo stated. *"I've got to run. Lot's of packing to do."* He started to walk away. Half way to the exit he turned and came back to the bar. He planted a kiss squarely on Teracita's quivering lips. *"When I get situated I'll send for you,"* he announced. *"Give me two weeks, okay? Oh by the way... I love you, Teracita!"*

With that he was gone. Teracita sat at the bar with tears streaming down her face. She'd feared the worst. Returning to Delicias in shame to work alongside her parents was to be her fate. Her time as an Au Pair was limited. Why she hadn't been let go yet she wasn't sure. It was becoming unbearable just the same.

Carlo was an immigration lawyer. He'd told Teracita he had the power to keep her in the country long after her visa expired. She didn't know the law, but she knew she never wanted to go back to Mexico. Once she'd had a taste of life on the outside she knew she could never go back. Anywhere had to be better...even Daytona Beach.

Daytona wasn't at all like Carlo had envisioned. Yes there were biker bars, and NASCAR definitely put its stamp on the area, but there was so much more. Upscale golf course communities lined the coast from Edgewater to St Augustine. Top notch institutions like Embry Riddle University, Bethune Cookman College, Stetson University, and Flagler College provided students with excellent educational opportunities. The area was loaded with dozens of top notch restaurants and nightlife. There was even a newly built kennel club and poker casino to endeavor in.

Carlo found a cute little bungalow one block from the beach for Teracita. It would be convenient having her close by for those times when he needed companionship. Just not to close. Carlo liked having Teracita in his life...but he lived alone.

He waited a couple weeks before arranging for Teracita to join him. He took advantage of the time off between jobs to cruise the beach and check out the sights. They were plentiful. Daytona Beach wasn't South Beach or Haulover, but the women were just as attractive, and easier to impress. With a seven mile swath of beach front resorts and bars to check out, Carlo kept busy.

The Cuban masochist wouldn't have the luxury of melting into the background here. It wouldn't take long for his face to become recognizable to the locals. As an upstanding member of the legal community he'd have to stay out of the limelight. Of course there was always Jacksonville or Orlando he could visit. Both cities had populations bordering one million, and no one knew him in either town.

Teracita was finishing up the Conti's laundry when Carlo called. She hadn't heard from him in over a week and she was beginning to wonder if she ever would. He'd formulated a plan. Carlo wanted her to leave the Conti estate and join him in Daytona.

Ramone normally dropped Teracita off for her class at Miami University. It was held on Thursday evenings. Instead of going to class Teracita was to make her way to University Station Metro and take the train to Palmetto. From there she would transfer to a Tri-Rail line heading to West Palm International Airport. Carlo would pick her up there. They'd drive the rest of the way to Daytona. Carlo assumed the Conti's would file a missing person report. He intended to leave a difficult trail for the authorities to follow.

Teracita waited at the coffee shop inside West Palm's main terminal, just as Carlo planned. She hadn't taken her first sip when her cell phone rang. Carlo was at the short term parking lot on level four. She was to make her way there. It was nearly 9:30 in the evening when the two finally hooked up.

Carlo exited the interstate a half hour north of West Palm and pulled into a Days Inn parking lot. He'd already booked a room. The latin lover had champagne on ice awaiting their arrival.

Teracita had packed but a few articles of clothing in a small bag, wanting to remain incognito. She'd withdrawn fourteen hundred dollars from her bank account, planning to use some of it to buy new clothes. The two of them celebrated Teracita's new found freedom by polishing off a bottle of Martini & Rossi. Afterwards they engaged in some good old fashioned sex.

Carlo exited I-95 at ten o'clock the next morning. He drove past the famous Daytona International Speedway and headed east. When he got to the beach Carlo parked his Mercedes and got out. It was low tide, making the wide expanse of sand quite impressive. Teracita couldn't have been happier.

She and Carlo walked along the shore. He pointed out the famous Daytona Beach Pier to the north. It had recently undergone a multimillion dollar refurbishing. The pier featured a seafood restaurant with a rooftop bar. Carlo told her you could see the Bahamas from up there.

Carlo turned and pointed in the other direction. His condo was a few miles south of where they were standing. Not sure how to avoid the subject any longer he blurted out *"And your place is just down the road."*

"My place," Teracita questioned? *"I thought we'd be together."* She'd never spoken to Carlo so boldly before. Her reaction even surprised her. The look on his face told her all she needed to know. When he lifted his arm with his fist clenched she backed off, then turned and walked back to the car.

It was in silence that Carlo drove the three quarter miles to Teracita's bungalow. The white stucco structure had a terra cotta tile roof and a broad front porch. The house was located one block from the ocean. It featured a small screened swimming pool, and had ceramic tile floors. There was a galley kitchen with modern stainless steel appliances. A loft bedroom overlooked the living area below. Despite her initial agitation Teracita was impressed with the place. Carlo didn't mention he had a month to month lease agreement on the property.

Carlo intended to seize control of every aspect of Teracita's life. He meant to instill fear. Make her reliant on him for her very being. One way to accomplish that goal was to use her immigration status as a weapon against her. He knew her biggest fear was being forced to return to Mexico. Carlo confiscated Teracita's visa, explaining it was important she be untraceable. He suggested she use an alias, and avoid public contact.

They agreed on a name. Teracita would henceforth be known as Bonita. The name meant *Pretty One* in Spanish. Bonita was to relax, enjoy the comforts bestowed upon her, and lay low. Carlo convinced her if anyone learned of her true identity she'd be deported.

Teracita *(Bonita)* realized she didn't have it to darn bad. She was living in an adorable little place ten minutes from the Atlantic Ocean. Her rent was paid for by a handsome sexy lawyer who called on her several times a week. Carlo even provided her with a stipend to cover groceries and other bills. It was enough to live on without being so much she could save for a rainy day. Things were just as he'd planned. Teracita spent her time reading, walking the beach, and exercising. She made no friends, as instructed...though she was friendly.

Carlo put in quite a few hours at work. He needed to establish himself as a go getter, and he worked hard to bring in new revenue. Headstrom & Downs took out several half page ads in the local newspaper introducing Carlo to the community. He in turn met with leaders of the Spanish Action League and other Latino organizations in the area seeking out potential clients.

He managed to take Teracita out to dinner a few times a week, and he spent the night at her bungalow on several occasions. For the most part though, she was alone. There were several ocean front resorts within walking distance of her bungalow. Teracita discovered they had Tiki Bars that were open to the public. She began to visit them on occasion.

She learned there were a couple neighborhood bars close by too. Mostly catering to the local crowd. Teracita found herself gravitating to them as a way of maintaining some semblance of social connection. For some reason Teracita felt the need to hide this fact from Carlo.

On more than one occasion Carlo tried unsuccessfully to reach Teracita. He'd paid to have a landline installed in her bungalow so he could reach her when needed. The fact she didn't answer made him suspicious. He started driving by the bungalow late at night to see if she was home, and if she was alone.

One night he saw Teracita walking along A1A. He discreetly followed her to see where she was headed. She stopped at a local night spot called *The Blue Whale*. Carlo pulled into an adjacent lot and waited. Two hours later Teracita came walking out of the bar with a young man. She jumped on the back of his motorcycle and off they went.

The biker dropped Teracita off in front of her house. Teracita waited till he removed his helmet then kissed him on the cheek. The two said their goodbyes and the young man drove off into the night. Carlo waited at the end of the street for ten minutes, then came to her door.

He let himself in with his key, then stood and listened as Teracita freshened up in the bathroom. After a moment Carlo disrobed and turned out the lights. He hid round a corner until Teracita came out. When she entered the dark hallway he grabbed her from behind and covered her mouth with his hand. Then he whispered in her ear, *"Who's your little boyfriend?"* Carlo roughly cupped her throat with his other hand and in a menacing voice asked, *"You fucking him?"*

Teracita nearly had a heart attack. ***"Ay que la changeal"*** she yelled out in Spanish, ***"What the fuck."*** Carlo spun her round to face him, then kissed her hard on the mouth. ***"No, I am not fucking him,"*** she screamed when he released her, ***"and I'm not fucking you either... You scared the crap out of me."***

When Carlo heard that he took it as a challenge. Women didn't say no to Carlo, especially little Mexican girls from the barrio. Teracita had changed into her nightshirt and panties while in the bathroom. The muscular lawyer found it easy to wrestle Teracita to the floor and pin her down.

168

While sitting on top of her Carlo reached down and removed her panties, then insensitively pinched her nipples through her nightshirt. Teracita winced at the painful nip, which sent a ripple of excitement through him. He bent over and took a nipple in his mouth and bit down. Teracita let out a scream, more out of surprise then pain. The bite hurt, but pleasurably so. Carlo pulled her nightshirt up and licked the swollen nipple he'd just bitten, then moved to the other one.

Alternating between breasts, Carlo roughly licked and sucked each one, sinking his teeth into each delicious morsel. When he finished he looked her in the eye and repeated his previous question, "A*re you fucking him?"* Teracita just laughed, thinking it a ridiculous question. Carlo didn't much care for her response. He backhanded her hard across the mouth. ***"Don't you laugh at me... Whore,"*** he yelled.

Teracita didn't know what to say. Did she love this man, or fear him? They'd engaged in some rough sex at times, but he'd never hit her. Not like this. The other times had seemed playful. This time it hurt. Teracita teared up. She told Carlo the guy who'd given her a ride home was just a boy. They'd talked inside and when she got up to leave he offered her a ride. *"I love you, Carlo,"* Teracita told him. "*You must know that by now."*

She could see him begin to unwind. Carlo had been tense, on edge, like an expectant father in a maternity ward. The muscles in his face relaxed and his shoulders slackened. He flipped Teracita over on her belly and entered her, slowly and methodically. After ten minutes of vaginal massaging, Carlo turned his attention to her bottom.

They'd had anal intercourse a few times. Though Teracita didn't particularly like it she would partake. She knew Carlo enjoyed it. Minutes after entering her he was finished. Carlo rolled over and laid there, not saying a word. Ten minutes later he was gone.

Over the course of the next month or two Carlo became more and more compulsive. His obsessive jealousy was more than Teracita could bare. The more he tried to persuade her to stay home the more she resented it. Even her fear of deportation didn't sway her from venturing out when the loneliness became too unbearable.

Carlo could have easily avoided the issue by spending more time with her, but he resisted because to do so would be to give up control. They continued to have sexual relations once a week, but even that became increasingly uncomfortable. It would be hard to say they made love, though that's what Carlo called it. The man's proclivity towards deviant behavior was becoming more and more pronounced. His acts of bondage were becoming excessively humiliating. The masochistic acts themselves were becoming more painful and unpleasant.

Where could she go? Teracita relied on Carlo for everything. Her housing, her food, spending money. Her very freedom was dependent on Carlo's good will. Still, this cycle of abuse had to stop. It was robbing Teracita of what little self respect she had left. The next time Carlo paid her a visit she would talk to him. He would have to understand!

The next morning Teracita took a long walk on the beach. It was a beautiful day. The ocean breeze was warm and refreshing. As she waded in the surf a guy came up and started a conversation with her. He was good looking. An Afro-American around twenty-five years of age. His name was Terrance. He said he was from Winter Park.

Terrance spoke in a soft voice. It gave the impression he was well educated. Teracita, as instructed, introduced herself as *Bonita*. She told Terrance she lived here in Daytona. He asked her if they could walk together for awhile. The two headed down the beach towards the pier.

When they reached the pier Terrance said he was getting hungry. He asked *Bonita* if she'd join him for lunch. She hesitated at first, afraid to start something she knew couldn't possibly last. Terrance persuaded her to relax and enjoy the moment. After all, it's just lunch.

They headed over to the Hilton Resort located a few steps from the pier. The hotel featured a steakhouse with an outdoor patio overlooking the beach. As they walked Terrance mentioned he had a room at the Hilton if she wanted to freshen up. Teracita declined, choosing to use the ladies room located in the lobby.

Terrance went to his room and made a quick outfit change. He would meet Teracita on the hotel patio. They'd agreed if she got there first she'd order drinks.

After freshening up Teracita made her way to the patio bar. As she approached she heard someone calling her name. Expecting to see Terrance behind her, she turned towards the voice. Instead it was Carlo standing there. He had a puzzled look on his face.

"What the hell are you doing here," he asked. Teracita told him half a lie, saying she'd been walking on the beach and decided to stop for a drink. *"I come here with clients,"* he angrily replied. *"I'm here with two clients now, and one of the partners from the firm. I can't very well introduce you to them dressed like that."*

Teracita was wearing a revealing bikini and beach sandals. She had an opaque wrap tied around her waist. *"Please leave,"* Carlo insisted. *"Now, before you embarrass me."* Teracita rushed out of the patio bar and down to the beach.

Terrance arrived just as Teracita rushed off. Unable to get her attention he called after her, *"Bonita... Bonita, stop."* Then he turned to Carlo, who was glaring back at him. Terrance considered asking Carlo what his problem was, but chose to walk away instead.

Carlo returned to his table inside the steakhouse and deftly morphed back into his lawyer persona. He'd deal with his whore later.

A full week passed before Teracita heard from him. Carlo showed up at her door one night with a double order of chinese and two sets of chop sticks. *"Hungry,"* he asked? After finishing off the fried rice with a bottle of pinot the two snuggled on the sofa. Neither of them mentioned anything about the rendezvous at the Hilton the week before. Teracita worked up the nerve to talk about their relationship. She told Carlo she missed the days when they just had regular sex, suggesting it would be great if once in a while they could make love like normal lovers do.

Carlo responded by taking Teracita in his arms. He whispered sweet nothings in her ear and softly kissed her neck, gently rolling her nipples in his fingers. When she reached down to touch him he lurched back and turned away. Teracita realized he hadn't gotten an erection.

"It's okay baby, don't worry about it," she told him. *"You'll always be my man."* With that Carlo hauled off and punched her square on the jaw. Teracita fell back against the sofa, tipping it over in the process. As she lay sprawled on the floor Carlo stood above her in a rage. She thought he was going to kill her. Instead he rushed out!

The next morning Teracita got dressed in a conservative black dress and called a cab. When the taxi arrived she instructed the driver to take her to the closest catholic church he could find. The driver told her the *'Little Lamb of the Sea'* was just across the bridge.

The cabbie dropped her off in front of a little run down church. Few attended the church with any regularity these days. It was scheduled for closure. To the rear of the church sat a rectory. It had been battered by age and neglect. In fact it didn't appear to be inhabited. Some of the windows were shuttered, and the large porch was barren of furniture. Teracita entered the church. After looking around a moment she dipped her hand in a ceremonial bowl of sacred water, then made the sign of the cross. She bowed in reverence, then proceeded down the aisle.

She didn't know it, but Carlo had been watching her place since early morning. He suspected she might do something stupid. He worried she'd call the cops, maybe even call her black boy friend to come save her. He'd followed the taxi across the Silver Beach Bridge and watched from the street as she entered the church. By the time he made his way inside Teracita was in a prolonged conversation with an elderly priest. He couldn't make out what they were saying, but he could tell Teracita was sobbing. He hid behind a large ornate pillar as the two walked back up the aisle towards him. They stood at the entrance of the church. Carlo heard the priest say, *"When you're ready my child, God is there for you. So am I. Now go...and sin no more."*

Teracita walked back home. Her face throbbed and her heart ached. What had happened between her and Carlo? Was avoiding deportation worth what she was experiencing? Was there any chance she could return to Miami? Perhaps Mr Conti would help her?

Carlo had told Teracita she'd broken the law by not reporting her whereabouts to the authorities. He'd said she could go to federal prison. She'd serve time, only to be deported upon her release. She tried telling herself if she just went along with his sexual agenda maybe he'd straighten out. It was obvious regular vanilla sex didn't do it for him any more. Teracita felt she had nowhere to turn for help. As she walked across the bridge she began to pray. *"God... Lord Jesus... Mother Maria... Help me."*

Several days passed before Carlo called to ask if he could come over. He apologized for hitting her, and promised to never strike her again. When he arrived that evening he brought a bouquet of roses and a bottle of champagne. Teracita told him she was willing to put up with some of his peculiar tendencies, but she had limits. The two made love that night. Carlo avoided using any restraints, nor did he hurt her in any way. He was able to get and maintain an erection, and successfully brought Teracita to orgasm. When it came time for his own, he faked it. Although unable to complete what he started, at least he was able to avoid the embarrassment and shame of her knowing, or so he thought!

Carlo left the bungalow around midnight. He told Teracita he had a big day coming up. Teracita showered and went to bed, for once happy and content. She was concerned for Carlo. He hadn't been able to climax with her, and that was a problem. At least he'd suppressed his anxiety and anger over it. If they could hold it together for a while, she was certain he'd work it out.

It was a cool moonless night. A northern breeze blew across the peninsula. Teracita shut the windows and curled up in a blanket. Surrounded by blackness she quickly fell asleep. She dreamed about Terrance, the black guy she'd met on the beach. In the dream she'd accepted his invitation to go to his room to freshen up. Once there he seduced her. Teracita spent the rest of the afternoon in his King size bed.

The bed wasn't the only thing King sized, as she'd come to find out. Still in a dream state, Teracita felt her hands being bound. Terrance was mounting her from behind. She couldn't move. She didn't want to. Suddenly a searing pain ripped across her buttocks. Teracita woke to her own voice, screaming in bloody agony.

Someone pulled her hair, forcing her head back. A cloth was stuffed in her mouth. When she tried to scramble away she couldn't. Her wrists had been tied to the bedpost. Red hot lashes blistered her bottom, biting into her flesh as they hit. Her attempts to scream were muffled by the cloth that gagged her. Teracita's upper thighs and ass cheeks were repeatedly flogged. The pain seared deep into her flesh.

For a moment the beating stopped. Teracita could hear her heart beating in her chest. She could feel the throbbing in her buttocks. Just when she thought it might be over a large powerful fist crumpled the side of her face. Several teeth separated from their sockets. She felt blood soak the cloth that gagged her. Her bottom burned like it had been set on fire. The brutality seemed to go on forever, but in actuality lasted just five minutes...Then it was silent.

Teracita lay there for a long time. When she finally did get up it took her thirty excruciating minutes to loosen the rope that bound her to the bedpost. She struggled to put on a dress and shoes. After tossing a few articles of clothing in a bag she retrieved her jewelry and cash box from their hiding place and left. She didn't even bother to shut the door on her way out.

It was nearly three in the morning when she left the torture chamber her bungalow had become. She could see the lights of the bridge in the distance. House boats that lined the marina on the mainland side of the bridge twinkled like stars in the moonless night. Her ass was on fire as she crawled slowly down the street. Not a car was in sight, not a house light lit at this hour. The whole world was sleeping, oblivious to the assault on her person. It was an hour later when she found herself standing outside the Little Lamb of the Sea Catholic Church.

Teracita pounded on the church door. She attempted to holler for help but it hurt to much. After five minutes of futile pounding she tried the rectory. She banged on the door till a porch light came on. *"Padre,"* Teracita weakly called out. ***"Help me!"***

Father Branigan made his way to the door to see what all the racket was about. When he saw Teracita he rushed to her side and helped her into the rectory. It was obvious she'd suffered a horrific beating. Her swollen face and blood encrusted lips were a telltale sign. The priest led Teracita to a chair and motioned for her to sit. She told him, *"I can't, Padre. It hurts."*

The Father told Teracita he was calling the police. She begged him not to. *"I don't know who did this to me,"* she claimed. *"It was so dark...and I was sleeping. It must've been an intruder. Padre, please don't call the police. I'll be deported!"*

Did she have any family? Any friends? When asked, Teracita shook her head no. She told the padre she was alone. *"Where do you live,"* he asked? Teracita hesitated before answering. She told him she'd been staying with a friend, but they'd argued and she was told to leave.

As of today she was officially homeless. Literally and figuratively. She had no place to go. *"I should take you to the hospital so they can check you over"* the priest declared. *"Were you raped?"* Teracita insisted she'd not been, though the priest persisted in asking. She told him she just needed some time to sort things out in her head. Father Branigan responded, *"I know what we're going to have to do."*

The priest went to his desk and fingered through a rolodex until he found what he was looking for. A business card from the Volusia County Domestic Abuse Council. He fetched Teracita a cup of tea, then made the call.

"I have a young woman here. She showed up on the church doorsteps this morning. She's been badly beaten. She claims she

176

doesn't know her attacker, but she has no place to go. I suggested calling the police but she begged me not to, saying she wouldn't cooperate with them if I did. Can you help her?"

Father Branigan was told to bring Teracita to the women's shelter on Beach Street. He knew the place from previous visits. He thanked the lady who assisted him, then hung up the phone. He told Teracita they were good people. They would help her, but they'd want to know who did this to her.

They arrived at a large building surrounded by a six foot high iron gate. It looked like a nursing home or a private school of some type. When Father Branigan pulled up to the gate a security camera swiveled around to film him. Then a voice from nowhere asked, *"How can I help you?"*

Once inside the facility Teracita was taken to a medical office where a nurse did a complete examination. Her face was cleaned up and gauze placed in her mouth. Her contusions were treated with a soothing antibacterial ointment. After a pelvic exam revealed she hadn't been raped she was treated to a warm sits bath. After drying off someone helped Teracita get dressed. Then she was visited by a shelter counselor.

The counselor was an overweight woman in her mid thirties. She had blonde hair with dark roots, and spoke in a nasally voice. Not bothering to look up from her note pad she asked personal questions about the attack, writing down Teracita's responses as she gave them. It all seemed quite routine. Then the social worker put down her pad and pen. She looked directly at Teracita and asked her point blank, *"Do you know the man who did this to you?"* Teracita shook her head vigorously...*No!*

"You don't know" the woman questioned, her disbelief apparent? *"You're kidding, right Hon? Tell me you're kidding!"* The counselor was used to hearing that refrain from victims. It was

177

amazing how many women came to the shelter beaten and battered by total strangers. It was enough to make one afraid to venture out alone. *"Okay, Sweetie. When you're ready to tell me, we'll talk. My name is Jewel. For now let's get you settled in."*

A volunteer was paged to bring Teracita to a room. She was fortunate in that one had just opened up. Like most days of the year the shelter was at full capacity. If people would only treat others as they themselves would like to be treated none of this would be necessary. It was approaching day light. Teracita had gotten very little sleep. The aide told her breakfast was at eight, then turned out the light. Teracita collapsed on the bed...face down!

EARLY RETIREMENT

MURDER IN DAYTONA

20

With Doris Van Fleet missing the Veronica Steven's homicide case turned cold. Detective Brooks racked his brain trying to come up with leads. He contacted Pam Sykes up in New York to ask whether she'd heard from Doris. The detective told her there was a warrant out for Doris on an unrelated charge, and reminded her it was a felony to harbor a fugitive from justice. As far as he knew Pam Sykes was the only person from Doris' past she kept in contact with.

Brooks drove out to Mt Dora to discuss the case with the police chief. They considered the possibility there might be a Mytilene connection. After all Doris had to have some friends in the area, she'd lived there for over a year. Somebody had to know where she was. Brooks was certain of it.

The chief offered to drive Detective Brooks out to Mytilene so he could talk to the folks in the management office. He figured they would most likely keep information on renters there. He told the detective he was surprised Mytilene even allowed renters, being it was such an upscale place.

Brooks was eager to talk to the homeowner who rented the cottage to Doris. The latino housekeeper had told the Mt Dora police chief she was out of the country indefinitely, visiting Paris or something.

The detective told the chief he would love to get a chance to snoop around a bit, maybe get a look inside the cottage. To avoid attention they drove there in the chief's personal car. He dropped Brooks off at the house on Boreas Lane then went back to talk to the girls in the sales center.

The property manager was off for the day, but the receptionist was helpful. She was a young woman, cute, with short dark hair. The chief thought she had a very flirtatious voice. He never would've guessed she was a gay woman. He asked her about the regulations on homeowners renting out properties. The seductive receptionist told him renting wasn't allowed. Hearing that, the chief suggested the regulations must not be strictly enforced, because he knew of at least one instance where someone had rented out their place.

"Not possible," he was told. *"Renting isn't allowed here!"*

The chief informed the receptionist that 28 Boreas Lane had a tenant, one Doris Van Fleet. *"No, no"* she replied. *"Ms Van Fleet stays in the gardener's cottage out back. Besides I don't think she pays rent. She's more of a guest. You see, the homeowner spends most of her time back in Texas. That's where she's from."*

Sounded plausible. The chief thanked the receptionist for her help. He'd considered asking her out but quickly changed his mind. She was far to young for him, not to mention way out of his league. Little did he know!

He drove back to the house on Boreas Lane, arriving just as the detective was exiting the cottage. *"Door was unlocked,"* Brooks said, shrugging his shoulders. *"Didn't find much though... How about you?"* The chief told Brooks he'd had a long conversation with the receptionist. She'd informed him there were no renters in Mytilene, it was against their policy. Evidently Doris wasn't renting. She was considered a guest of the homeowner.

180

The two lawmen got back in the chief's car and headed for the exit. As they turned onto Zephyrus Boulevard the chief mentioned the woman who owned the home at 28 Boreas Lane was a Texan. He said the receptionist told him she lived in Texas much of the time.

"What's she doing in Paris then," the detective wondered? As the chief drove past the sales center Brooks suddenly hollered, ***"STOP THE CAR!"***

The rear tires left a long black trail of rubber when the chief slammed on his brakes and squealed to a halt. *"What's her name,"* Brooks asked him? The chief looked at Brooks like he was crazy, then muttered something about running over a friggin' cat!

The detective asked him again... This time even more adamantly. The chief answered, *"I didn't asks her name, but I sho' as hell wanted to. Dat was a purdy lil lady!"*

"Not the receptionist," Brooks loudly corrected him... *"The homeowner... What's the homeowner's name?"*

Brooks had realized no one thought to ask for the name of the homeowner who rented the cottage to Doris. He got out of the car and rushed to the sales office. The short haired receptionist was sitting at her desk playing a game on her computer when the detective stormed in.

"I'm Detective Dan Brooks," he stated, just a little bit winded. *"I need some information."* The receptionist asked him how she could help. Brooks recognized her voice. It was the same voice he'd heard when he first came to Mytilene. The one on the speaker phone that so eerily sounded like the voice on his GPS. Again it unsettled him a little. After regaining his focus the detective asked, *"The homeowner at 28 Boreas Lane... The one that rents the garden cottage to Doris Van Fleet... What's her name?"*

"You mean Vanessa," the receptionist answered. *"Vanessa Del Rio... She's not here this time of year. She's back home in Texas."*

He asked the receptionist if she might have this Del Rio lady's address out there in Texas. She strolled over to a metal file drawer sitting next to the water cooler and pulled out a community data sheet. After jotting down an address on a post-it note she handed it to the detective. Brooks thanked her for her trouble then turned and rushed out of the sales office as quickly as he'd rushed in.

"Holy Mother of God," Brooks yelled when he got outside. He ran back to the chief's car and loudly exclaimed, *"Paris... Chief! The God Damn woman is in Paris all right... Paris Friggin Texas!"*

The Mt Dora police chief asked the detective what the hell he was talking about. Brooks laughed... *"The woman who rents the cottage to Doris... The homeowner... Her name is Vanessa Del Rio...and she's in Paris all right. Paris Fucking Texas!"*

The chief started the car then looked over at Brooks with a worried look on his face. *"I knows dat name, Detective. Vanessa Del Rio be dat woman I was tellin ya'll about. She dat oil baroness turn reel estate developer dat started Mytilene. Ifin your suspect be mixed up wid her you's gonna have your hands full. Dat be a lady wid some major clout behine er."*

They were quiet the rest of the way to the station. Once they were out of the car Brooks thanked the chief for everything he'd done and gave him a bear hug. Just before leaving he turned and said, *"Hey Chief... At least she ain't in France!"*

The chief answered that comment by telling the detective she may as well be, for all the hoops he'd be jumping through trying to get to her!

182

When he got back to his desk Brooks contacted the Paris Police Department. He was given the name of a detective. Bubba Johnson was a former college football player, having started at tight end for the Southern Methodist University Mustangs in the mid eighties. The SMU football program was shut down by the NCAA for rules violations following Bubba's freshman year. He did get to play in the Aloha Bowl against Notre Dame though, catching the winning touchdown pass as time expired.

SMU won that game 27-20. Bubba Johnson was christened 'Long Neck' by his teammates for the way he stretched out his body making that final score. In Paris Bubba was something of a celebrity. After a short conversation with him Brooks wondered if he might be better off working the case alone.

The brawny Texas detective spoke with a slow drawl. He took little seriously. Brooks first impression of Bubba was that he seemed as happy go lucky as a rooster in a hen house. He knew he needed local law enforcement's cooperation, but this guy might be more than he could handle.

Brooks gave Bubba a quick synopsis of the case and told him he'd be taking an early flight into Dallas the following morning. Bubba offered to pick him up at the airport, mentioning an old Texas diner out on Highway 19 where they could grab breakfast.

Being it was a two hour drive each way, Brooks thought it was a generous offer. He accepted. The detective later doubted his judgement after considered what spending two hours in a confined space with Bubba might be like.

After arriving at Love Field the detective made his way to the lobby. He saw this big ham hock of a man with a crew cut holding a cardboard sign that read **BROOKS.** The guy was dressed in a cheap black suit and wore a big Texas size smile on his face.

The two investigators greeted one another. Bubba told Detective Brooks everyone calls him *Long Neck*. Brooks response was to tell Bubba he'd just call him Detective Johnson if that was okay.

They got in Bubba's unmarked squad car. It was parked at the curb just outside the terminal. The detective had used police privilege to circumvent the airport's parking policy. Bubba justified his actions to the airport security guy, saying he had a two hour ride back to Paris.

Taking the Lyndon Johnson Freeway to escape the congestion the detectives were soon on their way out of town. Bubba told Brooks about the diner just outside Sulpher Springs they'd be stopping at. If there was one thing he appreciated it was a hearty breakfast. *"We are about an hour away from the best damned hash n eggs breakfast you ever tasted,"* he insisted. *"Besides, they got the purdiest waitresses you ever gonna see too!"*

Brooks worst fears were coming true. Bubba was a master communicator. He rarely came up for air. The bulky ex-jock talked about everything from his college football days, to living in Paris, to Texas barbeque. Seems *Long Neck* Johnson was an expert on all three.

Eventually Brooks was able to get the detective to concentrate on the subject he'd flown there for, the Veronica Stevens homicide. He explained he was in town to gather information on his chief suspect, a woman named Doris Van Fleet. He had reason to believe she might be hiding out in the Paris area. Specifically with a lady named Vanessa Del Rio.

"Del Rio," Bubba exclaimed! ***"Did you say Del Rio?"***

Detective Brooks looked at his counterpart questioningly, then said he understood Ms Del Rio was a woman of some substance around these parts.

"I'll say," Bubba replied. *"Del Rio got more clout round these parts than the football coach over in Austin! Ms Del Rio is as politically connected as anybody in this state. She made a fortune investing in oil, like most of the millionaires round here."*

The big balooka repeated the name to himself over and over as he shook his head. *"Vanessa Del Rio?"* Then he did something very unusual... He got quiet.

The Lone Star Diner sits midway between Dallas and Paris on State Route 19. There were a few dusty pick up trucks parked near the front entrance when the detectives pulled in. The stuffed head of a huge long horn steer was centered over the door. Its horns extended six feet, tip to tip.

They sat in the parking lot for a moment before Bubba spoke up. *"All that talk about Ms Del Rio done sorta killed my appetite,"* he said to Brooks. The Florida detective responded, saying it looked like it had killed his gift for gab too. With that Bubba Johnson broke out in laughter. His funk was over. He slapped his guest on the shoulder and said, *"Come on, Brother. Let's eat."*

A middle aged waitress greeted them when they walked in. Her name tag read *Lola.* She had long shapely legs and platinum blonde hair, which was piled high on her head. She flirted with Bubba as she led them to a booth. Brooks overheard her say, *"Is that a big gun in your pocket, Detective, or are you jus*t *happy to see me?"*

Bubba smiled, but he didn't respond. Rather than scan through the menu he told the waitress we'd both have the house special. When she left Bubba explained their relationship.

Brooks learned their so called relationship consisted of once a week trips to the diner for breakfast, followed by a romp in the back seat of Bubba's patrol car.

The detective was able to bring the conversation back to his investigation. He told Bubba he wanted to question Ms Del Rio, and possibly stake out her home in hopes of sighting Doris. He knew he needed the big goofy cop to cooperate. He had no jurisdiction in these parts.

Bubba told Brooks there was no fucking way he was getting caught up in an investigation of Vanessa Del Rio without definitive proof she might be involved in a crime. *"Harboring a fugitive from justice is a crime,"* Brooks reminded him. Of course he knew no charges had yet been filed against Doris. Hence no such crime had been committed.

Between heaping spoonfuls of beef hash and Texas toast Bubba asked his guest if his suspect and Del Rio were lovers? Detective Brooks asked him why he might think so. Bubba replied, *"Rumor has it Ms Del Rio is a lesbian. Ain't nobody ever seen her with a woman mind you, but she ain't never seen in the company of no man neither. She ain't married, so I was wonderin is all."*

Detective Brooks told Bubba the wealthy oil baroness had developed a high end community back in Florida, and that it was built exclusively for women. So it was possible she is a lesbian. Brooks added he had no definitive proof.

"That would be a damn shame," Bubba replied. *"A fine Texas woman like her bein a damn queer."* After a moment of reflection he added, *"With all the cowboys round these parts seems she coulda got herself some decent dick somehow!"*

Bubba finished off his hash and ordered more coffee. Brooks ate half of his then chowed down the last of his Texas toast. *"That was some breakfast, huh detective,"* Bubba bragged. Detective Brooks checked his watch and mentioned they should get going. When the check came he paid it, then thanked Lola for the great service. Bubba thanked Brooks for buying breakfast, then turned to the waitress and said, *"I'll be stopping by a little later with your tip, Sweets."*

The next forty minutes was spent driving twenty miles an hour over the speed limit. Bubba talked non stop the entire time. Brooks decided despite his counterparts propensity for talking too much, he was an okay guy. Perhaps being opposites would work in his favor. They could pull off the *Good cop - Bad cop* routine quite convincingly. Of that he was sure. If only he could talk Bubba into questioning the Del Rio woman.

Paris, Texas is a small city. It's located ninety miles northeast of Dallas, and is home to about 28,000 residents. As they reached the city limits Bubba drove past a sixty foot tall replica of the Eiffel Tower. It had a giant red Stetson cowboy hat sitting on top of it. Bubba told Brooks the Stetson lights up at night.

He bragged about Paris being named *Best Small City In America* by some national magazine. When they arrived at the station Bubba parked in his spot and hopped out. As the two detectives made their way inside they were stopped by a couple guys on the street. They wanted to talk SMU football. Bubba Johnson was indeed a popular figure in town. He seemed to know everybody, and everybody knew him.

Once inside Bubba wasted no time. He called in two colleagues and filled them in on the situation. Unbeknownst to Detective Brooks Bubba had already decided to set up twenty-four hour surveillance to watch the Del Rio property.

Vanessa lived in an exclusive area known as River Valley. Her forty-five hundred square foot ranch sat on two acres of land on the cities northern edge. As private a setting as it was the home was still within walking distance of Culbertson Square, the center of activity in the small city. The four of them they would alternate staking out the Del Rio property. If Detective Brooks suspect was identified she'd be taken into custody.

The team would work six hours on, six hours off. Brooks was somewhat surprised at the level of professionalism Bubba and his team demonstrated. The equipment used to conduct the operation was top notch. It included high resolution cameras and infrared video recorders for night vision.

It was three days before a sighting was made. Late one night the home's privacy gate opened and Vanessa Del Rio appeared behind the wheel of a luxurious gold colored Cadillac STS. When she did the infrared recorder picked up the image of a woman standing just inside the gate. She was tall and thin with short hair. She was smoking a cigarette. The woman waved at the driver of the Cadillac as the vehicle left the property.

It was at daybreak Detective Brooks got a phone call telling him the good news. The two junior detectives working the case were enjoying coffee and donuts inside the surveillance van when the woman they'd seen the night before came strolling out of the gate. They zoomed in on her face and verified she was the suspect in question. One of the detectives exited the vehicle and followed her on foot while the other one stayed back some distance and followed in the car.

The suspect stopped to buy a newspaper from a vending machine several blocks away. When she did the detective following on foot walked up and identified himself as a police officer. Expecting the suspect to try to flee the detective driving the car sped to the scene and jumped out to assist. It wasn't necessary. Doris gave no resistance. Matter of fact she was quite calm.

Brooks had just stepped out of the shower when he got the call. Bubba was on the line bragging about how the Texas Rangers had got their man again. *"You telling me you got her"* The detective exclaimed! *"You are sure it's her? Be very careful. She can be violent. I don't want your boys getting hurt."*

Bubba assured him it was Doris Van Fleet they'd taken into custody, adding she'd offered no resistance. *"Okay... I'll be there in ten minutes,"* Brooks excitedly yelled into the receiver. Before hanging up he said, *"I owe you a great big thank you, Long Neck."*

An hour later Detective Brooks and Bubba Johnson were sitting across the table from a very angry Doris Van Fleet. *"What the fuck is this,"* she screamed at the detective? *"I am going to sue your ass off, you son of a bitch."* The detective let her rant awhile before finally telling her to hush up. Brooks reminded her of the appointment she missed back in Daytona. He asked her why she missed it. *"Fuck you. I Forgot,"* Doris smugly replied.

Bubba sauntered over to where Doris was seated. He stood staring at her for a while, then bent down and asked her what her relationship to Ms Del Rio was. ***"Fuck you, Tex,"*** Doris angrily replied. *"Who is this asshole,"* she said to Brooks? *"Can't the big ugly moron afford a decent fucking suit?"*

The big Texas detective laughed. He introduced himself, telling Doris all his friends call him *Long Neck.* He said his suit was a whole lot better than the garb she'd be wearing sitting in the Texas State Penitentiary. Then he got right in her face and told her what he really wanted to know was if her and Ms Del Rio was lovers, cause if they was ... he wanted to watch!

Brooks pulled out the warrant that had been filed against Doris when she failed to appear in court to answer the traffic citation she'd been issued. *"I guess you forgot about this too,"* he calmly teased. *"Seems you have an issue showing up when you're supposed to, Ms Van Fleet. Not a problem though. We just come and get you is all."*

Doris sat quietly stewing for the next hour or two. Eventually her tone changed. She started whimpering she hadn't done anything wrong, and that she wanted to go home. *"You should have come when I asked you to, Dear."* Brooks told her. *"I went to a whole lot of trouble finding you. Now that I have, I think we'll get to know each other a little better. That is, if my friend Long Neck here releases you to my custody."*

EARLY RETIREMENT

MURDER IN DAYTONA

21

Carlo tried staying away from Teracita for as long as he could. He'd gotten carried away that night three days before. He half expected the police to show up at his door. Not that she hadn't deserved it. Teracita was proving to be an unappreciative little bitch. Just like the others. She'd disobeyed him. Carousing the bars at night and having hotel rendezvous with other men... Black men no less. Now running to a priest? Her latest transgression had sent him over the edge. The time had come to take control. Possession was ninety percent of the law, and Teracita belonged to him.

Teracita couldn't even be sure it had been him that dark moonless night. Even if she did know she couldn't prove it? Why not blame the attack on an intruder? If she questioned him about why he hadn't come around the past few days he could blame it on his job.

When Carlo went to the bungalow the landlord was there cleaning up the mess. He told Carlo he'd been summoned by a neighbor because the front door of the bungalow had been left wide open for several days. *"When I got here the lights were on, but no one answered my knocks,"* the landlord told him. *"It looks like a war zone in here. If I find any damage someone's going to have to pay."*

Carlo apologized for the trouble. He assured the landlord he'd cover any damages. He asked him if Teracita's personal effects were gone. The landlord motioned for him to come inside.

Most of Teracita's belongings were still there, but it was clear she was gone. Carlo was devastated. His little Mexican *chingona* had disappeared into thin air. Carlo didn't have time to play games. His position at Headstrom & Downs demanded he put in long hours. Especially with all the new business he was attracting. Fortunately much of his time was spent away from the office.

Carlo visited clients in latino neighborhoods throughout the area. He even billed a few clients for some of the time he spent fucking Teracita. Talk about getting your cake and eating it to!

Where to search? Teracita had no friends here, and no family. She'd avoid returning to Mexico. Carlo was certain of that. Perhaps she'd gone back to Miami. Possibly even returned to the Conti's, though that would be a mistake. She'd be deported for sure.

Then Carlo remembered Teracita's visit to the little church across the bridge. What was it that priest had said to her? Oh Yes..."*When you're ready child God is there for you...and so am I.*"

He waited until it was dusk before parking his Mercedes across the street from the church. Carlo approached the rectory cautiously. He'd brought an old business card from his days with the Rose Law Firm with him. When the priest answered his knock Carlo presented the card and introduced himself. He was an investigative attorney from Miami working on a missing person's case.

Carlo asked the priest for a few minutes of his time. Father Branigan showed him in. He lead Carlo to a seating area just off the foyer then went for iced tea. It was a warm night.

The priest returned with two glasses of ice and a carafe of tea balanced on a metal tray. As he set it down Carlo went into his spiel. "*I represent a prominent family from South Florida. My clients hired a young Mexican woman as a nanny. This young lady has gone missing and the family is quite concerned. They fear she may have been taken advantage of. I've been hired to locate her."*

Father Branigan was suspicious. Could this have anything to do with the poor child who showed up on his stoop several nights ago? He questioned the lawyer's assumption that something sinister had happened to the missing woman. Had he considered the possibility she just got homesick and returned to Mexico? Had anyone tried contacting her parents? There was more to this story. The priest sensed it. He asked his visitor how long the young lady had been missing?

Carlo could tell the priest wasn't buying his fabrication. He decided a story line made up of half truths would be more palatable to the old geezer. *"Okay, Padre, You got me,"* he said. *"The truth is the young woman has been missing for nearly four months. Her name is Bonita Suarez. She was hired through the American Au Pair program run by the State Department. As her sponsors, my clients are responsible for her while she's in this country. Now they are facing criminal charges for failing to notify the INS when their Au Pair went missing. It is my client's identity I was trying to protect."*

The priest fell for it. What lawyer worth his weight couldn't lie through his teeth. Carlo ranted on. *"My clients assume Ms Suarez has returned home, but they are afraid to contact the parents in case she hasn't. Being public figures, it would be very embarrassing for my clients if they were forced to appear in federal court to answer charges."* It was obvious Father Branigan took the bait. He leaned forward as Carlo reeled him in.

Carlo told the priest he'd spent the past month following leads. The trail had brought him to Daytona. *"Today I spoke with an acquaintance of Ms Suarez,"* the lying attorney continued. *"She told me she saw Bonita a week ago, and that she'd mentioned visiting a priest at a parish across the bridge. I assumed that parish was this one...and the priest was you."*

The attorney's story sounded plausible, and the priest bought it. Father Branigan told Carlo the young woman had shown up in the middle of the night a few days ago. She'd been badly beaten. The girl had claimed she didn't know her attacker, and begged him not to call the police. She was being housed at the domestic abuse shelter. Father Branigan said he wasn't at liberty to divulge the location.

Carlo thanked the padre for the information and got up to leave. When the two men reached the door Carlo offered his hand in gratitude. He told the priest his clients would be happy to hear Teracita was safe. Father Branigan froze. He let go of Carlo's hand and asked, *"Who did you say was safe?"*

The attorney looked at the priest oddly, then realized his Freudian slip. The priest recapitulated what he'd heard. *"You referred to the young woman as Teracita... You meant your clients would be happy to hear 'Bonita' was safe... Didn't you?"*

Carlo shrugged his shoulders. He made some half ass excuse about trying to keep names straight, then tried to change the subject. He asked Father Branigan if anyone else lived in the rectory. *"No... It's just me these days,"* he answered.

The issue had been eating at Father Branigan for some time. He'd spent over twenty years in that rectory, and now they wanted to close it. He felt compelled to complain. *"They tell me my church is no longer satisfying the needs of the community. The diocese plans to lock the doors once I retire. That's why it's in such disrepair. They don't want to put money into a place they plan to shut down."* Then he interjected, *"I guess the Little Lamb and I will be going to the slaughter together."*

A bead of sweat formed on Carlo's forehead. He wiped it away, while suggesting the priest turn up the air conditioning. Father Branigan told him it had malfunctioned months ago and the diocese won't get it fixed. A disquieting smile spread across the evil attorney's face. *"Damn budget cuts,"* he uttered as he started towards the door. Just before leaving Carlo turned back and said to the priest, *"To bad, Padre... It's going to be a warm night."*

Carlo didn't have to search for the location of the shelter. As an attorney he had privy to such information. He would set up surveillance and stake out the sight. He owned equipment that would help. The last time it had been used was several years back, when he was gathering evidence in a kick back scheme involving several immigration officials at Miami International Airport. That case had won him notoriety amongst the partners at Galen Rose, and the admiration of the *Los Norte* cartel.

The shelter sat on five acres of land south of downtown Daytona Beach. It was surrounded by a tall wrought iron fence. The fence had a voice activated security gate with motion detection cameras situated on either side. The facility had additional cameras strategically placed around the perimeter of the property. There was a police satellite office located on site also, staffed by citizen cops who fancied themselves *Officers of the law.*

Bordering the shelter property was a densely wooded area that overlooked the facility's parking lot. Carlo would have no trouble concealing surveillance cameras amongst the brush. His equipment would allow him to remotely monitor anyone entering or leaving the property. He could follow the activity on his laptop and use his attorney privilege to access data on any one he chose to. It was amazing how much information could be gathered from a license plate number. That was tomorrow's toil. Tonight's work was still unfinished. He had a little surprise in store for Teracita.

EARLY RETIREMENT

MURDER IN DAYTONA

22

Veronica spent most of the day working on the Diedra Daniels case. As a court advocate it was her job to assist a victim, inform her of her rights, and provide support. She wasn't allowed to address the court per se, but often times judges would suggest victims talk with an advocate prior to addressing the court.

It was women like Diedra that motivated Veronica to volunteer. Forced to do what she'd done to survive, Diedra had fallen through the cracks. Her situation, caused by a company she'd given twenty years of her life to, was not unique. It was one of those stories that rarely gets told, or falls upon deaf ears when it does.

Like so many others who'd lost their jobs to corporate greed, Diedra had picked up the pieces of her shattered life and moved in search of a better life. Little had she known when she left North Carolina that she'd end up homeless, much less beaten and raped. Nor had she foreseen she'd be living in a shelter for battered women.

Veronica had introduced Diedra to Teracita just days before. The two women seemed to hit it off despite the difference in their ages. Teracita was slow coming out of her shell at first, but she eventually allowed Diedra to get close. She even admitted knowing the man who'd beat her.

Diedra's hearing was being held at the County Courthouse in Deland. Veronica asked her case manager for permission to bring Teracita along, thinking the experience might help her. The three women could ride together in Veronica's car. Afterwards they'd celebrate Diedra's victory with lunch at Giacobbe's, a New York style eatery that Veronica had been yearning to try.

Veronica arrived at Teracita's door the next morning expecting to find her dressed and ready to go. Instead Teracita wasn't there. The door to her room was wide open so Veronica stepped inside. Clothes were thrown everywhere and Teracita's furniture was overturned. Veronica went searching for her.

She found Teracita curled up on the sofa in the community room. She was lying in a fetal position. Veronica rocked her in her arms awhile. Eventually Teracita calmed down enough she could ask her what happened.

Teracita choked back a few tears and pointed to the television, which Veronica hadn't even noticed was on. A Disney commercial was playing, followed by a weather update. It was going to be another warm muggy day in central Florida.

When the weather forecast ended a television reporter came on the air with news of a deadly early morning fire that had claimed the life of a catholic priest. The reporter said the fire had destroyed the rectory of the Little Lamb of the Sea Church in Daytona Beach. Veronica felt Teracita tighten up again.

Father Benjamin Branigan, a priest who lived alone in the rectory hadn't survived. The reporter said a faulty air conditioner was determined to be the cause of the blaze. He mentioned the church was due to be closed within a few months.

Veronica recalled Teracita had been brought to the shelter by a priest. She sat staring at the television screen, stunned. Could it be a coincidence? Could the very priest Teracita had gone to for help come to such an unlikely death? Obviously Teracita didn't think so. Her reaction spoke volumes as to what she believed.

"Is there anything you'd like to tell me," Veronica asked? *"Do you know someone who might have had something against this priest, Teracita?"* She waited for a response but none came. *"You know the fire marshals have blamed the fire on a faulty air conditioner? They have ways of determining if someone tampered with it."*

She waited a moment, then added, *"Perhaps we shouldn't jump to conclusions. After all...fires happen...and people die. Sometimes bad things happen to good people."*

Veronica knew she was running late. She had to get going. Diedra's hearing was scheduled for ten o'clock and it was a half hour drive to Deland. She brushed Teracita's hair away from her face and told her to get some rest. They'd talk when she got back this afternoon.

She went to the dining room where she found Diedra entertaining the other residents with stories about life on the street. The woman's resilience was inspiring. Veronica thought back to what she'd told Teracita moments before... Sometimes bad things happen to good people!

It was nearly half past nine when the two women exited the side entrance of the shelter and got in Veronica's car. If she hurried she'd just make it to court on time. Most days the courts had a full docket, but domestic abuse cases usually got priority over many others. She assumed it was because the judges felt victims had suffered enough without the added hassle of spending all day waiting for a hearing. Truth was county court took care of county business first, followed by attorney represented cases, then those appearing without council.

As Veronica drove out of the parking lot and through the security gate she passed a silver Mercedes parked on the side of the road. The driver of the Mercedes had come with surveillance equipment, intending to install it in the thick brush that bordered the parking area of the women's shelter. Carlo smiled as he thought about the reaction Teracita must have had when she heard the news about the fire at the rectory. Such a terrible tragedy! Of course he knew that she knew it wasn't accidental... No one could prove it!

He found a well concealed tree branch fifty feet from the shelter's fence. It provided an unobstructed view of the parking lot and employee entrance. With his motion activated surveillance camera in place Carlo could monitor the shelter from the comfort of his office or his living room. Anywhere really. The entire installation took him less than twenty minutes. He made his way through the wooded area to a side street, then hightailed it back to his car. Ten minutes later Carlo was sitting in his office billing the time it had taken him to install the equipment to one of his unsuspecting clients.

EARLY RETIREMENT

MURDER IN DAYTONA

23

They arrived at the courthouse with five minutes to spare. Veronica asked Diedra to sign them in while she went to park the car. Diedra's hearing was scheduled behind two others, giving them plenty of time to prepare.

Veronica coached her client on what to say in court. She wanted Diedra's attacker brought to justice and her client protected. Government funding was available to help victims like Diedra become independent. Veronica thought she might qualify for enough to get her set up in an apartment.

Criminal charges hadn't been filed against the man accused of attacking her. Circumstances surrounding the case led the district attorney to believe Ms Daniels was not without some fault. For one thing she hadn't been cooperative during the investigation. The police report stated she'd refused to specify where the alleged attack took place. She also refused to answer when asked if she'd been raped.

As for the attack itself, the report stated that when the alleged perpetrator tried to kiss the plaintiff she'd bit him on the tongue. The D.A. suggested the alleged attacker may have been within his rights to protect himself.

An investigation conducted by the Volusia County Sheriff's Department determined the plaintiff had known her attacker for several months. The two squatters lived together in a ramshackle building off State Route 40. An automobile found on the property, identified as belonging to the plaintiff, had been seized by the sheriff's department. They justified their actions by saying the vehicle had been used during the commission of a crime, i.e. trespassing and unlawful entry.

Veronica was fuming when she walked out of the courthouse. The judge had ruled against the plaintiff. There was no proof the alleged attacker wasn't acting in self defense. There also wasn't any proof Diedra had been sexually assaulted. The fact she wasn't brought up on criminal charges herself was a blessing, in the judgement of the court.

The only thing that might have saved her ass was that the owner of the orange grove didn't want to press charges. On the other hand the decision to seize her automobile and sell it at auction was upheld by the judge. He did approve a request that Ms Daniels be granted a one week extension before she had to leave the shelter however.

Both women walked to the parking garage in a daze. Veronica was visibly more upset than Diedra. Her faith in the system had been shaken. They sat in the car for ten minutes as Veronica went on and on about the unfairness of it all.

She eventually pulled herself together. Veronica asked Diedra if she still wanted to have lunch. Any thoughts of a celebration were put on hold, but Giacobbe's beckoned. It was only a five minute drive to the center of town.

Veronica parked her beetle opposite the restaurant and the two women made their way to the crosswalk. As they stood waiting for the light to change Veronica saw a vaguely familiar face on the other side of the street. A woman close to her age stood waiting to cross, aided by a walking cane. She was tall and thin, and had short blonde hair. When she looked up their eyes met. It couldn't be possible... Doris Van Fleet... Here in Florida?

When the sign flashed *WALK* Veronica made her way across the street while the woman with the cane waited. When she got there the two embraced. It had been over twenty years since they last saw each other, and they hadn't exactly parted friends. Even so, their greeting was genuine.

"I heard you'd moved to Florida," Doris said. *"Heard you're retired now, same as me!"* Doris glanced over at Diedra admiringly and asked her one time lover, *"So who's your friend here?"*

Veronica introduced Diedra, and said they were about to have lunch at Giacobbe's. After a moment of contemplation she asked Doris to join them. It felt weird running into Doris so far from home so many years later. *"Divine intervention,"* Doris joked. *"You still a Holy Roller, Vee? You were a born again Christian as I recall."*

While the three women waiting for a table Veronica gave Diedra a short synopsis of her and Doris' relationship, explaining *"It's all in the past now. Life goes on."*

Not one to let an opportunity pass her by Doris chimed in, *"Since you brought it up, how's your husband? What's his name... Oh yes... Richard."*

Rather than take the bait Veronica changed the subject. She told Doris about her volunteer work at the women's shelter, adding she was there in Deland today because Diedra had a court hearing. To her credit Doris was more than a little interested in learning the details.

Her disgust of the evil doings of man was apparent. When Doris heard about the judge's ruling she slammed her fist on the

202

table in anger. The action caused the lady seated behind her to stop her conversation mid-sentence and glare over at her.

Doris didn't pay her no mind. She reached across the table and ran her fingers over Diedra's injured eye socket. *"You poor girl,"* she said. *"It don't take away from your good looks though. Not one bit, Hon. With your figure no one's gonna notice a minor thing like that."*

After she finished eating Diedra excused herself and went to the ladies room. Doris took advantage of the fact she was alone with Veronica. She took her hand and said, *"Honestly Veronica, it's okay. I've happy with my life, and you're happy, right? So things worked out."*

The two seemed more like old friends than bitter ex-lovers. Doris hadn't changed much though. She told Veronica, *"Your friend has a hot little body. I do like younger woman you know... She deserves better, the poor kid."*

Doris mentioned she had a small place over in Mount Dora. It was owned by a friend of hers. She'd moved there after retiring. Doris neglected to mention her back injury, or the fact she was on permanent disability.

Veronica never asked about the cane, thinking it inappropriate. When Diedra returned from the restroom they ordered coffee and discussed her situation. Veronica mentioned the fact Diedra could be homeless soon. Doris suggested she might be able to help her out. She had acquaintances who were small business owners.

Doris leaned across the table and whispered, *"That is if you don't have a problem working for lesbians. The good thing is they'll treat you fair, pay you a decent wage, and won't concern themselves with your personal life."*

Diedra responded a little to loudly, *"NOT A PROBLEM MS VAN FLEET... I LOVE LESBIANS!"* Two women seated at a nearby table heard Diedra's boisterous response and started giggling. One of them gave her a hearty thumbs up.

Before leaving Doris took down the number of the pay phone at the shelter. She said she needed it in case she had to contact Diedra with information about a job. After some coaxing she swapped Facebook addresses with Veronica. The volunteer advocate suggested they keep their rekindled friendship secret until she had time to break the news to her husband. Doris was certain it would be met with resistance on his part.

She told Veronica to tell her hubby he had no cause for concern. His wife was to damn old for her. Doris hugged Diedra goodbye then whispered something in her ear. Diedra nod in agreement. Veronica couldn't help but notice the affectionate way the two women related to each other. She'd have a serious talk with Diedra on the way back to the shelter. Doris might seem nice, but Veronica knew the beast that dwelt within.

Carlo watched on his laptop as a red VW Beetle pulled into a parking space. Two women got out. The older one was well dressed. She exited the driver side carrying a briefcase. The passenger was younger. She was casually dressed and had short curly brown hair. Carlo thought she had a shapely body, but even from that distance he could see her face was pretty messed up.

He jotted down the car's license tag and added it to his list. So far Carlo had nearly a dozen numbers to research. He snickered at the thought of adding his play time to one of his clients accounts.

Veronica went directly from the parking lot to Teracita's room. She found her fast asleep. An aide told her she'd been sleeping all day, and wondered if Teracita was sick. Veronica assured her she wasn't. Just then her case manager happened to walk down the hallway. She saw Veronica standing outside Teracita's door and asked her how court went.

Veronica told her boss how bad the judge had treated Diedra. She pulled out notes she'd taken, with quotes made by the judge. She told her about the extension Diedra had been given before she needed to be out of the shelter. *"This poor girl has done nothing wrong, yet the judge threatened her with jail,"* she complained.

Her case manager reminded her she was just an advocate, with no power to change the system. Veronica responded, *"The bastard even let them confiscate her car, the one thing of value Diedra still owned."*

The next couple of days were spent trying to find Diedra a job. In less than a week she'd be tossed out on the street. In this economy jobs were scarce. Veronica knew people with college degrees who were bagging groceries or restocking shelves at Walmart. Finding a job that paid a livable wage, especially for a homeless woman with a questionable past, would not be easy.

Doris sent Veronica an email asking to be accepted as a Facebook friend. Veronica did so hesitantly, then immediately deleted the message. The two women would need to carry on their friendship in secret for now. Veronica was kind of surprised at how much Doris had changed. She knew she could never let your guard down though. Not with Doris. She was a sweet talking pussycat that could turn rabid in a heartbeat.

Diedra recieved several calls from Doris over the next few days. Doris told her she talked to some friends and got some feedback about a possible job. The brother of a lesbian couple she knew owned a wholesale flower business just outside Mount Dora. He was in need of someone to work in shipping and receiving.

The guy was willing to train the right person as long as they were honest and hard working. The job paid several dollars an hour above minimum wage, and came with benefits. The only catch was Diedra would need to relocate to Mount Dora. She wasn't going to be able to walk there from Daytona Beach on a daily basis.

When Veronica heard about the offer she was at first ecstatic, then suspicious. She knew Doris had a way of putting people in situations where they gave up control. If Diedra accepted this offer she'd be subjected to the lesbian lifestyle. Veronica wondered if it was deja vu all over again!

The three of them agreed to get together to discuss the pros and cons of the offer. Diedra wanted Veronica's input. She'd come to trust her judgement. Doris suggested meeting at the public library down the street from the shelter. They could use one of the conference rooms.

Veronica was leery about meeting so close to home, fearing her husband might find out. She asked if they could meet somewhere further away. Doris mentioned the library in New Smyrna Beach. It would be a bit of a drive, but no one knew them there. They agreed to get together at noon the following day.

Carlo had to meet with a client at nine that morning. The client was trying to bring his wife's family into the country, but he was getting flack from Immigration. Ever since homeland security took over immigration things had gotten much more difficult. The family was Brazilian, which didn't help. Tensions were running high between the two countries. The fact Brazil's new president had established close ties with Venezuela didn't sit well with the White House.

Hugo Chavez was head of the Socialist Party in Venezuela. He'd often stated his hatred for the United States and its military-industrial war machine. Again oil was at the center of the political decision making process. The up and coming Brazilian economy was reliant on a cheap and plentiful supplier. Chavez offered what they needed, more so then the freedom fighters to the North.

When his meeting ended Carlo decided to drive by the shelter. He parked on a side street with a view of the shelter's front gate intending to spend an hour or so watching people come and go. The surveillance camera was operating perfectly. Carlo was receiving a crystal clear picture on his laptop.

He wasn't there ten minutes when three women appeared on his screen. They came walking out the side exit and headed towards the red beetle he'd seen the other day. The older woman with the briefcase got in the driver's seat. The one with the short brown hair rode shotgun. The third woman was younger than the other two. She was dressed in a tight floral print jumpsuit and red heels. The dark haired beauty squeezed into the back seat. Carlo immediately knew who she was... Teracita!

As the three women approached the gate it slid open. Veronica stopped, looked both ways, then headed south on Beach St. Carlo glanced up from his laptop as she went past. He closed the lid and fired up the engine.

He could see the red VW in the distance. *"Slow down, Bitch,"* Carlo said out loud. Veronica tended to have a heavy foot... Old habits die hard.

Carlo followed the women down South Dixie Freeway. He caught a red light and watched his prey disappear in traffic. Filth spewed from his lips as he punched the steering wheel. An obvious overreaction to the situation.

When the light changed Carlo proceeded slowly, checking to his left and right hoping to see signs of a red VW Beetle. He fought the urge to speed up, thinking they may have pulled off somewhere. No such luck!

Just past the New Smyrna Beach Public Library Carlo caught yet another red light. He was seething mad. He was about to give up when he happened to glance in his rear view mirror. A glimmer of sunlight was reflecting off a shiny little red car sitting in the parking lot of the library. Carlo made a U-turn and circled back.

Knowing it made sense to sit tight and wait for the women to come out, Carlo went inside anyway. If Teracita caught sight of him she may react badly? He'd need to be careful. Carlo wandered around the library checking every nook and cranny. When he didn't see them he rushed back to the parking lot to see if they'd somehow left without being spotted. The VW was still there.

Reentering the building Carlo noticed a sign directing patrons to the library's conference room. He headed down a long hallway and saw light coming from one of the rooms. A large window allowed for visual observation of the room but no sound could be heard coming from it. Carlo peeked in. The three women were huddled around a conference table.

The older one with the briefcase sat at the head of the table. The woman with the short brown hair sat on the side facing him. Teracita had her back to the window. As Carlo peered in he was startled by someone brushing by him. *"S'cuse me, Buddy"* a woman with a cane bellowed as she squeezed past. The woman burst into the conference room and announced, ***"I'm here... Sorry I'm late."***

Carlo made his way down the hall, wanting to verify that it dead ended. The only way out was back through the main library. He returned to the lobby and took a seat in the magazine section. The spot afforded him a clear view of the hallway.

Veronica introduced Teracita to Doris and gave her a brief synopsis of her situation. Doris' response was to scold the young Au Pair. *"Why you girls put yourselves in these positions is beyond me,"* she told her. *"Any man pushes me around, I'll kill the mother fucker."* Veronica told Doris that comments like that were part of the problem, explaining it lays blame on the victim rather than the abuser.

Doris thought about what Veronica said. She conceded, sort of. *"You're absolutely right Veronica, but no man has a right to rough up a woman, no matter the reason. I'd kill the bastard!"*

Doris was sitting next to Diedra. She put her arm around the back of her chair and said, *"So Dee, I talked to some friends of mine. I can get you a job working at a flower shop. The pay is pretty decent...and they offer bennies. It's in Mount Dora though."*

Veronica piped in. She asked Diedra what she thought of the offer, reminding her the job was all the way out in Mount Dora. Diedra told her she'd never worked in a flower shop before, but it sounded good.

Doris turned to Diedra and clarified her statement, *"It's a wholesale flower business, Dee. They supply flowers to flower shops. You'd be doing shipping and receiving, but they'd train you!"* Diedra smiled a big wide smile and thanked her. Doris smiled back and said, *"Mount Dora's beautiful this time of year!"*

The women discussed Diedra's short term needs. She'd have to acquire some clothing and find a place to live relatively close to her place of employment. Veronica decided to take the bull by the horns. She asked Doris what her intentions were concerning Diedra. Doris responded, *"You know me. I plan to bring her over to the dark side."*

The comment brought a chuckle from the younger women but Veronica wasn't laughing. Doris got serious too. *"Diedra's a big girl. Ain't nobody gonna mess with her that she don't want to mess with. Besides, as far as I'm concerned I'm just helping out a sister in need."*

Veronica didn't respond to Doris statement. She more or less ignored it. She told Diedra she'd help her search for housing once her employment was secured. Doris arranged to pick Diedra up the next morning. She'd drive her out to meet her new employer. Doris told her she'd have to take a urine test, but other than that the job was a sure thing. With that they headed out.

Carlo held a magazine up to his face when he saw them coming. Veronica and Diedra headed towards the exit while Teracita and the skinny blonde with the cane went to the ladies room. He waited, hoping to get Teracita alone. It didn't happen. The two went in the restroom together and came out together. Carlo followed them out.

Veronica had pulled up to the front of the building. The passenger side door was open and the front seat pulled forward, allowing Teracita to jump right in. Carlo watched the red beetle speed off with his property inside. He saw the gimpy blonde with the big mouth walk to the far end of the parking lot. She got into a cream colored Jeep Wrangler with New York plates.

Doris started the engine and checked her rear view mirror. She saw the reflection of a well dressed Latino man. He appeared to be watching her. The guy was dressed in a silk suit and tie and wore his hair in a pony tail. She got out of the vehicle and yelled to him, *"Can I help you?"*

He smiled, then turned and walked away. Doris swore it was the same guy she'd passed in the hallway earlier. The one that had been peering through the conference room window. *"**Creep,**"* she

210

hollered after him before getting back in her Wrangler and driving off.

Carlo followed her from a distance. He didn't know who this woman was, or what her connection to Teracita was, but he was going to find out. She had balls, that he did know. If confronted she'd show no fear.

Doris turned on State Route 44 and headed west towards Deland. When she got to County Road 46 she made a right. She didn't have a clue someone was following her. Twenty minutes later she passed a sign that welcomed drivers to, *Mount Dora... The Little Gem On The Lake.*

Just past the sign sat the gated community of Mytilene. The entrance was quite impressive. A tall iron gate surrounded by a beautiful coquina stone wall. Carlo watched the jeep disappear behind the gate as he approached. *"End of the line,"* he said to himself. *"I'll be back... You filthy cunt!"*

EARLY RETIREMENT

MURDER IN DAYTONA

24

Roy Lane was the flower wholesaler who agreed to hire Diedra. He was a mild mannered guy around forty years of age. Roy ran another flower business up in Massachusetts, spending his time equally between the two. His employees were expected to be self managed and self motivated. Lane neither grew flowers, nor sold them retail. His was strictly a wholesale ship and receive operation.

Once she'd secured Diedra's employment Doris took her back to her place. The two enjoyed lunch together then took a tour of the gardens. Diedra had never been exposed to such enormous wealth, nor to the lesbian lifestyle. It was eye opening to see women expressing themselves so freely. Diedra observed women affectionately cooing one another at the pool. Some took turns massaging their partners with suntan lotion. As dusk fell Diedra gave in to Doris' flirtatious exploits. Her first lesbian encounter was simply another notch on Doris' belt.

When Veronica phoned the shelter the next morning she learned Diedra wasn't there. She contacted Doris and discovered her client had spent the night in Mytilene. Disappointed though she was she agreed to pick Diedra up and take her house hunting.

Mount Dora proved to be an expensive town to live in. Rental properties were scarce. The few that were available were well above Diedra's means. Fortunately a small affordable single wide in a trailer park just outside town had just been vacated. Veronica put up the first month's rent and security.

The women planned a house warming party for the following weekend. Veronica emptied her cupboards of extra dishes and cookware and at the crack of dawn she drove over to the shelter to pick up Teracita.

The poor girl didn't utter a word the entire way. Father Branigan's untimely death still weighed heavy on her mind. Arriving just after seven, Veronica planned to spend most of the day getting the trailer live in ready. Diedra had spent the night with Doris. Neither of them was there yet. Fortunately the front door was unlocked. The two went inside and got started.

An hour later someone pulled in the driveway and beeped their horn. The girls peeked out to see Doris behind the wheel of a rented cargo van. Diedra was directing her as she backed up to the doorway. After she was parked Doris unlatched the cargo door and slid it open. *"Furniture delivery,"* she hollered.

She'd found a used living room set for sale on Craig's List. The brown leather furniture was in near perfect condition, and cost less than half what it went for new. A stop at a local consignment shop added a small dinette set, as well as a used headboard, mattress, and small dresser to their haul. Diedra was well on her way to claiming independence.

By noon the entire trailer was spic n span. Diedra joked she could eat off the floors, but thanks to Doris she wouldn't have to. Doris walked over and gave the beaming woman a great big hug. Veronica thought it lasted for an uncomfortably long time. She also thought she saw a twinge of hesitation on Diedra's part before she hugged back. When the much older dyke finally released her grip she turned and asked if anyone was getting hungry. All three women answered in unison, *"I am!"*

Doris said she had to return the cargo van and pick up her car. On the way back she'd stop at the supermarket. When she left

Veronica cornered Diedra in the bedroom. She asked her how she was doing. *"I'm doin' all right,"* she answered. *"Why?"*

Veronica told her she was concerned about her, explaining she knew Doris' mode of operation. *"She might be quite a bit older now,"* she warned, *"but a leopard doesn't change its spots."*

"I owe her Veronica," Diedra responded. *"I owe her a lot. Doris wants me to admit I prefer girls, but I'm just not feelin it. You know what I mean?"* Veronica did. More than she could know.

Diedra felt the need to explain further. *"She's so much older than me. I mean she has to use a cane to get around. Doris is a nice lady and all, and she's sorta attractive, but you know... What am I gonna do?"*

Veronica told Diedra she'd talk to Doris if she liked, adding it wouldn't be the first time she'd burst her bubble. *"She's a big girl,"* she said. *"Doris can take it."* They went back to the kitchen to set the table for lunch. When they got there Teracita already had.

When Doris got back they had lunch. While feasting on tuna salad sandwiches and potato chips the girls listened to country music. Doris had Garth Brooks playing on her CD player. She'd bought a case of Rolling Rock when she went to the market. After tipping a few down she leaned her cane against the table and got up to dance. *"C'mon ladies,"* she said to the others. *"Don't just sit there. It's Garth Brooks for Christ sake."*

The four friends held each other shoulder to shoulder and danced around the tiny living room while Garth sang to them. There's bound to be rough waters, and I know I'll take some falls; But the good Lord is my captain, so I'll make it through them all...

The remainder of the day went much the same. Veronica was happy to see Teracita loosen up a bit. She'd sang and danced some. Even laughed a little. She was amazed this was the same girl she'd driven there that morning? Teracita even knew the words to some of Garth Brooks' songs! If nothing else, that alone made the effort worth it.

On the drive back to Daytona the two of them continued their tribute to country classics, each taking turns choosing tracks. Somewhere between the towns of Eustis and Cassia Veronica said, *"I think you may have seen the forest, Hon. It's not so scary when you're not lost anymore, is it?"*

Teracita smiled. She recalled her friend's attempts to help her calm her fears. Then she closed her eyes. She didn't open them again until the security gate of the shelter slid open to allow them inside.

Carlo hadn't seen them leave that morning. The attorney had been spending so much of his time performing surveillance he was falling behind at work. The misguided miscreant would have to spend at least part of his weekend at the office playing catch up.

He was well aware the law firms partners kept tabs on who was putting in the hours. His presence at the office wouldn't go unnoticed. Just having his car in the parking lot would garner him accolades. It's an amazing thing... Appearances!

Carlo arrived shortly after noon. Around three o'clock he heard a tap on his office window. He looked up to see a familiar face peering at him through the tinted glass. Jose Gacha, an old client from his days at the Rose Law Firm stood in the alleyway outside. He was accompanied by two thugs. Carlo leapt to his feet and sprinted to the back door. *"Senor' Gacha... What are you doing here, Sir"* he asked, obviously surprised by the visit?

Jose Gacha was the head of *Los Norte del Valle.* The last remaining remnant of the once powerful Medell'in drug cartel. Headquartered in Little Havana, the displaced Columbian crime ring was moving into other areas of opportunity.

Gacha had worked his way up the organization's chain of command by being a proponent of these changes. The vast amount of money the cartel made in narcotics was as plentiful in human trafficking. Gacha ordered his two bodyguards to return to the car. He wished to speak to his attorney alone.

They went back to Carlo's office, where Gacha took a piece of paper and wrote the words '**ARE WE ALONE.**' Once he was assured they were El Padrone spoke. It was in an unusual mix of Columbian spanish and broken english that he did. *"You forgot te veo luego... To say goodbye, Senor' Santiago."*

Carlo apologized profusely, telling Gacha he'd had to leave Miami expeditiously. He'd been given an opportunity here in Daytona, but he'd had to be available immediately. The lawyer suggested it was here he could make partner someday.

"Partner," Gacha angrily exclaimed! *"Yo creado identico, yo coasociado! Averno... I could've made you a King."*

Carlo told Gacha he appreciated everything he'd done for him, but he'd wanted to try to make it on his own. *"Ni siquiera uno... No one makes it on his own,"* Gacha erupted. *"Even I don't make it on my own... Comprende?"*

The powerful cartel boss softened his stance a little. He looked his attorney in the eye and asked, *"Por que abandoner... Why did you really leave, Carlo? Did it have anything to do with that Culona Chica? The woman-child they pulled out of that dumpster in Overton... Messy deal that was, Muchacho. The rats got to her before the cops did!"*

Carlo was stunned. How in hell did this guy know that? Senor' Gacha continued. *"What? You don't think we know about your little...problem?* **Christ sake, Hombre... Los Norte knows all!"**

The crime boss wasn't finished. He went on with his contemptuous onslaught. *"By the way, Senor' Abogado... Mr lawyer man... The little girl you dumped in that trash can was seventeen years old. Her Papa is a police captain in Lawrence, Kansas."*

Carlo buried his face in his hands and began to sob. The El Padrone grabbed him by his pony tail and yanked his head up. He slapped him hard across the face, then hollored, **"Knock off the bullshit, Carlo. I need to talk to you."**

Gacha had spent over a million dollars bribing high level homeland security officials in order to move his merchandise. A number of them had insisted on free samples. His merchandise? Little girls and boys... Some as young as ten years old.

They'd been purchased and traded for. Others handed over by duped parents. Some had been outright kidnapped. Regardless of how they'd been obtained the fact was they were being used to provide sexual gratification to those with the means to pay the price.

The cartel boss explained how the operation worked. Parents and relatives in eastern bloc countries were put in compromising positions. Often they were provided with drugs or jobs. Sometimes even sex. In exchange they would turn a child over to a decoy.

The unsuspecting youngsters were told they were going to America or Europe so they could have a better life. Some were to be adopted by wealthy couples. Others were told they would be trained as domestic workers. Teenage girls were often lured with promises of modeling careers. Many were simply taken by force.

"The gringo's had it coming," Gacha told Carlo... *"What goes around, comes around. That's how the world works, Muchacho!"*

He told his trembling attorney human trafficking is a forty-billion dollar a year business, adding most industrialized nations are involved in one way or another.

Some food for thought; A recent study done by the U.N. estimates the number of human beings living in slavery has reached twenty-seven million worldwide. Eighty percent of those are women and children. Many fall into the category of *'slave labor.'* That is they are forced to work against their will for no pay.

Over three million people are used in the sex trade alone. According to FBI estimates some twenty-thousand human beings are smuggled into the United States every year for the express purpose of providing sex for money.

Organized crime has a foothold in the human trafficking business, but they are not alone. The practice has afforded numerous nations the ability to purchase arms on the black market. The U.N. recently released a hot list of countries known to be involved. Among them is Iran, Syria, North Korea, Burma, Laos, Cuba, and Venezuela. Clearly the trafficking of human beings has become the commodity of choice for organized crime, replacing narcotics as the face of evil.

Jose Gacha needed someone he could trust to handle his legal immigration issues. Friends, relatives, and acquaintances from Columbia were desperately needed in Miami. Millions of dollars were being lost every single day because *Los Norte* didn't have the man power in place to control their interest. Some things needed to be handled legally. That's where Carlo Santiago came in.

Carlo suggested the Galen Rose Law Firm had the manpower and knowledge to handle Senor' Gacha's immigration issues. He told El Padrino it would be unethical for him to take business from his previous employer. Gacha replied pointedly, *"It is unethical to rape a seventeen year old girl, then beat her to death and toss her body in a garbage dumpster to be devoured by rats, Mr Santiago! No... You are my lawyer. You will handle my legal issues. Comprende, Senor?"*

Of course he would! Was he not his personal attorney? Carlo walked Senor' Gacha to the door and thanked him for his visit. When he returned to his office he laid his head down on his desk and whimpered like a sissy. He must have been crazy thinking he could just drive up the coast and disappear into thin air.

Gacha had assured Carlo no one would be coming after him for ethical misconduct or breach of contract. Anyway, his current boss would be pleased as punch. Representing someone like Jose Gacha was worth a fortune in new business. The concern he felt began to dissipate. Carlo realized with *Los Norte* protecting him he could probably get away with anything... Including murder!

He flipped his laptop open and rebooted. The shelter parking lot held the same cars that had been there before Gacha's visit. Carlo had been monitoring the lot since arriving at the office, with the exception of the hour that was interrupted by his highness. He decided to call it a day. The partners would be impressed by his work ethic. Imagine one of them spending a Saturday at the office!

Arriving back at his condo Carlo grabbed a cold beer from the fridge and flipped the television on. After watching the news he opened his laptop and brought up the image of the shelter parking lot. He sat back in his recliner and closed his eyes.

Three hours later Carlo woke to the sight of a red VW Beetle pulling into a parking space at the shelter. Checking the time at the bottom of the screen he noticed it was half past nine in the evening.

Veronica got out of the car and walked around to the passenger side. A beautiful girl with long dark hair stepped out. Carlo winced as the older woman wrapped her arm around her. Wide awake now, the attorney touched the screen and finger followed the two women as they walked arm in arm towards the entrance. Veronica held the door for Teracita and they disappeared inside.

Yes, he knew her name...Veronica Stevens of Ormond Beach, Florida. She was married to a Richard Stevens... Carlo stroked his ego. He was after all... A lawyer!

He'd begun his surveillance when he got to the office today. The two women must've left before then. *Who the hell gets up early on a Saturday,"* he wondered. It bothered him that he hadn't seen them leave. Still Carlo was glad he had a name to go with the face.

"Ve-ron-ic-a, Ve-ste-ee-vens," he mockingly sang to himself. He hadn't had as much success identifying the driver of the other vehicle though. The cream colored Jeep Wrangler with the out of state plates posed more of a problem. Carlo had limited access to information from outside Florida. Important thing was he knew where the Bitch lived. It was only a matter of time. He would enjoy seeing that cunt go down. What was it she'd called him? Oh yes... *CREEP.* Little did she know!

EARLY RETIREMENT

MURDER IN DAYTONA

25

A certified check made out to Headstrom and Downs Law Group arrived in the mail. An accompanying letter explained the $100,000 check was a retainer for the services of one of the firms associates, Mr Carlo Santiago. It was signed by Senor' Jose Gacha of Miami, Florida. The letter further stated Mr Gacha's desire that his legal matters be handled exclusively by Carlo Santiago.

The letter went on to explain their new client owned a thriving import/export business in south Florida. Gacha was hopeful Mr Santiago could assist him in bringing family members from his native Columbia to the United States. Included with the certified check and letter of introduction was a waiver of services signed by Senor' Gacha's previous attorney. Mr Galen Rose.

Senior partner Jim Downs asked Carlo to join him for lunch that afternoon. They braved the late summer heat and walked to the Daytona Hilton. The men dined in the steakhouse overlooking the beach and boardwalk. *"I received an interesting letter today,"* the senior partner announced. *"From a Mr Jose Gacha of Miami, Florida. It included a sizable retainer...and a request that you represent him."*

Carlo squirmed in his seat. He sipped his margarita as his boss continued his speech. *"We appreciate the business son. We need it. What concerns me is this Gacha fellow is a client of Galen Rose, your previous employer. You do understand it's unethical to hire an attorney from another firm with the intention of stealing away potential clients?"*

Carlo started to explain, but his boss cut him off. *"The letter stated Mr Gacha is no longer represented by the Rose firm. He attached a waiver signed by Galen Rose himself, releasing him as a client. Now would you mind telling me what the deal is between you and this client of yours?"*

The lying attorney shrugged his shoulders, then smiled and said, *"The old man trusts me, Sir!"* Downs looked at Carlo intently, then repeated his explanation back to him... *"Yes, Sir"* he answered. *"Senor' Gacha trusts me... You have to understand Sir, these old Columbian tradicionalista's are set in their ways. Mr Gacha is very old country. When he makes a pact with someone... It is considered unbreakable."*

Carlo explained how Galen Rose had assigned him to represent Senor' Gacha at his deportation hearing. *"We were successful in defending him in a case brought by the INS, Sir. Columbian officials in Bogota wanted him extradited to face charges there."*

Having his bosses ear, Carlo continued his diatribe. *"You see Sir, in Latin America it's common for government officials to go after wealthy expatriates. If they were successful they'd have put Gacha in prison until he agreed to release his assets. Then they would have dropped the charges. He'd be free, but completely penniless!"*

Downs considered his young associate's response. Who was he to look a gift horse in the mouth? The senior partner responded, *"Well in that case I'm glad to have him as a client."* He took a bite of steak, then facetiously asked Carlo, *"Got any more millionaires you care to send our way?"* The two men laughed and ordered more drinks.

Downs told Carlo he'd heard he spent most of the weekend at the office. *"That's exactly what we need more of around here, Son. Exactly the reason we brought you on board. You sort of remind me of... Well... Me!"*

With that the boss got up to leave. The firm had an expense account so it wasn't necessary to wait for the check. He slapped Carlo on the back as he rose from his seat, saying to him, *"Young man, we've never had a minority partner at Headstrom & Downs. Looks like that'll be ending soon."*

Carlo was walking on air as the two lawyers made their way back to the office. He envisioned the new company letterhead in his mind. **Headstrom, Downs & Santiago; Attorney's at Law.** He figured it was only a matter of time!

Once back in his office Carlo opened his laptop and resumed playing the role of private investigator. The red beetle was still sitting in the shelter's parking lot. He already knew the registrant, as well as her address and phone number. What he didn't know was her connection with Teracita.

Carlo spent the next several days researching license tag numbers. He discovered several of the cars in the shelter's parking lot were owned by single women. If he could just connect with someone inside it would make his next move so much easier. Picking up women had never been a problem for him. Fact is it was something of a curse. Carlo's problem was ignoring the one's he thought deserved his brand of *special treatment...*

After carefully considering the choices Carlo decided on a heavy set blonde. He knew from experience chubby women were easier to please. He also knew they were often attracted to men of color. His caramel complexion and green eyes would set her heart a pounding. Carlo was convinced when she found out the size of his endowment she'd be creaming her panties.

Jewel Abernathy was a thirty-six year old transplant from Iowa. She'd moved to Florida ten years before, newly married to an aeronautical engineer. Her husband had accepted a teaching position at Embry Riddle University, bringing his new bride to Daytona just weeks after the wedding. The marriage only lasted a few years. It turned out her husband was a closet homosexual who'd been cheating on her from the outset.

The poor bastard had been outed by the jealous fiance of one of his students. She'd unexpectedly shown up at her boyfriend's apartment one day to find him on the sofa engaging in copulation with his professor. Both men were wearing women's lingerie.

The girl eventually forgave her boyfriend after he convinced her he'd been duped by the lure of his cross-dressing professor. He'd claimed he was in danger of flunking out. When his professor offered a passing grade in exchange for sex he took the bait. That bit of information didn't stop the girlfriend from contacting Jewel and telling her all about her husband's sexual preferences.

His choice made, Carlo worked till mid afternoon then left for the day. He drove to the shelter and parked on a side street, then pulled out his laptop. The surveillance camera continued to work like a charm. It wasn't long before Jewel appeared on his screen. She came walking out of the shelter and squeezed her fat ass into a royal blue Ford Mustang. Carlo watched her drive through the gate and followed, careful to stay some distance back.

She stopped at a McDonalds drive thru. The attorney watched from across the lot as the plump blonde sat in her car wolfing down a Big Mac. When she finished she drove to a work out facility just down the road. Jewel pulled a gym bag out of her trunk and disappeared inside. Carlo parked his Mercedes along side his next victim's Mustang, then followed her in.

A tattooed woman at the counter offered to give Carlo a tour of the facility. He declined, asking if he could just meander around himself. He explained he wanted to get a feel for the place without the pressure of a sales pitch.

Scanning the room for his prey, he spotted her on a treadmill in the far corner of the gym. He made his way towards the back, stopping to admire a well muscled woman in the heat of battle with a machine. Eventually he got to where Jewel was working out.

She pretended to read a magazine as he approached. Jewel had been watching Carlo out of the corner of her eye ever since he walked in, drooling over his good looks. The shelter employee wore headphones, but turned the volume down when she saw him walking towards her. Carlo stood looking at the machine next to hers for a moment, then turned and smiled.

Jewel returned his smile, then went back to her magazine. Her heart was pounding. Carlo got on the adjoining treadmill but acted as though he didn't know how to turn it on. Jewel giggled, then hit the stop button on her machine and went to his aid.

In a nasally voice she said to him, *"You really shouldn't use gym equipment in street shoes. Don't you own any sneakers?"* Carlo explained he'd only stopped in today because he was thinking of joining a gym. *"Well you look like you're in decent shape,"* she responded. *"You obviously work out."*

Carlo told her he sometimes used the weight room at his condo, but thought he needed something more intense. *"Really,"* she flirtatiously replied. *"So you like intense?"*

The evil attorney could tell this was going to be easy. *"Yes,"* he told her. *"I like intense work outs. Intense movies. Intense women!"*

Jewel bit. She asked him what his interpretation of an intense woman was. *"Well,"* Carlo responded, *"An intense woman has curves...but she likes to keep them toned... Like you!"*

The chubby social worker blushed, then turned to leave. *"You going someplace,"* Carlo asked? Jewel didn't respond. She just looked over her shoulder and smiled as she walked away. Carlo called out after her, ***"Do you like movies?"***

Jewel stopped. She turned and responded in that irritating nasal voice of hers, ***"Yes... Intensely!"*** Carlo laughed. He liked this one, even if she was as fat as a friggin pig.

Carlo winked at the tattoo queen working the counter as he followed Jewel out the door. Watching her walk across the parking lot he thought to himself, *"Fat girls need lovin' too once in a while."*

When she got to her car and saw that Carlo had parked right next to her she thought it ironic. At the same time she was totally impressed with his wheels.

"Some things are meant to be," Carlo explained as he flirted with his prey. *"Shall we pick up a bottle of wine and a movie?"* Jewel suggested he follow her. She drove to a market up the street. Carlo ran inside for wine while Jewel chose a movie from the outdoor kiosk.

She lived in an apartment complex off Williamson Boulevard. A tiny one bedroom unit with paper thin walls and cheap carpeting. A couple black guys were shooting hoops when they pulled in. A netless basketball rim had been set up in the parking lot. White kids were skateboarding nearby. They stopped to watch as Carlo followed Jewel into the lot and parked his brand new Mercedes next to her aging Mustang.

This neighborhood didn't see many Mercedes C550's. It was more of a Chevy/Pontiac type neighborhood. Carlo locked his car then followed Jewel up a flight of stairs. When they got to the door she reached up and felt around the casing for the key. Carlo made sure to compliment her on having great legs while making a mental note of the location of the key.

Once inside Jewel went to change into something more comfortable. She returned wearing a loose silk jumper and curled up on the sofa with a bag of chips. Carlo opened the wine and sat beside her. *"So what do you do,"* she asked him in her nasally voice. *"For a living I mean?"*

Carlo wanted to punch her in the face, maybe clear up her nasal passages so her voice wouldn't annoy him so much. He fought the urge. He told Jewel he dealt in luxury automobiles, explaining it was a seek and find type service for wealthy clients. She responded *"That explains the Mercedes."* He feigned a laugh and admitted he could never afford a car like that otherwise.

He knew Jewel, like most women, liked to talk about herself. Carlo started to ask what she did for a living but before he could utter a word Jewel volunteered the information. *"I'm a social worker,"* she said. *"I like to help people."*

She went on for some time, telling Carlo stories of life as a counselor working with abused women. He pretended to be interested, hoping to lead her into divulging some information he could use. He listened as Jewel reiterated stories of young girls who'd been abused by controlling boyfriends or sexually assaulted by despotic stepfathers. Many of her clients had been emotionally mutilated by their psychotic parents. She spoke as though none of the little whores had enjoyed it. Carlo knew better.

Eventually they got cozy. Carlo suspected it had been a while since Jewel had enjoyed the company of a man. He found upon close investigation that she'd neglected to put anything on under her silk jumper. It provided him easy access to her large breasts and private areas.

Her tits were big and heavy, with huge brown nipples that swelled and hardened at his touch. She was an old fashioned girl down below. Most women were into the Brazilian wax thing these days, but Jewel was hairy as a sheepdog. Carlo envisioned tying her up and binding her tits till they turned purple. What fun it would be to bite into her swollen flesh.

Instead he settled for some finger fucking while she jacked him off. The look on Jewel's face when she unzipped his trousers was worth her weight in gold. It was as if she'd never seen a man's cock before. Her breathing increased and her chest heaved as she worked his shaft for all it was worth. He couldn't help thinking if she'd only work that hard at the gym she'd lose fifty pounds.

Amazingly, Jewel got off exactly when he did. With Carlo providing just the right clitoral stimulation, she gasped in orgasmic delight just as he unloaded all over her.

Carlo finished his wine, then said he had to be going. Jewel had stars in her eyes as she walked him to the door. On the landing he told her, *"Guess I made a mess, but you got me so excited I couldn't hold back."* Jewel giggled and apologized, like it was her fault. *"What a dumb cunt,"* he thought.

Carlo told Jewel he'd like to see her again. She wrote down her cell phone number and instructed him to call... Anytime! Carlo mentioned he was fascinated with the stories she'd told him about her work. He said he couldn't wait to hear more. Jewel watched as he walked down the stairs and crossed the parking lot. Just as Carlo was about to get in his car she yelled out...*"CALL ME!"*

His plan seemed to be coming together rather nicely. Carlo had successfully tracked down Teracita to the women's shelter by way of The Little Lamb of the Sea Catholic Church. He'd identified the person responsible for keeping them separated, a shelter volunteer named Veronica Stevens. He'd established a relationship with an employee of the shelter, a social worker named Jewel Abernathy. With luck she'd be the one counseling Teracita... Carlo would definitely be counseling Jewel!

For whatever reason this Veronica Stevens woman had chosen to butt in where she wasn't wanted. Carlo wondered if she was queer for his Teracita. The fact she'd wasted her weekend taking the young Au Pair out somewhere was puzzling. It certainly went beyond the scope of what a volunteer advocate's job duties were. Carlo knew government employees who sponged the system for everything they could squeeze from it. He figured if Veronica Stevens was putting forth this much effort there must be something in it for her.

Carlo knew the younger woman with the brown curly hair often accompanied her. Then there was that old blonde gimp with the cane. He disliked her the most! Carlo didn't know her identity yet, but he knew she was trouble. Between the three of them bitches his little Mexican flower wouldn't stand a chance of coming to her senses.

Now Carlo had an accomplice too. She'd help him rescue Teracita from their clutches. The attorney started spending less time performing surveillance and more time with Jewel. He took an avid interest in what she did for a living. He asked her all kinds of questions about the shelter and its occupants. The stupid slut was more than willing to talk about herself and her job.

Carlo cleverly feigned outrage for the victims and their situations. He wanted to know more about the younger women, especially those of latino descent. He asked if any clients ever got deported? If some received government services? He asked Jewel if photographs were taken when women came to the shelter after being abused, and if she was allowed to take files off the property?

He was a master manipulator, experienced in exploiting dim witted women. Carlo made Jewel feel as if he was engrossed in her work. As if she had the most important job on the planet. He discovered it was Jewel who originally interviewed Teracita the night she was brought to the shelter.

Jewel told him she wasn't assigned the girl's case, but she was familiar with it. She knew Teracita had been viciously beaten, and that she'd refused to name her attacker. She was aware the client was in the country illegally, though shelter policy dictated she was not to concern herself with that. A victim was a victim, end of story.

Things couldn't have fallen into place more smoothly if Carlo had planned it. He took that as a sign. His mission became less and less about Teracita and more about himself and his ego.

He got Jewel to eavesdrop on Veronica Stevens conversations. The axiom *The Walls Have Ears* was never more true. It was amazing what some women would do for a man. Carlo was able to train Jewel like a dog. The more useful the information she provided, the more she got fucked!

Jewel befriended the case manager. Eventually the two women became thick as thieves. The counselor would watch from her office window for her to arrive for work, then she'd make her way down to the manager's office to shoot the shit.

Much of their conversation revolved around the shelter's clients. Jewel made sure she asked about Teracita, the poor Mexican girl that had come to the shelter so badly beaten. She feigned interest by letting the manager know it was she who'd interviewed Teracita when she first arrived.

Veronica had no reason to be suspicious. She enjoyed Jewel's visits almost as much as her case manager did. She even told Jewel about the Diedra Daniels case, mentioning a friend of hers had helped place Diedra in a job. Veronica was proud of her work with Diedra. A homeless woman who'd arrived at the shelter beaten and abused only to have the system turn her away.

There were few success stories when it came to domestic violence. Most of the women had '*I am a victim*' patches sewn on their sleeves, or so it seemed. Many of them blamed themselves for their predicaments. The fact Diedra was self sufficient, a working woman with a place of her own, made it all worthwhile. Veronica had Doris to thank for that. It made her feel much better about her.

Jewel was smooth when it came to asking questions. No one would have suspected her ulterior motives. She showed an honest to goodness interest in learning more about this woman who'd helped a client find employment. She'd heard Carlo talk about her, saying he'd do anything to get her address. She knew if she got it she'd be in for the best sex of her life.

How many women in her shape were getting what she was getting? Carlo was a love god. He could fuck for hours...and he had the equipment to make women squeal with delight. He could take his partner over the edge on time...every time.

She managed to obtain Doris Van Fleet's phone number. When Carlo heard that he knew getting an address to go along with it would be a cinch. He concocted a plan to get even with the crippled bitch. She'd regret the day she ever laid eyes on him. She never should have angered him to begin with. He'd wanted to stuff that cane of hers right up her ass the first time she pushed by him at that library in New Smyrna Beach.

Knowing what he knew now perhaps he should have shoved it up her pussy instead. It might have been a life changing event for her. Carlo recalled following the old gimp out of the library that day. He couldn't believe she'd gotten out of her vehicle to confront him. The fucking dyke had balls. What was it she'd called him... Oh yes, *"Creep!"*

She had no idea how creepy Carlo could be. He had to fight the urge to drive out to her place and rape the piss out of her. When he was finished he'd dump her body in a swamp and let the alligators do the rest. The lesbian bitch was messing with his life. She was in cahoots with that other queer at the shelter. The two of them were messing up Teracita's head. They were keeping her away from him. They'd pay dearly for that.

Carlo talked Jewell into setting up a meeting with Veronica. She was to confide in her. He concocted the perfect fodder. Jewel would say she'd been engaged to someone a few years ago. She broke up with him because he physically assaulted her just days before they were to be married. Now he was back in town and he wanted to rekindle their relationship. She'd need to convince Veronica that she was once in love this guy, but now she feared him. She could say he wouldn't take no for an answer.

Veronica was on the floor filing documents into the bottom drawer of a metal filing cabinet when Jewel walked in. She told her the manager wasn't in today, then went back to filing. Jewel explained she didn't come to see the manager. *"I came to talk to you."* Veronica closed the file drawer and extended her hand so Jewell could help her up.

When she started talking the lies rolled off Jewel's tongue as though she believed them herself. She could have won an Oscar for her performance it was so dramatic. She didn't just repeat the story Carlo fabricated. She took it a step further.

Jewel embellished how her ex fiance would fly off the handle without provocation. She said the closer it got to their wedding day, the worse he got. Their marriage plans came to a grinding halt the day he smacked her across the face. *"He sent me sprawling across the floor and blackened my eye,"* she lied. *"I got a bloody nose and my face swelled up. I wasn't going to marry a man who beat me."*

She told Veronica he'd apologized, and promised to never lay a finger on her again. Then Jewel went into a rant. *"I'm a social worker for God sake. I'm employed by the domestic abuse council. I can't have a man using me as his punching bag. I broke off the engagement and told him I never wanted to see him again."*

After stopping to wipe tears away with a tissue Jewel continued. *"That was two years ago. I had to get an injunction to keep him away from me. He would call my house at all hours of the night telling me if he caught me with another man I'd be sorry. Sometimes I'd come out of the grocery store or the gym to find a note on my windshield. They were always full of violent threats and promises of how he would change. Finally he moved away. I heard he went to Tampa... Well, he's back!"*

Veronica took the bait. She told Jewel it sounded like her fiance followed the typical pattern abusers use. *"They strike, then apologize, then makes promises to stop, then strike again."*

Jewel told her she was afraid to stay alone at her apartment. That prompted Veronica to offer refuge at her place. Of course that wouldn't fit into Carlo's grand scheme. Jewel quashed that idea quick, saying she wouldn't dream of doing that. *"Besides,"* she said, (get ready because here it comes) *"I have a plan!"*

"I'm going to stay at a motel for a while," Jewel claimed. *"Long enough for my ex fiance to give up* and *go back to Tampa. I*

don't care if the place is four stars, as long as it's clean and I feel secure."

Jewel knew Veronica believed her. She figured the volunteer advocate was either very gullible or just plain dumb. *"I think I may have found just the right place too,"* she announced. *"The Pelican Inn. It's across the street from the ocean on A1A. He would never expect me to stay there. There is one catch though, Hon. I need to ask you a big favor."*

Veronica was willing to do whatever was necessary to help a friend in need. She was asked if she would consider getting the room in her name. Jewel explained it was important she remain anonymous. She told Veronica it wouldn't surprise her if her ex called every motel in Daytona Beach trying to track her down.

The plan was to have Veronica book the room for two nights, giving Jewel time to evaluate the place and decide whether she would consider staying there indefinitely. They could drive over to the motel together at lunchtime. Veronica would pay for the room with her credit card, then they'd return to work. Jewel would return later in the evening with her things. She asked Veronica if she would stop by in the morning to check on her. She could ask for two keys when she booked the room. That way she could let herself in.

Carlo's scheme was put in motion. After the two women booked the room they returned to the shelter and went back to work. Jewel spent the remainder of the afternoon fantasizing about the sex she and Carlo would be having that night. He would be so happy with her. Jewel knew when Carlo was happy... She was happy!

She didn't know what he had up his sleeve, and she didn't really care. Whatever it was it paid dividends to her. Jewel assumed Carlo must have a score to settle with Veronica or her husband. He

234

wasn't the kind of man who forgave debts. Anyway, she'd done her job. Tonight she'd reap the rewards!

Carlo met Jewel at the door when she got home from work. He had a strange contorted look on his face. It frightened her. Rather than enter the apartment Jewel took a step back. Carlo asked in a low monotone voice she didn't recognize, *"Do you have something for me?"*

Jewel knew what he was looking for. She felt around in her purse and pulled it out. Carlo snatched the key from her hand and examined it as if checking to see if it was real. It had an inscription on the plastic ring it was attached to. Property of the Pelican Inn ... Daytona Beach, Fl.

"My Little Tamale," Carlo exclaimed! The contortion on his face disappeared. He pulled Jewel inside and passionately kissed her. Like an animal in heat he tore her clothes off, squeezing and probing every inch of her ample body. He called her filthy vulgar names as he filled her with the entire length of his cock. *"Fat whore, Fucking pig, Cock worshipping cunt!"* The filthier Carlo spoke the more aroused she became.

They spent the next several hours performing acts Jewel had only fantasized about. They bordered on deviancy. The pounding she took brought Jewel over the edge and she had a mind blowing orgasm. After she came for the third time Carlo sat on her double chinned face and made her lick his asshole. Caught up in the heat of her lustfulness, Jewel darted her tongue in and out of his anal cavity with such gusto Carlo couldn't control himself. He spewed cum all over her.

The lust continued late into the night. Carlo didn't take long to reload. When he did, Jewel was ready. She was fucked every way imaginable, and Carlo made sure she came every time. The tub of lard was multi orgasmic. Jewel had an insatiable appetite. She didn't know what she'd do if Carlo ever stopped coming over.

She did know she could never go back to playing the dating game again. The only men Jewel ever seemed to attract were limp dicked momma's boys. Even her ex-husband had turned out to be a fag. She'd tried self stimulating herself with various devices but they hadn't done the job. Sex was a mind game, and Jewel needed the real thing. Now that she had a man who could satisfy her she'd do whatever she had to do to keep him coming back for more.

During a time out from their proclivities Jewel told Carlo Veronica had mentioned something about her husband going fishing the next day. She'd said she had to be home in time to cook dinner. Carlo took note of the information. He'd been hoping for an opportunity like this. It fit nicely into his grand plan.

He got up early the next morning. He slipped out of bed and got dressed. To avoid waking Jewel Carlo decided to forego taking a shower. He grabbed the key to the motel room off the night stand along with the note he'd printed off Jewel's computer. Then he headed out.

Carlo borrowed Jewel's Mustang and drove east. He parked on a side street a block away from the motel. He planned to slip in unnoticed.

He'd chosen The Pelican Inn specifically because of its location. The empty lot the seedy motel bordered provided easy access from the street. He could sneak in and out in relative obscurity. This was going to be fun. This old hag had done him wrong. Nobody fucked with a Santiago. His father had taught him that lesson as a child. He'd never forgotten it.

EARLY RETIREMENT

MURDER IN DAYTONA

26

Carlo was born in Havana. He was the seventh son of Rinalto and Juanita Santiago. His father worked at a meat packing plant, earning meager wages for the long hours he put in. His mother earned several national pesos a week doing the laundry of prominent families in the area. They lived in a rented shanty in the La Habana District, which borders the northern bank of the Almendares River.

Two of Carlo's brothers were involved in criminal activity. They were low level soldiers of *La Coporacion,* the Cuban Mafia. Both died when Carlo was just a small boy. They'd taken money for ratting out a man named Jose Battle, *El Padrino* of the Miami faction of *La Corporacion.*

The family of a close friend they'd known since childhood had been executed on orders given by *El Padrino.* Carlo's brothers provided information that resulted in Battle's arrest. For their trouble they were paid two-thousand American dollars.

Originally charged under federal RICO laws, Battle's lawyers negotiated a deal with the D.A. Their client eventually pleaded guilty to a reduced charge of obstruction of justice. He served three years in a medium security facility located outside Tampa, Florida.

When *El Padrino* avoided the murder rap the men who ratted him out were finished. Rinalto Santiago found his two eldest sons hanging from meat hooks at the processing plant where he worked.

They'd been skinned alive and left to rot over the 'National Day of Rebellion' holiday weekend.

Carlo's father swore revenge. It might take him a lifetime but he'd make those responsible pay. From that moment on it was drilled into his remaining sons heads. *No one fucks with a Santiago... No one!*

Rinalto's anger spilled over to his relationship with his wife. He started beating her regularly. It got so the remaining Santiago children couldn't sleep at night, the sounds from their parent's bedroom torturing them. Juanita Santiago's submissive nature wouldn't allow her to fight back. She tried to hide the scars and bruises she suffered, but her children knew.

She was an attractive woman. Though she'd borne seven children Juanita maintained a shapely figure. She had beautiful chestnut brown hair that stopped just short of her waist, and big brown eyes. Her large breasts continued to produce milk long after her last child was born, thanks to her husband's quirky desires.

One day she was collecting laundry from one of her prominent clients and her breasts leaked. The client got excited by the sight and made a pass at her. He happened to hold a powerful position as Undersecretary for the Municipal Assembly of Cuba. He also chaired the Committee for the Defense of the Revolution. Juanita was flattered to draw the attention of such an important man.

She understood the politician's attraction to her breasts. They were the source of life. She allowed her pursuer to suckle them. It felt good to have them emptied by someone other than her abusive husband. The two made love that afternoon, and made plans for future engagements.

Shortly after the affair began Juanita's lover noticed she had bruises on her body. The purple welts excited him more than her lactating breasts had. Juanita found his excitement excited her. The oppressive punishment her husband inflicted was unsolicited, but she looked forward to the erotic beatings her lover provided. After submitting herself to his crop he would suck the milk from her tits before untying her. Then the two would engage in heated bliss.

Rinaldo's anger ate at him. His inability to punish the people responsible for murdering his sons caused him to lash out at his own family. He turned to alcohol as a respite from the pain. He would often come home from a late night binge and rape his wife.

His remaining sons knew what was happening but they felt helpless to stop him. As a ten year old Carlo would lay in bed at night listening to his mother's whimpers as her husband forced himself upon her. In the morning after his father left for work he'd go to her room and cuddle with her. After a while Juanita started positioning herself so *her baby* could feed from her nipples. It became a regular routine.

At age twelve Carlo became suspicious. Several times a week his mother would leave to go collect laundry. She'd be gone most of the day but then come home empty handed. This one day he decided to follow her.

Juanita left early that morning. She walked nearly a mile before coming to a large hacienda that sat at the crest of a hill overlooking *La Viega Habana,* Old Havana. Carlo watched his mother enter the house without knocking. He snuck around to the side and found a window to peek through. What he saw would change his life forever.

His mother was being fondled by some man. A naked man. It was obvious he was excited by her presence. The man had a huge erection. Carlo watched as he disrobed his mother and tied her to a chair. His first inclination was to rush in and rescue her, but then he saw the look in her eyes.

He was immediately aroused. Carlo felt himself grow a huge erection of his own as the man got down on his hands and knees and put his face between his mother's legs. The boy took his swollen cock out of his pants and feverishly worked its shaft. When the man finished he untied the big breasted woman and led her to an adjoining room. Carlo rushed to secure a view.

Juanita was hoisted up and shackled to an iron swivel hanging from the ceiling. Carlo couldn't believe what he was seeing, or how much it excited him. His mother was dangling there several inches off the floor, stark naked.

Then the man picked up a rider's whisk. Carlo watched in shock as he started lashing his mother with it, leaving red welts across her bottom. He closed his eyes and masturbated to the sound of the whisk whipping his mother's ass cheeks. When the whipping ceased Carlo reopened his eyes. His mother had been taken down from the swivel and was now in her tormentor's arms. They were kissing passionately.

Without warning Juanita suddenly looked up and caught her son standing at the window. Their eyes met. Mother and son froze for a moment. Then she smiled, closed her eyes, and went in search of her lover's waiting mouth.

That night Carlo heard his parents fighting like never before. Normally Mrs Santiago submitted to her husband like a good catholic wife should. This night was different. She was screaming at him. Using all sorts of vulgar profanities. Carlo's father had come home drunk again, like he did many nights...and like many nights he started beating on his wife. This time she struck back.

In anger Carlo's mother told her husband she'd taken a lover. A man of importance. She didn't spare his feelings either. Juanita described in detail her lover's attributes and his ability to please. Rinaldo called his wife a liar, questioning who would want such a

240

hag. She laughed in his face. *"Don't believe me,"* she quipped? *Just ask your son!"* Then she walked out.

It was the last time Carlo ever saw her. Juanita disappeared without a trace. Come morning Rinaldo Santiago gathered his five remaining sons around the kitchen table to break the news. He told the three oldest it was time they fended for themselves. He gave each of them fifty pesos he'd put away for their weddings and led them to the door. He told his two youngest to prepare for a trip. He was taking them to Saint Elvira's, an english speaking school in Varadero, located on the outskirts of the city of Havana.

When they got to the school Rinaldo left the boys outside while he went inside to talk to the Headmaster. Fifteen minutes later he returned. He explained why he brought them there. He had business to attend. Important business that couldn't wait. The boys were to listen to the Headmaster. Rinaldo wanted them to work on their english speaking skills. He promised the boys he'd return for them when he could...

Carlo's father foresaw the day when Cuban men would be free to go wherever they pleased. He knew a better life could be found in the United States. Rinaldo apologized to the boys for their mother's behavior, and told them she wouldn't be coming back.

Before he left he took Carlo aside. Rinaldo confessed he knew what his wife had been doing, and asked his youngest son how it was he knew too? Carlo told his father he'd become suspicious. He decided to followed his mother to see what she was up to. *"Where did you follow her to, Little man"* his father inquired? Carlo told him about the large hacienda at the crest of the hill overlooking the old city. Rinaldo pondered for a minute, then said, *"You mean the home of the Undersecretary? Mmmmm... Good boy."*

A light went out in his father's eyes. Carlo saw it. A slight twinge caused the iris surrounding his pupils to go dull. He asked his father if everything was going to be okay. Rinaldo assured his son it would.

"Carlo," he told him, *"I want you to remember this always... Never ever trust a woman...and never ever let anyone fuck with you! Do you understand what I'm saying?"* Carlo assured him he did.

Rinaldo hugged his sons goodbye. Carlo sensed he would never see his father again. The thought frightened him. When the broken man released his grip on the boys he had tears in his eyes.

Carlo's fear came true. That was the last time he ever saw his father. He and his brother remained at Saint Elvira's until they were eighteen. Carlo was very intelligent. He excelled academically, easily passing every subject he took. His brother on the other hand struggled in the classroom. Vidal excelled in sports!

The boys were in their teens when they first learned their father had murdered someone. A political figure. Rinaldo had assassinated the Undersecretary of the Municipal Assembly of Cuba. He'd been hung for his crime.

Carlo knew the man his father killed was the same man he'd seen his mother with that day so many years ago. The man who'd tied his mother up and beat with a horse crop before making love to her. He remembered what his father said to him... You don't fuck with a Santiago!

Upon his graduation from Saint Elvira's Carlo was chosen to attend the University of Havana. In Cuba students didn't choose schools. Schools chose students. Because of his academic ability he was placed in an accelerated program.

Vidal hadn't been selected to attend university. He became a mechanic's apprentice learning how to maintain and repair diesel engines. The training helped him secure a position with *Empresa Caribe,* a commercial fishing outfit in Santa Clara. Cuba's second largest city was located about three hours from Havana.

Empresa Caribe had government approval to fish throughout the Caribbean. Thanks to a trade agreement with Canada the company was also allowed to fish Canadian waters. Carlo's brother made regular trips to Canada to perform maintenance on Cuban trawlers. He enjoyed his work, and was very good at it. The pay must have been good too because Vidal lived a very comfortable lifestyle when not at sea.

One day Carlo went to visit Vidal in Santa Clara. He asked his brother to help him get out of Cuba. Carlo seemed desperate.

He reminded Vidal it had been their father's dream that his sons go to America. Carlo wanted to bring that dream to fruition. He knew there were thousands of Cubans living in South Florida. He would have the best chance of assimilating into American society if he went there.

Carlo was smart. He figured Vidal was involved in something illegal in order to live so extravagantly. He just assumed it must be smuggling. People paid sea merchants a lot of money to smuggle them out of the country. Vidal had been living high on the hog ever since taking the job with *Empresa.* Carlo knew he couldn't pay for that lifestyle on a diesel mechanic's salary.

Vidal told Carlo he could make four times what he earned fixing engines by smuggling malcontents out of the country. Most commercial fishing vessels were involved with smuggling in some form or other. Companies like *Empresa Caribe* paid government officials large sums of money for their silence. He'd be glad to help his youngest brother get out.

Carlo neglected to tell Vidal the true reason he was so damn desperate to leave. He'd been struggling with an inner demon lately and the demon had won. He was at a disco in Old Havana a few nights before, intending to do a little drinking and carousing. He saw a woman there who reminded him of his mother. She was big breasted, at least forty years of age, and had long brown hair. Carlo watched her make a spectacle of herself, flirting with every guy who would give her some attention.

She was dressed in a red miniskirt with black fishnet stockings and high heels. Carlo thought she looked like a ten dollar hooker. At one point during the evening he caught her eye. At the time she was slow dancing with some grease ball half her age. The scum bag had his hands all over her ass. The woman looked over at Carlo and winked, then turned back to the slime ball she was dancing with.

He'd wanted to puke! Carlo turned away in disgust. The filthy whore had no way of knowing she'd opened a can of worms. Memories of his mother hogtied to a chair flooded Carlo's brain. This woman was probably married with children at home too. What the hell was she doing acting like a whore with men half her age. Carlo's demon spoke...

He left the disco and crossed the street, biding his time by hiding in the shadows in a dark alley. Nearly an hour passed before anyone else came out of the club. Once they did, the place emptied quickly. People were singing and laughing as they headed in various directions. Everyone it seemed, but the one Carlo was waiting for.

Finally it happened. The forty year old whore stumbled out, her slimy friend close behind. They stood on the sidewalk for a few minutes, talking. Carlo couldn't make out what they were saying. Suddenly the grease ball turns and walks back inside the disco. The miniskirted whore leaned against the building waiting for her meal ticket to return. A moment later he did, with two buddies in tow.

The four of them stepped off the curb and crossed the street, headed straight for him. Carlo back peddled further down the alley. He was totally hidden in darkness. If he hadn't accidently bumped into a trash can no one would have had a clue he was there. The sound of the metal lid crashing to the pavement reverberated loudly down the alley.

The whore and her three patrons stopped dead in their tracks. Carlo heard one of them say, *"It's just a bloody alley cat, is all."* The voice spoke english, The Queen's english! The others laughed. A moment later Carlo heard the same voice. *"Ere little kitty... Ere, pussy pussy pussy."*

They four of them were standing just inside the alley entrance. One of the Englishmen looked up and down the street, then took the whore by the arm and led her into the darkness. Carlo could make out their silhouettes, thanks to a street light in the distance.

He watched the old slut get down on her hands and knees and bury her face in the Englishman's now exposed crotch. The sound of her slurping could be heard in the crisp quietness of the early morning. Several minutes later the Englishman backed away and buttoned his fly. He patted the woman on the head as if to say, *Good dog!* Then he called out, *"Who's next, Mates?"*

The other two Englishmen took turns, each spending less than five minutes standing in the shadows getting a Cuban blow job. When they were finished they headed off down the cobble stoned street, leaving the whore sitting alone in the alley. Carlo could hear them laughing as they disappeared into the night.

He approached the bedraggled woman and unzipped his pants. When Carlo pulled out his cock the whore looked up at him and smiled. A cum chain was dripping from her chin. She wiped it off with the back of her hand then smugly asked, *"Did you enjoy the show, Big Boy?"*

Carlo was repelled. He wanted to beat this sexy looking middle aged slut to death. At the same time he desperately wanted to fuck her. The demon won...!

He ordered the disco swine to open her mouth, then proceeded to piss all over her face. Rather than be repulsed, she seemed to enjoy it. When Carlo had completely emptied his bladder the whore stood up and looked him in the eye.

Carlo found himself staring into his mother's large coffee colored eyes. Her high caramel colored cheeks were partially hidden by long manes of brown hair. Semen and piss was dripping from her chin, disappearing into her bountiful cleavage below. She leaned forward and lustfully whispered into Carlo's ear, *"Yum... Got any more?"* Carlo lost control!

Tribuna De Le Habana ran the story on its front page. A woman was found strangled in an alley off Calle Obisbo. She'd been brutally beaten about the head and torso. Cuba's National Revolutionary Police Force was investigating the crime. They had no comment at this time.

Carlo read the afternoon edition of the newspaper while sipping a cosmopolitan at a martini bar around the corner from his apartment. The story mentioned the NRPF didn't release crime statistics, but Cuba was reported to have the lowest crime rate in the western hemisphere. The agency took particular interest in keeping crime rates low in the nation's capitol.

According to the newspaper, witnesses reported the woman was seen dancing inside the Atelier Disco. The club is located at 77 Calle Obisbo. Several stated she was in the company of three men.

They appeared to be foreigners, possibly English sailors. A number of witnesses said the men spoke english. Little was known about the victim. She appeared to be in her mid forties. The National Police were asking anyone with information about the crime to come forward.

EARLY RETIREMENT

MURDER IN DAYTONA

27

THE MARCELINA was scheduled to depart at 1500 hours. The forty meter long freezer trawler was powered by a series 60 Detroit diesel engine, and outfitted with RSW tanks for keeping the catch fresh during extended days at sea. The sophisticated wheelhouse had modern contemporary navigational technology and computerized fish detection systems. Crew quarters below the bridge provided sleeping bunks for ten, and included a modern galley. The twelve man crew worked two six hour shifts, leaving room for four guests on each outing. Vidal Santiago arranged for his brother to accompany the crew on this trip.

THE MARCELINA's official log showed a navigational course heading southwest, with stops in Grenada and Barbados. The trawler would then sail due north to Bermuda. Gulfstream waters held abundant supplies of grouper and blue fin tuna, which would be caught, processed, and stored for sale to Canadian wholesalers.

When the ship's holds were full, THE MARCELINA would make her way to the North Atlantic to deliver her bounty. Once empty the ship would spend several weeks in dry dock in the seaport village of Cavendish, PEI. The engine room was scheduled for an overhaul. When maintenance was completed the crew would fish the Gulf of St Lawrence for mackerel and cod before returning to its home port, Santa Clara, Cuba.

The captain of THE MARCELINA kept a *'rough'* log which often didn't mirror the *'official'* version. As prosperous as commercial fishing could be, Cuban fishermen worked in a system that didn't allow for personal gain. In Cuba business entities were in reality, State run. The real money was made on the black market.

Smuggling goods on the high seas was a serious crime, but one that was difficult to detect. It was a simple case of too much ocean and not enough man power. THE MARCELINA was transporting contraband to the Bahamas that would bring its captain and crew the equivalent of three months wages.

Carlo and three other Cuban defectors were making their way to Miami. The odds of being caught were relatively small given the connections his hosts had. The crew of THE MARCELINA did this for a living, and they knew what they were doing. The cost each passenger was required to pay for their fare was five thousand dollars, American... In advance.

Vidal had put his finder's fee towards Carlo's passage. Half the remaining balance was covered by his crew mates, who'd waived portions of their pay outs. Carlo borrowed the remainder from his brother, with a promise to pay it back within the year.

After dropping anchor in Cat Island Bay several crew members readied their human cargo for transfer to another vessel. Ten minutes later an inflatable raft showed up off the leeward bow. Two english speaking Bahamians helped the Cuban defectors board their vessel, then covered them with fish netting and headed back to shore. Once in New Bight the three compatriots were split up. Carlo didn't know either of his countrymen's names, nor did he ever see them again. He was taken to a marina on the far side of the Island and put on a thirty foot Shuttle Cat.

The catamaran was piloted by a middle age man with a french accent. He was accompanied by an attractive blond half his age and a young Bahamian boy. Two minutes after Carlo stepped foot on board they set out.

The Cat's two 150 horsepower Honda marine motors cut through the aqua blue Caribbean Sea with ease. Two hours later Carlo was handed a beach bag and told to get ready. The bag contained a bathing suit, a towel, a tube of suntan lotion, and a bottle of Perrier.

The catamaran pulled into a marina and docked. The blond, now wearing a string bikini and sunglasses, handed Carlo a key card and said, *"Act like we are lovers and follow me."*

They stepped onto the wooden dock. Carlo held out his hand to assist his attractive benefactor. Once she was clear of the gangway she took Carlo's arm and pointed towards a pink stucco colored building at the end of the pier.

The Key Largo Colony Resort was a four star establishment that catered to upscale families on vacation. No one seemed to notice the couple as they made their way through the lobby and down an adjoining hallway. The bikini clad blond motioned for Carlo to use his key card to open the door to the suite. Once inside he let out a big sigh of relief.

Carlo was amazed at the ease in which he was able to leave Cuba. He really hadn't known what to expect, and though his brother was involved he'd feared the worse. He looked at the curvaceous young woman standing before him. A fleeting thought crossed his mind, but before he had a chance to act on his impulse she spoke. The blond's english was peppered with a french accent, which only heightened Carlo's state of arousal.

"You will stay here tonight, Oui? A limousine will peek you up tomorrow, eh... Comprenez-vous? Nine sharp, Yes!"

Carlo smiled at her and took a step forward. The blond put up her hand to slow his progress and said, *"Non, non Monsieur... Nine sharp."* Then she was gone.

Carlo spent the remainder of the day in his room. He'd have loved to sit by the pool and order an icy cold margarita but he didn't dare. He turned on the television and ordered a cheeseburger from room service. It came with a side of cole slaw. His new life had begun. He was eating American food, In America... Carlo had made it. He was in the land of opportunity. Not to mention the land of debauchery, corruption, and decadence. *Home Sweet Home!*

He spent the next few months kicking around Miami enjoying the freedom his new home provided. Not having documentation, Carlo found work as a stablehand at Calder Race Course. When the racing season ended he traveled with his employer to Hawthorne Race Course in Illinois. It was a learning experience. Carlo had expected thoroughbred horse racing to be legit, but he found it to be anything but. Things went on inside his employer's horse stalls that sickened him.

He worked for a trainer named Jim McGarrity. McGarrity often pressured the owners of his horses to let him shoot their animals full of drugs. Lasix to control blood pressure, and Bute to control pain. In moderation the drugs could be beneficial to a race horse, but the doses given to McGarrity trained horses was criminal.

Some owners even allowed him to force-feed their horses cortico-steroid enhanced milkshakes, in an attempt to increase their stamina and control swelling. Carlo saw more than a few sprinters run themselves to death. The vessels in the horses lungs would hemorrhage. They'd literally drown in their own blood.

It wasn't just what happened at Hawthorne that bothered Carlo. The track was located just outside Chicago, in the town of Cicero. The area has a notoriously high rate of crime. Originally the home of crime boss Al Capone, Cicero is now overrun by Latino gangs and the Mexican Mafia. Over eighty percent of its residents are of Spanish heritage. Street drugs like Crystal meth, Mad momma's, and H bombs are openly sold at nearly every major intersection.

The drugs made the medications being force fed to the horses seem like aspirin. Carlo couldn't stand seeing how perverse a significant part of his culture had become.

He returned to Miami. Carlo held a degree in communications from the University of Havana. He decided it was time he put it to use. He applied to Florida International University, hoping to further his education. After speaking with a school counselor Carlo agreed to take a placement exam. When the results came back his score was off the charts. The counselor asked him what his long range goals were. He suggested Carlo apply to the University's Law School.

An illegal immigrant who'd defected from communist Cuba after murdering a street whore was about to embark on a journey that would lead him to the pinnacle of American success. The seventh son of poor Cuban parents, one a convicted murderer who'd hung for his crimes, the other a masochistic slut who'd abandoned her family, was well on his way to living the American dream.

EARLY RETIREMENT

MURDER IN DAYTONA

28

Despite Carlo's excellent grades job offers didn't exactly pour in. He found himself competing with other law school graduates he considered inferior. Classmates with connections in the local legal community didn't appear to be having placement problems. Even those who'd barely earned their JD. There was definitely a lesson to be learned here. In America it wasn't what you knew as much as who you knew that mattered. He'd learn to maneuver through the obstacles placed in his path.

Carlo took a position as a law clerk with the Greater Miami Legal Aid Society. The job was far beneath his ability, but it paid the rent. His duties included preparing briefs, researching judicial decisions, and recording case information. Being bilingual made Carlo a valuable commodity. It was only a matter of time before someone would realize his true potential.

The Legal Aid Society offers the indigent of South Florida representation on a sliding scale. The organization depends heavily on the good will of local attorneys for the majority of the services it provides. It does keep a few lawyers on staff, but they mostly hold administrative posts.

The Miami-Dade County Bar Association encourages its membership to offer services *pro bono,* seeing it as a way to cultivate relationships and enhance professionalism. The bar's stated goal was to promote the administration of justice. Galen Rose is the sitting president of the bar. He sets the example.

The Rose Law Firm is a prominent fixture on South Florida's legal landscape. With a staff of nearly one-hundred attorneys they offer the gamut of legal services. The firm's specialty happens to be immigration law. It was while working on an immigration case for Legal Aid that Galen Rose first met Carlo Santiago.

The young law clerk impressed Mr Rose with his good looks, his charming personality, and his attention to detail. Carlo had taken a special interest in the case because it involved a young compatriot of his. A Cuban boy named Frederico .

The boy had been smuggled into the United States on a flotilla. The U.S. Coast Guard intercepted the flotilla as it made landfall in the Florida Keys and escorted its contingent of refugees to an internment camp to await deportation. Frederico's case received special attention because it mirrored a similar situation that got national exposure a few years earlier.

In that case an eleven year old boy named Elian Gonzalez was returned to Cuba by the Immigration and Naturalization Service under the direction of U. S. Attorney General Nancy Reno. She was reacting to a decision by the United States Court of Appeals, which denied the boy's immigration status. Notoriety came when the U.S. Border Patrol raided a home in the Little Havana section of Miami because it was rumored family members were hiding the child there. The feds rushed the home carrying semi automatic weapons after the occupants refused them entry. A subsequent search of the premises found the boy cowering in a bedroom closet.

Photos of the event were taken by an organization called the Free Cuba Committee. Several of its members *just happened* to be there when the federal agents arrived. The pictures were sent to independent news outlets nationwide, some of whom published them.

The photographs showed heavily armored border patrol SWAT team members bullying their way into the home, violently shoving residents aside in the process. The frightened child was hustled out the front door and shoved into a police car. The attorney general's actions resulted in several days of violent political unrest by Cuban American protesters. At the height of the riots a ten block section of Little Havana was closed off as thousands of demonstrators voiced their disapproval of the government's decision.

It was an election year. The national exposure may have cost presidential candidate Al Gore the White House. The Democrat lost the highly contested election after conceding defeat in the state of Florida, where numerous recounts gave a slim victory to Republican candidate George Walker Bush. With close to a million Cuban American voters in Florida, the election could have easily turned in Gore's favor.

Post election news reports stated Al Gore's flip flop on the Elian Gonzalez case cost him the Cuban American vote, which in turn cost him the State. Ultimately it was Florida that gave George Bush the electoral college votes needed to put him over the top.

Thanks to Galen Rose this recent case had a happier ending. The attorney was able to secure the child's release from federal custody and have him placed with relatives while his immigration status was reviewed. Immigration and Naturalization was no longer under the auspices of the U.S. Attorney General. Following the events of *9/11* the INS was transferred to The Department of Homeland Security.

In some ways the switch made immigration to the United States more difficult, but it also took it out of the courtroom. With conservative republicans controlling the political arena Rose felt confident he'd win litigation, and four months later he did!

Carlo, being far to intelligent to remain a law clerk, set out to impress Galen Rose. The Rose Law Firm was the preeminent choice of monied Cuban society in south Florida. The fact Galen was a homosexual only made Carlo's job easier. He was no fairy, but for a crack at the big time the eager young lawyer could tiptoe through the tulips with the best of them. It wasn't long before the two became *close* friends.

When Frederico's immigration case was settled in his favor Galen Rose got the credit. He and Carlo celebrated the victory with a night on the town. The morning after was spent eating breakfast on Galen's patio overlooking the Grand Canal. The gorgeous 'millionaires row' waterway wound its way across Los Olas Boulevard then turned east towards Ft Lauderdale Marina. Eggs Benedict accompanied by champagne mimosas were followed by a deep back massage.

Carlo made it perfectly clear he wasn't interested in a relationship with Galen, nor did he consider himself gay. Their sexual liaison had been the result of a night of binge drinking and cocaine inspired euphoria. Carlo's plan came to fruition when Galen peeked over the top of his morning newspaper and asked him if he'd be interested in coming to work for him.

An entry level attorney in the Rose Law Firm earned over one hundred grand a year. A twenty percent bonus was payable at year's end. Carlo jumped at the chance.

He spent the next few years perfecting his trade, winning case after case. His productivity was rewarded with monetary bonuses and expensive gifts. Mr Rose came to accept the fact Carlo was never going to be his boy toy, but they remained close friends.

When Mr Rose was approached by members of the Jose Gacha family he knew just the person he should turn to. Gacha was a high ranking member of Columbia's *Los Norte Del Valle*, easily the most influential drug cartel in the world. The organization rose to power after the Medell'in Cartel fragmented. Local headquarters are located in Little Havana. The cartel works closely with the local Cuban-American community. Galen Rose figured his talented young associate would be perfect for the job.

The Gacha family was having immigration issues. Jose Gacha was being hounded by Homeland Security, who was attempting to have him expelled from the country. Gacha's ties to *Los Norte Del Valle* were well known to the feds. The agency knew the easiest way to get rid of him was by using INS. Though he hadn't been linked to any crimes Gacha was kept under constant surveillance. Homeland Security officials thought their prayers were answered when INS received an extradition request from the Office of the Minister of Justice in Bogota, Columbia.

They were wrong. You see Carlo came up with the idea of using *Los Norte* connections within the Columbian government to make it appear as though Gacha would be in danger if he returned to Columbia. An extradition order was signed by the Columbian Minister of Justice requesting the United States place Gacha under arrest and turn him over to Columbian authorities.

Los Norte Del Valle paid the high level Columbian minister handsomely for his cooperation. Of course the minister was well aware what could happen to him if he refused to cooperate.

Accidents happened all the time in Bogota. More times than not the cartels didn't even bother making assassinations appear accidental. After all, it's hard to make a car bomb seem like an accident.

Carlo's strategy revolved around the idea there was so much corruption within the Columbian judicial system that to honor the extradition order was tantamount to signing Gacha's death warrant.

He fed the INS hearing officer a line of bullshit about certain members of the Columbian government going after the assets of wealthy expatriates who chose to live abroad. *Los Norte Del Valle* fed the flames by seeing to it certain enemies of the cartel did have their assets confiscated by government authorities. Carlo requested political asylum for his client and his immediate family.

The case ended successfully. Not only was Jose Gacha given asylum. Lines of communication were established with Columbian government and banking officials, as well as high ranking officers in the country's national police force.

A significant number of American officials were also put on the *Los Norte* payroll. The cartel was in position to overtake the *La Corporacion* as the leading player on the Miami scene. The only thing stopping it was lack of man power. Homeland Security had effectively shut the door on immigration. The agency developed a list of undesirable foreign nations whose citizens weren't welcome in the United States. Thanks to its inability to thwart the criminal activities of organizations like *Los Norte Del Valle*, Columbia was one of those nations.

Gacha told his lawyer he'd be well taken care for his efforts. Carlo had a burning desire to have a legitimate career in law. He really didn't want to be associated with one of the largest cartels in the world. That didn't stop him from asking the Columbian drug lord for a favor.

Carlo wanted Gacha to put a contract out on Jose Battle, the head of the Cuban Mafia's *La Corporacion.* He was also the man responsible for savagely murdering his two older brothers. Carlo blamed Battle for destroying his family and robbing him of his childhood. He would never forget his father's parting words. *Nobody fucks with a Santiago!*

The lawyer questioned Gacha about *La Corporacion,* asking him if he foresaw trouble down the road as the two entities fought for territory. Carlo thought he noticed his client's ears perk up when he mentioned the name Jose Battle. He assumed Battle was still running the crime syndicate. He knew the only way a cartel boss would be replaced was is if he died.

Gacha told Carlo the *El Padrino* was no longer active. Jose Battle had been diagnosed with stomach cancer a year ago. He wasn't expected to survive more than a few months longer. Carlo longed to avenge his family, but the thought of Battle suffering a slow painful death was enough to quench his desire. He'd let fate do his dirty work for him.

Carlo spent the next few years accumulating wealth, fucking women, and feeding his gambling addiction. He was living a life he could have only dreamed about back in his native Cuba. Having acquired a taste for culinary delicacies, the successful lawyer became a regular at some of the most expensive restaurants in south Florida. He bought himself a Ferrari and started spending weekends in South Beach. He found it was easy to pick up starry eyed young women impressed by his playboy persona and good looks.

The demon living inside Carlo was a sadomasochist. The attorney would often introduce one of his female admirers to the erotic world of bondage and humiliation. Occasionally he'd overstep the boundaries. The result would be a well deserved beating as the rage within was released.

He would use drugs and alcohol to prepare them for their evening of fun and games. That way they wouldn't be able to clearly recall any details. Those nights usually ended with Carlo driving his freshly beaten piglet to some remote location and dumping her on the street to sober up.

After a while Carlo began to realize the majority of the women he chose for his special treatment resembled his mother. They all had dark brown hair and brown eyes. They were all buxom. They were all whores. He started avoiding them.

Friday afternoons were spent playing the horses. Carlo knew from his days working the circuit that races were often fixed. He would pay young jocks and horse trainers for tips on that days winning entries. They usually came in. When time allowed he liked to visit Haulover Beach. The clothing optional park allowed him an opportunity to show off his masculine features. It was there Carlo met the woman who'd become his passion... Teracita Goncalves.

EARLY RETIREMENT

MURDER IN DAYTONA

29

Detective Brooks felt a full measure of relief and satisfaction when he walked into the station with Doris Van Fleet in tow. The plane ride from Dallas to Daytona Beach had been uneventful. In fact the detective's prisoner hadn't uttered a single word. He assumed the wrist shackles binding Doris to his side had managed to effectively silence her mouth as well. Few passengers on the flight even noticed the restraints. After some initial curiosity the ones that did seemed to forget about it.

Word of their arrival spread fast. Brooks humbly made his way through the throng that had gathered in the hallway. Everyone wanted to catch a glimpse of his prey. Someone applauded as they walked by and others picked up the queue. By the time they reached the processing area Brooks was the recipient of a crescendo of applause.

Doris was booked on the misdemeanor charge of failure to appear in court to answer a traffic citation. The fact she'd fled the state was grounds to hold her in custody. She was also wanted for questioning in the murder of Veronica Stevens, but she had not been charged with the crime... Not yet. The district attorney would determine if there was enough evidence to make a case. In the meantime Brooks could take advantage of the situation. He knew Doris had a short fuse and an explosive personality. He intended to strike the match that would light that fuse!

As part of his investigation the D.A. requested a search warrant allowing authorities access to Doris Van Fleets place of residence.

The evidence on hand, though circumstantial, was enough to persuade a judge to approve the request. The little stucco cottage that sat in the gardened grounds of the Vanessa Del Rio estate in Mytilene was about to be inundated by a team of investigators and forensic experts intent on tying Doris to the crime.

A parade of patrol cars and tech vans rolled into the quiet lesbian community. They didn't go unnoticed. Word spread like wildfire. It wasn't long before a large throng of women were congregated outside 28 Boreas Lane.

Moments later Mount Dora's police chief arrived, followed by television news crews from the surrounding area. It wasn't long before the place swarmed with reporters and sightseers. CNN even had a helicopter circling overhead feeding live coverage to affiliates around the country.

Vanessa Del Rio watched the entire event hidden away inside her home in Paris, Texas. She'd already contacted her attorneys, insisting they put a stop to the media circus being played out in her back yard. Ms Del Rio also contacted the Presidium of the quasi secret lesbian society she belonged to. The Sisterhood of the Skull and Roses would want to know if one of their own was in trouble.

With thousands of members across the country The Sisterhood could be useful. They had a legal defense fund that could be tapped if needed. Many of its members were attorneys. There was sure to be a few who would provide counsel *pro bono*. The society had dozens of members with close connections in the political arena too. They could pull a few strings. With enough interest the entire investigation could be made to look like a witch hunt.

As the scene unfolded outside Doris Van Fleet's home Dan Brooks and his team were busy going through every inch of space inside. They hoped to find something that would link Doris to the crime. Something that would implicate her in some way. Success beyond anyone's expectations came when one of the investigators found an old leather trunk stored under a bed in an upstairs bedroom.

A metal coffer found inside the trunk contained numerous items, including a stack of unsealed envelopes bound together with a red rubber band. None of the envelopes bore postage, but they were all addressed... To Veronica Flowers. The investigator wasted no time alerting Brooks of his find.

The detective opened the envelopes. Each contained a neatly folded one page letter, all signed by Doris Van Fleet. Most of the notations professed love for the addressee, and regret for having messed things up. Several spoke of the passion the two shared, and the sexual awakening Veronica had experienced under Doris' loving guidance. One note, a plea from a broken heart, begged for a second chance. The last letter was quite venomous in nature. It was filled with ridicule and contempt. The writer mocked how easily she'd replaced Veronica, and denounced her as a filthy hole for a cock to discharge in. The closing sentence brought immediate attention. *"When you come crawling back to me on your hands and knees stinking of semen I'll put you out of your misery!"*

Other items found inside the trunk included a Smith & Wesson 38 Special hand gun, a photo album filled with pictures of Doris and Veronica obviously taken during happier times, and a logbook. Doris had written down the names and addresses of dozens of women she'd '*banked,*' as she put it. Each entry came with a star rating.

Brooks chuckled to himself as he recalled the testimony of one of the women who'd come forward with information. She'd shown up at his proteges office back in New York wearing her nurse uniform. She claimed to have had sex with not only Doris, but Veronica as well. What was her name...oh yes, Betty! The detective couldn't resist looking to see if Nurse Betty had been rated in the logbook. Sure enough she was there... With five stars.

Lifting the heavy metal coffer out of the trunk Brooks noticed a sunken wooden panel on its underside. The detective knew the panel indicated a false bottom, and probably concealed a hidden compartment behind it. After fidgeting with the panel for a few moments he was able to access the compartment. The detective slid the compartment forward exposing its contents. He reeled back in disbelief.

The chamber held what appeared to be a wedding ring. The gold cincture had a single row of diamond chips. On the underside of the ring was an inscription, 1cor:13. That isn't what shocked him though. Lying next to the ring was a key. It was attached to a plastic chain. Printed on the keychain were the words... Property of the Pelican Inn ... Daytona Beach, Fl.

"JESUS CHRIST," Brooks uncharacteristically yelled out, followed by, *"MY GOD... WE GOT HER... Boys we got her!"*

A sense of deliverance overflowed the room as investigators came running in response to the detective's outburst. The evidence, though circumstantial, was strong enough to put Doris away for a long long time. Her attorney may even try to plea a deal to avoid her getting a death sentence.

"Not a word of this to the media," Brooks instructed those within ear shot. *"We'll announce our findings at a press briefing in the morning. This will get those SOB's off our backs! We've been fighting an uphill battle since this thing started. Now they can all go to hell..."*

Forensics continued their dactylography tests, while numerous investigators sifted through drawers and closets looking for more damaging evidence. Brooks walked out of the cottage holding the metal coffer close to his chest. Upon seeing him a herd of reporters advanced, blocking the detective's path. With microphones pressed to his face Brooks used his girth to push through the crowd.

As he progressed towards the street he politely announced the investigation was ongoing. He had no comment at this time. An attractive young woman identifying herself as a reporter for CNN asked the detective about the box he was carrying. Brooks smiled and answered, *"Oh this? It's just an early retirement present."*

When he reached the street the detective was met by the Mount Dora police chief. He grabbed Brooks by the arm and said, *"Ya'll need to git ouda here."* Brooks climbed into the chief's SUV and the two headed out, siren blaring and blue lights flashing. Once they left the coral colored gates of Mytilene behind the chief killed the light bar and siren. *"So, what's ya got dere, Detective,"* he asked pointing to the metal box on Brooks lap.

"Evidence my friend," the detective answered. *"Evidence! I have Ms Doris Van Fleet sitting in a cell on a misdemeanor charge of failing to appear in traffic court. This little box is going to keep her there permanently."*

Brooks told the chief how much he appreciated his assistance, and apologized for usurping his authority. *"I knew it was her... I just knew it. This time I got one over on Jordan. Do you know Jordan, Chief,"* he asked? *"Jordan Downs. He's a famous psychic. We've worked on a number of cases together over the years."*

The chief told Brooks he knew the name, but he'd never called upon him personally. *"Buncha baloney if ya asks me,"* he said. *"It don' replace good ole fashion po'lice work. No Siree... It don't."* Brooks laughed, then picked up the box sitting on his lap and kissed it. *"I done seen da lil feller on TV dough,"* the chief went on. *"He's a strange lil bastard if ya asks me."*

When they got to the station the chief pulled into his spot then sat there for a moment looking at the metal box on Brooks' lap. Finally he said, *"Glad I could help ya'll out!"*

Ten minutes later the detective was sitting in an unmarked patrol car being chauffeured back to Daytona. He pulled out his cell phone and tapped Jordan's number. After several rings he heard his impish friend answer, *"Hello, Detective."*

Brooks was hoping to surprise Jordan with the news of Doris' arrest, and he wanted to ask him to attend a major press conference in the morning. Before he could get the words out the psychic said, *"You've arrested the wrong person, Dan!"*

Brooks stumbled for words to counter his friend's speculation. *"I have evidence, Jordan..."* The psychic just snickered. He told the detective what he had wasn't evidence. It was circumstantial. He repeated his earlier claim insisting the murderer was a man. Brooks was adament he had proof. *"I can put Doris Van Fleet at the scene of the crime, Jordan. Jesus, Man... She had the fucking room key!"*

Jordan countered. *"Dan, you're my friend. I know you want this. I know you NEED this, Brother...but I'm telling you, Doris Van Fleet did not murder Veronica Stevens."* He waited for the detective to respond, but only heard silence.

"You know me, Dan" he continued. *"I wouldn't mislead you. If I didn't know it in my heart I wouldn't be so adamant. I've seen the killer... I know who the killer is...and it's not Doris. You may have damning evidence, my friend. You may even get a conviction...but she didn't do it!"*

The Detective was stunned. On one hand he had what was to him, solid evidence. On the other hand he knew Jordan was right ninety-nine percent of the time. Brooks had never known Jordan to

266

name an innocent person. In truth, he'd only known of one case the psychic didn't successfully solve. What was he supposed to do, release a suspect based on a psychic's *conjectural impulse?* No way! This case was coming to a close, and Doris Van Fleet was going down.

Doris was brought to an interrogation room for questioning. Detective Brooks was waiting there, sitting in a chair biting his fingernails when she arrived. He motioned for her to sit across from him, and instructed her to speak into the microphone. A female officer sat several seats away, quietly but intently paying attention. Doris was informed the conversation was being tape recorded, and that anything she said could be used against her in a court of law. Brooks asked Doris if there was anything she'd like to tell him concerning her involvement in the death of Veronica Stevens.

Her response didn't come as a surprise. *"Fuck you, you finger sucking asshole,"* Doris hollered. *"You've got absolutely nothing on me. My lawyer is going to sue the shit out of you, you no good bastard!"*

Doris looked down the table at the female officer. The bitch hadn't moved a muscle since she'd arrived. *"Who the fuck are you,* she angrily asked? *Why don't you fucking speak? Tell this asshole he can't hold me here like this. I haven't done anything wrong."*

"So you don't want to cooperate, is that it," Brooks asked. *"I didn't think you would, Doris...but I do have news for you. We've been out to your little cottage in Mytilene. You surprise me, Ms Van Fleet. I'd have thought you'd be much more careful than that."*

Doris quieted down a bit, shifting her gaze back and forth between Brooks and the female officer at the far end of the table. She repeated her intention to sue Detective Brooks when this was over. *"Over,"* he responded. *"Dear lady, your problems have just begun."*

Brooks asked Doris if she wanted to talk about the contents of the trunk under her bed. He was hoping to see alarm flash across her face. That might confirm she knew he had her between a rock and a hard place. He saw only complacency.

Doris sighed. *"You mean the 38 special? So you found my gun, Detective. Good police work... I have a legal permit for it, you dumb dickwad."*

Brooks was unfazed by the name-calling. He told his prisoner he was aware of that, but the gun was not legally registered in the state of Florida. He informed Doris her New York State gun permit didn't mean squat down here. *"So what,"* she mockingly responded.

The detective told Doris he wasn't playing games any longer. He said the evidence was overwhelming, and that she'd better wake up and smell the roses. Doris screamed, ***"That is total bullshit, Detective. You don't have a God damn thing on me, because I didn't do anything,"***

Brooks stood up and leaned across the table. In a quiet whisper he stated, *"For the record... You are under arrest for the murder of Veronica Stevens."*

Detective Brooks instructed the female officer to read Ms Van Fleet her Miranda rights, then have her taken back to her cell until arrangements could be made to transfer her to *The Resort*.

The next morning a podium was set up in the lobby of the Daytona Beach Public Safety Building. Brooks superiors suggested the announcement be made to coincide with local television's midday news broadcasts. When the detective appeared on the

268

podium a few minutes before noon he was accompanied by his division captain, the police chief, and the district attorney.

The media had been told an announcement was going to be made concerning the Veronica Stevens homicide investigation. With the attention given this case by the fourth estate, the lobby was jam packed full.

Standing to the right of the podium speaking to a contingent from the local Fox affiliate was Jordan Downs. He happened to look up just as Brooks noticed him standing there. The wide bodied clairvoyant smiled at the detective, then winked and mouthed the words, *"Fuck you."* The detective smiled back and gave his friend a two fingered victory sign as he stepped to the microphone. Invited to attend that announcement was yours truly, Richard Stevens.

Detective Dan Brooks acknowledged the men surrounding him on the podium. Then he said what everyone had been waiting to hear. *"Ladies and gentlemen, we invited you here today because we wanted to announce the results of a search warrant that was executed at a residence outside the village of Mount Dora, Florida yesterday afternoon. Evidence was found inside the home that directly links a suspect in the brutal murder of Mrs Veronica Stevens."*

Brooks paused as reporters pressed forward, their microphones held high to capture the moment. The case had seemingly taken on a life of its own. Even independent news agencies like Gannet and Reuters had correspondents there to capture the latest news. When it seemed appropriate to continue the detective revealed the identity of the suspect.

"Doris Van Fleet, a fifty-eight year old part time Florida resident from New York State has been arrested and charged with

the homicide. She is being held at the Daytona Beach Detention Center located off International Speedway Blvd."

Pandemonium broke out as reporters rushed in every direction wanting to be the first to break the news. Brooks looked back at his captain, shaking his head in bewilderment. His captain encouraged him to continue. After contemplating for a moment on how best to proceed the detective simply said, *"Thank you all very much for coming,"*

Following the announcement Detective Brooks had to take questions from the few remaining journalists in attendance. He hated this part of his job. Time spent answering stupid questions asked by idiotic members of the news media was an exercise in futility. If he didn't give them the answer they wanted they just ignored his response. He decided to avoid the situation altogether and made for the rear of the podium. Before he could get away his captain intercepted him. *"Detective,"* he told him, *"give them ten minutes, answer a couple questions, then meet me in the conference room upstairs."*

His superior officer told him they needed to verify the supporting information used to make the arrest. *"We don't want any mistakes, Dan. No misinterpretations. No excuses. We don't need egg on our faces."* The captain started to walk away, then turned and added, *"We have to be together on this, Detective."*

Brooks had been hoping to gather his team for a celebratory salute. He told his captain so. Despite what had been written in the papers he knew the effort his team had put into the case. *"It'll have to be another time,"* his superior officer told him. The detective, not one to rebel against authority, deferred.

He was completely unaware a party had been organized in his honor. His entire team was congregated in an upstairs conference room awaiting his arrival. The room had been adorned with

270

western style decorations spoofing the investigator's chosen mode of dress. Everyone was donning cowboy hats and large comical sheriff badges furnished by a local costume store.

The detective's favorite restaurant, *The Cactus Flower,* had been hired to cater the event. On the menu was braised beef brisket, pulled pork, black beans and rice, and Brooks' favorite, green chili stew. A three tiered cake formed in the shape of a badge was placed in the center of the conference table. It was created by a local baker and inscribed DBPD / RETIRED.

I'd been notified the day before. Someone from the department called inviting me to attend a retirement luncheon for Detective Dan Brooks. It would take place immediately following a major press announcement, which they also wanted me to attend. Even though I'd always felt Detective Brooks didn't like me, I did respect him. If he found the person responsible for my wife's murder, I loved the guy!

A citizen volunteer rescued me from a horde of reporters and escorted me to the conference room. The announcement shocked me at first. I hadn't expected Veronica's murderer to be someone from her distant past, but the more I thought about it the more it made sense. Veronica had always been a little afraid Doris might try to hurt her someday. Anger grew in the pit of my stomach as I made my way to the party.

When I entered the conference room I saw several familiar faces, but I was in no mood to be cordial to anyone. After learning who had been charged with Veronica's murder my nerves were shot. The psychic the detective worked with was standing in a corner munching on appetizers. The guy irritated the hell out of me. I decided to head off in the other direction.

That's when I saw Duval, the police interrogator who'd befriended me at *The Resort.* He was chewing on a cream cheese covered celery stick. The son of a bitch had chewed me a new asshole when I refused to sign his damn confession that day. I told myself he was just doing his job...

Being surrounded by a room full of law enforcement personnel was intimidating. As far as I knew most of them had no clue who the hell I was. A few of them did come over to offer me their congratulations. I fought the cramps ripping through my gut long enough to thank them for their perseverance and hard work, not knowing who they were or what they might have contributed to the investigation.

Ten minutes went by. Ten long minutes... Then someone announced, *"Okay fellas, he's on the elevator."* The hallway was quickly cleared of minglers and the conference room door shut. I heard voices approaching from down the hall. The moment the door opened everyone in attendance broke into applause.

Detective Brooks had a look of shock on his face. It was easy to pick up because he towered half a foot above everyone else in the room. A really bad rendition of *For He's a Jolly Good Fellow* broke out, followed by calls of *"Speech... Speech."*

I discovered something about police officers that day. They can eat! The spread laid out along the conference room wall was depleted in no time. Being a visitor I waited until the boys in blue made their initial pass before grabbing a paper plate and partaking.

I wasn't really hungry but I felt obliged to indulge because I'd gotten a special invitation. A single serving of black beans and rice remained, along with most of the green chili stew. I put some on my plate and returned to my seat by the door. Mistaking the stew for something edible I shoveled a spoonful in my mouth.

The spicy concoction set fire alarms off in my brain. I choked up what I could, using my paper napkin to catch the cud as it

272

spewed out. I looked up through tearing eyes to find Detective Brooks and his buddy Jordan Downs staring down at me. Both had big grins on their faces.

Brooks stuck his big ham hock out for me to shake. When I took it he said, *"Welcome to my world, Mr Stevens."* Despite a running nose and scorched lips I thanked the detective for all he'd done to catch Veronica's killer. He patted me on the back and asked me how I was doing. I told him my nerves were shot, but that I wouldn't have missed this day for anything.

The detective pointed to my half full plate of green chili stew. *"Personal favorite of mine,"* he said. *"Nobody makes green chili stew like they do down at the Cactus Flower."* I suggested they may have used a little to much chili powder, then changed the subject.

"I can't believe it was Doris," I said to the detective. *"After all this time... Why?"* With those words the raw emotion came rushing back. My body trembled and the knot in my stomach tightened. Fighting back tears I asked Detective Brooks how he knew it was her.

He bent down and looked me in the eye as he said, *"Follow me."* The detective led me out of the conference room and down the hall. We entered a large open room through a set of reinforced glass doors. **HOMICIDE** was written boldly across the top in big block letters. Fiber covered cubicles lined the outer perimeter of the room. Brooks led me to one then sat me in a chair.

"Damn good police work, Richard. That's how we knew it was her. Good police work. Plain and simple." The detective absolutely believed what he was saying. He continued. *"We couldn't have made an arrest without solid evidence, and we found it, thanks to a great group of highly dedicated men and women."*

"Evidence," I responded? Brooks explained he'd zeroed in on Doris early in the investigation. There were just way to many loose ends, or so he claimed.

"When she failed to report to my office for questioning my antennae went up," he explained. *"Why run if you're not guilty?"* The detective told me Doris fled the state, taking up refuge in a rich woman's mansion in Paris, Texas of all places.

"Turns out she had an outstanding warrant, Richard. Failed to appear for a traffic ticket. When she crossed state lines she opened the door for any police agency to make an arrest. Illegal flight to avoid prosecution. I took advantage of the opportunity and asked the D.A. to request a search warrant. We went out to her place in Mount Dora and searched every inch of the place. One of my investigator's found a storage box under her bed. Upon further investigation we learned it contained numerous items of interest. Certainly enough to ask a Grand Jury to issue an indictment!"

Good police work? It seemed to me perhaps Lady Luck might have had something to do with it. Doris hadn't crossed state lines to avoid prosecution for a traffic citation... She'd simply panicked! She must have felt the authorities were trying to point the finger at her for Veronica's murder. I figured she just got scared and took off.

That is until Brooks announced what he found in that storage box. I was stunned! Doris had the key to the motel room where Veronica was murdered. Not only that, she had Veronica's wedding ring!

The detective was taken aback when I told him it was Veronica's ring. He had no idea my wife's wedding ring was missing. *"Why the hell didn't you mention that sooner,"* he asked me? *"You knew your wife's ring was missing and you didn't say anything to anyone?"* I told Brooks I felt it was my one link to the crime, explaining if I could find the ring, I could find the killer.

I asked him why no one had noticed my wife wasn't wearing it the night they found her on that bed beaten to a bloody pulp. Everyone knew she was a married woman. All Brooks could say was *"I don't know. Somebody fucked up, Mr Stevens."*

Anyone could see Detective Brooks was visibly shaken. I felt guilty bringing it up. He told me he accepted the blame, that he was the officer in charge at the scene. I tried to tell him it wasn't anybody's fault. That nothing was going to bring Veronica back. As I prepared to head out Brooks said. *"I'm submitting those retirement papers tonight."*

EARLY RETIREMENT

MURDER IN DAYTONA

30

It was a few minutes past eight when Veronica left the house. She'd promised Jewel she would stop by the motel to check on her before going to the shelter. The poor woman was so afraid that her old boyfriend would find her. The odds seemed rather small, but Veronica understood how fear can muddle a person's vision. She drove straight to the Pelican Inn.

She parked her VW between an old Ford pick up truck and a rusty Volvo then made her way up to the second level. Veronica didn't see Jewel's car in the lot. That made her wonder if her friend had changed her mind. When she knocked on the motel room door no one answered. Strike two... For a split second she thought about leaving, but then Veronica slid her key in the lock. When the door opened she heard the shower running. That made her feel a lot better.

Veronica tossed her purse on the bed and looked around the room. It was neat as a pin. The furniture was worn a bit, but you'd expect that in a place like this. Quality comes with a price. There was a lounger by the window, and a little kitchenette. Two coffee mugs were sitting out on the formica countertop, along with a hand written note. Veronica walked over and picked it up.

Good morning, the note said. *Thanks for coming. I made a pot of coffee. Pour yourself a cup and I'll be right out.* It wasn't signed.

After pouring a cup of coffee Veronica took a seat in the lounger. To kill time she scanned the parking lot for signs of her friend's blue Mustang. Not seeing it she hollered out, *"What did you do, Jewel... Walk here?"*

The lounger was quite comfortable. Veronica pushed herself back and rested her feet on the footrest. When she took a sip of Jewel's coffee she thought it tasted a tad funky. Not that it was disgusting, but it wasn't exactly Starbucks either. Veronica was the Queen of coffee. She knew brew like an accountant knows numbers.

Writing it off to 'cheap motels serve cheap coffee' Veronica shrugged her shoulders and continued sipping. Within minutes she started feeling drowsy. Without thinking why, she closed her eyes.

She realized she was feeling very sleepy. Veronica attempted to open her eyes but found she couldn't. Her lids were sealed shut, as if held closed by some invisible weight.

Was it possible she had fallen asleep? How long had she been sitting in the lounger? A crusty coating lined her eyelids. Her lips felt dry, and when she tried to speak her words came out slurred. Drool dribbled from the corner of her mouth when she attempted to call out Jewel's name. It was as though she'd been given a double dose of some super muscle relaxant.

As out of it as she was, Veronica realized she no longer heard the shower running. She tried to climb out of the chair but her feet got tangled in the footrest and she stumbled. Someone caught her just as her head was about to hit the floor. Whoever it was, was strong. With big, muscular arms. The person drew her close. So close she could feel his breath on her neck. His body was wet, like he'd just stepped out of the shower.

"Hello, Veronica" the man said in a soft calm voice. He had a hint of an accent. Spanish, she thought. Veronica tried to ask him where Jewel was...but she couldn't. The words just came out slurred. It felt strange to be so mentally aware and yet unable to see or speak.

Without warning the man suddenly grabbed Veronica's arm and led her towards the bed. At that moment all sorts of scenarios went haywire in her brain. Who was this person? What did he want? Was she going to be raped? Was he going to kill her? Veronica panicked...

The wet naked stranger pushed her back on the bed and removed her shoes. She heard them clack on the ceramic tile floor. *"Are you comfortable,"* he asked? *"Why don't you let me help you with that skirt?"* Veronica felt helpless. The man unzipped her skirt and slid it down around her ankles. That was the last memory she had before slipping into unconsciousness.

In her sleep state Veronica wondered if she'd died. Physically comatose, the frightened woman considered the possibility this was what death was. Lost in a dimension somewhere between what was real and what was imagined. She only determined it wasn't possible when she realized she could hear her heart pounding in her chest. Veronica slept to the rhythmic drumming.

When she woke the clock on the night stand read 12:28PM. It took several minutes before Veronica could focus her eyes enough to see it. Her eyelids were still crusted over, and her pupils were dilated. She was lying on her stomach, completely naked. When she went to turn over on her back she wasn't able to. Confused at first, Veronica soon realized why. Her wrists had been bound to the headboard.

She struggled to free herself from the bindings, but they only tightened. Her squirming caused them to bite into her skin even more. The realization of her predicament scared her senseless.

Without warning her tormentor pounced. Violently yanking a handful of hair he pulled her head back and stuffed the panties she'd been wearing down her throat. She gagged on the silky material. The man put his mouth near Veronica's ear and whispered, *"Relax and breath normal, Mrs Stevens. Otherwise you're going to drown in your own vomit!"*

Veronica reacted just the opposite. She freaked out. She kicked her legs violently and tried to scream through the silky gag stuffed in her throat. The effort soon tired her and she stopped resisting. That's when she felt the first flesh ripping bite sweep across her buttocks. The blow sent her into a state of shock. She passed out.

Twenty minutes later Veronica came to. The effects of the drug she'd been given were beginning to wear off, with the exception of a faint salty taste that lingered on her tongue. She opened her eyes to see a naked man sitting in the lounger by the window staring at her with a grin on his face. She thought she recognized something behind his evil smile. Yes, it was there... Pain!

"Welcome back," Carlo said. *"I'm so glad you're here. We have a lot of work to do."*

Her tormentor was quite handsome, which seemed terribly odd. She didn't know what to expect, but it hadn't been this. His long black hair was pulled back in a pony tail. It revealed a man with a chiseled face and a dark complexion. He was well endowed, and she couldn't help but notice, quite erect. Veronica thought he looked to be in his late twenties.

The man was holding a leather strap in his right hand. He walked over to the night stand and picked up a wire bristle brush with the other. It was then Veronica noticed he was wearing thin opaque surgical gloves. Stranger still, the man was wearing a condom. Veronica remembered something her husband once told her. *Monsters don't necessarily look like... Monsters!*

He pulled the bed pillows from under her head and shoved them under her belly. *"You're probably wondering who I am,"* Carlo asked? *"Well, let me introduce myself, Mrs Stevens... **I'm your worst fucking nightmare!"***

With that the monster let loose with the leather strap. Blow after horrifying blow swept across her ass cheeks and upper thighs. The pain intensified with each swing. Veronica had never known such agony. She felt as though she'd been doused with gasoline and set on fire. Her nose started to bleed as the pressure to breath built up from the inside out. It mixed with gobs of snot that streamed across her face and hardened there. Eventually her attacker tired and stopped swinging. After coughing up some phlegm he let his breathing return to normal. The smile returned to his face.

"Tell me," Carlo said to his tortured victim, *"have you ever wondered what a spiny hair brush would feel like digging into raw nerve endings? Lets find out together, shall we?"* Veronica closed her eyes and wished she'd died. When the needles of the brush ripped across her already raw ass cheeks the pain cut like a knife. She was convinced this fucking devil had been sent to make her pay for her sins. If there was ever a time to repent it was now.

Carlo slammed the brush down hard and pulled the sharp bristles across the width of Veronica's bottom. Her entire body went into spasm. The pain of sharp needles rubbing across freshly exposed nerve endings was indescribable. After numerous swipes her torturer switched gears. He used the brush to paddle the backs of Veronica's upper thighs till they looked like swollen shanks of meat.

The day was coming to an end. Carlo sat back down in the lounger and admired his work. Veronica's buttocks were rippled with deep purple welts. Thousands of tiny raised dimples quivered like a recently plucked chicken being prepared for the evening meal. Lines of ripped flesh ran across the backs of her thighs. Her body twitched involuntarily. When the air conditioner kicked on the cool air sent waves of excruciating pain through Veronica's body. She asked God to let her die.

It wasn't to be. At least not right away. Carlo started to talk. Veronica fought through the pain trying to hear what it was he was saying. *"Lets talk about why we're here, Mrs Stevens"* he said. *"Does the name Teracita ring a bell with you?"*

Carlo went on to tell Veronica how much he loved Teracita, and that he wouldn't allow her to be brainwashed. *"Who gave you the right to fuck with my life,"* he asked? *"You messed around with the wrong person this time. Do you understand me, Mrs Stevens?"*

Veronica knew she was in serious trouble. This madman was out of control. There didn't seem to be any way to stop him. When he went into the bathroom she desperately tried to free herself, but again the bindings bit deep into her wrists. This time they cut off her circulation. It was then she realized it was pantyhose that'd been used to tie her to the bed. She cursed herself for always carrying an extra pair in her purse. When the lunatic came out of the bathroom he was carrying a Swiss army knife and a wine bottle. He picked up where he left off.

"By the way, my name is Carlo Santiago. The young lady you are holding against her will is my fiancee. That fucking priest never should have brought her to that so called shelter. I'm sure you heard what happened to him. He made the same mistake you did, Mrs Stevens. Nobody fucks with a Santiago... Nobody!"

Carlo opened his Swiss army knife and located the little corkscrew. He stuck the tip into the wine cork and worked it for a few minutes until it came free. Then he sat the bottle down on the night stand and closed the knife. He lifted Veronica up by the hips and fluffed the pillows beneath her. Veronica's tortured ass was now fully exposed, properly propped up for display.

The madman straddled his victim, then twisted around and fingered her pussy till it was moist. It always amazed him how a woman could self lubricate even in the most dire of situations.

Veronica shuddered as Carlo slid his knife into her vagina. Holding the handle tight he pushed deeper and deeper, not stopping until his latex covered fist was entirely swallowed by her pussy. He freed his thumb from the wet crevice and slid it into her ass hole.

"Are you ready to die, Mrs Stevens" he asked? *"Shall I slice your gut open and let you bleed out like a pig?"*

In all honesty Veronica was ready. The torture had gone on long enough. There was no escape. She had no way out. This monster was going to kill her. Why drag it out and let him enjoy it any longer than necessary? She closed her eyes and prepared herself to die an agonizing death.

Carlo pulled the knife out, telling Veronica he'd only been kidding. Suddenly she felt a sharp pain under her right shoulder blade. It was accompanied by a bubbling sound. Moments later something warm and wet trickled down her back and gathered at the base of her spine. She realized she'd been stabbed.

Just when things couldn't possibly get any worse... They did! Veronica felt something being forced into her vagina. At first it didn't seem conceivable, but then she knew. This monster was stuffing the wine bottle up her pussy, and doing so bottom first. She felt the lining of her vagina tear as it made space for the
282

invading foreigner. With the bottle fully inserted, Carlo backed off to view his masterpiece.

This was a planned event. She knew because he'd brought a straw with him. Carlo bent down and stuck one end of the straw into the bottle, then wrapped his lips around the other end and sucked. After several draws he stopped, smacked his lips approvingly, then removed the straw.

He dropped it in a plastic baggie he'd left on the night stand, but replaced it with another. This straw was left dangling in the mouth of the bottle. The thought of Veronica's husband finding his wife in such a state excited Carlo to the point of orgasm. He closed his eyes and ejaculated into his condom.

Peeling the used rubber off his shaft he checked the time... It was quarter past three. *"So much to do and so little time,"* Carlo joked out loud as he dropped the condom in the bag with the straw. He continued talking as he walked to the bathroom. *"It has been fun, Veronica...but I must be on my way... I do hope you've enjoyed yourself."*

Carlo disappeared into the bathroom. Over the sound of the flushing toilet Veronica heard him say, *"I'd like to think you might consider coming back for another visit sometime."*

Was it possible she might survive this nightmare? Veronica thought about her mom and her sisters. How unique and special each one of them was to her. She thought about her daughter. What would happen to her if this was to be her fate? What about her husband? Who would take care of him? How she prayed she would see them all again.

Carlo had thoughts of his own in the moments he spent alone in that motel bathroom. Tormenting thoughts. He saw the lust in his mother's eyes as she hung naked from a ceiling hook while her lover lashed her with a horse crop. He remembered the pain on his father's face as he buried his two eldest sons after they'd been skinned alive by the Cuban Mafia. He saw the half eaten face of a teenage girl he'd tossed in a dumpster back in Miami. Carlo had left her there to be devoured by rats.

He reappeared at Veronica's bedside. After a moment he said, *"Don't be alarmed, Mrs Stevens. I wouldn't leave you here all alone. Your husband will be stopping by shortly to free you from your bindings. Please tell him your clothes are in the top dresser drawer. I folded them for you."* Then it got quiet...

So quiet Veronica could hear her heart beat. She could FEEL her heart beat. Was he gone? Had her prayers been heard? Through the blistering pain emanating from her ravaged bottom she felt herself smile. It was a timid, negligible smile, but a smile just the same.

Veronica could just barely see her hands stretched out above her head. Tethered to the headboard, they'd turned an unnerving shade of blue. Still, she was alive! This madman hadn't killed her. She closed her eyes and tried to relax her body. Help was on the way!

That's when the first blow struck. It landed with a sickening metallic thud. The back of Veronica's head compressed, then swelled to twice its normal size as it filled with blood. A moment later a second blow split her skull wide open. Blood and brain exploded from the gaping wound and sprayed across her face.

Her hair was coated with thick crimson liquid. It began to coagulate almost immediately. Grayish matter oozed from the deep crevasse in her skull, hissing as it exited like molten rock slowly crawling down the side of a rock face mountain... It is possible Veronica may have felt the first blow. The second one killed her instantly.

After congratulating himself on his handy work Carlo went through the room methodically checking for any trace of evidence. Once satisfied nothing remained he picked up his aluminum baseball bat by the tapered handle and stepped out onto the veranda. He scanned the lot below for any signs of life, then quietly closed the door behind him. Carlo made his way down the steel staircase and across the vacant lot, dropping the bloodied murder weapon in the scrub.

It was four o'clock. There was still time to place the note he'd printed the night before. Carlo climbed in Jewel's mustang and drove towards the Stevens' home. If his timing was perfect Veronica's husband would arrive home from his fishing trip, find the note Carlo left, and show up at his wife's motel room precisely when the cops did. His scheme was working just as he'd planned.

Getting into the retirement community undetected wouldn't be a problem. Carlo had discovered a way in while performing surveillance a few weeks before. There was a crumbling rock wall at a point close to where the Stevens' lived. It was well hidden by overgrowth. The wall had been built years ago. Back then it served a dual purpose. Keeping the livestock in while establishing a perimeter. The landowner didn't know it, but he did Carlo a huge favor.

Once the note was planted Carlo drove to a plaza just down the street and waited. At 4:30 he saw Veronica's husband drive by. He watched him turn into the gated community and disappear around the bend. Ten minutes later he drove by again, this time headed in the direction he'd come from.

Carlo waited another fifteen minutes then drove to a pay phone he'd seen at the rear of the plaza. His first call was to a local television station. He told the person who answered the phone he'd just murdered his wife. She could be found in a room at The Pelican Inn Motel on A1A.

After he hung up Carlo dialed 911. He reported the same crime to the emergency response dispatcher, only this time he provided the room number as well. It would be the first time he'd ever turned himself in. That evil grin returned to Carlo's face.

EARLY RETIREMENT

MURDER IN DAYTONA

31

Diedra Daniels was the first outsider Doris had seen since being arrested. She'd taken the day off from her job to drive over to Daytona for a visit. The once homeless street urchin was grateful to Doris for helping her find a job. The wholesale flower business proved to be right up Diedra's alley. She was exceeding all her employer's expectations. A woman who less than a year ago was trading her body for a meal now made nearly as much salary as she once did working at the furniture factory back in North Carolina.

Though she'd spurned the older lesbian's sexual advances they remained friends. When Diedra got to the jail she was disappointed to learn she'd have to communicate through a plexiglass partition. Still, they were happy to see each other.

Of course Doris pleaded her innocence. *"Those pricks want to hang Veronica's murder on me because I'm a lesbian. That's what this is all about,"* she insisted. Doris wanted to know what people were saying about her on the outside. She told Diedra she trusted her lawyer, but the woman didn't tell her shit. *"Everybody knows I didn't do this... Right"* she asked?

Diedra did her best to settle Doris down. She didn't mention the media was eating her alive. Reporters were claiming through reliable sources that evidence found inside the home of Doris Van Fleet would send her straight to the gas chamber. Some in the media were painting her as a modern day *Ailleen Wournos,* the serial killer who'd gained notoriety when portrayed by academy award winning actress Charlize Theron in the hit movie, *Monster.*

The local lesbian had been sentenced to death for murdering seven men in the Daytona area back in 1989. Ailleen Wournos spent nearly eleven years on death row before being executed on October 9, 2002. Now the media was preparing to hang Doris Van Fleet from the highest palm tree... Figuratively speaking.

"You have people on your side," Diedra encouraged her friend. *"Lots of people! You've got a great lawyer, and you've got The Sisterhood. Women across the country are prepared to march in your defense. Don't forget you've also got Ms Del Rio!"* After a moment Diedra added, *"and you've got me!"*

She tried to sound convincing, though she didn't believe a word of it. Truth be known Diedra thought Doris did murder Veronica. It was a classic case of jealousy mixed with pent up rage and opportunity that lead her to commit the senseless act. It was murder, and what murder ever made sense?

Doris had helped her when she was down. It was time to return the favor. An act of kindness should never go unacknowledged! Diedra only knew what she'd been told. Whatever it was that happened between Doris and Veronica all those years ago had set the wheels in motion. Perhaps it was fate. Who could say?

Forty minutes after arriving a female jailer came by and told Diedra her time was up. Then she turned to Doris and said, *"Let's go, Sweetie pie."* Doris looked at the burly black guard dubiously, as if to say, *"Fuck you... Bitch!"* When she didn't respond fast enough the jailer took Doris by the arm and ordered, ***"WALK ON, Dead Girl!"***

288

It would have been nice to get more visitors, but Doris knew her friends were few these days. Vanessa Del Rio wouldn't be coming to see her, but the millionaire land developer did pay for her legal representation.

Ruby Hines was a successful Dallas lawyer. She specialized in criminal law. Ms Hines was known throughout the state of Texas as a no nonsense win at all cost attorney. She came with glowing credentials. Ruby was a graduate of Southern Methodist University Law School. Her father was the Undersecretary of the Interior. Before accepting his political post he'd been a senior partner in a prestigious District of Columbia law firm.

Doris had a sense that with Ruby Hines representing her all would be fine. Hell, O.J. got off didn't he...and that asshole *WAS* guilty! It was only a matter of time.

Ten years out of law school, Ruby Hines was at the top of her game. Ms Del Rio hired the leggy redhead because she'd heard about the success Ruby had with high profile criminal cases. She was also a friend and financial supporter of Ruby's father. Del Rio offered to let the high profile attorney stay at her home in Mytilene, but Ruby declined. She took up residence at the five star Daytona Suites Oceanfront Resort instead.

Ruby's first order of business was to get Doris bonded out of jail. A release would be difficult, but doable. She set up a meeting with the district attorney the afternoon she arrived.

She provided the D.A. with an inventory of information she required for the case. Copies of search warrants, interrogation notes, interview tapes, photos of the crime scene, etc, etc, etc. Ruby wanted to know on what grounds her client was subjected to arrest and extradition from the state of Texas. Of course she knew the police were within their rights to detain Doris. All because of a fucking traffic citation no less.

The Grand Jury was hearing the case the following Tuesday morning. Exactly one week away. Considering the evidence being presented by the prosecution everyone involved expected an indictment would be forthcoming. Ruby spent the rest of the week getting to know Doris. She needed to know every detail of her personality and background.

Ruby liked Doris right away. She found her to be feisty and full of spirit. The attractive lawyer could see why her client would have no problem picking up women if she were so inclined. There was one question that remained unanswered... Where was Doris the day Veronica Stevens was murdered?

Doris hadn't answered that question when Detective Brooks asked it weeks before. She'd replied she couldn't remember. Now her life may very well depend on her remembering. Ruby asked her client if she would submit to hypnosis as a way of taking her back to that day. Doris froze up.

Truth is, Doris knew exactly where she was that day. It would be impossible to forget! The thought of someone else discovering the truth was devastating to her.

She'd spent the afternoon with a man she'd met on a plane. They were seated next to each other and he'd struck up a conversation. Both were returning to Florida after visiting friends in upstate New York. Doris found she was comfortable around him. It was the first time in her life she'd enjoyed being in the company of a man. Something about him seemed familiar.

His name was Clinton Dane. He'd told Doris he was a cancer survivor, claiming his cancer was in remission... That was a lie! Clinton was a retired marine biologist. He'd dedicated thirty years of his life to studying sea creatures, often spending months at a time at sea. The last few years were spent trying to keep an independent ocean research facility from closing.

290

The facility was located just south of St Augustine. It had been struggling to compete with larger corporate funded facilities on the eastern seaboard. When the owner announced the facility was being transformed into a marine park for tourist Clinton decided it was time to get out.

After their flight landed Clinton asked Doris if she would consider meeting him for lunch some time. She surprised herself by saying she would. They agreed to get together the following Friday at *The Hungry Whale* in New Smyrna Beach. Even though the oceanfront restaurant was within walking distance of his condo Clinton chose to drive there. He hoped to impress Doris with what he referred to as *The lady in my life.*

The lady in Clinton's life turned out to be a candy apple red 1967 Cadillac Eldorado. The automobile was in pristine condition. General Motors had completely redesigned the car for that model year. His was one of the first to roll off the assembly line.

Clinton went on and on with details only a dedicated car buff would understand. The Caddy featured front wheel drive, and came with a unified power plant. It had a THM transmission and a torque converter with a planetary gearbox. He was amazed Doris understood everything he was saying! She waited for him to finish before explaining she'd been a mechanic for over twenty years.

They were seated at a booth offering a gorgeous view of the Atlantic Ocean. Clinton ordered fish tacos and talked shop. Doris liked him. She considered Clinton a friend, albeit a male one. She dined on baked talapia and let him ramble on about cars, engines, and life under the sea.

Despite his medical condition Clinton was looking for more. He desperately wanted a relationship. Doris never said so directly, but she figured he was hoping to find someone so he wouldn't have to die all alone. The man was completely naive about the lesbian lifestyle. When he learned Doris preferred women he refused to accept it.

After lunch they took a ride to Canaveral National Seashore. The scenic park was only ten minutes from Clinton's condo, which he pointed out as they drove by. Once inside the park they made their way down to the southern tip. Clinton pulled his Cadillac into a small parking area and killed the engine, then asked Doris if she'd like to walk on the beach. She reached for her cane while he popped the trunk and took out a beach bag. He hadn't said so, but Clinton had planned to make this trip down the seashore. *"A scout is always prepared,"* he joked as they headed off.

That section of Canaveral Seashore is known as Apollo Beach. It's named after the space program that landed a man on the moon. On a clear day the NASA launch site is visible from the beach. Unbeknownst to Doris, Apollo is a clothing optional beach. She found that out shortly after stepping foot in the sand.

Clinton had gone into the restroom adjacent to the parking area when they arrived. He told Doris to go on ahead and he'd catch up, so she followed the boardwalk up over the dunes. She was standing on the beach watching a seaplane that had just taken off from a marina located a few miles south of them when Clinton walked up beside her. He was naked as the wind!

The sixty-two year old retired marine biologist was well built. Clinton had a barrel chest and powerful forearms that belied his age. A full head of wavy hair was just now beginning to turn grey. Doris found herself trying not to acknowledge his state of undress. It was a little embarrassing, especially considering Clinton was sporting an eight inch semi.

"Are you gonna get out of that garb, Woman," he asked? Doris told Clinton she didn't know there were nude beaches in Florida. She asked him if it was legal. *"I thought everyone knew about*

Apollo," he answered. *"Don't worry. There are no federal laws against nudity...and we're on federal property."* With that Doris tepidly peeled off her clothes. She put them in Clinton's bag, then they headed off down the beach.

The tide was out and the beach was wide. Before long Doris saw a few other sun worshipers laying in the sand. One guy was jogging down by the water, his cock swaying to the rhythmic pace he was setting. A quarter mile down the beach Clinton stopped and unfurled his beach blanket. He motioned for Doris to sit.

They watched sandpipers trying to outrun the waves crashing on shore. A dozen brown pelicans flew over head, like a squadron of B-52's sent on a do or die mission during the last world war. After a while Clinton put his arm around Doris.

She hadn't had a man put his arm around her since she was a little girl. Doris stiffened up, but she didn't tell him to remove it. Clinton pointed out a few cloud formations in the sky. One appeared to be the face of Abraham Lincoln, another a big puffy giraffe. After several minutes of gentle coaxing, Doris reclined...

Clinton was on top of her faster than a jackrabbit scurries down a hole. He planted a kiss squarely on the lesbian woman's mouth. For some reason Doris thought of Contessa, the housekeeper who worked for Vanessa Del Rio. The poor girl must've felt much like Doris did right now, restrained and forced to take a submissive role.

Why had she let this happen? Doris hardly knew this man. Clinton Dane was just a guy she'd met on a plane. They shared some friendly conversation and a meal, but she had no interest in him romantically. She was a lesbian! The only other man who ever entered her was her stepfather, and she was just a child at the time.

Doris liked Clinton, and she was sympathetic about his having cancer. Even if he was in denial. She knew very well she might be the last woman he'd ever fuck...

No way was she going to admit that in public. Doris had a reputation that had taken her a lifetime to build. What was worse... A headline that read *'Lesbian murders her ex-lover'* or *'Lesbian contradicts everything she ever believed in and has sex with a dying man while lying on a public beach?'* Exactly! So a hypnotist was out of the question.

Ruby was incredulous! Did this woman not understand the seriousness of the charges against her? Did she have a death wish or something? We're talking capital punishment here... The death penalty! The big city lawyer was trying to save this small town lesbian's ass. For all she knew Doris did it! Why else would she not be forthcoming concerning her whereabouts the day of the murder?

The Grand Jury would indict Doris, of that Ruby was certain. She'd seen the evidence. Still, it was mostly circumstantial. As damning as it was the prosecution had no fingerprints, no forensic examples, no eye witnesses, and in her judgement, no case. Ruby's biggest fear was that she wouldn't be able to save Doris from herself.

After working five straight eighteen hour days Ruby decided to take Sunday off. She was in Daytona after all. It was time to relax. Go to the beach, catch some rays, and swim in the ocean. The resort she was staying at had an exclusive spot on the beach, and offered its guests a plethora of shore amenities. Beach loungers, sun umbrellas, towels and bikes, they were all complimentary. The resort also featured a tiki bar out by the pool. It's there she met the man she'd choose to spend the night with.

He was Latino. Tall, dark, and handsome. The guy appeared to be in his mid-thirties. Ruby was laying in a lounger sipping on a frozen margarita when he approached. As attractive as she was, Ruby was used to men flirting in a seductive manner. Normally she just blew them off. Her legal career came first, and she put in very long hours. This time was different.

Carlo was taking an early morning jog on the beach when he noticed the long legged redhead. She was making her way across the pool patio. He watched as she settled into a lounger and ordered a drink from the waiter. The fact she was staying at this particular resort told him she came from money. With all the choices available to vacationers only the well heeled chose the three hundred dollars a night and up high end resort.

Carlo had never gotten over his penchant for showing off. Women just seemed to be wooed by his physique, complexion, and cool attitude. He was a man comfortable in his own skin. He sauntered up to the tiki bar and ordered a Havana cooler and a frozen margarita, then he made his way to Ruby's lounger. *"May I offer you a refresher,"* Carlo asked with a smile? *"Margarita, frozen, no salt."* He held the concoction out for Ruby to take. He knew if she accepted she was his. It happened all the time.

Visions of long, shapely legs tightly wrapped around his waist flashed through Carlo's mind. He could imagine the puff of red hair that surrounded her manicured pussy and the long fleshy labia he'd be sucking on tonight if he played his cards right... Perhaps he'd shove a broom handle up the rich bitch's cunt and spin her around. She'd look like one of those ceramic horses you see on a carnival carousel. Something for the kids to hold on to. God he'd been blessed with a vivid imagination!

Ruby took the drink. In a sweet Texas twang she said, *"That's pretty smooth, Cowboy... Pretty smooth."* She'd never had a Latin lover. Kind of unusual considering she lived in Texas. This one was definitely her type. Muscular, good looking, and assertive. It was her experience that assertive men usually backed it up. She wondered if guys got their confidence from the size of their cocks. What the hell, Ruby thought to herself. It's Sunday.

The two of them spent the rest of the day together. Carlo ordered more margaritas and did his thing. They discovered they were alike in many ways. Both were connoisseurs of good food, both appreciated well made clothing, and both of them drove a Ferrari. Neither one mentioned what they did for a living, though Ruby did say her father was in politics. Carlo just naturally assumed being from Texas, Ruby came from oil money.

As midday turned to late afternoon Ruby knew she had to make a decision. It'd been awhile. She could use a good fuck. She hated having sex on the first date, but then she wasn't actually dating this guy. Ruby didn't know anyone else in town, besides, she was a big girl. She invited Carlo to join her for dinner in her suite.

Ruby's suite was located on the top floor of the resort. When they walked in she pointed towards the kitchenette and told Carlo to make himself a drink. She was going to take a shower. A mini bar was stocked with a selection of beer, wine, and mixers. Carlo made himself a bacardi and coke, then stepped out on the balcony. From the fourteenth floor it offered a splendid view of the coast.

Ten minutes later Ruby appeared wearing a satin bathrobe and black stiletto heels. Her heels clicked on the bamboo floor as she walked across the room. When she reached Carlo she took his drink from his hand and said, *"Come here, Handsome."* Carlo wrapped his arms around the curvaceous attorney's body and pulled her tight. Ruby could feel his excitement! Carlo was standing at attention, and it definitely got hers...

Women are so easy, Carlo thought. Young or old. Short or tall. Rich or poor, it didn't matter. They all wanted to get laid. He would have liked to introduce this one to his special treatment. This one had class. He'd fuck her like she'd never been fucked before, then kick the shit out of her. Carlo knew he couldn't take it that far though. He couldn't afford to draw to much attention right now. Besides, *Little Miss Texas* had connections. Her father was a big shot politician up in D.C.

Carlo kissed Ruby till she purred... He was well versed in how to please a woman. He believed if the pleasure wasn't as fervent as it could be, the pain wouldn't be as harsh as it should be. In his head the two were intricately connected. He took Ruby's hand and lead her back inside. They sat on the sofa and picked right up were they'd left off. After several minutes of intense petting Ruby took over.

She'd done this before! Carlo was blown away at the boldness and skill in which Ruby worked. The woman took his manhood down her throat without so much as a whimper. Ruby Hines could suck cock. She'd been practicing since the eighth grade. By the time she was a junior in high school she'd developed a taste for it. Nothing had changed her mind since then.

When Ruby finished rocking Carlo's world she got up and made a drink. *"How was that,"* she asked when she returned to his arms? Carlo told her it was amazing. *"Good, because it happens to be my speciality,"* she bragged.

Carlo wasn't finished. He told Ruby he had a specialty too. She looked down to see he was fully erect again. She was amazed at how quickly he'd recovered, and thrilled that he wanted another go. *"I just need a little stimulation,"* he teased.

"Looks like you're plenty stimulated to me," Ruby responded. She put her head back and gasped as Carlo filled her.

The sex continued for the next couple hours. Ruby could feel Carlo fill her with each manly thrust. She put her hands on his bottom and encouraged him to probe even deeper. Eventually the pulsating onslaught filled her midsection and she released herself completely. Carlo felt the rhythmic beat of Ruby's orgasm and let himself climax at the same time. They lay there for quite a while, silently reviewing the evening's events. Then Carlo got up and went to take a shower.

He admired himself in the mirror as he dried off. There was a bathrobe hanging on the back of the door. It matched the one Ruby had been wearing earlier in the evening. Carlo slipped it on then popped his head out the door and asked Ruby if she wanted to go get something to eat.

She said she would prefer to eat in. There was a room service menu in the top drawer of the bedroom night stand. Carlo went to retrieve it. After making his selection he put the menu back in the drawer. That's when he noticed a briefcase on the floor next to the bed. It was open. Carlo could see it held a thick file folder and a legal size yellow tablet. They were sticking up in the air just begging to be read by a set of curious eyes. Carlo looked towards the door then quietly lifted the tablet from the briefcase.

"What the fuck," he said aloud once he realized what it was he was looking at. Written on the tablet were the words... *Veronica Stevens - homicide - November 13 - Daytona Beach Fl.* Below the inscription was a mess of undecipherable scribbling mixed with crudely drawn stick men and smiley faces. Carlo removed the file folder from the briefcase and opened it. Stapled to the inside corner was a business card. It identified Ruby Hines as a criminal defense attorney from Ft Worth, Texas. A quick check of the folder verified she was in Daytona working on the Veronica Stevens murder case. She was representing the woman who'd been charged with the crime.

Carlo rushed out of the bedroom. Standing there like a deer caught in someone's headlights he blurted out, *"I forgot to lock my car. My damn briefcase is on the back seat."* He grabbed his shorts and found his shoes, then turned to Ruby and said, *"I'll be right back."* Then he was gone!

No kiss good bye... No, *that was fun...* No nothing! Ruby didn't see Carlo after that. He never came back. Room service brought their food order, but she ate alone. Ruby knew men were strange creatures! Fortunately she only needed them occasionally... When the mood stuck.

EARLY RETIREMENT

MURDER IN DAYTONA

32

News of Veronica's murder swept through the facility like a Florida brush fire on a warm windy day. The shelter's director had hoped to make an announcement before word got out but she never had time. Loose lips sink ships, and this flotilla was going down fast. Teracita Goncalves was shocked when she heard about the brutal homicide of her friend from a gossip mongering fellow resident. A Jamaican woman named Flo.

It was common to see Flo hanging around the hallway outside the director's door. She was there when word of the murder first came in. Knowing that the murdered volunteer and Teracita were on friendly terms she went looking for her. Flo found the young Mexican woman in the community room reading a book. There were half a dozen other shelter residents there too. Some were playing cards, others watching TV.

Flo charged in announcing the murder as if it were a juicy story from some gossip magazine. She did so in her normal, hard to understand Jamaican-English accent. *"Memba mi teall you dis. Dat dum azz that wuks here. Dat Veeronika wooman. She be down! Oh zeen, me sey she murdahd! Alla dim goodaz whites girls gits it ventully. I nose dat."*

Within minutes word spread through the entire facility. The director arranged emergency counseling for any resident wishing to participate. A few girls filtered in, but most dealt with the news their own way. Teracita went into a state of denial. She got real quiet. She isolated herself in her room and refused to admit it even happened. She had to wonder, if Veronica was murdered, would she be next?

It was hard to hide from it. The story was carried on every television channel from Orlando to Jacksonville, as well as many of the cable news networks. The local newspaper ran front page lead ins and full page articles for several weeks following the murder. Word on the street was out. This case could prove disastrous for the already failing Daytona Beach economy.

A few weeks after the murder took place Teracita decided drastic action was necessary. She'd woke up in the middle of the night in a cold sweat. After calming herself with a cup of hot tea Teracita had a heart to heart conversation with herself. The way she saw it, she could either go back to Carlo... or run.

She'd run! If Carlo caught her he'd kill her for sure...and it wouldn't be pretty. Teracita knew her demise would make Veronica's murder seem like child's play. She was convinced Carlo murdered Veronica, just as she knew he started the fire that took the life of the priest she'd confided in. She also knew she was next.

She couldn't go to the cops! Carlo was a well respected attorney with important friends and acquaintances. She was a foreign domestic worker who'd terminated her right to be in this country when she ran off with him.

The fear of deportation loomed large. Returning to Delicias was out of the question. To return there would be to die there! No... Teracita would disappear into thin air. She couldn't rely on anyone to help her. Carlo would only use them to find her. He had access to information not available to most people. She knew from her days back in Delicias that the drug cartels could find anyone... It would be best to avoid the obvious!

Strange as it sounds Saint Paul, Minnesota is home to a large contingent of Mexican immigrants. Teracita had looked it up. One more would surely go unnoticed. She had money hidden away. Enough she figured, to buy a bus ticket there. The only problem was once in St Paul how would she survive?

Before she was murdered Veronica told Teracita there was an emergency cash drawer inside the director's office. She understood the frightened girl's predicament. Of course it was a serious crime to take it. She'd stipulated that it only be used under the strictest of extenuating circumstances!

Teracita would need to alter her appearance to shield her identity, but her plan seemed feasible. She'd wait until Saturday. The office staff didn't work weekends. The shelter custodian usually waited until then to do a thorough cleaning. Veronica had pointed out that the keys to the front offices were left on the janitor's cart when he took his lunch break. She felt bad that the poor guy would probably lose his job when the cash came up missing, but this was a life or death situation... He'd find another job!

There was four hundred and thirty-eight dollars in the cash drawer, as well as three dimes and three pennies. Teracita put the thirty-three cents back, but then changed her mind and took it. *Every penny counts,* she surmised.

While confiscating the cash she'd seen a pair of scissors on the director's desk. She stole them too. Later that night when everyone else had gone to bed Teracita took the scissors and went into the bathroom. Ten minutes later her long beautiful hair lay in clumps on the bathroom floor. The self produced boy cut looked quite stylish on the young Mexican woman. Next came a dye job. Teracita settled on red, thinking no one would ever recognize her. She nearly didn't.

A few days before the soon to be woman on the run had gone to a thrift store a couple blocks from the shelter hoping to find clothes to travel in. She'd found several masculine looking outfits that fit. The transformation was stunning. She looked a little like Hillary Swank playing that girl turned boy in the movie *Boys Don't Cry,* only a lot bigger on top. Come the crack of dawn she'd pack her new used wardrobe in a backpack and make her way to the bus station.

A Google search told her a one way ticket to Minneapolis cost one hundred and ninety-two dollars. It would take approximately forty-one hours to complete. Her bus was scheduled to depart at 7:00AM. She would arrive in Minnesota two days later, right around midnight. Not a soul on earth would know where she was. It had to be that way!

When she boarded the bus Teracita had her pick of seats. She took one a few rows from the back, preferring to be near the toilet. The bus was comfortable and the seats were roomy. She spent most of the morning looking out her window daydreaming of her new life.

As the day progressed Teracita watched the flora change. It went from live oak, to hardwood pine, to alabama hemlock. She'd never seen America, except on the television down at the bodega. This trip would take her through eight states. She was excited about the adventure. Eventually Teracita dozed off to the rhythmic cadence of the bus wheels rolling beneath her seat.

She woke to the sound of gun shots. At first startled, Teracita quickly realized the commotion was coming from a twenty inch movie screen that hung from the ceiling three rows forward. She recognized the characters on the screen, but not the actors playing them.

Mr T was arguing with Murdock as he haphazardly flew his helicopter at treetop level. Murdock completely ignored his nemesis' pleas to straighten out and fly right. Meanwhile Face was hanging out of the side of the helicopter by his fingertips, all while a dozen soldiers were firing automatic weapons at him. Finally Hannibal ordered them to knock it off. Mr T told Murdock, *"I'll deal with you later, Sucka,"* then he reached out and hauled Face back inside the chopper.

This was the theatrical version of the hit television show, *The 'A' Team.* The actors weren't the same ones Teracita was familiar with, but they were true to character.

The seat next to hers had been empty when she dozed off. It was now occupied by a young man, and he was completely engrossed in the film. Teracita thought he looked to be around twenty-five years of age. He had shoulder length blond hair and a full beard. His bare feet were pushed up against the back of the seat in front of him. It was several minutes before he realized the sleeping beauty sitting next to him had woke up.

"Hi," he said, *"I'm Aaron...and you are?"* Teracita blushed. Without thinking she blurted out her name. The moment it came out she realized she'd blown her cover. *"Well, young lady. You are missing a great flick... I used to watch The 'A' Team faithfully when I was a kid. Best show ever... So where you headed, Teracita?"*

When he heard where Teracita was going he laughed loudly. *"Girl, are you insane. You're going to Minnesota in December?"* He told Teracita he was from Clay County, Missouri. He was a marketing rep for a greeting card company there.

Aaron was quite perceptive for a young guy. He could tell Teracita was excessively anxious for some reason. He surmised she must be running from something. *"If I get up to Minnesota I'll have to look you up,"* he said. *"My accounts tend to take me in the opposite direction. I travel through northern Alabama, Tennessee, and western Kentucky."*

After a while Aaron went back to his movie. Occasionally he would look over at Teracita and smile. A few times she caught him checking out her boobs when he thought she wouldn't notice. It had been a long time since Teracita had been with a man. Carlo had introduced her to some very hard core stuff. She'd become used to frequent sex. Something stirred inside when she noticed, innocently enough, that the young man was sporting an erection inside his tight fitting jeans.

Tedium set in as Monday morning turned into Monday afternoon. The skies remained overcast all day, which only added to the problem. It was broken when the bus driver announced he was stopping at a diner in a small town just south of St Louis.

It seemed as though time here stood still. A gas station directly across from the diner had a giant metal winged horse on its roof. There was a single gas pump, which was staffed by an attendant. He actually checked your oil and washed your windshield as you gassed up. Two mechanics were busy servicing vehicles in the garage stalls.

A general store sat kitty corner to the diner. A blackboard sign advertised its fine collection of Deruta pottery and locally made crafts. Teracita was amazed when she saw a horse and buggy come clopping down the road. It pulled up in front of the general store. The rig was driven by a teenage boy wearing a wide brim hat and overalls. He was accompanied by two small children similarly dressed. Aaron noticed Teracita's interest and told her the kids were Mennonites. The area was full of them.

Until now Teracita had relied on the food she'd confiscated from the shelter's kitchen to tide her over. When Aaron offered to treat her to a *'real'* meal, she accepted.

They were seated at a blue vinyl booth towards the back. It featured a wall mounted Rockola. The antique juke box still played 45's for a quarter. Aaron pulled some change from his pocket and had Teracita select one. After scanning the menu Teracita decided on the St Louis style ribs. Aaron ordered Kansas City meat loaf with mashed potatoes and corn on the cob.

The two youngsters felt a little awkward at first. Aaron tried making small talk, explaining some of the nostalgia surrounding them. The black and white checkered floor, the chrome stools, and the wall art. There were a lot of photos on the walls. Most featured singers from the 1950's.

Teracita told Aaron when she was young she used to watch Elvis movies on Saturday afternoons. All the kids used to gather in front of the television set down at the bodeguita. It was the only TV in the barrio. She used to watch the 'A' Team there too. All the kids in Delicias did. They'd buy penny candy and watch TV. It was a tradition.

Aaron told Teracita he was of Irish decent. He'd grown up in Kansas City, at the point where the Missouri and Kansas Rivers converge. His parents had joined the Mormon church before he was born, hence the name Aaron.

His last name was Collins. He said he'd grown up poor too, but he'd been lucky enough to go to college on a scholarship. He earned a B.A. from Missouri Southern University, a small school up in Joplin.

When the bus driver announced it was time to hit the road a mass exodus took place. Ninety percent of the diner's customers rose in unison. Aaron and Teracita remained seated while the crowd exited. Once the other passengers were gone Aaron got up. He took Teracita's arm and escorted her out of the diner.

The bus driver stood at the bottom step of the bus welcoming each passenger back as they boarded. As Teracita and Aaron approached he said to them, *"I thought for sure I was gonna lose you two lovers."*

They were scheduled to arrive in Kansas City around 6:00PM. Teracita watched out the window as the plains of the Missouri countryside passed by. Eventually she drifted off to sleep. Just east of Kansas City she woke up. Her head was resting on Aaron's shoulder. He'd fallen asleep too. Someone had placed a blanket over them. She drank half a bottle of water then pulled up the blanket and snuggled into her new friend.

About thirty minutes later the bus pulled into the station. Teracita shook Aaron to tell him he was home. He rubbed his eyes, stretched, and looked out the window. *"This ain't home,"* he said. *"Not anymore!"*

The condition of the bus station was deplorable. Homeless people were spread across benches meant for customers waiting on buses. Garbage from a Burger King across the street littered the grounds. The scene was grimy at best, down right depressing at worst. Aaron looked at Teracita and whispered, *"For everything there is a reason. We all have a purpose under heaven."*

He stood up and gave Teracita a hug, then told her to stay on the bus. *"Nothing around here for you to see anyway. You don't want to use the restrooms here, that's for sure."* He took out his wallet and pulled out a business card and handed it to her. *"My phone number is on it,"* he said. *"Call me when you get to Minnesota... Just so I know you're okay... Okay?"*

Teracita watched him walk away. She felt a pang of remorse. He was such a nice guy. She would miss him. There were still six hours to go before she reached Minneapolis. Fear set in as Teracita recalled the events leading up to her current situation.

Her mind played tricks on her. She progressively got more and more paranoid. It seemed every man who looked at her had evil on his mind. Teracita closed her eyes but she couldn't escape the vision of Carlo leering over her with his fists clenched.

Fortunately no one who boarded the bus in Kansas City occupied the seat next to her. Teracita spread out and waited for the movie screen to drop down. Perhaps a flick would take her mind off things and allow her to escape reality for a while.

Pan's Labyrinth was being shown. It's the poignant story of a young girl being raised by a sadistic stepfather whose only escape is to enter into a fantasy world of horror and fascination. She must prove herself worthy in order to take her rightful place as Princess and be reunited with her father the King.

As captivating as the film was, Teracita drifted off to sleep. She was awakened by a voice telling her it was the end of the line. She gathered her things and stuffed them in her backpack, then walked off the bus.

It was late, and it was cold. A building across from the bus depot flashed the time and temperature. It was seventeen degrees outside. Teracita saw a line of taxi cabs up the street and headed for them. A cabbie approached her and said, *"Where you headed, Toots?"* Teracita told him she needed to find an inexpensive hotel for the night. The cabbie drove her to a place a few miles from the depot. The inn cost sixty bucks a night, but that included a modest continental breakfast.

She'd done her research. Teracita knew her final destination was West St Paul, a suburb a few miles south of Minneapolis. The city had a large Latino community. It would allow her to melt into the background, or so she hoped. After breakfast Teracita took advantage of the Twin Cities public transportation system. She walked eight blocks to a metro station and boarded a bus.

Two bus transfers and a twelve minute light rail train ride later and Teracita was in West St Paul. She found the city of some 20,000 residents to be quite vibrant. People hustled around her as she stepped off the train. It wasn't long before she realized they did so in part to keep warm. The temperature had only gone up ten degrees since last night.

Looking around she noticed a bakery and made her way to it. As if by design, a spanish language help wanted sign was in the window. Teracita went inside and ordered a loaf of pan dulce sweet bread and a cup of coffee, then she inquired about the job.

The middle aged baker who owned the store asked Teracita if she had references. *"No, I just arrived here,"* she answered. *"I'm from Kansas City"*

The baker told her he was sorry but no references, no job. Teracita thought a moment, then remembered Aaron. She told the baker she'd be back, then left to find a pay phone. After several rings Aaron picked up. Teracita told him she needed his help. After explaining the situation, Aaron came up with a plan.

He concocted a story about owning a small greeting card shop in Kansas City. Teracita had been a clerk there. She'd left when a sick relative asked her to come to Minnesota. Having no other family around, she'd agreed. Aaron said he would email a letter of reference to the baker, or telephone him if need be. With Aaron's fabrication fresh in her mind Teracita returned to the bakery.

The baker was busy waiting on a customer when she arrived so Teracita talked to his wife. The two women bonded immediately. Maria was a middle aged Mexican immigrant. She reminded Teracita of her mother. Warm and eager to please, willing to help anyone. Teracita told Maria the story Aaron had concocted. The baker's wife hired her on the spot.

Maria wanted to know if Teracita had a place to stay. *"No... Excepcion,"* she replied. *"I hope to find one soon."* The woman took Teracita by the hand and lead her behind the counter. The baker stood by helplessly as they disappeared behind the door and into his home. He just shook his head. *"Asombrosa,"* he said to himself... *"Amazing!"*

The baker's wife showed Teracita a cute little studio apartment. It was accessible from the back of her apartment. You just exited through the kitchen door and walked ten feet down the hall. The apartment was furnished with traditional Mexican furniture. A wrought iron bed took up most of the space. The galley kitchen featured a hand painted ceramic bowl sink. There was a small fridge, a microwave, and a stove top to cook on. Everything anyone could possibly need was there, right down to the dish towels.

Maria told her new employee the job paid $150 per week with the apartment, or $250 without. Teracita took it with the apartment, inferring the little studio was a Godsend. The baker's wife agreed. It was... Divine intervention.

Teracita took a few days to get familiar with her new surroundings. She learned how to operate the cash register, and how to deal with difficult customers. It was apparent her days as an Au Pair were over, so it was just as well. She worked a split shift. That way she was there during the busy periods. Early morning, lunch time, and late afternoons. The shop was closed on Sunday and Monday.

Over the next few months the baker and his wife grew fond of Teracita. They understood she was in the country illegally, as were many others in the community. The baker paid her off the books, and in cash. Teracita rarely ventured out, other than to attend mass at the Church of St Joseph on Sunday mornings. Sometimes she accompanied Maria when she went to the mall or needed help grocery shopping.

Teracita never dated anyone. She never even talked about a man. It was obvious she was running from something, but the baker and his wife never pried. They watched over her and treated her like the daughter they never had. Perhaps Maria was right... Maybe it was divine intervention!

EARLY RETIREMENT

MURDER IN DAYTONA

33

Ruby Hines arrived at the court house early. She'd reserved work space in a room just down the hall from the judges chambers. Gwen, her paralegal assistant, had flown in the night before to assist with paper work and research. She was staying at a motel near the airport. Gwen phoned Ruby first thing that morning. She wasn't at all surprised to hear that her boss was already on the job.

The Grand Jury was scheduled to convene at 10:00AM. At quarter past seven Ruby placed a breakfast order with a local restaurant that advertised free delivery. *"Red pepper quiche, paired with garlic butter croissants and fresh squeezed orange juice, please. Oh...and black coffee... Bold!"*

After reviewing the documentation for the umpteenth time Ruby live streamed the local news on her laptop. She watched intensely as the female anchor baited her audience with promises of coverage from the steps of the district courthouse. The Grand Jury would be hearing the Doris Van Fleet murder indictment.

After interjecting two non related stories between three sets of commercials the anchor finally said, *"And now we go live to the Seventh Judicial District Courthouse in Daytona Beach. Good morning, Yolanda."*

A very attractive television news correspondent appeared on the screen. She was wearing a short red chemise with matching heels. The young woman was standing on the top step of the county courthouse facing Orange Avenue. She'd just started talking about the Veronica Stevens murder investigation when a brisk wind coming off the ocean suddenly lifted her dress up around her waist. Her camera operator quickly panned to the marina across the street. As he swung his lens around viewers got a look at the Daytona Beach skyline.

Once the wind died down the recomposed reporter reappeared on the screen as if nothing had happened. Yolanda Gibson was a twenty-one year old college intern. She'd only been working at the station a few months when the manager gave her the prestigious assignment. Rumors ran rampant as to what Yolanda may have done to persuade him to do that. Whatever his reason, she was very good in front of a camera. The young woman exuded confidence. She handled the *upskirt* incident like a seasoned pro. It was for all intense and purposes her 'Marilyn Monroe' moment!

She told her viewers local police agencies had difficulty trying to identify a suspect, but one was finally in custody. *"A woman named Doris Van Fleet has been charged with the murder of fifty-two year old Veronica Stevens of Ormond Beach. The victim was found dead in a beach side motel this past November. The unsolved crime had put a damper on the Christmas holidays locally, and was promising to negatively impact the upcoming tourist season."*

Yolanda went on to tell her audience that reliable sources are reporting the police have uncovered what is said to be damning evidence inside the suspect's home. Evidence that could positively link her to the crime. She said the woman charged with the crime was a lesbian, and that the alleged perpetrator and the victim were once lovers. She inferred this case was similar to the so called *'Monster murders'* committed by lesbian serial killer Ailleen Warnous back in the eighties.

Gwen showed up with two cups of coffee she purchased from the Starbucks around the corner from the courthouse. Ruby took one of the cups and told her assistant she was headed for the rear entrance of the building. She wanted to be there when Doris was escorted in. She instructed Gwen to continue monitoring the news, and to annotate anything she considered significant.

A police van arrived just as Ruby stepped off the elevator. The rear doors swung open and two muscle bound deputies escorted the prisoner into the building. They were accompanied by a female jailer who was carrying Doris' walking cane. Ruby rushed over and identified herself as Ms Van Fleet's attorney, then notified them she would be accompanying her client to the holding cell.

When she and Doris were alone Ruby explained the procedure in detail. She wanted Doris to know what she could expect once they were in the courtroom. She instructed her not to answer any questions or make any statements to anyone without her being there.

Ruby again asked Doris where she was on the day of the murder. When Doris replied with a shrug of her shoulders the attorney gave her a warning. *"You should know the grand jury will most likely come back with an indictment. The prosecution has more than enough circumstantial evidence to make a case. Just not enough to convict... Not in my opinion... If you are indicted we will plead not guilty!"*

At 9:55 Ruby told Doris it was time to go. She gave her a hug and said she'd see her in the courtroom. Ruby walked up the two flights of stairs and made her way to the front of the building. Gwen was seated at the defendant's table reviewing documents when she walked in. The jury, which consisted of eight men and four women, was already seated and waiting on Judge Walker's arrival. Ruby smiled at them as she took her seat next to Gwen.

At 10:05 a bailiff walked out of the judges chambers, closely followed by a black man in a black robe. He turned towards those assembled and said, *"All Rise."*

The honorable Halstrom Davis Walker was the first black man to graduate from Florida State University's College of Law. He'd been an assistant district attorney in Tallahassee for twenty-two years when he decided to run for city mayor. After being voted in he served two terms. The judge then accepted a seat on the bench of Leon County's Court of Appeals. He became State Justice for the Seventh Judicial District in 2005. Halstrom Walker was known locally as 'The Hanging Judge.'

The charges against the defendant were read aloud in the courtroom. *"Murder in the 1st degree; Unlawful detention and false imprisonment; Use of a deadly weapon in the commission of a felony; Sodomy; Lewd & lascivious behavior; Cruel & inhuman treatment; Failure to appear in defiance of an outstanding warrant; Interstate flight to avoid prosecution.*

The state prosecutor introduced the evidence that had been used to justify taking Doris Van Fleet into custody. Ruby knew he had a good case. Some of the evidence could be damning. She chose to make the jury wait before responding. It was a ploy she used sometimes, believing the tactic could cause a juror to become distracted. Three minutes passed before Ruby finally stood and approached the jury.

"Did any of you folks happen to notice the cane my client uses to assist her walking," she asked? *"Do any of you truly believe this woman has the physical ability to commit the offenses she has been charged with? Did the district attorney present a single witness that can place my client at the scene of the offense? Did he present a single fingerprint? Did he offer even one single piece of forensic evidence? I suggest the prosecution is grasping at straws, ladies and gentlemen. They simply have no case!"*

Ruby gave the jury time to let her words sink in. She made eye contact with each individual juror before proceeding. *"They've provided you with an orange cart full of circumstantial evidence that I intend to tip over and spill across this courtroom floor. If you choose to let the state continue with its lesbian witch hunt then I suggest you tread carefully. Oranges rot easily in the hot Florida sun. You all will be knee deep in tangelo mash before it's over."*

The attorney turned and walked back towards her client. She gave her a wink, then grabbed Doris' cane and turned back to the jury. *"Consider the victim's size,"* she said. *"Veronica Stevens was five foot five inches tall. She weighed one hundred fifty pounds. Could my client physically manipulate an adult size body at her age and condition? I suggest she could not. The prosecution hasn't offered one single ounce of verifiable evidence in this case, ladies and gentlemen. Ms Doris Van Fleet **did not...I repeat, did not murder Veronica Stevens**. If indicted... **WE WILL PLEAD NOT GUILTY!"***

The jury deliberated. Ruby Hines had made a good argument. The evidence was circumstantial, and taken alone was probably not enough to indict. One glaring fact posed a problem. The attorney for the defense never alluded to the whereabouts of her client on the day of the murder. If Doris Van Fleet had nothing to do with the crime, why didn't she have an alibi? If she wasn't at the scene at the time the crime was committed, then where was she...and who was she with?

The key to the puzzle was literally found hidden under the suspect's bed. Why would she be hiding a key to the very motel room where the victim was found? Why would she even be in possession of such a key? Circumstantial? Perhaps, but damning nonetheless. The jury pondered, but in the end they knew what they had to do.

Three hours after deliberating the grand jury returned to the courtroom. All twelve members were in concordance. They'd signed an indictment charging Doris Van Fleet with murder in the first degree for causing the death of Veronica Stevens. Judge Walker read the indictment aloud then set a date for the defense to offer its plea. This case was going to trial.

EARLY RETIREMENT
MURDER IN DAYTONA

34

Carlo laid low in the days following his sexual encounter with Ruby Hines. He'd had an enjoyable time before learning who she was and why she was in town. Fortunately for her his discovery had negated the beating he'd planned to surprise her with. She was the type he usually chose too. A woman with no local ties, no morals, and a superior attitude.

People at the resort had seen them together, but Carlo wasn't concerned about it. As an attorney he knew total recall was almost none existent in eye witness accounts. Most people gave varying physical descriptions that rarely matched the testimony of other witnesses. Even fewer ever matched time lines or other crucial facts. Chances are they were just faces in the crowd.

He knew the grand jury was deliberating that morning. Carlo arrived at his office around eight o'clock. The charming despot greeted the receptionist with a kiss on the cheek, then told her he was working on an important case and didn't want to be disturbed. Once sequestered behind his desk Carlo unfolded the newspaper he brought with him from home.

The paper featured the Stevens murder story on its front page. The headline read, *'TILL DEATH DO US PART.'* Underneath the headline was a subtitle, *'Lesbian Lover Faces Death Penalty.'* Carlo read the article nonchalantly as he sipped his coffee.

He seemed impervious to any feelings the story may have stirred. When he finished reading he just smiled...then opened his laptop. He surfed the web for a few minutes, looking for newly posted pictures of young women in various sadomasochistic poses. After selecting a few for his personal file Carlo changed gears.

A small flat screen television was mounted on the wall opposite him. Carlo reached in his desk drawer for the controls and tuned in a local news broadcast. A young female correspondent appeared. She was standing on the steps of the courthouse prepared to tell viewers about the impending decision the Grand Jury would be making this morning concerning the Veronica Stevens homicide. Carlo adjusted the volume so he could listen in.

Just as she was about to give her report a gust of wind suddenly blew in off the ocean and lifted the reporter's dress up, exposing her for all to see. Once his laughter subsided Carlo felt a familiar tinge in his gut. She was delectable. He'd have to remember this one!

The story was given *'special'* status by the television news division. This meant as information became available the station would interrupt its local broadcast to give viewers up to date reports. Carlo kept the television on so he could watch the story develop.

Around 9:00 the sexy on site news correspondent reappeared on the television screen. A police van had just arrived and officers were escorting Doris Van Fleet into the courthouse. One of them walked ahead and held the door open for the prisoner. When he did Carlo saw Ruby Hines. She was standing just inside the doors, waiting as her client slowly made her way towards the entrance. Once the prisoner disappeared inside the building the camera operator panned back to the reporter, who gave a brief synopsis of the event.

Carlo telephoned Jewel to ask if she'd seen the news. Jewel hadn't realized what she was getting herself into when she agreed to do Carlo's bidding. She'd only wanted to make him happy so he'd make her happy. Now she was beginning to understand how serious her involvement could be. If she were to be caught her conviction could result in a very long prison sentence. She had no choice but to go along.

Carlo reassured Jewel he knew what he was doing. It was a game to him, and he played to win. All Jewel had to do was, *"Keep on keeping on!"* He told her no one would suspect anything if she just acted normal. She just had to continue going to work, remain friendly with the case manager so as not to raise suspicion, and be prepared to answer any questions that might arise. He'd take care of the rest.

Naturally Carlo knew Jewel was scared of him. He liked it that way. Of course it didn't stop the little piglet from fucking him every night. She was a needy woman. Carlo would take advantage, but eventually he'd have to deal with the situation.

At half past three a *'special report'* interrupted programming again. Yolanda Gibson appeared on camera with news of the indictment. Doris Van Fleet had been formally charged. The Grand Jury found sufficient evidence to proceed with a trial. The devious attorney grinned from ear to ear. *"Call me a creep now,"* Carlo said aloud... *"You fucking dyke!"*

His plan was coming to fruition. The only thing lacking was Teracita. Carlo's next step would be to free her from the bondage of the shelter. He assumed she'd be brainwashed by now. She may not even recognize him anymore. Carlo called Jewel and told her about the grand jury's decision. *"I told you everything would be okay,"* he said. *"I know what I'm doing, Babe!"* Jewel was silent on the other end. After a few awkward moments Carlo said, *"I'm going to need your help getting Teracita out of the shelter."*

Jewel never mentioned Teracita was no longer at the shelter. She knew Carlo would freak when he found out. He'd most likely leave her. Jewel was afraid he might even kill her, just like he'd killed Veronica. Her hope had been that once he got used to being with a 'real' woman he'd forget about the Mexican teenager.

Teracita had left the shelter shortly after the news of Veronica's murder first spread through the facility. She just vanished into thin air. Most of the residents thought she had something to do with the robbery of the cash drawer in the director's office because she'd disappeared the same day the theft was discovered. Unfortunately the custodian had been blamed. He was the only person in the facility that had keys to the office. After an investigation showed there was no sign of a break in he'd been dismissed.

Now that Doris Van Fleet had been indicted for **his** crime Carlo could turn his attention back to Teracita. He'd devise a plan to get her away from the shelter. Perhaps Jewel could arrange to take her shopping at the mall. It would be easy to snatch her away and take her somewhere to be detoxified to his way of thinking.

Carlo celebrated that night. He raided Jewel's liquor cabinet, drinking far more than a man with his secrets ever should. He let his guard down, mentioning this wasn't the first time he'd killed someone. Jewel must've had a look of horror on her face because Carlo caught himself mid sentence and dropped it. He was drunk, but not that drunk.

It was better Jewel believe Veronica Stevens had been the only casualty to suffer the wrath of Carlo Santiago. The last thing he needed was to frighten his accomplice away with grisly stories of past deeds done. To take her mind off it Carlo did what he does best. He took Jewel in his arms.

By early morning the passion had subsided. Carlo lay quietly beside his sleeping paramour. The smile on her face was a telltale sign she'd gotten exactly what she needed. Exactly what she craved... Carlo too was completely relaxed. He breathed slow, deep breaths. Looking straight up at the ceiling he said aloud, *"Teracita, my love. Tomorrow I bring you home."* Then he drifted off to sleep.

When Carlo woke Jewel poured him some freshly brewed coffee. She knew he wasn't a breakfast person. She'd already eaten, having been up for over an hour. How she wished last night could last forever. In her heart she knew that wasn't going to be. Then he said something that caught her completely off guard. Something she never thought she'd ever hear. *"I love you, Jewel."*

The words rolled off his tongue like he really meant them. Carlo needed Jewel's cooperation to bring his plan to a successful conclusion. She was his means to an end. In a way he did love her. Just not in the normal sense. He loved how desperate she was for attention. How insecure she was about her appearance. How she could be used and abused without fear of reprisal. Love has many wonderful applications. The trick is in knowing how to apply them.

Jewel teared up. Why now? Why did he have to say those words then? Where were the *I love you's* last night? She considered the ramifications of her next act, then acted. Jewel told Carlo she'd checked Teracita's file before leaving work the previous day and gotten quite a shock. *"She's gone, Carlo... Teracita took off a couple months ago. A few weeks after Veronica and I went to the motel. No one knows where. She just disappeared!"*

Carlo never even blinked! He stood perfectly still, like a cold stone statue. Jewel told him about the theft from the director's office. *"Over $400 dollars was taken from the emergency reserve cash drawer"* she said. *"The custodian got blamed because he had a key to the office, but most of the residents think Teracita took it because she went missing the very day the money did."*
Without uttering a word Carlo got dressed and walked out. Jewel peeked out the corner of the living room window curtain as

he got in his Mercedes and drove away. When it was gone she breathed a sigh of relief. She'd expected him to blow a gasket. If this was the end, so be it. She was ready to move on.

Carlo had plans for Jewel. Plans he'd been formulating for weeks. She was becoming a nuisance. A ball and chain. She'd served her purpose, now it was time to cut her loose. He'd miss the sex. Jewel was insatiable. He would've liked to keep her as a pet, but it wasn't in the cards.

His client and confidant Jose Gacha owed him a favor. The Columbian crime boss had been busy establishing *Los Norte* as the main trafficker of human beings in south Florida. The cartel had made hundreds of millions of dollars in the drug trade, but RICO laws had changed the tide. Human trafficking was the new money making machine in organized crime.

It would take years before laws were passed to control the trade. So much emphasis had been put on stopping international narcotic trafficking that no one saw it coming... Almost no one! Jose Gacha did, and he was now in position to be a major player.

Gacha had connections. Politicians, police commissioners, judges, padrones. He even had the Russian mob and leaders of rival cartels cooperating with him. Senor' Gacha had become a very influential man.

Human beings were being trafficked for a variety of reasons. Slave labor, forced bondage, illegal adoption, even as a supply line for body parts used in medical transplants. The majority however were women and children supplied for the sexual gratification of men. Carlo was hoping Gacha would find a place for his Jewel. Perhaps in an eastern European whorehouse, or sold as property to some rich South American philanderer.

Carlo found the thought of Jewel being turned into a sex slave amusing. He knew she'd be popular on the meat market, even at her age. Women with huge tits and big asses always were. Carlo knew the pimps and videographers who worked the black market had ways of turning even the most innocent of girls into coital pigs. She would be easy. Jewel was a natural. It wouldn't surprise him if she ended up in hardcore underground porn videos, or worse. She deserved it! Jewel had deserted him when he needed her most.

EARLY RETIREMENT

MURDER IN DAYTONA

35

I watched the proceedings intensely, absorbed in seeing my wife's killer finally brought to justice. The prosecutor and the attorney for the defense seemed to be watching just as closely. Judge Walker questioned each potential juror. He wanted to be absolutely sure they met all the qualifications necessary to serve in his courtroom. The *Voir Dire* examination was something of an art. The judge knew a potential juror's body language was often more revealing then his verbal response. Once he was satisfied, the attorney for the defense was allowed her turn.

I noticed how closely the redheaded barrister studied each person as they took the stand. I could tell her mind was working overtime, even as she appeared to be completely relaxed. A few of her questions perplexed me. For example one juror was asked where she shops for shoes, while another was asked how often he trims his beard. She asked two female jurors if either of them followed specific diets.

Ruby Hines encouraged the pool of potential jurors to speak freely. She used tactics like nodding her head yes as she spoke, and waited patiently for the quieter ones to formulate a response in their minds before answering. The attractive attorney smiled at the female candidates, and borderline flirted with the men. On one occasion the judge requested she refrain from *'coaxing'* the jury.

Ms Hines was young, but oh how she reminded me of my Veronica. From the red hair and nails to the funky outfits and high heels. How I wished she was the prosecutor rather than the defense attorney. The contradiction was painful in a way. It was as if a younger version of my wife was defending the person who'd murdered her.

After Ruby Hines finished questioning a potential jurist the prosecuting attorney would take his turn. His questions were more direct and to the point. Did the juror believe in God? Did they believe in the principal of an eye for an eye? What did he or she do for a living? Had anyone in their family ever been convicted of a felony? Were any of them homosexuals? This back and forth pattern of questioning went on for several hours. At the end of the day eighteen potential jurors had been excused. Twelve for peremptory reasons and six as a challenge for cause made by the respective attorneys. Only five were chosen to serve.

This procedure went on for several days. Eventually a jury of twelve was chosen, along with six alternates. It consisted of seven men and five women. The average age was fifty-three, though one juror was twenty-six and another seventy-two. I attended every session, as did Chief Detective Dan Brooks. We greeted one another daily but sat on opposite ends of the gallery.

For the first time I realized Brooks was a nail biter. I watched as he unconsciously gnawed on his fingertips, completely absorbed in the proceedings. The big detective seemed quite a bit older than I remembered. In actuality we were relatively close in age, but for some reason I'd always thought of him as much younger than myself. In my mind Brooks was more masculine, more virile, and more vibrant then I. Looking at him now I couldn't help but think the case had aged him. The thought lifted my spirits in an odd way.

With the jury selected the trial was scheduled to begin the following Monday morning. The local Fox affiliate announced plans to carry the trial live. The atmosphere was sure to be circus like. People were expecting a show.

The center ring would feature the actual trial, while the side rings would attract the lesbian agenda and the domestic abuse connections. Other lesser interests would bring their followers too. The death penalty crowd, the born again Christians, the tourism industry folks, even the local elected officials.

I would be in attendance for sure. Playing the role of resident torchbearer, I'd be cheering the good guys on to victory. I'm not a violent person, but I wanted justice. I didn't care who the defendant was or what her sexual preferences were. I didn't care if it was a crime of passion or a random act. The only thing I cared about was seeing my wife's killer put down.

The proceedings were scheduled to begin at nine o'clock in the morning. Knowing the interest the trial had generated I planned to arrive a half hour early. When I turned onto Orange Avenue I saw a huge throng of people standing in front of the courthouse. Many of them were carrying signs claiming affiliation with one group or another. Being for or against the accused determined which group one belonged to.

Traffic was being directed into a single lane as I approached the courthouse. I put my turn signal on, intending to pull into the courthouse parking lot, but I was rebuffed by a traffic cop. He motioned for me to go straight. When I tried to explain I was there for the trial he barked, *"Move it,"* then turned away.

As I approached the Orange Avenue Bridge the traffic came to a standstill. On the beach side of the street people were parking in the empty lots of boarded up businesses. The economic climate in this part of the state provided ample room for all.

My failure to foresee the level of interest in my wife's case caused me to miss most of that mornings proceedings. There were approximately sixty seats in the galley. Half were reserved for witnesses and family members. The remainder went to members of the media and casual spectators. Dozens camped out overnight hoping to secure one of the seats. By the time I parked and walked back across the bridge it was nearly ten o'clock.

I made my way through the ever increasing crowd, taking in the carnival atmosphere as I pushed myself towards the courthouse steps. It reminded me of the midway at the New York State Fair on a Saturday night. A mass of people milling around, most with no particular destination in mind. There were people holding picket signs, some for the death penalty, some against. A few held signs warning of the coming rapture, others simply read JOHN 3:16. A contingent from the rainbow coalition showed up to support gays and transgenders.

The kicker was when I saw this guy pushing vacation time shares right in front of the courthouse. A short tour would net me a free movie pass and lunch at the Ocean Walk. Declining his offer I made my way to the front entrance. Another ten minutes was spent emptying my pockets and removing my shoes so I could pass through security. It was nearly eleven o'clock when I finally made it to the courtroom. I no sooner arrived when I was met by a rush of people spilling out into the hallway.

The proceedings had started with the arraignment at precisely 9:00AM. The charges had been read by the prosecuting attorney, a man named Uriah Wells. Wells possessed a calm demeanor and a slow southern drawl. His non assuming nature gave credence to the phrase, *'Talk softly and carry a big stick.'* The silky smooth orator was personally responsible for putting more than a dozen men on Florida's death row.

Once charges were formerly lodged the judge asked the attorney for the defense how her client was going to plead. *"We plead not guilty, Your honor"* she replied, before adding... *"As promised!"*

328

The preliminaries over, Judge Walker instructed the prosecutor to give his opening statement. He did so in textbook *Uriah Wells* style. He never referred to Doris Van Fleet by name, choosing instead to refer to her as, *The Killer.* Uriah knew the importance of having the jury identify the defendant with the negative *'Killer'* label. It was a psychological ploy that often worked. It's a scientific fact that once an image is formed in someone's mind it is difficult to dislodge.

When describing the victim Uriah used words like, *'nurturing mother, loving wife, compassionate volunteer.'* The prosecutor's goal was to portray Veronica in as positive a manner as possible, imprinting a good impression of her in the minds of the jury. Unlike defendants, Uriah always referred to victims by name.

He described the scene of the crime to the jury, asserting the reality of the brutal murder with adjectives like horrific, agonizing, and despicable. The prosecutor painted a mental picture for the jury, turning the modest motel room into a torture chamber, where the atrocities suffered by the victim were inflicted over the course of many hours.

Uriah informed the jury they'd be shown graphic photographs, warning them they'd be shocked and sickened. He explained the importance of understanding the nature of the crimes committed. He told the jury evidence would be presented that would directly implicate the defendant as the killer. Evidence that could not be explained away or ignored.

The prosecutor masterfully walked the jury through the case. He referred to Veronica's earlier involvement with the defendant, suggesting it was a case of youthful experimentation by a young woman confused by the lack of affection she received from her father. Uriah told the jury the defendant on the other hand had a history of violent behavior and a demonstrated lack of self control.

"The defendant's inability to accept reality and get on with her life, even after all those years, led her to a desperate conclusion. If Veronica Stevens wouldn't love her... She'd love no one."

Uriah Wells proposed the defendant had recently found out her ex-lover was living near Daytona Beach. Less than an hour's drive from her home in Mount Dora. He told the jury he intended to provide evidence proving the defendant was void of normal human emotions. He would show she was quite capable of carrying out such a dastardly deed.

"Murder, ladies and gentlemen of the jury, is very often a crime of opportunity," the prosecutor explained. *"When Veronica Stevens accepted an early retirement offer from her employer and moved to Florida... The door of opportunity opened."*

He went on. *"Let me ask, did you ever have a sore that just wouldn't heal? A sore that festers, no matter how much ointment you put on it. There are folks who have contracted diseases. They carry the symptoms of those diseases their entire lives... Just when they think their symptoms have cleared up a stressful situation arises and low and behold, they reappear. If you had sores like that wouldn't you want to get rid of them, once and for all?"*

Uriah had the jury right where he wanted them! He continued. *"Just get rid of them, so they couldn't keep coming back to cause you more pain and embarrassment."*

The metaphorical comparison was ingenious. It painted a picture truly worth a thousand words. Doris Van Fleet suffering from an incurable venereal disease. Years spent trying to separate herself from the pain and suffering, only to have it come back worse than ever. Finally, when opportunity allowed her to rid herself of it once and for all, she did. Who could blame her? Everyone deserved some measure of peace and tranquility, right?

So when the time came she hacked it off, and with a vengeance...
Guilty as charged!

The prosecutor told the jury he would show that the defendant had the motive, the means, and the wherewithal to commit murder. *"Physical evidence was found in her possession that irrefutably links her to the scene of the crime,"* Uriah insisted. *"When this trial has concluded I am sure you will find you have but one choice, ladies and gentlemen. To find the accused guilty of murdering Mrs Veronica Stevens in cold blood."*

If the trial had ended with the prosecutor's opening statement it would have been cut and dry. Uriah Wells made Doris Van Fleet look like a vindictive, venomous, vengeful woman. Disillusioned and hell bent on getting even for past inequities. Fearing jurors would view her physical limitations empathetically, he used them against her. Rather than show pity on her, the prosecutor told the jury he would establish that the defendant used her liability like an albatross.

"The Killer's medical issue was another source of anger and frustration that built up over time. I will present eye witness accounts," Uriah informed the jury, *"of our supposedly handicapped defendant violently hurling her cane in an episode of uncontrolled rage. Do not be fooled,"* he warned them. *"Testimony given by medical doctors and physical therapist will substantiate without a doubt that the defendant is physically capable of committing the crimes she has been charged with."*

At the conclusion of the prosecutor's opening statement Judge Walker called for a twenty minute recess. It was during this recess I arrived. Fortunately I was able to find out some of what had transpired in my absence. I watched as a television news reporter gave an account of the proceedings to her audience. She spoke of the drama unfolding in the courtroom. How smooth the prosecutor was, and how eloquently he spoke.

331

She gave viewers a description of the defendant, telling them how Doris was dressed and what jewelry she wore. Specifically a necklace. A thick gold chain with an unusual pendant. It featured a skull smiling up at a bouquet of roses.

Out of the corner of my eye I saw Detective Brooks. He was watching me watching the newscaster. He smiled when I nodded at him, and motioned for me to come over. *"What do you think so far, Stevens,"* he asked? *"That prosecutor is smooth as a baby's bottom, don't you agree?"* I had to explain my tardiness, and the fact I'd missed the morning's entire proceeding. *"Too bad,"* he replied. *"You'd have been pleased."*

The detective filled me in on what had transpired during the morning session. Just as he was finishing someone in the crowd announced court was back in session in five minutes. Everyone shuffled back inside and took their seats. I was escorted to a reserved seat by a female bailiff.

"All rise," an officer of the court announced as a stately black man dressed in a ceremonious black silk robe appeared from a door to the right of the bench. *"The Honorable Hiram Walker presiding over the Seventh District Judicial Court."*

I recognized the judge from the indictment hearing. He was an imposing figure, and I felt a sense of pride and satisfaction as I thought about what Veronica's reaction would be to a black man presiding over her killer's trial. My wife always had a heart for the oppressed. She constantly reminded me of her belief that Black America would eventually rise above the shackles of bondage that tried to keep them in their place. She'd truly be pleased today!

"Is the defense ready to present its opening statement," the Judge asked? Ruby Hines stood and answered affirmatively. I watched as she bent down and whispered something in her client's ear. I'd only seen pictures of Doris. It felt odd seeing her in person.

I thought she looked frail. I'd expected a vibrant looking woman. Attractive, but in a masculine way. Instead I saw a thin lady about my age dressed in a gabardine pantsuit with a matching silk chiffon blouse.

Ruby paced back and forth in front of the jury box. When she stopped she looked directly into the eyes of each juror. I found myself doing the same thing. I was sure I recognized some of them from the indictment hearing. I made a mental note of which ones I'd agreed should be on the jury. After Ruby made eye contact with each juror, she spoke.

"Ladies and gentleman, allow me to thank you for your service to your community and to this proceeding. My client and I are grateful for the sacrifice each one of you has made to be here today. I'm sure the family of the victim is appreciative of your efforts as well." Then she turned and looked at me.

"Mr Stevens, I would like to extend my deepest sympathy to you and your family for your loss. I'm sure this is a difficult time for you. I assure you it is my goal to get to the truth during these proceedings." After a perfectly timed pause, Ruby turned to address the jury again.

"Ladies and Gentlemen, the prosecutor has provided us with information this morning which, taken out of context, could lead one to conclude my client had something to do with the death of her friend, Veronica Stevens. I intend to prove he is mistaken. The so called evidence the prosecutor will present to you is highly circumstantial, innately subjective, and perception based. The proof is in the pudding, ladies and gentleman. I will not allow my client to be served up as dessert for a prosecution that has no factual basis to make their case. The law demands there be proof beyond a reasonable doubt... It simply does not exist!

The attractive attorney was good at her job. I was impressed, not only by her conviction but with her ability to persuade. Ruby Hines was tough as a bucket of nails, while simultaneously as feminine as a blossoming flower. I'd hired old Arty Sheckstein to represent me. Thankfully my alibi got me off, because I wouldn't have stood a chance against the likes of someone as competent and skillful as this lady.

I wanted to dislike her. I was supposed to dislike her, but I didn't! On the contrary, I was damn turned on by her. As Ruby continued her opening statement to the jury I slipped into a fantasy laced trance.

The navy blue pinstripe skirt Ruby was wearing fit like a glove. It sat on her hips like hot fudge on a sundae before drizzling down around her vanilla ice cream thighs, stopping several inches above her knees. She filled the garment out in a way only a woman could. The attorney's unbuttoned waist length pinstripe jacket hinted at the large round breasts hidden beneath her camisole. Navy blue stiletto heels not only completed her ensemble... They set it off.

When Ruby walked across the hard wooden courtroom floor the clickety-clack sound of her heels made my stomach flutter. I'm convinced I wasn't alone. The room stirred with her every step. I watched her mouth as she spoke, but honestly didn't hear a word. I was mesmerized by the shape of her lips, and the glossy lipstick that covered them. Her red fingernails matched perfectly. I envisioned them digging into my back as I penetrated her.

The sound of the Judge Walker's gavel striking its wooden block snapped me out of my trance. I'd missed most of the defense attorney's opening statement. Now court was adjourned. Everyone stood as the judge made his way to his chambers. I glanced over at the defendant's table and saw Ruby looking back at me. The moment our eyes met she turned back to her client. Doris was being prepared to be taken back to her holding cell by a female jailer. Her ankles were shackled and her wrists handcuffed. Once chained, the jailer grabbed Doris by the elbow and helped her up.

Court had recessed for lunch. The proceedings would begin again at 2:15PM. I made my way to the front of the courthouse and exited the building. My position on the top step offered a gorgeous panoramic view of the marina across the street. The throng that had gathered in front of the courthouse that morning had dissipated. I decided to take a walk around the perimeter and enjoy the display of boats sitting in their slips.

I've always enjoyed being around boats. When I lived up north I used to attend classic wooden boat shows. Veronica and I once thought about buying one, until we realized the work involved in keeping them maintained properly.

It dawned on me the last time I was on a boat was the day I'd found my wife's body. It had begun with me joining my neighbor on a fishing trip. The smell of mahogany was fresh in my mind as I reminisced about his *'Salome,'* She was a beauty, and he cared for her like she was his most precious asset. I remembered he'd lost his wife. I was saddened that I'd now joined him in that classification...

It was all still very real. The smell of death and the grimy feel of cheap accommodations. The shame of being placed under arrest and questioned like a common criminal. The realization that through no fault of my own I was for all intense and purposes, alone in the world. My soul mate had been stolen from me by an *unnamed* thief.

The time went swiftly. I heard a church bell chime in the distance. Two gongs told me it was time to get back. I returned to the courthouse with a new found vengeance. The thief who'd stolen my life *was* named, and she was sitting at the defendant's table.

Doris Van Fleet had once been Veronica's lover. She'd introduced her to the lesbian lifestyle, and tried to turn her into something she was not. When Veronica couldn't fake it anymore Doris made her feel like a failure. She became abusive, and subjected Veronica to all kinds of mental cruelty. When she could no longer take it, Veronica ran. When she did, she ran to me!

I never saw it coming. I knew my wife feared Doris, but it'd been years ago and miles away. How could I protect her from such evil? Who knew her ex-lover, her implacable nemeses, lived just down the road in Mt Dora? I made a vow to see this trial through. To not let my weakness for beauty affect my judgement. Ruby Hines was not on my side. She was defending the person who'd tortured my wife to death. I needed to hate her!

EARLY RETIREMENT

MURDER IN DAYTONA

36

Carlo watched the events unfold from the comfort of his law office. The local news channel carrying the trial treated it much like one of its mainstream competitors reality shows, right down to the sexy flamboyant correspondents. The more he watched, the more Carlo felt compelled to be there.

He'd wait till the end of the week, giving himself time to alter his appearance. It was imperative that he remain anonymous. Carlo visited a men's boutique located across the street from his condo. He told the obviously gay hair stylist he wanted to make a drastic change, while still maintaining his good looks. The stylist looked Carlo up and down admiringly before suggesting a tuxedo cut. He said he'd add some tinting and a blow dry. Carlo was convinced the little fag wanted to blow dry more than his hair. This first visit would be his last visit... Then he saw the results!

His long ponytail was gone, replaced by a medium length blown back hair style that featured silver highlights. The nouveau cut gave Carlo a modern, sophisticated look in a trendy sort of way.

The sadistic lawyer normally dressed in high end clothing. He'd pair Armani dress slacks with Gucci animal print pullovers, or Gloria Vanderbilt silk tee's under a Brooks Brothers blazer. For the trial Carlo bought Dockers and button down shirts purchased at the local Walmart. To further shroud his identity he grew out his facial hair. Standing in front of the mirror that Friday morning Carlo barely recognized the person staring back at him.

By weeks end the crowds that gathered in front of the court house had dwindled. Carlo figured if he arrived early enough he could secure a seat in the spectator's gallery. Hoping to avoid attention he parked his Mercedes a couple blocks away and walked. After going through security he made his way to the courtroom.

When he got there a few people were milling about in the hallway waiting for the doors to open. Carlo leaned against the wall and quietly stared down at the floor. He went over details in his mind, reassuring himself he'd covered all his tracks. Twenty minutes after arriving a court attendant came by to announce there were eight seats available in the spectator's gallery. All other seats were reserved for witnesses, family members, and members of the media. She passed out numbered cards to those who'd arrived early enough to get a spot. Carlo secured number four.

At 8:45 the court attendant began escorting witnesses and family members to their seats, followed by the well connected. Once they were seated she announced spectators could take their places in the remaining seats at the back of the gallery.

Carlo saw Ruby the moment he entered the courtroom. She was seated at the defendant's table reviewing documents. A plain looking woman sitting next to her behaved as if she were waiting for instructions. Ruby pointed out something on the document she was reading and the two woman giggled. Moments later a door to the left of the judge's bench opened and two deputies appeared. They escorted the defendant to her seat, then knelt down and unshackled her.

Doris poured a glass of water from the carafe in front of her, then turned and looked around the room. She didn't make eye

338

contact with anybody, but Carlo put his head down anyway, wanting to avoid any chance of recognition. He saw Ruby take Doris by the hand and mouth the words, *"No fear."* Doris smiled and mouthed back, *"No shit!"*

A minute later the jury filed into the courtroom and took their respective places in the jury box. Carlo watched Ruby watch the jurors. He could tell she was fixated. This woman could intimidate the biggest of bad asses. She was a good looking woman. Tall and busty, and full of piss and vinegar. He'd have loved the chance to beat that piss out of her back in her hotel room that night. His unexpected discovery had ruined the opportunity... Unfortunately. Perhaps there'd be another? One never knew!

His concentration was interrupted by a voice. *"All rise."* The judge entered the courtroom and took his seat behind the bench. Comically, everyone who'd risen sat back down without waiting for instruction, as if they were puppets. Everyone except Ruby Hines that is. She hesitated!

The defense attorney did a visual '360' of the room before taking her seat. Unlike Doris, she made eye contact with people. Carlo didn't look away as he had when Doris scanned the room earlier. Ruby was captivating. What man could resist? She looked at him fleetingly, unknowingly, as if she'd never laid eyes on him before. After she finished scouring the room she sat down. The judge spoke up. *"Are you ready, Counselor?"* Ruby replied she was. *"Then you may proceed,"* he instructed.

Ruby came forward. She smiled at the jury, then turned to address the judge. *"The defense calls Doctor Jane Felder, your Honor."* Doctor Jane Felder had testified for the prosecution the previous afternoon. She was a behavioral psychologist employed by the Florida State Department of Corrections. She specialized in determining a person's ability to reason normally. Dr Felder's job was to evaluate prisoners for the purpose of placing them in the general prison population.

Felder had examined Doris Van Fleet. The state wanted to determine whether Doris should be considered a flight or suicide risk. She'd testified the previous day that in her professional opinion the defendant could be both. It was Dr Felder's opinion that if given the opportunity the defendant would try to escape, and under certain circumstances, could attempt to injure herself or others.

Ruby began her cross examination of the witness by asking Dr Felder two simple questions. *"Do you attend church regularly?"* and *"Do you believe homosexuals will go to heaven when they die?"*

Both questions were met with vehement objection by the prosecutor. Uriah Wells had to take a moment to compose himself after leaping from his chair, red faced and livid. He asked for permission to approach the bench. When granted, the prosecutor apologized for his behavior. *"Your Honor, what in our Lord's name is Miss Hines doin' askin' this here witness a question like that? What the blazes does Doctor Felder's religious beliefs or personal feelins towards homosexuals got to do with her testimony as a behavioral psychologist?"*

Judge Walker peered at Ruby over his glasses and said, *"Well, Counselor?"* Ruby told the judge she thought it was obvious why she would ask those questions. She followed that up by asking him whether the prosecutor was going to object to every question she posed. Then she explained...

"My client is not a believer in the Christian sense of the word, Your Honor. Doris believes there is a God in some form, but she doesn't buy into the philosophy of the holy trinity." Ruby hesitated, as taught in college law 101, then said, *"Doris is a gay woman,*

340

Your Honor... Openly and without remorse, but that don't make her a killer! Hell it don't even make her a bad person! The prosecutor would like the jury to believe she is both. "

Ruby paused, counted under her breath, again as taught in college law 101...then continued, *"I can only surmise, so would Doctor Felder."*

The judge smiled at Ruby, then turned to the prosecutor and told him his objection was overruled. The seasoned attorney gestured to Judge Walker by bowing her head respectfully, then turned back to the witness. She held out her hands mockingly, as if to say, *"Well, Doctor?"*

Doctor Felder blushed a little, then answered, *"Yes... I go to church. I'm a born again Christian."* The psychologist explained that her faith taught her homosexuals were an abomination to God, and that sodomy was an abhorrent behavior unacceptable in God's eyes.

Ruby turned towards the jury. As she did she asked, *"Tell me Doctor Felder, is it true as far as you know being a behavioral psychologist, that twenty-five percent of the population in America has had at least one homosexual experience?"*

The question brought a groan from the prosecutor's table, but no objection. The witness hesitated. She looked up at the judge for some sign of guidance but got none, so she answered. It was Doctor Felder's understanding the number was closer to ten percent of the population.

The defense attorney was quick to correct her, explaining the ten percent estimate came from a study done by Alfred Kinsey way back in 1948. Ruby stood in front of the jury box and announced, *"Ladies and gentlemen, the times they are a changin!"*

This line of questioning continued into the afternoon. Ruby was determined to free her client from the bondage of her sexual preferences and religious beliefs. It was not a crime to be skeptical of religion, especially these days. Nor was it a crime to be gay or lesbian. In fact it was, one could say, a God given right. Her client might be found guilty of murder, but she would not face the gas chamber because she happened to be a non believing lesbian. Not if Ruby Hines had any say in the matter!

Carlo was impressed. This woman was a good lawyer. They'd have made a great team under different circumstances. It was odd having her look at him without recognition. He could describe her in detail, right down to the little birthmark that ran along the inside of her butt cheek. Either his makeover was really convincing, or he'd failed to make the impression he thought he had.

During breaks in the news coverage Carlo made creative use of his time. He placed several phone calls to Jose Gacha at *Los Norte* headquarters in south Florida. When *Los Norte del Valle* replaced *La Corporacion* as the top crime syndicate in Little Havana the one time cartel lieutenant's star was on the rise. Gacha made untold millions for the cartel by leading them into the human trafficking trade. For his efforts he was made El Padrino of *Los Norte* operations in south Florida. Gacha was virtually untouchable.

Carlo had a favor to ask, and he knew Gacha had the means and wherewithal to grant it. He wanted someone to disappear. Preferably kidnaped and forced to work in the sex trade. Senor' Gacha agreed to his lawyer's request, reminding Carlo he always remembered his friends... Carlo knew the crime boss never forgot his enemies. He'd risen through the ranks of the Columbian cartel by living up to that creed.

Carlo made a second request. He wanted Gacha to find his Mexican girlfriend. This time the lawyer needed his client, rather than the other way around... Jose Gacha was happy to oblige. The first request was granted as a payback. This one came with strings. Carlo would be his! Once somebody was indebted to the cartel it was a lifelong debt.

The young lawyer had saved *El Padrino's* ass. Gacha's attorney was in many ways responsible for his success in America. It was Carlo's defense strategy during his extradition hearing that had provided the opportunity to make the connections necessary for Senor' Gacha to set up shop in Little Havana. For *El Padrino,* it was a winning hand. Gacha would repay his attorney for helping him get established, while at the same time enslaving him to the cartel.

Gacha was somewhat reluctant to turn Jewel into a sex slave. Not that there wasn't a market for chubby white women her age. There definitely was! Men in the Middle East would devour a woman like her. A white woman, especially an American, would be a very valuable commodity indeed. Gacha's problem was he knew that she knew things... He knew she could be linked to a murder!

El Padrino knew if there was one thing that could bring him down it was a witness with loose lips. *Loose lips sink ships!* Gacha wasn't about to have that tub of lard floating around waiting to torpedo his luxury cruise liner. Better to dispose of her. He would tell Carlo she was sold to a wealthy Syrian sheik who had a thing for fat white women. He'd say the shiek went through them like water and was always in the market for more. With that out of the way he'd order his soldiers to take Jewel on a one way boat ride to the middle of the Everglades.

Gacha did know a sheik who bartered for white women on the black market. In fact *El Padrino* had recently sold him a young girl of fifteen. The teenage runaway had landed in Miami Beach after hitching rides on southbound semi's traveling from Indiana to Florida. She'd managed to make the trip on the twenty-eight dollars she'd earned baby sitting the week before.

Now her life would be spent staffing the spigot in the palace squat toilet. Gacha knew when he sold her she'd eventually kill herself. He'd seen it happen dozens of times.

Teracita Goncalves was different. His attorney's teenage girl-friend had disappeared into thin air. Finding her would be more difficult. Gacha would start by talking with his connections in Mexico. He had people imbedded within the Juarez organization. The Vicente Fuentes led cartel controlled the main transportation routes for billions of dollars worth of illegal drugs entering the United States. Now that *Los Norte* business centered around human trafficking the two criminal enterprises could assist one another on occasion. Getting a little information for an associate such as Jose Gacha should be a simple procedure. Surely her family knew where she was?

EARLY RETIREMENT

MURDER IN DAYTONA

37

Three grisly desperadoes brandishing automatic weapons showed up at the Goncalves home in Delicias, Mexico. They pushed their way inside as Teracita's parents gathered her three youngest siblings and sheltered them from the onslaught. One of the invaders, a slime ball with greasy long hair and a pock marked face, seemed to be the leader. He threatened to shoot Teracita's father if he didn't tell him where his daughter was.

Believing the man was referring to Antonetta, his sixteen year old daughter, Mr Goncalves told the bandito she was still in school. *"No...el mas viejo,"* the thug shouted. *"The older one!"* Initially confused, Goncalves realized the man was talking about Teracita. He told him she was in America, and that he hadn't heard from her in months. *"Es un mentiroso,"* the thug shouted. *"You're a liar!"*

The disheveled desperado shoved Goncalves with the barrel of his weapon, sending him sprawling on the living room floor. *"Le asesinara,"* he yelled, *"I will murder you!"*

Mrs Goncalves jumped between her husband and the greasy mercenary. She pleaded with him, screaming *"Dice la verdad... He tells you the truth!"*

The thug backed off. He warned Mr Goncalves that his daughter shouldn't mess with cartel business. He told him she'd gotten herself in trouble up in America and was wanted by the *El Padrino* himself. Looking back at his compadres, the desperado laughed loudly as he said, **"hego carajo ella tambian...** *I'd fuck her too!"* Mrs Goncalves looked at him disgustingly, which made the desperado laugh all the harder.

Without warning the ugly cartel soldier took a step forward and viciously kicked the woman in the stomach. Mrs Goncalves rib cage was no match for the desperado's military style boots. The leather footwear featured steel toe reinforcements that could knock the wind out of a horse. A bone chilling crack split the air as the bandito's boot made contact with the woman's midsection. She doubled over gasping for air as her diaphragm went into spasm. The trauma of having her ribs smashed sent waves of pain ripping through her body.

The other two desperadoes pointed their weapons at the family, who was now huddled around their injured matriarch. The two home invaders lunged towards them, hesitating only when the tyrant who appeared to be in charge stopped them. He seemed to consider his options, then motioned it was time to leave.

The bandito turned and walked towards the door. Just as he was about to open it a little girl came rushing in unexpectedly. She ran right into him. The despot dropped his automatic weapon, which discharged the moment it hit the floor. The little girl was Teracita's seven year old sister.

Blood sprayed from her neck. It looked like a water hose when someone places their finger over the end of it. A torrent of red splatter painted the living room wall behind her. A large puddle formed around the little girl as she crumbled to the floor in a heap. Her carotid artery was severed. Teracita's sister bled out in less than thirty seconds.

When the other two desperadoes saw what happened they burst out laughing. The bandito who'd dropped his weapon turned to Teracita's parents and shrugged his shoulders. He bent down and

346

picked up his gun, wiped the blood splattered handle on his pants, then said to his compadres, *"Vamos... Let's go!"*

Nothing could be done. The Juarez Cartel owned the *Federales* in Chihuahua. Murder was rampant throughout the province. Those desperadoes could have assassinated the entire Goncalves family and it would have been dismissed as a non investigative crime by the authorities.

Mr Goncalves lay his wife on the sofa then went for a blanket. He wrapped his seven year old daughter in it and walked the two miles to Our Lady of Guadalupe Catholic Church. The church was located in the center of town. Onlookers made the sign of the cross as he passed by, knowing what had happened before asking.

When the grieving father arrived at the church he handed the blanket holding his lifeless child's body to the padre. The priest took the bundle to the sanctuary and performed last rites. Then he initiated a quick burial on the consecrated grounds of the church cemetery. The family had no money to pay for a service, so the child was laid to rest without a vigil or liturgy. A simple prayer of intercession was made on the dead child's behalf.

Jose Gacha was not happy when he learned the details of what happened at the Goncalves home. At first his lieutenant thought he was upset about the accidental shooting that had taken the life of the little girl. Then he realized *El Padrino* was upset with the misfits who'd been sent to get the information he wanted. They'd left without securing the location of Teracita Goncalves. Their failure would be their funeral.

Gacha had no patience for weak minded morons who couldn't follow instructions. He telephoned Vicente Fuentes, his Juarez Cartel counterpart, to tell him so. Fuentes in turn contacted the politician who had budgetary control over the Mexican police force. After a short conversation with the ranking legislative member of the Chamber of Deputies he called Jose Gacha back to assure him his complaint had been handled.

An hour later *Federales* raided a home in the Colonia Mirador, a section of the barrio in the city of Chihuahua. They'd received a tip that members of the Juarez Cartel were hold up there. The cartel was responsible for murdering hundreds of civilians over the past year. Three men, four women, and six children were taken into custody. The women and children were released thirty minutes later. The men were told they were being transported to Aquiles Serdan Prison, a maximum security facility just outside the city limits. They never made it!

The official story was that the three prisoners had escaped, assisted by other cartel members who'd bushwhacked the security detail as they made their way to Serdan Prison... Unofficially, the three were taken to a remote location and executed.

A rumor was circulating that one of the thugs, the one with long hair and a bad complexion, had offered to rat out his superiors in the cartel in exchange for his release. When his proposition was refused he'd pissed his pants and wept like a baby. According to the rumor the other two desperadoes were blindfolded and shot, but the rat was buried alive up to his neck in the Sonoran Desert.

The rumor did have some merit. What actually happened was the pock faced bandito was forced to dig his own hole in the hard desert floor. Then half a dozen *Federalas* took turns kicking his head in, breaking bones and knocking his rotting teeth out in the process. He was left to rot in the hot sun. If he was lucky he'd die before nightfall. That's when the nocturnal feeders come out to prey. Diamondbacks, coyotes, wolves..... It was justice, Mexican style!

EARLY RETIREMENT

MURDER IN DAYTONA

38

The trial didn't take long. Two and a half weeks after it began the jury was sent to consider its verdict. Due to the high publicity the case had generated Judge Walker sequestered them. The twelve jurors and two alternates were transported to different locations throughout the area by plainclothes deputies in unmarked cars.

Of course the paparazzi managed to find them. Freelance journalist and photographers showed up regularly to pester them with questions and snap unsolicited photographs. Because of the judge's ruling the established press was dependent on the paparazzi to furnish them information, reluctant to go against the court's orders themselves.

The prosecutor based his argument almost exclusively on circumstantial evidence. With no eye witnesses, no forensic evidence, and no admission of guilt, Uriah Wells still managed to present a strong case. So strong in fact, the only saving grace for the accused was that she had Ruby Hines for an attorney.

Ruby had raised doubt in the minds of many who watched the trial. There was however one lingering fact that everyone struggled with... The key to the motel room where the murder took place was found hidden in the metal storage box found under the bed of the accused. That one fact, along with Doris Van Fleet's failure to offer a verifiable alibi for her whereabouts on the day of the murder was hard to disregard.

The jury spent several days pouring over court transcripts, discussing testimony, and considering the case. On five separate occasions they asked Judge Walker to clarify legal and procedural issues. The prosecutor's main fear was that the jury wouldn't come to a unanimous decision. The last thing Uriah Wells wanted was to have to retry this case. He believed if he wasn't successful in getting a conviction now the accused would get away with her crime. Unless hard evidence were found, there would be no retrial.

A conference room on the third floor of the courthouse served as home base for the jury. They convened each morning at nine o'clock. Lunch was catered so the jury wouldn't be accessible to the press. The room was air conditioned, though windows were opened to allow for some fresh air. It was furnished with high quality pieces. A red mahogany conference table and chairs had been imported from the Philippines. Wood plank floors cut from american black cherry were buffed and waxed to a mirror like sheen. Solid mahogany panels covered the walls.

A large mosaic of the Great Seal of the State of Florida was featured on the wall opposite the windows. It depicts a Seminole Indian spreading hibiscus flowers along the shoreline while two Sabal Palms stand at either end in the distance. In the background a steamboat makes its way up the St Johns River as the sun rises on the horizon. Written in big block letters above the depiction are the words, **FLORIDA - THE SUNSHINE STATE.** Beneath the inscription it reads, **THE 27th STATE OF THE UNION - 1845.**

The jury worked diligently, reviewing what evidence was presented and discussing amongst themselves the facts of the case. They seemed to be deadlocked. Ten of them were in agreement. Two were not. Florida law required all twelve be unified in its decision.

One jurist held up the proceedings for an entire day. Scarlet Mason was a twenty-six year old stay at home mother of two.

350

Scarlet agreed with the majority concerning guilt or innocence, but she wrestled with the idea of the death penalty. Eventually she was persuaded to cast her vote with the others after they convinced her the death penalty argument was a separate issue.

The other dissident came from the other end of the age scale. Harry Callahan was a seventy-two year old retired school teacher from New Jersey. He believed the defendant was not guilty. Plain and simple! No amount of argument or persuasion could convince him otherwise. If it hadn't been for Scarlet Mason's issue with the death penalty there would have been a hung jury and the defendant would have been set free. Her indecision caused an additional day of deliberations, which ultimately proved to be a death blow to Doris Van Fleet.

Let me explain. Like every day since the deliberations started a sheriff deputy was scheduled to pick up Mr Callahan at his hotel and transport him to the courthouse. Normally Harry would be sitting in the lobby awaiting the deputies arrival, but this morning he hadn't shown. When he didn't see him in the lobby the deputy inquired at the front desk. No one had seen him. The clerk said Mr Callahan hadn't shown up for the complimentary breakfast that morning. That was something the old man never missed.

The deputy instructed the hotel clerk to accompany him to Mr Callahan's room. Upon entering they found Harry lying on the bathroom floor. He wasn't breathing. The officer performed CPR while the clerk dialed 911. Unfortunately he was long gone, having suffered cardiac arrest some time during the night. The jury would have to go to an alternate if the trial were to continue. Two had been sequestered in the event something like this happened.

Paul DeWayne was the first alternate. He was a tool and dye machinist for a local ball bearing manufacturer. The forty year old was just as familiar with the trial as any of the others. Still, the judge spent an hour discussing the situation with the prosecutor and the attorney for the defense. He wanted to review the law as it pertained to the situation. It was Judge Walker's responsibility to ascertain the appropriateness of continuing the trial. In the end he decided he was comfortable proceeding.

Paul DeWayne was convinced Doris Van Fleet was guilty, and he had no problem with the death penalty. In fact he supported it. Mr DeWayne joined the others in the conference room that Friday morning. By mid afternoon the jury was ready to announce a verdict.

EARLY RETIREMENT

MURDER IN DAYTONA

39

Due to the large population of Mexican immigrants living in the Minneapolis-St Paul area the local cable television provider dedicated several channels of programming in Spanish. One of those channels was the Telemundo News Network. Many residents of West St Paul watched the network religiously.

TNN broadcast its live feeds from the *Estado Libre* facility in the Baja. The rest of the network's lineup featured taped segments dedicated to events of cultural importance.

Teracita Goncalves had put in an especially long day at the bakery. Everyone in town was preparing for the Cinco De Mayo celebration. The shop extended its hours to accommodate the long line of last minute shoppers. Customers snaked out the door as they stopped by on their way home from work.

Teracita waited on customers while the baker's wife manned the register. Her husband remained in the kitchen making fresh conchas, mantecado, and bigote rolls. After the shop closed Teracita cleaned up in the front of the store while her employers tallied the day's reciepts. They'd all have the next day off to celebrate Cinco De Mayo.

When Teracita got home she made a pot of coffee then turned on the television. She went directly to TNN. The Mexican news channel was the one connection she still had with home. Watching developments in her native land helped keep Teracita centered, but it also made her homesick. How badly she missed her family. Her hope and prayer was that one day she'd be able to let them know she was all right. Trying to do so now would be too risky. For the time being the less they knew the better!

Telemundo was airing a documentary on the origins of Cinco De Mayo. Mexico's convincing defeat of invading French forces in the battle of Puebla on May 5, 1862 is one of the country's largest celebrations. Cinco De Mayo in Spanish translates to, *The 5th of May.*

Many historians agree the United States survived the American Civil War in tact because of Mexico's victory over the French that day. They base their assumption on the fact Napoleon III would have established a Mexican empire to serve French interests had France won the battle. Most believe he would have attempted to sway the outcome of the Civil War by supplying the confederate army with weapons and supplies in support of their fight for secession.

Napoleon III believed breaking up the Union would limit America's opportunity to become a world power. The fact he was forced to dedicate his troops to battle the Mexican army allowed President Lincoln time to quell the confederate uprising. A year after Mexico's victory at Puebla the Union army defeated the confederates at Gettysburg.

After the documentary ended Telemundo aired a special report on the warring factions along the country's northern border with the United States. Rival drug cartels intent on controlling the transportation networks supplying the billion dollar drug trade into America were considering a suspension of hostilities during the Cinco De Mayo holiday. Teracita watched the report with interest. She knew it affected her family. Her home state of Chihuahua was at the epicenter of the drug trade.

Even one day of peace would be welcome, as not a day went by without some form of violence being bestowed upon a rival cartel. Often it was an innocent bystander who suffered for the cause. Teracita knew many families who'd lost loved ones who just happened to get caught in the middle of an outburst and were gunned down. Mexican authorities were powerless to stop the cartels. The criminal enterprises vast man power, availability of weapons, and endless supply of cash were far superior to that of the police.

The Juarez Cartel, under the leadership of Vicente Fuentes, was the main source of income for many of the young men in Ciudad Juarez. In their eyes he was more than a man... Fuentes was a God!

Rival cartels were pushing Fuentes for a slice of the pie. The Sinaloa, Los Zetas, and Familia Cartels were all well established. They were also blood thirsty. The vast amount of money involved made the battles worth fighting. Juarez had become the most dangerous place on earth. The murder capital of the world. Its death rate was nearly five times the national average. More people in Ciudad Juarez die from unnatural causes than any other reason.

Teracita watched the screen intently as a news correspondent stood in the streets of Juarez telling viewers about the opportunity for a cease fire over the Cinco De Mayo holiday. He interviewed several bystanders, each of whom gave accounts of loyalty to their patron, Vicente Fuentes. Then a segment recorded the previous day was shown. It was preceded by a warning from the correspondent that some scenes could be disturbing to viewers.

The reporter was interviewing a man who claimed to be a supporter of a rival faction. The man told him police officers had used force to take three men into custody several days ago. He said the men were taken from their home and driven into the desert, where they were executed by Federales. The man was emphatic that none of the men was given a trial.

He further stated the murders were carried out under orders from Vicente Fuentes. The television reporter promised to investigate the man's claims, and thanked him for his bravery.

Teracita adjusted the volume on her television set so she wouldn't miss any of the dialog, then went to replenish her coffee cup. No sooner had she turned around when she heard what sounded like an automatic weapon popping off rounds. The loud noise startled her so much she dropped to the floor. It was hard to tell if the gunfire came from the television or outside her window.

The television screen went black. Teracita could hear the cameraman swearing in the background as he struggled with his equipment. A few seconds later he refocused his lens and panned the surrounding area. The correspondent was kneeling over the bleeding body of the man he'd just interviewed. He was clearly dead, having been hit at least a dozen times.

When the disturbing segment ended viewers were treated to a commercial for *Negra Modelo* beer. The dark beer with the creamy taste was caricatured in the body of a big black bull, inferring sexual overtones. American style marketing had found its way south of the border. The special report continued several minutes later. The television correspondent who'd witnessed the execution of the man he was interviewing the previous day was now standing inside a police station accompanied by the Deputy Chief of Police.

The reporter questioned the Deputy Chief about claims being made by some locals that *Federales* had taken justice into their own hands. As expected the Deputy Chief quelled the rumors, claiming the men in question were taken into custody for murdering a little girl in the city of Delicias.

They'd invaded the home of a working family there, severely injuring the female head of the house and murdering the young child, who'd been shot in the head. Their motive was unclear but it

356

was believed to be a personal matter. Unfortunately the men who perpetrated the crime had escaped while being transported to Serdan Prison to await trial.

Teracita was stunned by the news. Why would a trio of men assault a working family in Delicias? What could the family have possibly done to warrant such an attack? It had to be drug related. Almost all murders were. It never crossed Teracita's mind the family who'd been attacked might be her own. She watched as the news correspondent asked the Deputy Chief if his claims could be verified. The second in command answered, *"Ciertamente... Certainly! Talk to the family. The Goncalves live on Calle Real Di Nieca, in the north sector. I doubt if the little girl's mother will be able to speak to you. She was badly injured. Her husband should be able to tell you everything you need to know."*

"DEMONIOS," Teracita screamed! Her baby sister had been murdered? Shot and killed by an intruder? Her mother was badly beaten? Teracita was beside herself with grief... She let out a guttural scream and fell to the floor.

The butcher's wife ran in, alerted by the screams coming from down the hall. She found Teracita shaking uncontrollably on the floor. Moments later her husband arrived, holding an unloaded revolver in his hand. *"What happened... Is anyone hurt,"* the baker inquired? His wife looked at him and shrugged.

After some time passed Teracita composed herself enough to point to the television screen. The special report was just ending. The news correspondent was reminding his audience to tune in next week when the show would be broadcast live from Tijuana. They would be discussing the *gringo friendly* nature of the city, and the potential impact American tourist dollars have on the local economy. As the closing credits rolled visions of the war torn streets of Juarez were shown onscreen, followed by pictorials of the leaders of the Mexican drug cartels.

Teracita lay on the floor weeping. The baker and his wife still had no clue what had caused the turmoil. Eventually Teracita stopped crying. She attempted to explain, and insisted she had to get in touch with her father.

EARLY RETIREMENT

MURDER IN DAYTONA

40

The Goncalves family attacked by members of the Juarez Cartel? Why would they? Cartel soldiers didn't invade homes and murder innocent children for no reason. It is true many innocents had died, caught in the middle of warring factions or because they were related to the wrong person, but there would be no reason to force their way into the home of a poor family in the barrio and selectively murder a child.

Teracita's employer knew if her family was chosen for a personal visit from the cartel there had to be a reason. He also knew the cartel had connections in Latino communities throughout the United States. West St Paul was not without its share of street gangs, and those gangs were heavily influenced by the cartels back home.

The baker and his wife sat in Teracita's living room listening as she told them how she'd been recruited out of high school to work as an Au Pair for a wealthy family in south Florida. She explained how she'd fallen in love with a lawyer she met in Miami Beach. He specialized in immigration law, and had promised he would help her obtain her green card and become a permanent resident.

She told them the man turned out to be an abusive tyrant. He'd savagely beat her and threatened to kill her. Teracita explained how she'd gone to a priest for help, and that the padre had taken her to a domestic abuse shelter. She confessed to stealing money from the shelter so she could run away, and that she was deathly afraid her lawyer/boyfriend would track her down. She insisted Carlo was capable of murder, claiming that he'd killed before.

At first the baker thought his employee might be exaggerating a little. Embellishing her story in lieu of what had happened to her little sister back in Mexico. He asked Teracita why she thought cartel soldiers would attack her family without provocation. Was it possible her father was involved in the drug trade in some way? Teracita emphatically answered...No!

"How about your boyfriend," the baker asked? *"Does he have any connections to the cartel? After all, he is a big time lawyer in Miami. "* The baker leaned forward in his chair and reminded Teracita, *"Miami IS the drug capital of America."*

She sat stone faced, trembling and red eyed. Teracita thought back to some of her conversations with Carlo. She tried to recall things she'd overheard from behind closed doors. The baker asked, *"Is it possible this lawyer may have gotten your parents involved with illegal narcotics in some way? Perhaps trying to help them financially on your behalf? It would make sense ifffff..."*

The baker stopped mid sentence. He turned to his wife with an alarmed look on his face. She saw the fear in his eyes and instantly the same thought crossed her mind. Was it possible this lawyer had hired the Juarez Cartel to find Teracita for him?

It made sense. A Miami lawyer was bound to have connections with the drug underworld. Especially a Cuban that specialized in immigration law. He'd have the money, and from the way Teracita described him he wouldn't hesitate using some of it to reclaim his property. The baker knew if the Juarez Cartel was involved they wouldn't stop until she was found. He stood and motioned to his wife. It was time to leave...

As they were leaving Teracita told her employer she really needed to contact her father, bur her family had no phone. The baker suggested she send a telegram, but warned it could be intercepted. Same with a letter. In fact any normal means of communication could be traced back to her. Perhaps it would be better to wait.

Teracita felt very close to the baker and his wife. They'd taken her in. Given her a job and a place to live. They were like family, and she believed they felt the same way about her. The baker said he had an idea, but needed time to think it through. He suggested they all get some sleep, reminding them tomorrow was a holiday. *"We will talk more in the morning and come up with a plan."*

Teracita didn't know it but the baker had already formulated a plan in his head. He cursed the day the little *chica* first walked into his shop. If there was one person you didn't want to see heading your way it was a *soldado ombrero,* a cartel foot soldier.

The baker's life flashed before his eyes as he considered the ramifications of his actions. An act of kindness, like harboring a runaway and giving her a job so she might become self sufficient, was catamount to suicide when it came to cartel business. If the Juarez Cartel was searching for Teracita they'd find her...and it wouldn't take them long.

The studio apartment Teracita rented from the baker and his wife had been converted from what was originally part of the main house. Though it had its own separate entrance the apartment and the main house shared a bedroom wall. Most times it was quiet. The baker and his wife didn't have a television in their bedroom. The only time Teracita ever heard them was when they made love. The floor register was a good conductor of sound.

All was quiet on the other side of the wall tonight. Despite the solitude Teracita couldn't seem to fall asleep. She worried for the safety of her family, and grieved over the death of her little sister. She wondered why they'd been chosen for such an attack. In the silence she heard muffled commotion coming from next door.

Teracita listened as the baker and his wife argued in a very restrained, almost muted manner. Not able to make out the gist of their conversation Teracita lay on the floor with her ear to the register. What she heard shocked her.

Her employer was conspiring to turn her over to the cartel. Teracita heard Maria come to her defense as her husband railed against her. In muffled tones the two argued over whether to notify the Juarez Cartel of Teracita's location. They didn't know for certain if the cartel was looking for her, but if it was they didn't want to appear to be hiding her. It was too risky.

Approaching the street gangs was a dangerous proposition. These young thugs would shoot you just as well as look at you. None of them had the sense to fear death or incarceration. They viewed the grave or prison as their eventual destiny anyway. For most of them...that was true!

The baker knew The Latin Kings had ties to the Juarez Cartel. Many families in West St Paul came from Ciudad Juarez, and many were loyal to Vicente Fuentes. They'd left their homes and come to America precisely because of the never ending crime there, but somehow they managed to view Senor' Fuentes behavior as justifiable. To them he was not a criminal. He was a hero.

The Latin Kings were said to have well over two thousand members in the Twin Cities area. Nearly three hundred belonged to the West St Paul faction, known locally as *The 38s.* The name was said to come from the gang's preferred means of execution. The Smith & Wesson .38 special. The small lightweight handgun was easy to conceal, and it held five rounds. Plenty to carry out the job.

Teracita heard Maria cuss at her husband in spanish as she slammed the door behind her. The baker would be sleeping alone tonight. That much was evident. He'd told his wife he was going to talk to some guy named Rinaldo in the morning. That was enough to set her off.

Rinaldo Rodriquez was a popular West St Paul attorney. He provided legal representation to low level gang members charged with various misdemeanor charges brought by the police as a way of harassment. Rinaldo had a drinking problem. It's what kept him from taking more prestigious cases. His services were limited to defending clients against speeding tickets, loitering, possession, driving while impaired, minor charges like that. What made Rinaldo a household name in the barrios was the fact his older brother was the leader of *La Linea,* the most powerful street gang in Ciudad Juarez.

Teracita lay in her bed trembling. Her trusted employers, her new family as it were, was going to betray her. Where would she go? Who would help her? The U.S. immigration authorities would deport her for sure. Sending her back to Delicias would be catamount to signing her death warrant, and if she went back to Carlo she'd end up dead eventually anyway. She needed a plan... Fast!

EARLY RETIREMENT

MURDER IN DAYTONA

41

When the trial resumed the courtroom was filled to capacity. Ruby Hines stood facing the jury as they filed in, making eye contact with each juror. The attorney purposely wore a look of compassion on her face, pairing it with an air of confidence. Her intent was to send a message to each member of the jury. *Do the right thing!*

Uriah Wells sat quietly fiddling with his cell phone. Unknown to anyone else in the room, the celebrated prosecutor was making dinner reservations in advance of the guilty verdict he was quite certain was forthcoming. He looked up when the jury entered, gave them a halfhearted nod of recognition, then returned to his phone.

A moment later the officer of the court announced *"All Rise."* Judge Walker entered through his chamber door as everyone, well almost everyone...stood in unison. When the judge reached his bench he glared over at the prosecutor's table and cleared his throat. Uriah looked up to find everyone in attendance had their eyes on him. The normally passive/aggressive prosecutor quickly put his phone away and apologized. The judge then turned to the jury and asked them if they'd reached a decision.

The jury foreman stood and faced the judge. It was obvious how nervous he was. When the court attendant handed the man a mic he paused to gather his wits, then responded, *"Yeah, yes we ha, have... Your Honor."*

At that moment my heart raced. It felt as if I'd been shot full of adrenaline. Judge Walker instructed the weak kneed jury foreman to continue. The man cleared his throat. He glanced over at the defendant, then turned to look at his fellow jurists. Alternate juror Paul DeWayne nodded his head encouragingly. That seemed to help. The foreman announced the verdict.

"As to the charge of murder in the first degree, we the jury find the defendant... **Guilty***!"*

The room exploded! It seemed as though everyone in attendance reacted all at once. Some in celebration of the verdict, others shocked by it. Judge Walker slammed his gavel down half a dozen times, yelling, ***"Order in the court... There will be order in this courtroom!"***

He instructed the bailiffs to remove any person who failed to comply with his order. Half a dozen members of the media rushed out in the middle of the outburst, intent on being the first to announce the verdict to the public.

I wept... The feeling of euphoria I thought I'd experience never materialized. I should have been elated... I should have been celebrating...but I knew nothing was going to bring Veronica back. She lived now only in my dreams and memories...and in my heart.

Once order was restored Judge Walker instructed the foreman to continue. He started to announce the verdict to the next charge, but was interrupted. *"Speak into the mic, Sir,"* the judge instructed. The still nervous man had put the microphone down during the outburst and forgot to pick it up again. When he did a high pitched shriek bolted out of the sound system, sending shivers through the spines of everyone in the room.

People covered their ears. Others winced. Some doubled over, as if the screech could be avoided by laying low. You couldn't help but react. Judge Walker slammed his gavel down for a second time. Again he announced, *"There will be order in this courtroom."* Once order was restored the judge nodded for the jury foreman to continue.

*"As to the charge of first degree unlawful detention and false imprisonment, the jury finds the defendant... **Guilty.**"* The foreman looked up at the judge for his reaction. He didn't have one. Judge Walker sat stone faced as the foreman went on reading the charges and the verdicts. *"Use of a deadly weapon in the commission of a felony... **Guilty.** Cruel and inhuman treatment... **Guilty.** Lewd and lascivious behavior... **Guilty.** Sodomy in the first degree... **Guilty.** Interstate flight to avoid prosecution... **Guilty.**"*

The State of Florida had overwhelmingly proven its case, at least in the eyes of the jury. One of thirty-four states that still carried out capital punishment, the jury's verdict meant it was possible Doris Van Fleet could be sentenced to death for her crimes... Justice, American style!

Ruby Hines was stunned. It certainly wasn't the outcome the defense attorney had expected. There simply was no proof. When she reached over and took her client's hand Ruby started to tear up. She fought through a lump in her throat to tell Doris... *"We Will Fight This!"*

Judge Walker instructed the bailiff to take the defendant into custody. The same jailer who'd escorted Doris into the courtroom at the beginning of the trial brushed past Ruby with intent. It was her job to put the prisoner in shackles. She did so with ruthless abandon.

The woman seemed to mock Doris as she went to place her in handcuffs. Without warning the newly convicted murderer swung her free arm around and cold-cocked her ill mannered adversary.

Blood spurted from the wily jailer's mouth, as did several teeth and a few choice expletives.

Ruby tried to intercept her client's swing before it landed but she was too late. She somehow ended up at the bottom of the bruhaha. A huge male deputy had come rushing into the melee, intending to use his size and girth to pin the defendant down. He unintentionally took Ruby with him when he lunged.

The high heeled attorney was nearly crushed to death. Add to that a mad as hell three hundred pound female jailer and a falsely convicted lesbian dyke fighting for her life and you have the makings of a gruesome battle.

Ruby's injuries were significant. The most severe being a fractured collarbone and two broken ribs. What bothered her the most though was the split lip she suffered. It required a dozen stitches to close. The sexy attorney had an image to live up to. Those things matter!

Eventually order was restored. Hiram Walker remained at his post until Doris Van Fleet was shackled and hauled from the courtroom. Only then did he retire to his chambers.

None of the physical pain Ruby suffered matched the pain in her heart. The normally reliable attorney lost a very winnable case. Her client had not been proven guilty beyond a reasonable doubt. Not in her mind. There would be an appeal... There had to be!

EARLY RETIREMENT

MURDER IN DAYTONA

42

Aaron got quite a surprise when he answered the late night knock at his front door. He hadn't heard from Teracita since the day she asked for his help landing a job at that bakery shop in Minnisota. He'd hoped she'd stay in touch. Hoped they might get together someday. It was too late now. His girlfriend had just moved in with him the week before.

Rebecca was a typical midwesterner. She had freckles and red hair, not to mention a cute figure, but it was her bubbly personality that made her easy to like. It was nearly midnight. Rebecca was fast asleep on the couch.

Aaron lay next to her watching TV. One of the cable channels was showing *'True Grit'* commercial free. Who could resist John Wayne as 'Rooster Cogburn' being tamed by the likes of teenager Kim Darby. The 1969 film earned Duke the academy award for best actor that year.

Rebecca was awakened by the sound of Aaron talking with someone at the front door. When she got up to see who it was she got a surprise. A young Latino woman was standing there with tears in her eyes. It seemed like Aaron was trying to block the doorway, as if he didn't want the two women to meet. Rebecca pushed past him. She took the distraught girl's arm and invited her to come inside.

Teracita apologized emphatically for showing up at their door so late at night. She told Rebecca she'd go and come back in the morning, adding she didn't realize Aaron was married!

Rebecca would have none of it. She insisted the poor girl stay. The three of them spent the next hour emptying a bottle of wine and getting to know one another better. Rebecca explained her and Aaron's living arrangement. They'd dated for a few months and decided to move in together to save on expenses. Neither of them had discussed marriage at this point, but Teracita knew Rebecca was hoping.

She explained how she and Aaron met, telling Rebecca how friendly and protective he'd been on the long bus ride from Daytona. Teracita made sure her hostess understood they'd just been friends.

It was two in the morning when Aaron finally broke up the party. Rebecca prepared the guest bedroom, then joined her mate in the master. As they kissed goodnight Aaron whispered how much he appreciated her being so understanding. He assured Rebecca nothing had ever gone on between Teracita and himself. He'd simply reached out a helping hand. Rebecca reassured him back, saying she knew that. Teracita had already told her.

The two roommates lay quietly in the dark for a few minutes. Then Rebecca turned to Aaron and said, *"She is beautiful, isn't she?"* Aaron didn't answer. A short time later Rebecca drifted off to sleep.

Aaron lay awake for a long time. Too long it would seem, because Rebecca started snoring. He tried plugging her nostrils hoping to stop the annoying sound, but he wasn't successful. It's strange how Rebecca's snoring never seemed to bother him before tonight.

When it became intolerable Aaron grabbed a blanket from the closet and headed out to sleep on the living room sofa. On his way there he had to walk past the guest bedroom. He fought the urge to open the door and peek in.

Ten minutes later he heard Teracita get up and tiptoe to the bathroom. Aaron knew it was her because he could still hear Rebecca's snoring, though from the living room it wasn't nearly as loud. He faked he was asleep, keeping one eye open as he waited for his house guest to come out of the bathroom. A few seconds later she appeared.

The glow of a distant street light shined faintly in the window behind her. The effect silhouetted Teracita's dark form. Aaron could make out the defined contours of her breasts and the explosion of her hips where they met her waist. It made him squirm with desire.

He questioned his decision to ask Rebecca to move in. She'd originally balked at the idea, but Aaron had been persistent. He'd gotten tired of living alone, and they seemed so compatible. Who knew a week later this exotic beauty would show up at his door?

Teracita lingered in the hallway outside the guest room. Her appearance was almost ghostlike, her body haloed by the wispy white light of the street lamp. Aaron couldn't make out the features of her face in the darkness, but he felt her eyes upon him. The stirring in his loins had produced a throbbing hard on. Enraptured by the moment, he pulled back the blanket to expose himself.

Aaron didn't know if Teracita could see him in the darkness or not. Most women he'd been intimate with seemed impressed by his size. His job kept him on the road for weeks at a time and Aaron wasn't adverse to meeting a stranger now and then.

Teracita hesitated for a moment, then turned back towards the bedroom door. It wasn't that she didn't want to. God knows she did! It had been months since she'd known a man intimately. Aaron heard her whisper, *"Good night"* as she disappeared from view.

He woke before dawn. Rebecca had stopped snoring. When Aaron realized that he wrapped his blanket around his shoulders and headed back to bed. His erection hadn't slackened one bit. As he snuggled in behind his housemate he couldn't resist pressing up against her. The rhythmic throbbing soon woke Rebecca and she turned to receive him. Teracita lay quietly in the guest bedroom as her hosts consummated their relationship.

As the sun came up in the eastern sky Rebecca followed the aroma of freshly brewed coffee into the kitchen. When she got there she found Teracita had already set the table for breakfast. Several pieces of bread were browning in the toaster and a sausage and egg omelet was cooking on the stove. The two women gave each other a smile of acknowledgment, then Rebecca helped her guest finish up.

Once the toast was buttered and the juice was poured Rebecca went to wake Aaron. Teracita waited until breakfast was over before telling them of her predicament. The way Aaron reacted to it was almost as if he didn't believe her. The idea of drug cartels sending ruthless soldiers to murder innocent children was so foreign to him it didn't seem real. It sounded more like the script for a poorly written Hollywood 'B' movie. Teracita could tell she wasn't being taken seriously. Unfortunately her predicament was serious... Deadly so!

The one time Au Pair knew her abusive lawyer boyfriend represented members of organized crime. She knew he was well connected with the leaders of the cartels. Teracita had overheard some of his conversations. She'd seen documents she wasn't supposed to see. If Carlo hired the cartel to find her, they would. She understood that, and she had to make Aaron understand it too!

Teracita told him she was in imminent danger. She told him she was certain her family had been targeted. The cartel was searching for her and they thought her family knew where she was. *"Carlo hired the cartel to find me"* she insisted, *"and they won't stop until they do...."*

These thugs thought nothing of murdering innocent children. Their organization was so powerful it controlled the national police force. They kidnapped well to do citizens for ransom, then sent them back to their loved ones in little pieces. These are the people that were after her, and they could be knocking on Aaron's door any minute. When she put it that way he knew he only had one option. He had to get Teracita out of the country!

Aaron was adamant about that. She couldn't go back to Delicias, and she couldn't return to Florida. Those options were off the table. She certainly couldn't go back to Minnesota. That would be suicide.

"How about a Cruise!" It was Rebecca who first mentioned it. Though it sounded implausible at the time the more they weighed their options the more it made sense. A Caribbean cruise during spring break. Teracita was the perfect age. She'd melt right into the crowd.

A ship full of pesky partying college students was unlikely to draw the watchful eye of immigration. They'd pick a cruise line with multiple stops on its itinerary. With spanish being the main language of the islands it would be easy for Teracita to assimilate. They could tell no one about their plan. That way no one could be coerced into spilling the beans.

Teracita would need an American passport. Aaron would probably have to go underground for that. Lots of undocumented immigrants carried false identification. It was just a matter of finding someone professional enough in their craft to pull it off.

Aaron thought he knew a guy from his old neighborhood who could provide for their needs. It would cost some serious cash...but he was committed now. There would be no turning back. It was only a matter of time before the bad guys traced Teracita right to his front door.

EARLY RETIREMENT

MURDER IN DAYTONA

43

Carlo's reaction to the verdict was moderately subdued. He purposely withheld any outward signs of emotion, but inside he was giddy as a kid who'd just been handed a bag of cotton candy. All around him people jumped out of their seats, some in anger and some in celebration. It depended on their point of view. Not him. Carlo just sat quietly in the gallery soaking up the scene.

He couldn't help but laugh when pandemonium broke out at the defendant's table. A very angry Doris Van Fleet had slugged the female jailer who came to haul her away. Judge Walker started banged his gavel on his desk like he was hammering an iron spike through a railroad tie. He ordered his courtroom cleared.

Two bailiffs ran to the jailer's aid while two others began herding people towards the doors. Carlo stood to join them. He watched with amusement as half a dozen uniformed deputies attempted to rush in from the hallway to join the skirmish. The ensuing bottleneck was truly comical.

Just as he reached the door Carlo saw Ruby Hines go down in a heap. She'd been tackled by one of the deputies who rushed into the fray. *"To the victor goes the spoils,"* he said to himself as he made his way out of the building. He felt like a conductor directing a symphony. Amadeus Mozart reincarnated in the body of a gifted Cuban lawyer overseeing the majesty of his greatest work.

There'd been many loose ends to consider. He'd taken care of the *Jewel* issue. Senor' Gacha had assured him of that. In a few days she'd be on the other side of the world servicing Al-Qaeda militants, or so he believed! One could only imagine the treatment she'd receive from those insane camel jockeys. With no way out of her predicament she'd hang herself within a month.

With the Veronica Stevens homicide successfully pinned on Doris Van Fleet his work was nearly finished. The judge would rule on her fate at an upcoming sentencing hearing. The prosecutor was going to ask for the death penalty, and considering the violent nature of the crime Judge Walker was bound to honor his request. If no appeal was granted her sentence could be carried out rather swiftly. No sense in delaying justice!

Carlo could turn his thoughts to Teracita. Once he had her back where she belonged he could get on with his life. With the cartel searching for her he was certain it wouldn't take long.

The twisted attorney went straight from the courthouse to his office. With all his extra curricular activities to attend to he'd fallen drastically behind, though he was able to camouflage some of that with false billing. Fortunately he'd secured the Gacha account for the firm. That one deal made him practically untouchable.

A whole week went by before Carlo heard any news about the search for Teracita. He was sitting at his desk reviewing documents when his secretary buzzed him saying there was a Mr Mantivo at the front desk asking to see him. *"He doesn't have an appointment, Sir. He says you are expecting him?"*

Carlo had no idea what she was talking about. He wasn't expecting anyone today. He'd told his secretary to clear his schedule so he could get caught up. When he went up front to meet the man he didn't recognize him. He asked, *"Do I know you, Sir"*

The man handed him a card and responded... *"Si, Senor Santiago."*

After looking at the card Carlo told his secretary he'd return shortly, then the two men left. She watched them climb into the back of a silver colored cadillac with dark tinted windows. The driver pulled away from the curb and the car disappeared from view.

Santo Mantivo offered his guest a cigar, which Carlo accepted. He told him he'd been hired by an unnamed outside benefactor to locate a missing person, explaining it was unusual in that he was normally called upon to dispose of someone. In this instance he was only to find and apprehend his target. He didn't ask why. A contract was a contract. He'd come there today to inform the attorney of the whereabouts of his fiance, Ms Teracita Goncalves.

"Minnesota?" Carlo asked when he heard Teracita's location. *"My Bonita spent the winter in Minnesota? How the hell did she get there...hitch hike?"*

Mantivo told the surprised attorney his missing fiance was living in West St Paul, a small city just outside Minneapolis. He said the town was home to thousands of Mexican immigrants. *"Ms Goncalves works in a bakery shop there. She lives in an apartment located behind the shop. Her employer heard she was being sought by the cartel and wisely informed on her."*

The killer for hire explained what Carlo already knew. That his benefactor has affiliates throughout the United States. Latino street gangs loyal to Vicente Fuentes were at the organization's disposal. The arrangement was beneficial to both parties. The street gangs moved millions of dollars worth of cartel product and in the process became wealthy themselves.

Of course little of that wealth filtered down to the average street thug who risked life and limb everyday. Those guys never got more than a carrot on a stick. It was important they remain hungry... A hungry dog bites!

Carlo was hoping Mantivo would tell him he had Teracita in the trunk of his car. What he got was even better. The professional hitman wanted Carlo to accompany him to Minnesota so he could personally hand her over to him. He had a private jet sitting on the runway at the New Smyrna Beach Airport.

A vision filled Carlo's mind. In it Teracita answers a knock on her door only to find him waiting on the other side. At first she resists, having been brainwashed by those queers at the shelter. He'd fix that. All he wanted was his property back!

When Mantivo dropped him back at the office he went to see Jim Downs. He gave a courtesy knock on the senior partner's door, but instead of waiting for permission to enter he just burst in. Carlo told his boss he was leaving town for a couple says. When he was asked him why Carlo responded, *"Business, Jim... Jose Gacha business!"*

He didn't have to say anything else. His boss responded with a flippant, *"Okay... We'll see you when you get back."* A few minutes later he was back in Mantivo's silver colored cadillac headed south.

A Cessna Citation was sitting on the tarmac, its twin jet engines running. A few moments after boarding they were on their way. The Daytona International Speedway came into view as the pilot banked left. Carlo peered out his window to see what from there looked like hot wheel cars speeding around the iconic race track. Drivers were practicing for an upcoming event.

Two hours later the pilot started his descent into the Twin Cities area. Carlo thought the Minnesota terrain looked cold and barren. Florida always seemed so inviting from the air. Miles of coastline filled with high rise condos and sandy beaches. Inland were green patterned squares full of lakes surrounded by homes with glistening swimming pools attached to them.

The plane landed at a private airstrip thirty miles outside the city of Minneapolis. When Carlo disembarked he'd wished he'd remembered to wear a jacket. The temperature was thirty degrees cooler than when he left Daytona. Springtime in Minnesota meant you shouldn't pack your parka just yet! It could snow here in June, and it often did.

Carlo checked his watch. There was a one hour difference between time zones. It was nearly 3:00 PM here. The hungry attorney hadn't eaten all day. He asked Mantivo if they could stop to grab a bite somewhere.

Santo told him he could eat after they checked into their hotel. They were staying at a suite inside The Mall of America. It would be midnight before they'd make the drive over to West St Paul, so there'd be plenty of time.

The paid assassin told Carlo his plan. They'd enter Teracita's apartment using the key provided by the landlord. He would inject her with a harmless sleeping agent and they'd carry her away. Simple as that. When she woke a few hours later she'd be lying in Carlo's bed, or anywhere else he wanted her delivered.

If Carlo wanted him to Mantivo could arrange for his fiance to be deprogramed. In fact he could arrange to have her behavior altered in whatever way Carlo desired. He'd been involved in human trafficking for a long time. Along the way he'd picked up a few tricks.

Mantivo explained how effective mind control is achieved. Using intensive systematic indoctrination under very controlled circumstances almost anyone's attitudes and convictions can be replaced with an alternate set of beliefs. He'd once seen a catholic nun turned into a promiscuous nymphomaniac within days of being enslaved.

An hour later the two men arrived at their destination. Traffic had been light until they got close to the massive mall. Then it picked up. It took them twenty minutes just to maneuver their way through the parking lot.

While Mantivo checked them into the hotel Carlo reviewed a Mall of America brochure that had been sitting on the counter. He was amazed to find there were over five hundred stores in the mall. That was a good thing because he was going to be needing a warm coat. Carlo discovered there was an Armani Menswear shop on level two.

Mantivo walked over and handed him a key badge. They were staying in suite 408. Carlo pointed to the brochure and said he needed to shop for a coat, adding *"I can't believe how fucking cold it is here!"* The hired killer laughed. He told Carlo to take his time. He'd be at the hotel bar.

It must have taken Carlo twenty minutes to get from the hotel lobby to the men's store. Along the way he passed an aquarium, a Lego Land theme park, and a fourteen screen movie theatre. The Mall of America was a city unto itself...

After browsing through the store Carlo chose an expensive wool jacket. He picked that one because it featured a large hidden inside pocket roomy enough to hold his 357 magnum, a revolver nearly nearly ten inches long. The mistrusting lawyer wasn't going anywhere with Mantivo without it.

Santo was waiting at the bar just as he said he'd be, but he wasn't alone. A middle aged floozie in a short tight dress was sitting next to him. Carlo walked up behind them and jokingly asked if there was room for him. The redhead turned and smiled. *"Hi... I'm Ginger,"* she said. *"We can definitely squeeze you in, Handsome."*

Carlo felt a familiar twinge run up his spine. Another place, another time, and he'd have charmed the skirt right off this cheap hooker. First he'd have gained her trust, then he would have tied her up and kicked her teeth out. *"Pleased to meet you"* Carlo responded. Then he turned to Mantivo and said, *"So what's up, Compadre?"*

Mantivo told Carlo his new girlfriend was very talented, explaining she could balance a martini between her tits and walk across the room without spilling a drop. *"Is that so,"* the lawyer responded, pretending to be impressed.

He wasn't surprised to learn Mantivo had just lost a hefty bet to the redheaded bimbo. She'd performed the feat moments before he'd arrived. *"Let me buy you a drink to ease the pain,"* Carlo offered. After getting the attention of the bartender he ordered three fresh martinis.

"Two martinis," Mantivo corrected him. Then he turned to Ginger and said, *"Get lost."* She looked at him incredulously, but didn't move. The hired assassin repeated himself, only louder this time, ***"I said get lost...you dumb cunt."***

The ample breasted redhead slid off her bar stool and huffed off. Carlo watched her derriere sway from side to side as she walked away. *"What a waste,"* he mumbled to himself.

He liked this Mantivo character, though he didn't trust him. One thing he did know. Professional assassin or not he better not fuck with him. That would be a mistake. Carlo reminded Santo he hadn't eaten all day and offered to buy him dinner. Rather than grab a table the two decided to eat at the bar. They both ordered the blackened salmon with horseradish sauce.

It was nearly eight o'clock when the two men headed back to their suite. They discussed Mantivo's plan on the elevator. If they left the hotel at midnight they would arrive in West St Paul around 12:20. An alleyway ran along one side of the building. A side door would provide them with covert access. By 12:30 they'd be in Teracita's apartment.

They discussed the idea of letting her see Carlo's face for a second, just to see the fear in her eyes. Then Mantivo would force feed her a heavy dose of GHB. The *Mickey* would knock her out for hours. In the end they decided not to take a chance. If Teracita got off a healthy scream before they had a chance to overpower her it could prove disastrous.

Once she'd been drugged they'd carry her back through the building and place her in the trunk of the car, then drive straight to the airstrip. The Cessna would be on the tarmac waiting to take them back to Florida.

When they got to the room Carlo went to take a piss while Mantivo set the alarm clock next to his bed. Then he flopped down on the pillows and hollered out, *"Time to catch some Z's, Amigo."*

There would be no rest for the wicked. Carlo's nerves were to wired to sleep. His thoughts drifted back to the first time he ever saw Teracita. Her attraction was heightened as much by the fact she was as innocent as a lamb as it was by her amazing good looks. She was as fragile as a delicate flower. The type of woman one could possess and mold into his own creation.

When the alarm went off Carlo sprung out of bed. He glanced at the clock. It was quarter past eleven. He knew Mantivo was already up because the bathroom shower was running. Carlo couldn't help thinking this guy was cool as a cat. He grabbed a can of beer from the mini fridge and started getting dressed. At 11:50 Mantivo walked out of the bathroom and asked, *"You ready, Bro?"*

At the stroke of midnight they headed out. True to form snow flakes were falling. Fortunately they melted the moment they hit the windshield. Mantivo pulled out of the mall parking lot and hopped on Interstate 494 headed west. At precisely 12:20 they pulled into the alleyway next to the bakery shop.

Mantivo went over the plan one more time, reviewing every detail. It was a simple operation. One he'd carried out dozens of times before. When he was sure they were ready he acted...

Carlo followed him into the building. They quietly made their way down the dark hallway to Teracita's apartment. Once there Mantivo handed him the key.

When he turned the door handle it produced a loud sound that echoed down the hall. Carlo held his breath for what seemed like an eternity. When if felt safe to do so he reached out and pushed the door open.

It was pitch black inside the apartment. Mantivo hadn't really considered how dark it might be. He whispered to Carlo they needed a flashlight, saying he thought there might be one in the glove box. The lawyer quickly retraced his steps back to the alleyway.

When he returned a few minutes later Mantivo took the flashlight and scanned the room. No one was there. He looked in the closet, it held no clothes. He checked the dresser drawers...

Nothing... The bathroom... Empty! He turned to Carlo and said, *"What the fuck, Amigo. The bitch ain't here!"*

To say Carlo was disappointed would be an understatement. He was beguiled. Flabbergasted. He'd been looking forward to this moment since it was first mentioned. The usually aggressive lawyer looked at Mantivo and sheepishly asked, *"Could she be out? Maybe she has a boyfriend?"*

Of course he knew the truth. His *Bonita* had flown the coop. The bitch had disappeared. She'd bested him yet again!

Mantivo stood in the middle of the room contemplating the situation. He wanted to walk down the hall and put a bullet in the baker's head. *"De mierda bastardo debe haber sabido,"* he muttered to himself... *"The fucking bastard must've known."* He'd warned her they were coming...

Santo hadn't been hired to assassinate anyone this time. He considered himself a professional. He only killed under contract. No sense getting excited about it. When The Latin Kings got word of what happened they'd take care of business. Mantivo was certain of that.

Without warning some kid would walk into the bakery shop with an AK-47 and fire off a couple dozen rounds. He'd take out the baker and his wife with a hail of bullets, as well as anyone else unlucky enough to be buying a loaf of bread there that day. The entire episode would go down as a robbery turned bad. It wasn't Mantivo's mode of operation, but it was effective.

They hustled back to the car and headed out. Mantivo assured Carlo he would find his fiance, but secretly he was worried. It had been his idea to bring the lawyer along. He'd hoped to impress the personal attorney of Jose Gacha with his skills. The fact it wasn't an actual hit had caused him to relax. As a professional assassin he'd have carried out the execution and collected his pay in short order. This foolishness seemed like child's play to him.

Mantivo hoped his lieutenant felt the same way. This entire operation was being carried out because of a friendly deal between two cartel bosses. The two often worked together for mutual gain, each having something the other needed. This game of cat and mouse he'd been handed was just plain bullshit!

He knew Teracita had only been located because the baker was loyal to Vicente Fuentes. He'd approached The Latin Kings with the information out of fear he'd be seen as disloyal. The chances of someone else turning her in were slim. If *El Padrino* complained to Fuentes about Mantivo the cartel might cut him loose. The hired assassin wouldn't just be unemployed... He'd be dead.

EARLY RETIREMENT

MURDER IN DAYTONA

44

Brush Creek runs between West 80th Street and Blue Avenue. The creek's banks are home to some of the toughest street gangs in metropolitan Kansas City. None of them Black or Latino. These gangs are rooted in Irish heritage, sprung from the working class neighborhoods that surround the district. They are descendants of Irish immigrants who left New England after the Civil War in search of opportunity.

In the 1970's good paying union jobs started drying up. Many of the district's blue collar workers had to take whatever jobs they could find to support their families. The children of these workers found that crime often paid more than the meager salaries their parents could earn performing menial tasks. They eventually organized into well run gangs.

Unlike their counterparts in the ghetto the Irish street gangs often cooperate with each other. Because they do law enforcement finds it extremely difficult to infiltrate them or break them up. Truth be known, many of the cops have family in the gangs.

Aaron drove into the city and parked his car near the affluent Country Club Plaza. From there he walked the dozen blocks to his old neighborhood. He didn't dare park on the streets along Brush Creek. The minute he turned his back his car would be stripped down to the hull.

His family had left the neighborhood during his senior year in high school. He'd be a stranger now, and Aaron knew outsiders weren't welcome here. The minute he crossed West 73rd Street he felt eyes upon him. Word of his arrival preceded his appearance.

When he walked into Malone's Bar three blokes met him at the entrance. The Irish saloon was home to a street gang known as The Blue Bloods. The largest of the three stepped forward. He was young, Aaron guessed about nineteen, but big as an Ox. He stood at the doorway blocking Aaron's progress. *"Ha dere, Mate,"* he said. *"What's the craic?"*

Aaron knew the lingo. He politely answered, *"got me a throat on"* as he pointed to the bar. He asked the bloke to join him for a pint. The fellow turned to his mates and whispered something under his breath, than he and Aaron took a stool.

After downing a Black & Tan Aaron told the gang member he had business there. He explained he'd grown up in The Creek, and mentioned a few names. The bloke asked the bartender for a pen and wrote an address down on a paper napkin. He handed it to Aaron and told him to be there in half an hour. Then he stood and extended his hand.

Aaron knew enough about street gangs not to extend his hand first. That would have been considered disrespectful in the gang environment. People who did sometimes left less healthy than when they arrived. As they shook the bloke said, *"Hope fer your sake you ain't talkin shite, Mate."* Then he rejoined his friends at the other end of the bar.

When Aaron got to the address written on the napkin he found he'd been sent to a vacant lot. Just as he was about to leave a car came barreling around the corner and screeched up to the curb. A darkly tinted rear window lowered a few inches and Aaron heard a familiar voice say, *"Get in, Butter face."*

He hadn't been called that since he was a kid. When the rear door opened Aaron was greeted by an old classmate of his, Clive Byrne. Clive had quit school at the age of seventeen. He'd been a very smart student. His grades rivaled Aaron's. There's no doubt he would have gotten a college scholarship if he'd remained in school. It was just a few months later Aaron's family moved out of the district. He hadn't seen Clive since.

Clive's father was supposedly in the IRA. Rumor was he'd served twelve years in an English prison for talking back to a British army officer. The officer retaliated by framing him for a robbery he didn't commit. It's said when Mr Byrne got out of prison he sought out the man who'd framed him and slit his throat.

His official position in the IRA was creating false documents. On occasion he produced counterfeit punts. Never anything under hundred pound notes. The reason Clive left school was to learn the craft from his father. He'd evidently learned well because the car he was being chauffeured around in sold for upwards of forty grand.

Aaron told his childhood pal he needed help procuring some identification documents for a friend. He showed Clive a picture of Teracita, explaining she was in trouble with one of the Mexican drug cartels. The forger wanted more information. He knew not to take unnecessary risks, especially with the likes of them.

Teracita's story was rehashed in detail. Aaron admitted his biggest fear was that the cartel might trace her to his door step. Clive stopped his one time pal mid-sentence. *"MIGHT,"* he questioned loudly? *"I hate to break it to you, Mate...but some slabber is bound to spill the beans. There ain't no MIGHT about it. The cartel will definitely trace her to your door step... You Butter face!"*

Clive told Aaron he'd have the documents ready in a couple days. It would cost him five grand. *"Half off for a friend,"* the forger added. Aaron understood now how Clive could afford that luxury automobile. Before parting Clive gave Aaron a warning. From one mate to another... *"Consider moving...and I mean out of the country!"*

The cost of the documents would drain a third of Aaron's savings account. He considered heading for the Canadian border. Common sense told him to think things through before doing anything rash. He'd pick up the forged documents on Thursday, then send Teracita on her way.

That night everyone went to bed early. The three of them were worn out. The girls had gone shopping while Aaron gallivanted around town. Teracita needed clothes for her trip. Rebecca took her to Zona Rosa, the premier outdoor shopping and dining destination in Kansas City. While there they visited a travel agency.

They learned that not only were cabins still available on a cruise ship sailing out of Galveston, Texas, but the price was being heavily discounted because the ship was full of college students on spring break. The cruise liner would be making ports of call in Jamaica, Belize, Curacao, and the Dominican Republic.

Several hours after retiring Aaron was awakened by Rebecca's snoring again. He went to the kitchen to get a glass of water and was surprised to see Teracita sitting there in the dark. She hadn't been able to sleep either. Dressed only in his boxers Aaron's excitement was immediately evident.

He looked into Teracita's eyes for permission to touch. The sound of his girlfriend snoring down the hall gave him the confidence to continue. Aaron took his beautiful Mexican visitor by the hand and led her to the living room sofa. They spent the next hour fulfilling their carnal desires while Rebecca slept.

When they finished they snuggled on the sofa and whispered sweet nothings into each others ears. In the still of the night they agreed to go to the Caribbean together. Aaron justified the plan in his head, harkening back to what Clive Byrne had suggested... *"Get out of the country!"*

When Thursday morning came Aaron made his way back to Brush Creek. This time he didn't park his car somewhere safe and walk. He drove straight to Malone's Bar. As he approached the entrance he was met by the same bloke he'd encountered a few days earlier. *"You be pullin a wally drivin down here, Mate"* the gangster warned him. *"Clive be in back. He's been waitin on ya."*

Aaron walked to the back of the bar and through a vestibule that opened into a meeting room. Clive Byrne was sitting at a large rectangular table downing a pint when he strolled in. Four of his fellow Blue Bloods were leaning against the wall behind him, two on either side.

Somewhat nervous about what he was about to do, Aaron reached inside his jacket and pulled out an envelope containing a wad of cash. Clive motioned for one of his underlings to bring him the manilla folder containing the documents he'd forged. *"These be fool proof, Butter Face"* he bragged as he plopped them down on the table.

Aaron opened the folder and compared the contents to his own documents. They appeared to be identical. It seemed to surprise him a little. He wondered what other types of forgeries Clive produced. Visions of hundred dollar bank notes danced in his head.

He reached across the table and offered his hand in gratitude. Clive didn't take it. He couldn't. That would go against gang protocol. The master forger walked around to the other side of the table and gave his childhood friend a healthy hug. *"Ya done yerself good, Mate"* he said. *"Now get out of the country fore de find ya.*

They'll eat yer head off, Butter face!" Aaron knew Clive's warning was genuine. He'd be heeding his advice.

EARLY RETIREMENT

MURDER IN DAYTONA

45

Rebecca was a nurse at Kansas City General. She was assigned to the cardiac ward. Her schedule required her to work three twelve hour shifts. This weeks rotation had her working Friday through Sunday nights. Aaron and Teracita took advantage of the situation.

Wanting to be sure Rebecca didn't walk in on them in the event they overslept, Aaron set the alarm clock. His efforts proved unnecessary. The two made love all night long. They took breaks in between of course, but neither of them fell asleep. Any *'down time'* was spent titillating and fussing over one another, the way young lovers do...

When Rebecca left for work Saturday evening Aaron and Teracita got on the computer and Google searched 'Islands of the Caribbean.' They learned it was relatively easy to travel between Island nations. There were dozens of couriers with sea planes and private boat charters one could utilize. The coconspirators planned their escape. Aaron would book himself a cabin on the same cruise Teracita was taking. To get a feel for the locales they'd disembark at each port of call. When it felt right they'd simply not return to the ship.

Aaron would drive them to Galveston. He'd leave his car at the airport and take a taxicab to the ship. Money might be an issue. After paying for the forged documents he only had ten grand left in his bank account, along with a couple credit cards. Perhaps he'd find work once they were settled. If things worked out it might even be possible to stay with his current employer.

His job as a marketing rep allowed him to take chunks of time off. Aaron was paid on commission. There were months when he had to be on the road pushing product, but late spring was always slow. Taking a few weeks off wouldn't be unusual.

He was thinking of approaching his employer with the idea of setting up accounts in the Islands. It was definitely something he'd pursue down the road. Right now he had to concentrate on just getting away.

Aaron hated the idea of leaving Rebecca high and dry. He'd coerced her into moving in with him, even though she'd initially said no. He liked Rebecca, but her snoring was getting under his skin. Even if Teracita hadn't shown up at his door he probably would have dumped her. One can go without sleep for only so long. Question was should he and Teracita do the right thing and tell her, or just sneak off like jackals in the night.

When Rebecca came home from work Sunday morning she found her suitcase packed and waiting by the door. It had been a particularly long night, having lost two patients to cardiac arrest. The last thing she needed was this!

Thing is she never saw it coming. Rebecca honestly believed Aaron and Teracita were just friends. She hadn't even wanted to move in with him in the first place... No matter, she was too damn tired to fight about it. Her parting words to Aaron were...
"YOU'RE AN ASSHOLE!"

WHEW... He really thought it would be much worse. Rebecca could get animated. Aaron thought for sure she'd be crying and pleading for a second chance. In a way he was proud of her. His girlfriend had basically told him to go fuck himself. It seems honesty was the best policy after all!

The ship wasn't due to sail until the following Monday afternoon. Both Aaron and Teracita were on edge. The question remained, would an assassin show up at their door before they had a chance to get away? Would it be wise to just pack the car and go? Better to arrive early then to stay put for an entire week wondering if they'd live long enough to make the trip at all. It would take two days of driving to get to Galveston. Once they were there they could hide out until it was time to set sail.

Teracita helped Aaron prepare the apartment for dormancy. His lease was paid through the summer so it wasn't necessary to give the landlord notice. After giving the place a thorough cleaning they packed the contents of the fridge in a couple plastic garbage liners and gave them to a young couple who lived across the street. Aaron knew the young man had lost his job a few weeks back. They were surviving on the girl's meager income. She worked as a file clerk in a law office downtown. Next morning they loaded up the car and hit the road.

It was seven a.m. when Aaron entered the southbound ramp leading to Interstate Highway 71. He dialed in a soft rock station and set the cruise control. The soothing sounds of Seals & Croft purred from the speakers as he settled in for a long day's drive.

At precisely the same moment Santo Mantivo was exiting the opposite side of the highway. The professional assassin had picked up Teracita's trail, having been furnished the information on her whereabouts by a member of a Kansas City street gang known as The Blue Bloods.

It was unusual in that Irish gangs rarely cooperated with the drug cartels. The Blue Bloods were a conglomeration of Irish working class skinheads. The offspring of the offspring of the original Kansas City immigrants. They hated niggers and they hated spics. As far as they were concerned the cotton pickers who invaded their city following the Civil War had caused their demise. The invasion by the unwanted southern Blacks was then followed by an influx of Wet-Backs from Mexico. The gravel bellies had been infiltrating Kansas City for the past twenty odd years. Latinos had taken over the entire northeastern quadrant of the city.

Blue Bloods were beholden to the IRA, and the one thing the Irish Republic Army needed more than any other was cash. What they didn't need was enemies. Especially organized enemies like the drug cartels. Though it was next to impossible to infiltrate the Irish street gangs, it was possible to recruit from within.

The bloke who'd first confronted Aaron at Malone's accepted payola from the IRA for information they wouldn't otherwise be able to divulge. Occasionally this information proved valuable. The fella knew from word on the street that the Juarez Cartel was searching for a girl. It just so happens he knew where this girl could be found. He had the license plate number of the car owned by the man harboring the girl. A few short phone calls netted him a couple hundred bucks, as well as continued good standing with his IRA handlers.

The IRA in turn offered to sell this information to connections within the Juarez Cartel. The offer was relayed to *Los Norte Del Valle,* who informed Senor' Gacha. A counter offer was made.

Gacha wanted the IRA to have the girl picked up and her companion shot. After some hesitation his offer was refused. Providing information for cash was one thing. Working with drug cartels was quite another. The IRA decided their best option was to provide the information pro bono as a jester of good will.

The cartel now knew where Teracita could be found. Santo Mantivo was given a chance at redemption. This time he traveled alone. The killer for hire flew into Wheeler Field, a small airport a few miles outside Kansas City. He rented a car and headed for pay dirt with instructions not to mess up. It was a few minutes past seven when he arrived at his destination.

There'd be no waiting until the middle of the night this time. The killer for hire would do his deed in broad daylight. He had orders to kill any inhabitants of the apartment and take the girl, with force if necessary.

Mantivo parked across the street from the house. He loaded his semi automatic with a fresh magazine then crossed over. The front door was locked. The assassin rang the doorbell but there was no answer so he made his around to the back of the building, trampling through a patch of freshly budding rose bushes in the process. That door was locked too. Mantivo took a boot to it and the wood door gave way.

The killer called out, *"Cualquiera aqui... Anyone here?" He* systematically moved from room to room, carefully checking for anyone who may be hiding in a closet or behind a door. When he reached the master bedroom Mantivo saw coat hangers strewn across the bed. The assassin got a bad feeling in the pit of his stomach.

He went back to the kitchen and opened the refrigerator door. It was empty. Completely void of food. Mantivo stared at the empty white carcass in disbelief. He realized the appliance wasn't even running. His anger got the best of him and he slammed his fist against the door, screaming at the top of his lungs, *"ME CAGO EN CHRISTO... I shit on Christ!"*

A plastic trash can sitting in a corner of the kitchen became the object of Mantivo's continued frustration. He kicked it across the room, spewing its contents across the floor. The hired gun was beat. He slumped down in a chair and laid his head on the kitchen table.

The little cunt had disappeared into thin air again. That was painfully obvious. The refrigerator was the telltale sign. Nobody unplugged their fridge unless they weren't planning on coming back.

Mantivo figured he was a dead man. Perhaps he should save his employer the trouble and just shoot himself right then and there. The assassin lifted the semi automatic to his head, prepared to do what must be done.

The cold steel barrel of Mantivo's weapon rested on his ear lobe as he surveyed the room. The faces of total strangers he'd slain for others began to appear in his mind like a deck of flash cards. The gunman's eyes glazed over and his hands began to shake uncontrollably. He was about to squeeze the trigger when something registered in his brain. Something that made him relax his grip.

On closer inspection he saw it. Mixed amongst the empty soup cans and rotting banana peels that spilled out of the trash can when he kicked it over was a neatly folded colorful brochure. Mantivo put his gun down on the table and walked over to pick it up. The brochure was from a Kansas City travel agency.

Mantivo saw the pamphlet was for a cruise line sailing out of Galveston. Stamped on the inside flap was the name of a ship. Below that was a cabin number and a sailing date. On the back of the brochure was a name. Ms Bonita Santiago.

"Bonita," Mantivo said aloud, trying to recall where he'd heard that name. Had Carlo Santiago not referred to Teracita Goncalves as his *"Little Bonita?"* Could she be using that name as an alias?

The hired assassin was convinced she was. *"What luck,"* he laughed. *"This fucking brochure is going to save my ass!"* Mantivo kissed the pamphlet's cover then stuffed it in his pocket. At least he had something to show for his troubles. He'd know soon enough.

EARLY RETIREMENT

MURDER IN DAYTONA

46

Aaron figured they'd make it as far as Dallas that first day but construction on the highway had forced them to take a detour. He'd been driving for nearly ten hours when he saw a sign advertising a Family Inn located at the next exit six miles ahead. They were still forty minutes north of Dallas, but that was close enough for him.

Teracita had fallen asleep some fifty miles back. They'd spend the night, have breakfast in the morning, then continue on to Galveston. There wasn't any hurry.

The motel sat just off the interstate. It wasn't anything special. Just one of those places that sprung up along the highway when it was built back in the late fifties. Aaron woke Teracita when they got there. They nibbled on snacks he purchased from the vending machines in the lobby, then turned on the TV and settled in for the night.

Aaron found he wasn't able to sleep soundly. He lay in bed listening to tractor trailers speeding up and down the highway. As a young man he'd worked as a *lumper,* unloading pallets with a lift jack while attending college back in Joplin. He'd once considered truck driving as an option if the college thing didn't work out. An owner/operator could earn a hundred thou a year, or so he'd read. Heck that was way more than he made as a marketing rep.

It was after midnight. The percolating sound of a diesel engine coming from an idling truck drifted across the nearly empty motel parking lot. Aaron was surprised a trucker would leave his engine running like that. It wasn't like he needed to. The temperature was a comfortable seventy-two degrees. He got up to take a look.

A flickering light was coming from inside the truck's cab. Aaron didn't know why he was so mesmerized, but the moment captured his attention. He closed the drape and went to the door. After hesitating a moment he slid the chain off the lock and stepped out onto the sidewalk.

In the quiet of the night Aaron thought he heard muffled cries coming from the direction of the semi. The more he listened the more he was convinced it wasn't just in his head. He started walking towards the idling rig. When he got close he stepped into the shadow of the motel's overhang.

Several light poles were inoperable in this secluded section of the lot. The bulbs had probably burned out long ago, but due to the fact no one ever parked that far from the lobby entrance the owners didn't bother replacing them. Aaron stood perfectly still and focused his eyes on the tractor trailer.

On the passenger side of the truck's sleeper compartment was a small window. Beneath it an airbrush artist had decoratively painted the words, `Amigo de Diablo`.

A depiction of a winged demon standing in the midst of a ring of fire was painted below that. The succubus had long black hair covering her breasts, and a sleek voluptuous body. Two small horns protruded from her forehead, and a human skull hung from a chain around her neck. It reached down to her navel. Her demonic eyes portrayed lustfulness.

Aaron was transfixed on the artwork. A sudden flicker of light from the sleeper compartment's window broke the spell. He looked up to see the face of a young girl pressed up against the glass.

The girl had closely cropped red hair. It framed a freckled face. Her features were contorted in a painful expression. Tears streamed down her cheeks and smeared the window. Aaron stepped out of the shadows and slowly walked towards her. As he did the child despairingly mouthed the words... *"PLEASE HELP ME!"*

Suddenly she was gone. Someone or something had jerked her back. The outline of the girl's nose was visible on the fogged glass, till the faint light that'd been flickering in the background was extinguished. Then all was silent.

Aaron stood in the dark parking lot looking up at the small rectangle window of the sleeper, hoping the girl might return... She didn't! The big rig sat idling like a giant sleeping ghost as he back pedaled to the safety of the shadows from hence he came.

He didn't take his eyes off the sleeper compartment window till he was some distance away. Then he turned and ran back to his room. After locking the door and setting the chain Aaron stood by the window, fighting the urge to look out.

When he was a kid his mother used to use a phrase on him. *"Curiosity killed the cat!"* Aaron had always been curious. Ever since he was a little boy. He was the type of kid who'd rummage through his parents closet during the holidays hoping to catch a glimpse of his presents before they were wrapped. As a boy he constantly hounded his mother with questions. *"What were you and dad talking about last night... I heard you both whispering? Who was that on the phone? Why was your bedroom door locked when I got home from school today?"*

She never would divulge. Instead his mother would tell him, *"Curiosity killed the cat."* He never understood that saying more than he did at this moment.

"I can't get involved," he told himself. *"My ass is on the line."* Last thing he and Teracita needed was exposure. Sure he could call the cops, but if what he'd seen was what he thought it was he'd surely become the focal point of an investigation... He forced himself to go to bed.

Aaron woke a few hours later. He went to take a piss, then checked the alarm clock. It was nearly 6:00 AM. He shook Teracita and told her it was time to get up. She mumbled, *"Despierto... Despierto... I'm awake."*

He quickly gathered their things and tossed them in his luggage bag. It was time to leave. Teracita sat up and stretched. She asked, *"Are we gonna eat something? I'm hungry."* Aaron ignored her and continued getting ready.

Ten minutes later they were in the car. Aaron tepidly glanced towards the end of the parking lot where the tractor trailer had been idling earlier that morning. It was gone. He drove to the spot where it had been parked and got out. Teracita asked him what he was doing. He shook his head and said, *"I'll explain later. Let's go eat."*

They found a diner just up the road. There was only a handful of customers when they walked in. Two old geezers were sitting at the counter huddled over steaming cups of coffee not paying attention to anyone, including each other. Another guy was sitting alone in a booth reading a newspaper. His face was hidden by a braided leather cowboy hat that sat low on his forehead. Aaron said good morning to him as they passed by on their way to be seated.

The cowboy looked up and nodded. The young buck had a nasty scratch on his face that ran from just below his left ear all the way to his nose. It looked like a fresh wound. Aaron presumed it was probably well deserved. In all likelihood it had been put there by some wild Texas filly after the cowboy put his hands where they didn't belong.

They were seated in a booth towards the back. Without asking, the waitress filled their coffee mugs and said she'd be right back with a menu. The fifty something waitress seemed the type who'd probably waited on tables most of her life. Aaron told her they didn't need a menu. They'd both have the breakfast special he saw on the board when he walked in.

Just then a guy came out of the men's room. He was dressed like a trucker, right down to the chained wallet he was wearing. He brushed past Aaron and joined the young cowboy at the booth near the front of the restaurant. Aaron watched as the cowboy leaned across the table and said something to his companion. The trucker turned and glared at Aaron with a malevolent look in his eyes.

Aaron quickly looked away. He hadn't been intimidated by anyone in a long time. He was a fairly big guy, and he was in fairly good shape. Like most kids growing up in The Creek he'd been in plenty of skirmishes as a boy. He knew he could hold his own. This time was different. Something about this trucker and his cowboy counterpart warned Aaron to avoid any altercation.

The waitress returned with their breakfast. She refilled their coffee mugs, then sauntered off. After she left Aaron glanced down at the booth where the two strangers had been sitting. They were gone! The trucker and his friend had slipped out unnoticed. For some reason that brought him relief.

He and Teracita finished their breakfast in relative silence, offering only obligatory exchanges when asked to pass the salt or ketchup. The waitress came back to top off his coffee, but Aaron declined. He asked her if she knew the two men who'd been sitting in the booth closest to the door. *"Never seen em before, Hon"* she answered. The waitress took a few steps, then turned and added, *"Good tippers though... They left me a sawbuck... Don't see too many truckers leavin ten-spots these days!"*

402

Teracita looked at Aaron questioningly. She asked him, *"What was that all about?"* He told her the two men in the front booth had given him the creeps. Especially the young one in the cowboy hat. She replied they had more to worry about then some ugly cowboy. *"The cartel would make those two hombres seem like boy scouts."*

Aaron slid out of the booth. He pulled a twenty dollar bill from his wallet and set it on the table, then announced it was time to go. Their new life was waiting for them at the end of the road. Teracita took a final gulp of coffee then slid out behind him.

As they headed out the door a big rig pulled around from the back of the restaurant. Aaron couldn't make out the driver, but he did recognize the truck. It was the same one that had idled in the motel parking lot all night. He knew because there was a sultry winged demon hand painted on its side just under the sleeper compartment window. He watched as the driver made his way to the highway entry ramp and headed north. The opposite direction he and Teracita were traveling.

Moments later they were on the Interstate driving south. In less than six hours they'd be in Galveston. *"So,"* Teracita asked out of the blue, *"You gonna tell me what's going on? You been acting weird all morning."*

Aaron tried to explain his behavior away by saying he'd just gotten the creeps. Probably a result of the stress he'd been under. He admitted feeling a few pangs of guilt over dumping Rebecca the way he had. Everything had happened so fast he really hadn't had time to digest it.

After a while he decided to come clean. He told Teracita he'd had trouble sleeping because a semi had parked in the corner of the motel parking lot with its engine idling all night long. He told her about the flickering light coming from the cab, and how it had captured his curiosity. He said when he went to investigate he saw a young girl peering out the sleeper compartment window. *"She seemed to be in trouble,"* he confessed. *"She was crying. I thought she might need my help."*

"So did you," Teracita asked? *"Did you help her?"* Aaron said he got spooked and ran back to the room. He didn't think he should get involved, especially considering the predicament they were in.

Teracita agreed. She told him it was probably a couple having a squabble or something. There were lots of married truckers teaming up these days. Tandem drivers could share driving duties and keep the wheels rolling. Miles were money. *"Can you imagine what it must be like being in such close quarters for so many hours at a time,"* she said. *"You're bound to get into squabbles."*

It got quiet after that. Aaron settled down to the task at hand. Galveston was their ticket to a new life. He'd felt a connection with Teracita the first time he ever laid eyes on her. When he left her on that Greyhound bus last winter he wasn't sure he'd ever see her again, but he hoped he would. His lack of patience had led him to ask Rebecca to move in with him. When the beautiful Mexican Au Pair showed up at his door he knew that decision had been a mistake. One that had to be rectified.

A quick stop at a rest area followed by a stop to refuel were the only breaks they took. By noon they were crossing the causeway to Galveston Island. The plan was to drive to the airport, pull the license plates, and ditch the car in long term parking. It would have been convenient to keep the car until they sailed on Monday but Aaron feared someone would trace it to them.

Scholes International Airport can be accessed from the causeway by taking the Gulf Freeway to 61st Street. Aaron pulled into the parking lot and took a ticket from the automated dispenser. He chose a space close to a shuttle stop. Teracita got their luggage out of the trunk while Aaron wiped down the inside of the car with disposable wipes he'd purchased for the occasion. He wanted to remove any trace of fingerprints on the steering wheel and dashboard. He wasn't sure why. It just seemed prudent.

When he finished he tossed the car keys in the trunk and closed the lid. Then they made their way to the airport terminal. Aaron noticed the cruise port could be seen in the distance.

When they got to the terminal the two separated. Aaron thought that seemed prudent too. He'd booked a room at the East Beach Resort, a three star property located directly on the Gulf of Mexico. Teracita would take a cab there. He would take the hotel's courtesy shuttle.

The resort was one of many that lined Seawall Boulevard on Galveston Island. The area was a tourist mecca, with plenty of restaurants and nightspots to spend time in. Aaron suggested they rest up from the trip. They could go out on the town tonight.

Ten minutes after arriving Aaron was fast asleep. It's no wonder. He hadn't slept a wink the night before. Teracita turned the television on, but kept the volume low so she wouldn't disturb him. A local news station was airing a story about the effects another oil spill could have on the areas fishing industry. The correspondent was explaining how the gulf shrimp business was still reeling from the last major spill.

After a commercial break a television news anchor appeared on screen with a disturbing story about a teenage girl whose battered body was discovered lying in a ditch in southern Cooke County. The girl was found by a passing motorist who'd pulled to the side of the highway to repair a flat tire he got while driving to work that morning. The man was employed at a large distribution warehouse a few miles north of the village of Sanger, Texas.

This was the third homicide involving a young woman in that town this year. There hadn't been a single murder in Sanger, Texas in the previous forty years. All three appeared to be connected in that the victims were young woman with no obvious ties to the area. Even so, the town's residents were sure to be frightened by this latest tragedy. After warning the television audience that the following report might be too graphic for some viewers the news anchor went live to a correspondent at the scene.

The reporter was standing in a ditch along Frontage Road. All around him police were busy looking for clues and securing the area. Behind him viewers could see what appeared to be a body wrapped in a plastic cadaver pouch. It was laying by the side of the highway awaiting transport to the morgue. The correspondent approached a state trooper and asked him if there was any indication what might have caused the victim's injuries, adding it had been reported she'd been beaten to death. The trooper stopped what he was doing to answer the reporter's question.

He confirmed the victim had suffered a horrendous beating. Unlike anything he'd ever encountered. He said no weapons had been found at the scene, but the investigation was ongoing. The trooper mentioned the case was similar to two previous homicides in the area, in that all three victims were young women unknown by local authorities. So far no one had come forward to claim the bodies or provide any information.

The trooper stated the victim was most likely a runaway or a prostitute. A small college located twelve miles south of town had been considered as a likely source, but the school hadn't reported any of their students missing. It seemed these young women had met their demise at the hands of a serial killer.

The correspondent gave viewers a detailed description of the latest victim, along with a hotline number to call if anyone had any information. He held up a picture drawn by a state police sketch artist. It showed a girl around fourteen years of age with short red hair and a face full of freckles.

Teracita let out a scream! What she saw shocked her. *"OH MY GOD... OH SHIT... QUI DIOS AYUDE A SU... GOD HELP HER!"*

Aaron was awakened by the noise. Teracita pointed at the television screen and hollered, *"IS THAT HER, AARON? IS THAT THE GIRL YOU SAW IN THE WINDOW OF THAT TRUCK?"*

The poor guy wiped the sleep from his eyes and looked at the TV screen. He caught a glimpse of the girl's face just before the image disappeared. *"Yes,"* he answered. *"That was her... What the hell happened?"*

Teracita told him the girl had been found dead. Someone had beat her to death and dumped her body along the side of the road. The same road they were on earlier in the day.

"I fucking knew it," Aaron said remorsefully. *"Those fucking bastards... It was that fucking cowboy..."*

They held each other. Aaron wept openly. *"I couldn't help her,"* he pleaded. *"We couldn't take the chance. That could be us if we're not careful!"*

Teracita stroked her boyfriend's hair and whispered in his ear everything would be okay. She told him when this ordeal was over they'd go to the cops and tell them everything. Aaron put his hands to his face and said, *"This whole thing is insane... Is this really happening?"*

The two lovers spent the rest of the day in bed. They ordered dinner from room service and watched pay per view movies to pass the time.

After the sun set they got dressed and went for a walk. There were several bars just steps away from the resort, and Aaron really needed a drink...

They avoided talking about what happened to the girl. Teracita tried to take Aaron's mind off it by teaching him to speak a few words in Spanish. He'd need to learn if he was going to live in the islands. They ordered a couple rounds to help calm his nerves. It worked. After a while the Irish Mormon began to unwind.

It was early morning when they staggered back to their room. Aaron went to take a leak. Teracita waited for him to shut the bathroom door then quickly changed into a sexy negligee she'd bought when she went shopping with Rebecca. At the time she had no idea she'd be wearing it for him.

She climbed into bed and spread herself across the mattress. When her boyfriend came out of the bathroom Teracita playfully asked, *"You ready for dessert, Guapo?"* Aaron smiled and crawled in beside her.

It was no use. The girl in the window haunted his thoughts. So much so he couldn't maintain his erection. Every time Aaron looked at Teracita he saw her. *"This isn't supposed to happen to a guy my age,"* he griped. After ten frustrating minutes he got up and went to take a shower.

Teracita removed her negligee and stuffed it back in the bag. She understood Aaron had much on his mind. Sex was ninety percent mental. They'd have plenty of opportunities to have fun together when this was over. Secretly though, she worried... Her boyfriend was right. That wasn't supposed to happen to a guy his age!

Aaron didn't approach Teracita in a sexual way the remainder of their stay. They spent the weekend sunbathing by the pool and walking along the beach. Evenings were spent enjoying dinner at one of the restaurants on the island and watching movies in their room. Things got so relaxed both of them forgot they were being sought by people who wanted to kill them. When Monday morning arrived reality reappeared. That's when they reverted to being desperadoes on the run again.

The plan was to board the cruise ship separately. They'd go to their respective until it was time for the captain's bon voyage party later that evening. Then they'd hook back up.

Teracita left first, taking a bus the cruise line provided to transport guest staying in area hotels to the dock. When she boarded the ship she made her way to her cabin, which was located on the lower level just above crew quarters. She'd seen no reason to be frivolous with her money since she'd be departing the ship before it completed its journey anyway.

Once she was gone Aaron had a long talk with himself. What in the hell was he doing? Why was he throwing away everything he'd worked for to be with this girl? How the fuck did he get caught up in this nightmare anyway? Why hadn't he acted when he realized that young girl in the truck was in serious trouble? Was he responsible for her death? **Why was his mother's bedroom door always locked when he got home from school?**

Aaron canceled the taxi he had planned to take to the cruise port. He arranged with the front desk to catch the hotel shuttle back to the airport. He'd done what he could for Teracita. From now on she was on her own!

His anxiety hadn't helped. A man his age with erectile dysfunction issues? Fuck that! He'd dumped two women in the span of one week. It was empowering in a way. He hoped he was making the right decision.

Aaron wondered if this whole Mexican drug cartel thing had been overstated. He didn't know if he'd ever find out. Then again, maybe he didn't want to. The fact of the matter was simply this. They were after her... Not him!

Upon reaching the terminal Aaron made his way to the long term parking lot. He could see his car in the distance. It was the only one without a plate. Remembering he'd tossed his car key in the trunk when they left he reached in his back pocket and pulled out his wallet. He kept a spare in the zipper compartment.

Aaron checked his watch. He knew Teracita would be onboard by now. She wouldn't miss him until later that evening when he failed to show up at the bon voyage party. He couldn't help but wonder if she suspected. He'd seen the disappointment in her eyes when he had his melt down, knowing full well she was used to a man who could perform. Might she be on the deck of the ship trying to spot him in the lines of people still going through the pre-boarding process?

From the upper decks of the ocean liner one would be able to see the airport. After all, cruise ships are nearly two hundred feet tall. That equates to a building over twelve stories high. The top deck would be quite a vantage point for someone seeking a view.

Aaron retrieved his other set of car keys from the trunk then tossed his suitcase in and closed the lid. He reached under the front floor mat and pulled out the license plate. After installing it he got behind the wheel.

Looking north towards the cruise port he could see the ship he was supposed to be on. She sat in her berth patiently awaiting her departure. Aaron could imagine the work that goes into preparing a ship that size to sail the seas with several thousand guests aboard. He opened the driver side window and hollered, *"I'm going to miss you, Teracita... BON VOYAGE MY LOVE...* Then he turned the key in the ignition...

Hundreds of people were relaxing on the Lido Deck when they heard what sounded like an explosion in the distance. Most of them jumped out of their deck chairs and rushed to the starboard side of the ship. Teracita was one of them. She saw a plume of smoke billowing up in the air, coming from the direction of the airport.

The distinct sound of sirens could be heard as a succession of fire trucks rushed towards the scene of the explosion. Someone ran by saying an airplane had crashed. Another was overheard saying the explosion came from the airport parking lot. He joked it was a hell of a way to get out of paying the parking fee.

Eventually the excitement passed. Everyone went back to enjoying the day as if it never happened, but it was hard to ignore the cloud that drifted from the area of the explosion and now hovered over the ship. Teracita took her drink and went back to her cabin. She wondered if Aaron had seen the explosion. She knew exactly what he'd say. *"There's a reason for everything... Everything has a purpose under heaven."*

EARLY RETIREMENT

MURDER IN DAYTONA

47

Carlo was elated when he heard the news. It had only taken Santo Mantivo a few days to relocate Teracita. She'd been staying at the home of a young man in Kansas City. Santo went there to dispose of the young man and bring the girl in but he'd just missed them, apparently arriving within minutes of their departure. The good news was he was able to ascertain their destination... The couple was headed to Galveston, Texas.

Mantivo said Teracita was boarding a cruise ship sailing out of Galveston Harbor that Monday afternoon. He even sent him a brochure with her boarding information on it. Her passage was booked under an assumed name, Bonita Santiago... *Bonita*! Carlo got a big kick out of that!

He was to meet Mantivo at the airport in Galveston early Monday morning. His boss surely wouldn't deny him a short vacation. Not after he'd brought a quarter million dollars worth of new business to the practice. The firm's only concern was being investigated by the feds. Carlo's boss was cautious to a fault. He'd always been vigilant in his efforts to avoid having any criminal activity linked to his law practice. Money laundering would be the obvious concern. Jim Downs took painstaking steps to inhibit the activity.

It would be a culmination of Carlo's hard work. The Doris Van Fleet sentencing hearing was scheduled for Friday morning. He had every intention of being there. With the distinct possibility she'd be given the death penalty there was no way he was going to miss it. He would follow that joyous occasion up with the trip to Galveston to reclaim his prize possession.

Carlo arrived at the courthouse early enough to secure a spot in the spectator's gallery. News reports were warning commuters to take alternate routes if they planned to be in the vicinity of the courthouse because large crowds were expected. Numerous self interest groups had organized bus trips in an attempt to capitalize on the publicity. National news networks were carrying segments of the hearing hoping to garner high ratings.

Throngs of people showed up for the festivities. By 9:00 a.m. the crowd lined both sides of Orange Avenue. The Doris Van Fleet trial had again created a carnival atmosphere. Every kook and clown in town came out for the show.

Lesbian factions from across the country arrived in force to provide support for their sister, who'd become something of a national poster child to them. They were joined by an even larger contingent from the National Organization for Woman.

Hundreds from the Christian Right showed up to spread the word of eternal redemption. Their spokesman proclaimed, *"If only one soul gets saved the angels will celebrate in heaven."* The movements *God is love* message was perplexing in lieu of its *An eye for an eye and a tooth for a tooth* tenet.

Conversely, hundreds on the Christian Left were calling for leniency and forgiveness. They were lobbying for a governor's pardon, intending to accomplish their agenda through mass prayer and the miraculous intervention of the Lord himself. Intermixed with these extremists were Satanist, Paganist, Atheists, Baptists, and the Overtly Curious. There was even a small group handing out flyers promoting DirectTV!

413

At 9:30 a.m. Judge Halstrom Walker entered the courtroom. He instructed those present to be seated, slamming his gavel down in a show of ownership. *"There will be NO outburst from anyone in this room today,"* the judge warned. *"Any display of behavior that I deem as unacceptable will be met with a charge of contempt."*

The judge looked down at Uriah Wells and asked him if there was anything further he wished the court to consider in conjunction with him making a ruling. The soft spoken southern orator stood and took off his glasses, then approached the bench.

"Most everyone here was witness to what transpired a few days ago in this very courtroom," he told the judge. *"It is unfortunate that some couldn't be here today, unable to attend due to injuries they suffered in the melee."* The wily prosecutor stopped his expose' for a moment to take a sip of water from a bottle that was sitting on his table.

The water bottle ploy was a trick the prosecutor often used to control his animation. The prop forced him into downplay mode, and made him appear more at ease. Uriah Wells had found success in part by keeping a calm demeanor and appearing to be in control.

When he was ready to continue the prosecutor directed his attention to the defendant's table. He pointed out the accused was without her lead attorney this morning. *"The reason for that is quite simple,"* he reminded the court. *"Ms Hines was caught in the middle of that ugly brouhaha instigated by her client at the end of the trial last week."*

Uriah glanced over at the attorney filling in for Ruby and said, *"I understand Ms Hines was severely injured in the process. A badly fractured collarbone I'm told... Is that not so, Counselor?"*

Getting no response, the prosecutor turned back to the judge. *"Your Honor, the defendant's actions speak volumes. It is apparent*

Doris Van Fleet is a very violent woman. One who is quite capable of committing atrocious crimes against society. As such she should be removed from that society!" He paused for effect, counting to five in his head before continuing.

"A jury of her peers has found the defendant guilty, your Honor. Guilty of committing the most heinous crime of all. Murder in the 1st degree! Who was the object of her wrath? A precious woman who ran in fear for her life. A life that was eventually taken, albeit years later."

The prosecutor turned to face the assembly. He scanned the galley until he found me sitting in the second row. *"You deserve justice, Sir"* he proclaimed. *"Your wife was taken from you, Mr Stevens. Gruesomely, I might add. Barbarically murdered by this MONSTER!"*

Uriah then turned to the judge. *"Your Honor, the Stevens family deserves justice. The State believes justice can only be served in this case if the punishment fits the crime."* The prosecutor was playing his role to perfection. Who could disagree with him? He continued. *"As the attorney chosen to represent the people of this State I respectfully ask the court to sentence Doris Van Fleet to death for torturing and murdering Mrs Veronica Stevens. A far more compassionate ending than the one she afforded her victim, I may add."*

Judge Walker thanked the prosecutor for his comments, then turned to the attorney for the defense. He gave him the same opportunity to persuade. At first Ruby's replacement didn't seem to have the same zeal she had. He informed the judge he intended to file a petition with the Court of Appeals requesting a new trial.

Then the attorney turned his attention to the jury. The only thing holding his anger back was a paper thin veil of professional etiquette. *"THERE WAS ABSOLUTELY NO PROOF OF GUILT,"* he complained. *"Where was the evidence? You can't say...and I'll tell you why. Because it doesn't exist. I assure you... Doris Van Fleet did not murder Veronica Stevens."*

The attorney pulled a handkerchief from his jacket pocket and wiped his forehead before continuing. *"With all due respect, ladies and gentlemen. The people of the State of Florida couldn't possibly want anyone, much less a woman, to be executed for a crime in which no substantial proof was presented! Let's review, shall we? There were no witnesses, no fingerprints, no forensic evidence presented whatsoever. My client's verdict was based on a presumption of guilt! All because a key was found amongst her possessions. That's what linked her to the crime. A key. Is that damning evidence? I think not... It is circumstantial evidence at best!"*

This guy was good. Perhaps Doris should've had him represent her. No matter... The trial had concluded and the jury had found the defendant guilty... It was time to pay the piper. Judge Walker thanked the attorney for his criticism and his comments. He asked that his deepest sympathy be relayed to his colleague, along with wishes for a speedy recovery.

Then Judge Walker instructed the defendant to stand and face the court. He asked Doris if she had anything she wanted to say prior to being sentenced. She said she did.

Doris apologized for causing the disturbance the previous week. She explained she was in a state of shock, saying she'd never seriously thought the jury would find her guilty of a crime she didn't commit. She thanked her attorney for his representation today, and told the court she was very satisfied with the job Ruby Hines had done on her behalf. *"God loves you Ruby,"* she proclaimed... *"She loves all of us!"*

With that the courtroom erupted in laughter. Judge Walker slammed his gavel down on its wood block and loudly stated, ***"There will be order in this court... So help me!"*** Then he glared down at Doris and asked *"Anything else... Ms Van Fleet?"*

Doris replied, *"Yes, one more thing."* Then she turned and scoped out the gallery until she spotted me. The words she spoke left me speechless. They also left me wondering if we'd convicted the wrong person.

"Veronica loved you very much, Richard. She told me so herself. You see...we were good friends. I loved her, but I knew she was not in love with me. I accepted that long ago. I admit I'm a little rough around the edges. Hell, I'm a dyke. I fight authority, but I'm no murderer."

I began to see how Veronica might have fallen for her all those years ago. The way Doris came across was nothing like I'd expected. I couldn't help feeling sorry for her as she continued addressing me. *"God knows how that key got into my home, Mr Stevens...but I don't. I can tell you this. A piece of my heart died along with Veronica that day, and I know you understand what I mean. She got to the both of us. She became a part of us, and when she left she took a part of us with her. I'm truly sorry for your loss, Sir."* With that Doris turned back to face the judge.

Judge Walker was visibly moved by Doris' speech. After clearing a lump in his throat he continued with what he had to do. *"Doris Van Fleet, you have been tried by a jury of your peers. They have found you guilty of committing premeditated murder in the first degree. In the State of Florida that is a capital crime. As such it is punishable by death. It is not within the scope of my jurisdiction to ascertain the validity of such a sentence, but rather it is this court's responsibility to carry out the work of the State in the best interest of the people. As such I, Hiram Davis Walker, sentence you, Doris Van Fleet, to death by lethal injection."*

The judge quelled the stirring that was breaking out in his courtroom with one swipe of his gavel. Then he continued. *"You have a right to the appeals process, Ms Van Fleet. Your sentence shall not be carried out until you or your representatives have exhausted all avenues at your disposal to dispute the sentence."*

With that said, the judge thanked the jury and excused them. Once they'd filed out he allowed everyone else to leave. The prisoner was reprimanded to the county lock up, pending transfer to the maximum security facility located up in Starke, Florida. Doris didn't resist when her jailer put her in shackles. She didn't struggle as she was led out of the courtroom. It was as if she'd reconciled herself to the fact this was to be her fate.

Life hadn't treated Doris fairly. As a little girl she'd been continually molested by a stepfather she hated. As an adolescent she'd been left unprotected by a mother who refused to face reality. As a teenager she knew she was different then her peers, at an age when being different meant to be disdained and disaffiliated.

She was a person who was never given love, and therefore never learned how to love, yet desperately yearned to be loved. Now she was paying the ultimate price for a crime she didn't commit! Life had indeed been unfair!

After the hearing I milled around the halls outside the courtroom. I wasn't certain justice had been served. Doris had managed to reach me in a way that was genuine. Was it possible an innocent person had been sentenced to die for a crime she didn't commit? Jesus, I hoped not!

I decided to avoid the lights and cameras surely awaiting my arrival in the lobby by finding solace in an upstairs men's room. I sat in a stall and cried. I cried for Veronica, and I cried for myself.

EARLY RETIREMENT

MURDER IN DAYTONA

48

Sitting there in the men's room I realized I wasn't alone. I could sense it. Someone had invaded my privacy while I was busy trying to eradicate the pain that had resurfaced over the course of the trial. I used a wad of toilet paper to wipe the tears from my face and mustered up the courage to utter *"Hello?"* For some reason I framed the word as if it were a question.

A moment later I heard a toilet flush, followed by the shuffling of feet as my silent intruder stepped out of the neighboring stall and made his way to the sink. I decided to face my embarrassment head on. I came out of my hideaway and walked over to wash my hands. When I looked in the mirror I saw the reflection of the man who'd overheard my meltdown. He returned my gaze.

The guy looked to be in his thirties. His dark hair featured silver highlights along the sides, and he had a neatly trimmed mustache. He was a pretty big fellow, quite muscular. It was obvious he worked out. I had no doubt the ladies found him attractive.

He nodded at me in the mirror, then turned and extended his hand. *"Hey...I'm Carlo,"* he said. *"I saw you in court today. You're the husband... I'm sorry for your loss, Sir. I'm sure it was a very unpleasant thing to have to sit through."*

Having come to grips with my emotions I asked him why he'd gone to the hearing? What interest did he have in the case? Carlo responded, *"I'm in my final year of law school, Mr Stevens. The trial was an opportunity for me to see how the legal system works from the outside looking in. I attended every session. As a matter of fact I was sitting a couple rows behind you!"*

I asked him if he'd learned anything from the experience? Carlo thought for a moment, then answered, *"Yes... I did. I learned you win some you probably should have lost...and you lose some you probably should have won."*

We walked out into the hallway together. I headed for the elevator while my new friend took the stairs. I was glad I had the chance to talk with him. It felt good to talk to someone, and he seemed like a pretty decent guy. When I reached the first floor I was surprised to see him standing at the elevator waiting for me. Carlo had run down three flights of stairs hoping to catch me before I left the building. He was a little winded, but no worse for the wear.

He wanted to apologize. He hadn't meant to infer he thought the woman who killed my wife was innocent. The young law student told me what he meant was he didn't think the prosecutor had proven the defendant was guilty beyond a reasonable doubt. He questioned the lack of evidence, agreeing with the defense attorney on that count.

I was about to tell him I had some doubts of my own when I saw Dan Brooks walking across the lobby. He was chatting with his psychic friend Jordan Downs. I quickly excused myself and hurried to catch up with them. When I was close enough so they could hear me I said, *"Hey, slow down. I need to thank you guys."*

Jordan replied first. *"You want to thank us? That's incredible. Brooks here had you thrown in jail, Mr Stevens. I was convinced Doris Van Fleet didn't do it...and now you want to thank us?"*

Detective Brooks wrapped his massive arms around me and gave me a hug. I felt like a rag doll engulfed in the bigness of his body. He asked me how I was holding up, but I didn't get to answer because Jordan interrupted us. *"Listen,"* he piped in, *"I'm happy for you. We're both happy for you... They got the Bitch. That's all that matters!"*

It was then I remembered my men's room cellmate. I turned to draw him into the conversation but he was nowhere to be found. *"That's strange,"* I said to the detective, *"I wanted to introduce you to Carlo, but it looks like he disappeared."*

Jordan interrupted again. He pointed his disfigured index finger towards the revolving lobby door and said, *"Your buddy Carlo went thataway... I saw him leave while we were talking!"*

"So who is he," Brooks asked? *"A friend of yours?"* I told him Carlo wasn't a friend per se. Just a guy I'd met in the upstairs men's room...

I guess I left myself wide open for the lampooning that came next. Detective Brooks got a big grin on his face. *"You met him in the men's room,"* he asked incredulously? *"Richard, we have laws against that in this town!"*

It wasn't until then I realized what *'Meeting a guy in the men's room'* must have sounded like. I bent over laughing.

It felt good to laugh... I hadn't laughed in months. It felt so good it hurt. When I finally came up for air Jordan spoke up. *"We were just getting ready to go over to Ramone's for a celebration. Care to join us? You know Brooks here has been around a long time... He's decided today is the day... The detective has submitted his papers."*

I looked at Brooks for confirmation, and got it. The detective said, *"It's true. I've investigated my last case... I'm officially off the clock. It would be an honor to have you join us, Stevens. Ramone's is just around the corner. Hell, it's ladies night... Ladies drink free. Maybe one of us'll get lucky!"*

Jordan took me by surprise when he grabbed the detective's arm and whispered, *"Jesus, Dan... The guy just lost his wife."* I didn't think he had a sensitive bone in his misshapen body. Brooks must've thought his pal was right because he turned to me and apologized.

"Listen you two" I responded. *"My wife might be dead...but I ain't! I like a little pussy now and the, just like the next guy."* Jordan looked at me like I'd committed adultery with my wife's best friend until I piped in, *"Veronica would want me to."*

"I guess that's settled then," the detective said. *"Let's head on over. The bartender is holding a couple bar stools for us."* We hadn't quite made it to the exit when Jordan Downs stopped dead in his tracks.

"Uh Oh..." the impish psychic said. *"Boys... I gotta take a crap. You two go ahead. I'll meet you over there. Gimme ten minutes."* With that Jordan waddled off in search of a bathroom. I hollered after him, *"There's a men's room on the third floor, just past the elevator."*

Brooks and I headed out. We weren't quite halfway there when the detective hollered, *"Last one there buys the first round."* Then he takes off like a bat out of hell. Like a damn fool I run after him. By the time we reach the place we're both huffing and puffing like a couple of old blow fish.

Standing outside the bar's entrance Brooks jokes, *"Yeah... We're really gonna impress the ladies with these tired old bones... My Ass!"*

We go inside and belly up to the bar. When I finally get the bartender's attention I order us a round. With my drink in hand I hold my glass towards heaven and honor my dear departed wife. *"Here's to you... My Love."*

Jordan was still in the third floor men's room back at the courthouse... He'd found an envelope lying on the floor inside one of the stalls. Assuming it must have fallen out of someone's pocket he held it up to his forehead, as if trying to *'see'* its contents. Of course it didn't work. The famous psychic chastised himself... *"Some psychic you are,"* he joked as he opened the envelope conventionally.

Inside was a brochure for a cruise line, along with a handwritten note. The name of a ship was listed inside the brochure along with a room number and sailing date. It was due to depart the following Monday afternoon from the Port of Galveston.

A name was written inside the brochure too. A woman's name... Bonita Santiago. The accompanying note read, *"Carlo, if you want your Little Bonita...come and get her."* It was signed *S.M.*

"Son of a gun," Jordan said to himself. *"This must belong to the guy Richard was with. I'm sure he said his name was Carlo. I should get a healthy reward for this find."*

Meanwhile back at Ramone's the bar's proprietor was proclaiming it *Detective Dan Brooks Night.* To do so he rang an old fashioned school bell he kept on the back counter. The bartenders normally used it to acknowledge large tips.

Most everyone there knew the detective. They applauded loudly, and several came over to offer their congratulations in person. Drink chips started lining up in front of him. Everyone wanted to buy the burly, good natured detective a round.

One of those people ended up being the young law student I'd met in the courthouse men's room. He came over to say he hadn't noticed me come in, claiming his attention was diverted by a woman he was sitting with at the other end of the bar. She was much older than he, but according to him, the old hag still had *IT!*

I tried to ignore his comment. It didn't sound like something the young man I'd met in the courthouse men's room would say. I asked him if he was a regular customer there. Carlo responded, *"No...but it's Ladies Night!"* He pointed to the woman he was sitting with and quipped, *"Except she ain't no lady, At least not when I get through with her."*

I introduced him to Detective Brooks, saying he was the person who solved my wife's murder. Carlo said he knew who the detective was. He'd followed the story in the newspapers. *"I was kind of surprised they got a conviction,"* he blurted out. *"Weren't you, Detective? I mean the evidence the jury based their verdict on was all circumstantial!"*

"WHOA," Brooks complained. *"Hold on there. That's my case you're talking about, Son! There was plenty of evidence to convict. You don't need to see a smoking gun to know somebody was shot. Blood spurting out of the hole is a pretty good indication."* Carlo put his hands up in mock self defense and told the detective he didn't mean it the way it sounded.

He asked me where the little guy was. The one he'd seen me talking with back in the courthouse lobby. I answered, *"You mean Jordan? He'll be along shortly. He got held up."* I immediately got this humorous mental picture of Jordan sitting in the bathroom stall with his feet dangling off the floor. The thought nearly had me cracking up. All I could imagine was him trying to wipe himself with those stubby fingers. Cruel, I know.

"Jordan is a psychic," I blurted out. *"A famous one. He's been on television. He helps Detective Brooks sometimes. Jordan's even worked with the FBI when they've had cases they couldn't solve!"*

Carlo seemed unimpressed. He congratulated Brooks on his retirement, then nodded towards the woman he'd been hitting on at the bar. He said he needed to get back before someone else took advantage of the empty stool beside her.

When he left Brooks said, *"That guy gives me the creeps."* I told him I found him kind of creepy myself. Just then Jordan appeared out of nowhere. The impish psychic had a big grin on his face. He'd overheard our conversation as he approached and he asked Brooks who gives him the creeps? *"Never mind,"* the detective answered. *"What you got there?"*

Jordan was holding an envelope in his hand. I found the fact Detective Brooks noticed it right away amazing. Jordan could have held that envelope in his hand all night long and I never would have noticed. The detective's investigative instincts were a part of who he is. Retired or not, he'd always be a cop.

The ever prodigious psychic raised the envelope up over his head and playfully waved it in the air, loudly proclaiming, *"I found it lying on the floor in the little boy's room. I think Richard's friend might be interested in it."* Then he turned to me and said, *"Your friend's name is Carlo, is it not?"*

Carlo must have heard his name mentioned because he came right over to inquire what everyone was talking about. Surprised to see the owner of the envelope there, Jordan replied, *"We are talking about you, Amigo. We were wondering if you might be missing something?"*

The attorney looked down at him questioningly and said he didn't think so. Jordan, being Jordan, decided to toy with him. He held the envelope out and goaded, *"Are you planning a little trip, Carlo? Going on a cruise maybe?"*

Blood rushed from Carlo's face. He became pale as a ghost. Jordan must have realized the guy was really upset because he immediately stopped taunting him with the envelope. He offered an explanation instead. *"I found the envelope on the bathroom floor. It was in the stall over at the courthouse. I almost wiped my ass with it!"*

The psychotic lawyer snatched the envelope out of Jordan's hand, nearly knocking him over in the process. *"Hey... Easy, Dude"* Jordan exclaimed! *"I thought I was doing you a favor!"*

Once the envelope was back in his possession Carlo seemed to relax a bit. He apologized for his behavior, suggesting perhaps he'd had one to many vodka shots. He thanked Jordan for finding it. To show there were no hard feelings he held out his hand for Jordan to shake.

That was a mistake. The moment he grasped Carlo's hand Jordan felt a strong emanation. There was no warning, it happened instantaneously... In the time between the click of the second hand on a clock. The lawyer, realizing the psychic could *'read'* him, attempted to pull away. Jordan held on. He might have been small in stature, but his grip was strong.

Carlo used his free hand to grab the psychic's shirt collar. He shook him violently until finally Jordan released his grasp. Carlo took a step back and said, *"What the fuck is wrong with you, Mano? You loco or something?"*

426

"I know you," Jordan replied. *"We have met before."* Carlo told Jordan he was crazy. He'd never seen him before tonight. At that point Detective Brooks interceded.

"What's going on here, fellas? You two having a lover's spat?" Carlo told the detective the little imp wouldn't let go of his hand. He said the little creep was freaking him out. Brooks tried to assure him Jordan hadn't meant anything by it. *"Poor little bastard just wanted to be friends. Aint that right, Jordan?"*

Jordan wasn't laughing. He eyed Carlo suspiciously, then turned to his friend and said, *"I know this guy, Dan."* The detective, still trying to lighten up the situation, kiddingly asked Jordan if that's why he was trying to hold hands with him. *"You don't understand,"* Jordan implored. *"I know this guy! I know his essence."*

Carlo took the opportunity to end the conversation. *"Look, Bro. I'm an attorney. Lots of people know me."* Brooks asked him if he could see the contents of the envelope, just to satisfy his own curiosity. The lawyer pulled out the brochure and handed it to him. After the detective read it he handed it back. *"So...you're meeting a girl on a cruise? Good for you, you Lucky bastard. Ever been to the Caribbean?"*

Carlo smirked. *"I'm Cuban, Detective... What do you think?"* Brooks chuckled at the rude remark, then suggested perhaps it was time for him to leave... *"I intend to!"* Carlo replied as he stuffed the envelope in his rear pocket. He took two steps towards the door then turned and said, *"By the way, you did a nice job investigating that murder, Detective... Thank you!"*

Brooks stood there bewildered. *"What was that supposed to mean,* he asked aloud? *"Thank you... The prick said thank you?"* The detective uncharacteristically rushed after his nemesis, who by now had left the premises. When he got to the door he hollered, *"have a nice cruise, you jerk"* then slowly sauntered back to the bar. *"That little prick,"* he repeated. *"What did he mean... Thank you?"*

Jordan and I didn't say a word. We just glanced at each other. All I could think was, *"What just happened? What had we done?"*

Brooks was still mumbling to himself when Jordan said he was heading out. *"You boys stay here and celebrate. You both have good reason to. Forget that Cuban piece of shit, Dan. You're retired now man. Screw it."*

He waited for a response from the detective. When none was forthcoming Jordan turned to me and said, *"Stevens... your wife's killer is sitting on death row. Pay back is a Bitch!"* Then he left.

EARLY RETIREMENT

MURDER IN DAYTONA

49

Jordan knew what Detective Brooks and I may have only suspected. Doris Van Fleet was innocent. After the famous psychic left Ramone's he got in his car and headed across the Orange Avenue Bridge. When he got to A1A he turned left and drove up the coast a couple miles, searching for the lime colored facade of the Pelican Inn. When he spotted it he pulled in.

Two vehicles sat in the dimly lit lot facing the building. Both had out of state plates. Jordan noticed several letters of the neon sign were still out, and the dumpster still overflowed with garbage. He parked his Mercedes underneath a pole light then made his way to the office. A small sign in the window instructed *RING FOR SERVICE.* Jordan rang the buzzer.

After a moment the office light came on and a drably dressed man appeared at the door. The unkempt employee didn't seem to enthusiastic about having a potential guest. It was keeping him away from his TV show, which could be heard playing in the distance. He waved Jordan in, then walked around to the back of the counter.

Jordan said he'd like a room. He only needed it for one night. *"Thirty-two bucks,"* the clerk burped as he reached for the registry log. Jordan pulled the cash out of his wallet then inquired about room twenty-eight. Was it available? The clerk recoiled. *"You want to stay in twenty-eight,"* he asked suspiciously? Jordan explained it was his lucky number.

The disheveled laggard pulled a key off a board hanging on the wall and handed it to his odd looking guest, then asked him to sign the register. As Jordan was heading out the door he heard the clerk mutter, *"Pleasant dreams, Pal."*

He climbed the steel deck stairs leading to the second level. When Jordan got to the door he stood staring at it, recalling the last time he'd been there. After some hesitation he slid the key in the lock and turned the door handle. The minute he did something strange happened.

Jordan felt a presence. It was ambivalent and alien, like the feeling you get at one of those Halloween Fright Night houses as you make your way down a dark hallway knowing when you least expect it some monster is going to jump out at you. Undeterred, he stepped inside.

The room came alive. Never before had Jordan felt his gift so abundantly. Even when assisting the FBI on a case that got national publicity had he felt this empowered. The effervescence bubbled in his veins. Jordan felt like he'd crossed a threshold into an alternate reality.

To the psychic everything in the room seemed to be in present time, while his own presence felt ghostly. As if he were having an out of body experience. Veronica Stevens was lying on the bed. She was naked, and her wrists were bound to the bedpost. The pain she was in showed on her face. It was contorted and full of fear.

Someone was taking a shower. Jordan slowly made his way over to the bathroom door and peeked in. He saw a man through the steamy mist. The guy was big and well muscled, and wore his hair in a pony tail. Leaning against the wall was an aluminum baseball bat. Jordan noted its taped handle. Laying beside it was a thick leather strap. A long handled bristle brush sat on the counter.

The renowned psychic stood there, mesmerized by the clarity of his vision. Suddenly the man turned the shower off and stepped out into the mist to dry off. Jordan quickly ducked back into the bedroom and looked for a place to hide, but he didn't get the chance. The guy came walking out of the bathroom naked as the wind.

Jordan recognized him immediately, though he looked different. It was Carlo, the guy he'd met at Ramone's... The guy whose envelope he'd found in the men's room back at the courthouse. The guy who'd offered his hand in gratitude. He was carrying the leather strap in one hand, and the bristle brush in the other.

It seemed Carlo was unaware of Jordan's presence in the room. The psychic watched helplessly as the naked man made his way over to the bed. He sweet talked Veronica, who shivered at the sound of his voice. The sweetness was short-lived. His banter became increasingly vulgar and more threatening. When Carlo lifted the leather strap Jordan cringed. The beating started.

The illusion seemed brutally real. The first swing of the strap bit into Veronica's buttocks, leaving a thick purple welt. Jordan realized she couldn't scream. Her mouth had been gagged. He could however, see the horrified look in her eyes. She drifted in and out of consciousness as her tormentor calculatingly instilled his wrath.

Unable to contain himself Jordan screamed at Carlo to stop. He threatened to expose him if the beatings continued. The psychic may as well have been screaming at a brick wall for all the good it did. Fact was, the three people in that room were locked in a surrogate point in time. Their dimensions couldn't be spliced, no matter how much screaming Jordan did or how hard he tried to intervene. He was there as a silent witness.

And witness he did! Jordan saw Carlo murder Veronica Stevens. The brutality of the attack was hard to fathom. The manner in which she died was heart wrenching. Bad enough she was beaten to a blistering pulp, but then to have her head smashed open and her brains spilled out. It was nothing short of overkill.

Jordan stood helpless as Carlo inserted a wine bottle bottom first up his victim's vagina. The neck of the bottle protruded from the opening like a colorful glass penis. To make matters worse the demonic attorney placed a straw in the bottle and shockingly took several draws. Some of the wine dribbled off his chin onto the sheets below. Then he stood back and admired his handiwork.

Stunned by what he'd just witnessed, Jordan walked over and looked the homicidal maniac straight in the eye. What he saw reminded him of a shark as it tears into the carcass of its next meal. Carlo's eyes were black and lifeless. Jordan watched them roll back in orgasmic ecstasy as the life of his victim flickered and went out.

The miscreant set about, methodically cleaning every square inch of the room. Then he gathered his weapons of destruction and prepared to leave. He stopped to prop his victim up on the bed for the benefit of her eventual discoverer, who he was hoping would be her husband. That was the plan.

At the very moment Carlo closed the door the motel room transmogrified back into a lifeless shell. The stench of death dissipated and the room took on the appearance of what one might expect to find in a thirty-two dollar a night motel. The entire event had been an apparition. A picture within a picture. Jordan felt like he'd just watched a movie, except from the inside out. Even though he knew the plot he was helpless to alter it, or change the outcome.

The disfigured psychic stepped out onto the dark veranda. He took in a big gulp of salt infested air and tried to gather himself together. The experience had been harrowing. Once his breathing returned to normal Jordan made his way back to his car.

He'd been right all along. The killer was a man. No sense rubbing it in now though. Nothing was going to bring Veronica Stevens back from the dead, and no court in the land would overturn Doris Van Fleet's conviction. Not based on the testimony of a psychic who witnessed the murder seven months after it occurred.

Driving back to his home in Boca Raton, Jordan went over the events of the evening in his head. He wondered why Carlo would be going on a cruise. He worried for the woman he was supposedly taking the cruise with. The guy had freaked out when Jordan held the envelope containing the cruise brochure up in the air back at Ramone's. Something about that cruise was suspicious. This was no ordinary vacation. This was a mission. He picked up his phone and dialed his travel agent.

Jordan discovered there were still a few staterooms available for the Monday sailing. He was warned the ship was carrying hundreds of college students on spring break. No matter, he wasn't taking a pleasure cruise. He was convinced Carlo had a dastardly deed up his sleeve. Somehow it was tied in with the murder of Veronica Stevens. He would get to the bottom of it, no matter the cost.

Though it wasn't his motivation Jordan realized he might even get a shot at a prime time television show out of this. After seeing Carlo do his thing in that motel room he was convinced he'd done it before. If the murderous monomaniac wasn't careful he might just find himself taking a long walk off a short pier. Jordan, being as irreverent as he was, jokingly nicknamed his effort *The Feed the Fishes Campaign.*

He called me the next day to inform me he'd reserved two seats on a redeye flight from Orlando to Galveston. One for him, and one for me. We were flying out Sunday morning. That news was followed by a plea to trust him. When I questioned Jordan's sanity he told me he had undeniable, unequivocal proof Doris Van Fleet did not kill my wife. He said it was up to us to make sure an innocent woman wasn't unjustly executed! I asked him why he hadn't gone to Detective Brooks with this information, but he blew me off.

We were staying at the lush San Luis Resort on Galveston Bay. The hotel sent a limousine to pick us up at the airport. Jordan spent the duration of our flight convincing me he knew what he was doing. He told me about his visit to the Pelican Inn, and what he'd 'seen' transpire inside the room. He was so damn sure of himself I had no choice but to go along.

I too had sensed something was amiss during the trial. Yes, Doris Van Fleet had been convicted, but by what evidence? Nothing substantial had been presented, other than her refusal to come up with an alibi for her whereabouts, and the fact a key to the room where the murder took place was found in her home. It was damning evidence, but it was circumstantial. Who's to say how it got there? Perhaps I had a bit of a sixth sense myself...

What shocked me was Jordan's assertion that the true assailant was none other than Carlo, the law student I'd met in the men's room at the courthouse. Of course I later learned he wasn't a law student at all, but a practicing attorney. Why he'd felt the need to lie about it I did not understand?

We remained in our hotel suite until Monday afternoon. That's when Jordan called a cab to take us to the cruise port. We didn't take the limo because Jordan feared it would draw unnecessary attention. It wasn't unusual for the quasi-famous psychic to be recognized in a crowd. As he explained, *"Some folks do watch those low budget late night cable shows you know."*

The goal of our trip was to determine if Carlo was on the ship. If he was it was important we locate the object of his attention. She could be in real danger. Professional accolades could come later.

Shortly after boarding we heard an explosion in the distance. Jordan immediately estimated the size of the explosive device in reference to its proximity to the ship. We stepped out onto the balcony of our stateroom just as a long column of smoke rose in the sky and drifted towards us. It appeared to be coming from the vicinity of the airport. Could it be the work of our nemesis? Who knew?

The ship departed precisely at 4:00 PM, moving ever so slowly from its berth. Upon reaching international waters the captain hosted a bon voyage party in the Rum Runner lounge. The room was large enough to accommodate several hundreds of people. Even though he felt out of place in the mostly college age crowd, Jordan attended. I remained in the stateroom, as instructed.

Most in attendance seemed delighted to be there. Tuxedo wearing servers roamed the floor offering complimentary champagne to their sandal wearing guests. White gloved waiters held trays of cheese and finger sandwiches as the throng of young party goers got into the spirit of the occasion. The captain shook hands with well wishers and enjoyed a glass of champagne before discreetly disappearing from the scene. It obviously wasn't his kind of crowd either.

Jordan couldn't help but notice an attractive young Latino woman standing alone against a back wall. Unlike everyone else her age, she was dressed to the nines. The girl seemed somewhat distraught. He likened her to a frightened kitten stuck in a tree.

He watched her for some time. She didn't talk to anyone, other than to thank a server who handed her a glass of champagne. The young lady seemed apprehensive. Jordan noticed how she kept her eyes focused on the lounge door, as if expecting someone. After a while he made his way over to say hello.

She didn't respond. The moment Jordan interrupted her the young woman looked down at the floor, then turned away. Unfettered by her initial rejection he tried again. *"Hello... I'm Jordan,"* he said, *"Jordan Downs...and you are?"*

The girl towered over him when he stood next to her. It was kind of comical. Her high heels made her appear even taller than she was. That didn't stop Jordan one bit. He carried on with his conversation as if he was at one of his impromptu book signings. *"It's Doctor Downs, actually,"* the well known psychic bragged. *"I'm a professor at Duke University. I assume you're on Spring Break?"*

Finally, she spoke. *"I'm Bonita,"* she replied. *"Bonita Santiago. I'm waiting for my fiancee. He should be here any minute now."* Jordan was stunned! He could barely speak. That was the name on Carlo's cruise brochure, standing before him in the flesh.

Never one who was able to hide his feelings, Jordan was sure she could read him like a book cover. He was right. She did! Teracita could tell whatever it was she'd said had shaken the little guy up...but what had she said? The fictitious name she was traveling under. That was all!

EARLY RETIREMENT

MURDER IN DAYTONA

50

Santo Mantivo used cartel connections to camouflage Carlo's embarkation. Fear could still open doors. Port security looked the other way when the lawyer boarded the ship along with forty-two other multinational service workers. Why not. They all had the same agenda. Someone had to clean up the mess.

Teracita Goncalves, using the pseudonym *'Bonita Santiago'* would be traveling alone. Unbeknownst to her, her companion had chickened out at the last minute. It was a stroke of luck that the greeting card marketing rep had woke up realizing this wasn't his battle. That decision made Santo Mantivo's life a lot simpler.

The assassin thought he might find Aaron's car in the airport parking lot. When he did he hardwired a bomb to the ignition, just in case something went wrong and the foolish Irishman made a run for it. When Aaron told Teracita *"adios and vaya con dios,"* the poor bastard sealed his own fate.

Had he not chickened out Mantivo would have had no choice but to go on the cruise too. It wouldn't have been prudent to let the lad stay on board and cause more grief. The cartel had alliances in the bowels of the ship that would've taken care of the body. Now that it was just Teracita, Mantivo figured Carlo could take over. After all, he'd been hired to find her...and he had. What the Cuban lawyer did with her from that point on was his business!

Carlo had her room number, he had her itinerary, and he had her attention. Teracita was scared shitless and he knew it. He also knew fear could be used to his advantage. Fear caused people to make mistakes. In this world the strong capitalize on the mistakes of the weak. It was a time honored tradition.

He considered attending the bon voyage party. With Teracita's supposed rescuer out of the picture she would be all alone. In the end he decided not to, realizing his appearance might cause a scene. Better to wait! When she discovered her lover boy had bailed her reaction would be more satisfying anyway. There was time... She had nowhere to run!

The bon voyage party ended at six o'clock. Schedules were tight on a cruise ship. Guests in early seating went directly to the dining room. Those in late seating headed down to the Stargazer Theatre.

Tonight's show was a musical conglomeration of love songs recorded by The Beatles. Put on by cast members employed with the cruise line, the show was an abbreviated version of the Cirque du Soleil production *LOVE,* developed for the Las Vegas stage.

Teracita decided to forgo the dining room, opting to grab a quick bite at Octopus's Garden Buffet. The restaurant was open twenty-four hours a day to cater to hungry guests. When she got there she was surprised to see many other passengers had made the same choice. Evidently spring breakers preferred pizza and burgers over torpedoes of tenderloin and escargot.

When she finished eating Teracita retired to her room. She was worried. Where was Aaron? She'd waited for him at the party like they'd planned, but to no avail. The thought crossed her mind he'd had a change of heart. They hadn't made love since Aaron had his erectile dysfunction issue. Had he decided he was in love with

Rebecca after all? Had he run back to Kansas City to try to win her back? She curled up on the bed and fell asleep.

Teracita dreamed. In her dream Aaron was standing on the pier blowing kisses up to her. Suddenly the ship started moving. The ocean liner floated from its moorings and turned towards the open sea. She considered jumping overboard and swimming back to him, but she knew if she attempted to she'd most certainly be killed. As the ship slowly made its way out of port Aaron became smaller and smaller, until finally he vanished from sight.

It was early morning when she awoke. Teracita lay in bed looking up at the ceiling. Her life was so confusing these days. She'd had a simple life up to the time she came to America. Maybe it was men, she thought? They were always leering, checking her out, making lewd comments. Men could be so deceitful. Even Carlo Santiago had seemed to be a perfect gentleman when she first met him.

In the quiet hours of dawn Teracita thought she sensed a slight rumbling, though in her somewhat indolent state it was almost undetectable. Whatever it was, there was a definite rhythm to it. The rumbling seemed to be coming from directly below her. A scary thought passed through her mind. What if it was demons from hell, clawing their way up intent on bringing her back with them?

"I should have made Aaron go to the police and report what he saw in the sleeper window of that tractor trailer," she told herself. *"Now God has forsaken my soul and Satan has sent his minions to claim it!"*

She glanced over at a half filled water glass sitting on the night stand and noticed ripples on the surface. Her room, being one of the least expensive bookings, was one deck above crew quarters and towards the rear of the ship. Teracita realized the rumbling was the ship's diesel engines turning the turbines that propelled the vessel forward. With that in mind she relaxed. Today would be a full day at sea.

After taking breakfast in her room she made her way to the pool deck. Relaxing in a lounger, Teracita closed her eyes and thought about the previous night's dream. Was it possible the explosion she'd heard while waiting for the ship to depart was Aaron's car going up in flames? If that was the case, was she supposed to be in the car with him when it exploded?

It was more likely he'd run back to Kansas City with his tail between his legs. Last she knew that tail didn't wag anymore anyway! She prayed it was the later, because if it wasn't she was in more danger than she'd realized.

The weather report was calling for partly sunny skies, with increasing clouds in the afternoon. Heavy thunderstorms were forecast this evening. A scheduled *'Dance Under the Stars'* was moved from the pool deck to the ballroom just to be cautious.

The event was scheduled to begin at 10:00 p.m. A twelve piece swing band would be playing golden oldies until two o'clock in the morning. Guests were encouraged to dress up in traditional 1950's garb. Poodle skirts, bobbie sox, rolled cuff blue jeans, and saddle shoes.

Teracita felt somewhat safe lying on the pool deck surrounded by hundreds of spring breakers. A cabana boy brought her a Naked Jamaican, the featured drink of the day. He tried to find out if she was cruising solo. Many women were this trip. At least that's what he told her, with a twinkle in his eye. The young attendant spent much of the day in the vicinity of Teracita's lounge chair. She figured he was harmless. Anyway, it might be good to have someone watching out for her. Just in case!

Kiosks at either end of the deck were serving burgers and hot-dogs, along with pizza and salads. Around noon Teracita got up to grab a bite to eat. At one o'clock a steel drum band arrived to entertain guests for the afternoon.

The staff played pool games with half intoxicated sophomores who couldn't drink back home because the legal age was twenty-one. Here on the high seas it was eighteen. One entertaining young man decided it would be fun to untie the bikini tops of the coeds trying to play volleyball in the pool. A couple of the girls snuck up on him when he wasn't looking and de-suited him. He ended up scurrying around the pool deck with his willy swinging in the air.

Teracita covered her face when the naked fellow ran past her. Finally one of the staff handed him a towel and ordered him to cover up. Some people think cruising is for old folks... Not this cruise! These kids were hell bent on partying till somebody came along and dragged them off the ship and sent them back to their ivy covered dormitories.

On the opposite side of the pool and one deck up, Carlo Santiago watched the entire spectacle from beneath a pair of dark sun glasses. His new look, the short stylish hair cut and neatly trimmed mustache, really changed his appearance. Teracita might not have recognized him if they passed each other in the hall.

Carlo was staying in a fellow crew member's berth, having commandeered the space by dropping the names Vicente Fuentes and Jose Gacha. He knew the mere mention of their names would stir fear in the hearts of the ship's mostly Latino employees. The head of the most powerful drug cartel in Mexico and the leader of *Los Norte Del Valle* were familiar to all. Their names could open most any door.

The corrupt attorney was able to do whatever he wanted on board. Workers jumped at the chance to be of service to him. If they were lucky maybe he would mention their cooperation to Vicente Fuentes or the El Padrino.

With nearly fourteen hundred guests on board it would be easy to overlook someone on the crowded deck. Jordan and I claimed a couple chairs along the rail overlooking the pool. Unbeknownst to us Carlo Santiago was less than a hundred feet away, hidden beneath a pair of shades and lounging in a pool chair. Had he chosen a spot on the opposite side of the ship chances are he would have recognized us. As it was we never saw him and he never saw us. We did however, see *Bonita.* We watched...and we waited!

By mid afternoon Jordan was ready to pack it in. The heat and humidity had gotten to him. He told me we would pick up the surveillance after dinner. I decided to wait it out. With clouds on the horizon and the wind picking up I figured it would cool off some. Besides, I was digging the calypso beat of the steel drum band.

As dinner time approached Teracita gathered her things and returned to her cabin. She'd decided to enjoy a real meal tonight. Truth is she'd be much safer in a crowded dining room than she was sitting all alone in her stateroom. I followed from a distance, hoping she might encounter Carlo along the way, if he were in fact on board. She didn't.

It was semiformal night. Teracita fingered her way through her wardrobe and picked out a casually elegant cocktail dress for the evening. She lay it down on the bed then went to take a shower. No sooner did she pull the curtain closed then the shower scene from Alfred Hitchcock's 'Psycho' popped into her head. The poor girl envisioned there was someone on the other side of the shower curtain waiting to slit her throat. Needless to say, she finished showering with her eyes wide open. It was a short shower!

When Teracita met her table mates she introduced herself as *Bonita Santiago*. They included a young couple from Houston who'd just gotten engaged, two guys from Chicago who everyone assumed were gay, and two female college students on spring break from a private university back East. For the most part they all seemed very nice.

She felt a tad embarrassed about sailing alone. As if she couldn't find someone to go with... Anyone who saw her would know that was impossible! After dinner the two college students invited Teracita to join them for the show in the theatre. An illusionist was headlining the entertainment. The guy was being billed as a famous Las Vegas act, but none of the girls had ever heard of him before.

I'd been watching Teracita since she entered the dining room. Jordan was still reeling from his overexposure to the sun and so remained in the cabin. When she and the other young ladies got up to leave I followed them. I stood in the rear of the auditorium and kept them under surveillance as the illusionist did his thing. Half way through his show the girls left. They went to the casino together.

They met a trio of off duty crew officers who happened to be gambling at the roulette wheel. The girls had stopped to watch the action and the guys starting flirting with them. I sat down at a slot machine and observed from a distance.

One of them got the girls to agree to hold a party in their room. That's when I decided to head back to report my observations to Jordan. I didn't see Carlo anywhere. I strongly suspected he wasn't even on the ship. This was turning into a wasted trip!

Crew officers are allowed to keep alcohol in their quarters. Several bottles made their way to the girl's cabin. After downing a few shots of *Jose Cuervo* Teracita found herself engaged in some heavy petting with one of the guys. Fortunately she didn't let things get out of control.

She knew it was time to go. This party wasn't a good idea from the start. She'd resisted her male suitor, who wanted her to go further than she had. When one of her new friends mentioned moving the party to the big dance being held in the ballroom upstairs Teracita took the opportunity to say she wasn't feeling well. Her admirer offered to escort her to her room but Teracita convinced him to go with the others.

On the way back to her room Teracita started feeling nauseous. She headed for the Promenade Deck to get some fresh air, but when she got there she found it was pouring outside. The weather man had been right for a change. She turned and made her way to the elevator.

Had Teracita opted to brave the rain and go out on the deck she might have bumped into Jordan and I. We'd gone there shortly after I got back to the stateroom that evening, in response to one of Jordan's clairvoyant visions.

While recovering from heat exhaustion Jordan had fallen asleep. He had a dream there was a woman being chased through the ship by a man hellbent on harming her. The tyrant caught up with the woman outside on the Promenade Deck. When I got to the stateroom Jordan told me about his vision. He said he sensed he'd watched his own demise.

The famous psychic was not only convinced that Carlo was on the ship, he was convinced whatever was going to happen, was going to happen tonight!

A knock on our stateroom door interrupted our conversation. A messenger from guest relations had been sent to inform Jordan his inquiry concerning a guest named Carlo Santiago had come

444

back negative. No one by that name was on board. In fact no one with that name had booked a cruise. Jordan thanked the messenger and closed the door. As soon as the fellow was out of hearing range he bellowed, *"BULLSHIT... He's here... I'm certain of it!"*

Jordan's plan was to camp out on the Promenade Deck. All night long if he had to! Someone had to stop this madman. He couldn't report it to ship security. There was no record of anyone named Carlo Santiago being on board. He couldn't even tell them about his concern for *Bonita,* Carlo's supposed target. He didn't know anything about her, other than her name. They'd think he was a madman!

Neither one of us had any way of knowing it at the time, but while Jordan was sleeping and I was busy keeping an eye on *Bonita* and her friends, Carlo was in Teracita's cabin choosing something for her to wear. The insane lawyer had used his cartel backed influence to acquire a key to her room. He rummaged through her lingerie drawer until he found just the right item.

It was nearly midnight when Teracita stepped off the elevator and made her way to her cabin. Carlo heard someone mumbling in the hallway just outside the door. The voice was female. Whoever it was sounded whimsical... Almost childlike. She was giggling and acting silly. Suddenly the door swung open.

Carlo ducked down along the side of the bed as the intruder walked in. She kicked off her shoes then went into the bathroom. He could hear her in there, mumbling and giggling as she peed.

When he heard the toilet flush Carlo got up and positioned himself between the cabin door and the bathroom door, effectively blocking the exit. The woman came out of the bathroom draped in a towel and started towards the bed. Carlo was surprised to see it was Teracita. He hadn't recognized her voice, and never seen her intoxicated. After a moment he spoke. *"Hello, my little chingona."*

Teracita, half drunk on tequila, turned to face him. This was a moment predestined to happen. She knew it, and Carlo knew it. Would he beat her? Would he kill her? Would he make love to her? Perhaps he'd do all three!

"You've been a very naughty girl," her relentless pursuer complained. *"You have caused me a lot of grief. What's the matter, Teracita? Don't you love me anymore?"*

Teracita couldn't talk... She couldn't move! Carlo tossed some sultry lingerie on the bed and said, *"Put this on. We're going to be making up for lost time tonight, Sweetie."*

The murderous madman unzipped his fly and fished around for his manhood. *"Remember this,"* he asked as he pulled out his cock? It was enormous. He wasn't even hard and it hung there like a stuffed sausage in a butcher shop. Eight inches long, and thick as a water bottle. Carlo scared some women off when they saw him for the first time. Fantasy was one thing, but this guy could do some damage.

Teracita's heart was racing. Fearing for her life, she put on the lingerie Carlo had tossed on the bed. She recognized the baby doll. It was one she'd purchased while shopping with Rebecca. Her dark skin glowed next to the fluorescent pink material. Her breasts overflowed the small cups. She looked... Delicious!

The evil attorney leaned forward and ran his fingers through Teracita's hair. Then he looked her in the eye and said, *"Treat me right and the world can be yours. Reject me and I'll cut your head off and send it to your mother in the mail!"* He gave his words time to sink in, then added, *"And If you ever run from me again, Lil One, I'll have every one of your brothers and sisters gang raped then taken to the desert and buried alive... Do we understand each other?"*

Teracita shivered. This monster made her feel subhuman. He made her feel filthy. She had no doubt he'd do exactly as promised. She hated him!

The frightened young Au Pair reached for Carlo's cock. She held it in her hand and massaged the head as it throbbed in her palm. Then Teracita stood and slowly circled around him, softly caressing his testicles as she moved. When her tormentor was fully between her and the bed she playfully put a hand on his chest and pushed him backwards. Carlo closed his eyes as he lay back on the pillow, prepared to get the best blow job of his life.

Teracita considered running. Nothing stood between her and the cabin door. It may have been her only chance to survive. Instead she took the full length of Carlo's manhood in her mouth and held it there, just as he'd taught her. The mad attorney's eyes rolled back in their sockets as his member throbbed deep in Teracita's throat.

Before he knew what was happening his reclaimed possession clamped her jaw down as hard as she could. Teracita's teeth sunk deep into Carlo's flesh as thick hot fluid filled her mouth. She jerked her head violently back and forth like a Great White attacking its prey. Blood gushed all over Teracita's newly purchased pink fluorescent baby doll. For a moment she thought she may have bitten his cock completely off.

Carlo looked down at his nearly dismembered manhood and squealed like a pig. He violently swung at Teracita's head, while using his other hand to grab his severely damaged crotch. Every time his heart beat more blood spurted out.

Teracita fought the urge to finish what she'd started. Instead she turned and ran. Carlo attempted to chase after her but he slipped in a puddle of blood that had pooled at the foot of the bed. When he fell his face slammed into the hard ceramic tile surface splattering his nose on impact. Ripples of pain shot through his body.

Before he was able to pick himself up and continue the chase Teracita was on the stairway leading to the upper decks of the ship. She tried to scream, but nothing came out. Fear had closed the passageways of her trachea. The sound just lodged deep in her throat.

Most passengers were attending the big dance being held in the Grand Ballroom on the opposite end of the ship, oblivious to the battle being fought seven decks below.

Before Teracita knew it Carlo was on her tail. The enraged masochist held his nearly severed penis in his hand as he took the stairs three at a time. Blood was flowing from his badly broken nose, smearing his white dress shirt.

As she reached the upper levels of the ship Teracita saw a sign pointing to the Promenade Deck. Gasping for breath, she ran towards the door. The moment it slid open she was met by a fierce wind and a blinding rain.

She knew her nemesis was gaining on her. Teracita could hear him wheezing as he gulped for air behind her. She thought she noticed someone standing in the shadows as she ran by and tried to shout for help, but it came out a hoarsely whisper.

The Promenade Deck didn't circle around the entire ship. It ended on either side. Eventually Teracita had no place left to run. She stopped and faced her assailant, whose face was contorted in a frightening mixture of anger and agony.

Skin and vein hung precariously from Carlo's nearly severed penis. It looked as if his manhood had been caught in a butcher's meat grinder, giving new meaning to the term decapitated. The

448

attorney's shattered nose sat cockeyed on his once handsome face, a reminder you should never corner a frightened animal. The blood that had drenched his white dress shirt was washed away by the driving rain. It ran down the grooves between the teak deck boards beneath his feet.

After a moment of remorse Carlo wrapped his hand around his one time girlfriend's throat and lifted her clear off the deck. As she dangled in the air he came around with a vicious right handed punch that sent her sprawling backwards. There was little doubt of his intentions. This was not going to end in a loving embrace or an appeal for forgiveness.

Jordan and I had been outside waiting for well over an hour, sheltered from the wind and rain by an overhang that jutted out from the side of the ship where it met the bow. We'd hid there in anticipation of the manifestation Dr Downs had seen in his dream earlier that evening. We were actually close to giving up when we saw the glass door slide open and *Bonita* came running by us in a frenzy. Jordan was about to rush out and join the fray when I grabbed him and pulled him back.

The little imp wouldn't stand a chance against the heavily muscled and much younger attorney. I yelled, *"NO WAY... HE'S MINE"* and charged into the darkness. It was difficult to recognize facial features in the swirling downpour, but I knew this was the same son of a bitch I'd met in the men's room back at the courthouse in Daytona...and I knew he recognized me too!

Carlo shouted something, but it was indecipherable in the harsh elements. The wind died down just long enough for me to make out a portion of what he said. *"Your wife begged me, Stevens!"*

I went into a rage. I swung my fists in a blind fury, intent on bludgeoning this monstrous demagogue to a bloody pulp. Unfortunately I was no match for him. This God of a man was strong and powerful, despite his recent run in with a human chain saw. When he wrapped his arms around my torso and lifted me up over his head my life flashed before me. I was looking straight down into the depths of the churning black ocean some ten stories below.

Jordan, still hidden beneath the overhang, had watched in horror as my nemesis manhandled me like I was SpongeBob SquarePants on one of his guileless adventures. He covered his eyes when I was lifted up and dangled over the side of the ship. As if to do so would somehow alter the reality of my predicament.

When Carlo released his grip my heart came up in my throat. Through the howling of the wind and the hard driving rain I heard a faint scream. I assumed it was my own. When my body hit the hard surface I immediately lost consciousness.

I awoke sometime later to the tender touch of an angel. The wind had died down some, and the rain had stopped. I was curled up in a fetal position. *Bonita* was holding me in her bosom and gently caressing my head. *"You're okay, Senor Stevens"* she said when she realized I'd come to.

After confirming I was actually still alive I asked her what happened... Where was Carlo? My angel hesitated for a moment, then answered... *"Carlo's gone,"* she said. *"He was going to kill you... I panicked, Senor. It was an accident... Honest it was!"*

What could I say? Who could explain such a turn of events? We sat there awhile, quietly listening to the wind speak its mind. Eventually Jordan broke the silence. *"Don't blame yourself, Dear Lady. You did what you had to do. We have you to thank, Bonita."*

She corrected him. *"No, el Doctor. My name is Teracita... Teracita Goncalves. I was traveling under the name Bonita, but that is not who I am."* She pointed to the spot where Carlo had been holding me over the railing and said, *"He gave me that name!"*

I discovered what transpired while I was struggling with Carlo. Evidently Teracita reacted to my impending doom by ramming into him. Though she's not a big girl, Teracita is strong. Strong enough, anyway. Carlo was sent toppling over the railing. Fortunately for me when she hit him he turned his body in a way that I somehow landed on the deck.

I got to my feet then held my hand out for Teracita. Jordan, feeling chivalrous, took his shirt off and wrapped it around her naked shoulders. *"Let's go inside,"* I suggested. We went back to our stateroom to sort things out before reporting what happened to the captain.

Jordan went into the bathroom and returned with dry towels, then took a seat by the balcony window. I sat on the edge of the bed and toweled off. Teracita sat next to me. She spoke first, telling us Carlo was a really bad person. That he was a sadist, and that he hated women.

"He hurt a lot of people, Doctor Downs," she said to Jordan. *"Carlo was an evil man. He used people, then discarded them like they were trash. I know he's killed before!"* Then Teracita turned to me. *"Carlo murdered your wife, Senor Stevens... She tried to help me. Veronica was my friend."*

I cried... I sat on the edge of the bed and wept like a baby. Jordan came over and put his hand on my shoulder. He attempted to console me, saying, *"Carlo would have killed you tonight if he could have, Richard. You and Teracita are both survivors. I think your wife is doing a little dance up in heaven right about now. You should be proud... Both of you... You never gave up!"*

Teracita leaned over and kissed my cheek, then put her head on my shoulder. The three of us sat there in total silence. My mind was racing. I reviewed every detail I could remember about the murder investigation. After a while I said, *"Veronica told me about you, Teracita. She said you'd been brought to the shelter by a priest, and that you'd been badly beaten by someone. I remember she told me you'd gone there frightened to death he'd find you."*

Several minutes passed. I'd gotten no response to my previous statement. Unable to put it to rest, I asked Teracita if she knew the woman who'd been charged with killing my wife. *"Do you know Doris Van Fleet"* I inquired? *"Does she have a role in any of this?"*

Again I got no response. I turned to see if Teracita had heard me. I discovered the poor girl had drifted off to sleep right there on my shoulder. I gently laid her head back on the pillow, then turned to Jordan to ask what he thought we should do about everything that had transpired. He held a finger to his lips and mouthed, *"shusssh."*

I bent over and whispered in Teracita's ear, *"Carlo Santiago won't ever hurt you again, Little Angel. Not you or anyone else... They can hang a sign in that law office of his cause he won't be going back to work. He's taken an EARLY RETIREMENT."*

TO BE CONTINUED...

ACKNOWLEDGMENTS

I would be remiss if I didn't thank the people who took time out of their busy lives to offer their advice and give me encouragement as I wrote my first novel. Portions of this book dealt with very uncomfortable subject matter. Though there was no intent to offend, I fear some may have been offended. If you were, I apologize. Thank you for considering my work as a piece of literature. Additionally, I want to thank the local writers groups in Holly Hill and Ormond Beach, Florida for allowing me an opportunity to sit in, learn, and share my thoughts and ideas.

Also the various police departments serving eastern Volusia County. You deserve to be recognized and commended for providing those of us who live here with a safe & decent place to raise a family and retire to. You are forced to deal with a large transient population that filters in and out of the area on a seasonal basis. That fact inherently provides opportunity to those who would prey on the unsuspecting before disappearing with the morning tide.

To the agencies and organizations who exist to help victims of violent crime, domestic abuse, and the homeless... THANK YOU! The need is far greater than the means, but your tireless efforts are not in vain. *What greater love is there than this... That we lay down our lives for our fellow man.*

SPECIAL THANKS TO:

Teracita; My friend and neighbor. A retired english teacher who dedicated her time to read and edit my work. You inspired me to continue writing when I struggled for words.

Karen; An avid reader of the genre, you encouraged me and offered support when I needed it the most.

Lois; A dear friend from across the street. Also a retired teacher and avid reader of the genre. You took time to evaluate my work and provide honest feedback.

Pamela; A talented artist and a gift to all who know her. For showing interest, offering advice, and believing in me. You aren't just my sister in law. You are my friend. A shelter from the storm.

Last, but certainly not least, Lorelei; You are my best friend, my confidant, and the love of my life. Thank you for allowing me to be me, and for giving me the courage to reveal my inner most thoughts.

You became a *writer's widow* the day I put pen to paper and left your world behind to enter my fictional universe. The sacrifice you made in time, companionship, and solitude so that I might follow my literary journey is a testament to your love and devotion. It was your experience as a volunteer court advocate with the Domestic Abuse Council that became the inspiration for my work.

Most Especially I want to thank the victims of domestic abuse;

Those of you who have suffered, both physically and emotionally, at the hands of an abuser. It is your story that needs to be told. Your suffering that needs to be recognized and dealt with. I dedicate this book to you...

Let us stand together and hold our heads high. Let us be heard!

F C HENDERSON

LOVE